Becoming

AN LA LOVERS BOOK

JOURDYN KELLY

Becoming
Copyright © 2018 by Jourdyn Kelly
Published by Jourdyn Kelly
All Rights Reserved.

No part of this book may be used or reproduced, scanned, or distributed in any printed or electronic form without permission. Please do not participate in or encourage piracy of copyrighted materials in violation of the author's rights. Purchase only authorized editions.

ISBN Number - 978-0-9982725-3-5

This is a work of fiction. Names, characters, places, and incidents either are the product of the author's imagination or are used fictitiously, and any resemblance to actual persons, living or dead, businesses, companies, events, or locales is entirely coincidental.

Cover Art by: Jourdyn Kelly
Interior Design by: Fictional Formats

Also by Jourdyn Kelly

Eve Sumptor Novels:
Something About Eve
Flawed Perfection

The Destined Series:
Destined to Kill
Destined to Love
Destined to Meet

The LA Lovers Series:
Coming Home
Fifty Shades of Pink
Coming Out
Becoming

Author's Note

I love being captivated by books that lead me into different, exotic places, and through impossible scenarios. I love being able to become someone else for a time. Reading has always inspired me to bring my own characters out to play. My hope is that *my* writing will inspire others, or at the least, give them a way to escape from everyday life for a little while.

Becoming

Chapter One
REBECCA

University of California, Berkeley – 1997

"Becca! Wait!"

Rebecca Cuinn slowed her pace marginally and let her roommate catch up. "What's up, Allie?"

"Geez," Allie wheezed. "Why do you always have to walk so fast?"

Rebecca slanted a look at her friend. It wouldn't do her any good to point out that she had been walking at a normal pace. Allie would just accuse her of calling her overweight, and Rebecca was not about to get caught in *that* trap again.

It had been a source of contention between the two since they became roommates in their freshman year. Rebecca had been far too nervous to notice anything amiss with her new roomie and never noticed the occasional glares. It took Allie two semesters to warm up to Rebecca, finally confessing that she had been jealous of her when they first met. As time passed and the two started to know each other a little better, Allie continued to compare her short, squat stature with Rebecca's equally short, yet svelte build. As annoying as it was, Rebecca would do the obligatory "you're not fat" speech—which she sincerely meant—and change the subject.

"Sorry." Rebecca slowed down even more, though at this point she could probably sit down and be moving faster. "Did you need something?"

Allie smiled enthusiastically. "*We* have been invited to a Gamma party!"

"Allie, we have a major test coming up..."

"On Monday! It's Friday, Becca. You can't seriously tell me that you're going back to the dorm to study *all* freakin' weekend."

Rebecca mentally patted herself on the back for refraining to comment on Allie's dire need to do exactly that. *She's probably going to ask for my notes Monday morning.*

"Not that I need to explain anything to you, but I'm going to study and read. It's been a long week, Allie. I've really been looking forward to just relaxing."

"You are so boring!"

"Thanks," Rebecca deadpanned.

"I mean it, Becca. We're in our senior year here and I haven't *once* seen you drunk or naked." Allie rolled her eyes when Rebecca raised her brows. "You know what I mean. You've never had a guy in our room. And, you've never spent the night with anyone. It's like you're a virgin!" Allie muttered to herself. "Yeah, right."

Stunned, Rebecca stopped in her tracks. She wasn't sure what she was most offended by. That she was being criticized for being good or that Allie literally scoffed at the idea that Rebecca could be a virgin.

"Hang on. What do you mean, 'yeah right'?"

Allie was ten feet away before she realized Rebecca was no longer next to her. She finally stopped and backtracked to the stupefied blonde.

"I mean, you're gorgeous. No one that looks like you is a virgin."

Rebecca peered down at her faded Levi's and t-shirt. Being on an accelerated course to get her Master's in Entrepreneurship, she never put much thought into clothes or make-up like other girls. Where Allie owned a ton of products that littered their room, Rebecca was content to keep it simple. Business plans were what she was interested in. Not parties, fashion, or boys. *Especially* not boys. Though that wasn't something she felt she needed to confide in Allie.

"Looks like me?"

Allie rolled her eyes again. A common occurrence with her. If they had been in a real argument, she would have followed it up with some muttered curse about how she had to always explain everything.

"I swear you're oblivious to the way people look at you. You're blonde, thin, have flawless skin, an ass for days, and those incredible eyes. Though I'm sure no guy is looking there when they can stare at your big tits."

"Why does it feel like your compliments are really criticisms?" *And why do I feel so dirty hearing you talk about my ass and tits?*

"I'm just saying, you're like every dude's wet dream. And, the *only* reason I'm invited to this party tonight is because you're my roommate and I said I could get you to go. So, do me a solid and go. You're too serious. Get drunk, get laid, and let me ride on your damn coattails!"

Rebecca shook her head and started walking again. "I'm not going to some lame frat party. I'm sorry. Why would you want to go anyway if you think they really didn't want you there?"

"Hello? To get laid! With enough alcohol, even someone like me could look like you."

"You sorely need to work on your self-esteem, Allie." Rebecca shifted her bookbag to her other shoulder. The only problem with accelerated courses was it felt like she was carrying double the books.

"Yeah, well, I can do that after I graduate."

I don't think graduating with a 2.7 GPA is going to help your self-esteem. "I'm just not interested," Rebecca said aloud.

"Buff guys, drinking, grinding all up on you. Did I mention buff guys?

How could you not be interested?"

This time, Rebecca rolled her eyes. *Zero interest.* "You've been watching too many movies if you think there are only 'buff guys' at these things. But, hey, knock yourself out. Go and have fun. Just be careful and don't leave your drink unattended."

"You're really not going to do this? Not even for me?"

Rebecca stopped once more and looked at her roommate. Even after the years they've been rooming together, she couldn't call Allie a good friend. Never once did Rebecca feel comfortable enough to tell Allie her deepest, darkest secrets. Truth was, Rebecca didn't have *any* true friends and she was happy that she was graduating soon.

"If you knew me at all, Allie, you wouldn't even be asking me to do this. Look, whether I go or not, you've already been invited. You don't need me."

"You're right. I don't need you," Allie huffed. "Go be your boring self." With that last barb, Allie stormed off in the opposite direction of their dorm.

"Being focused does not make me boring," Rebecca muttered as she continued towards her building. So what if she was still a virgin? That was her choice and she definitely wasn't going to lose that at some frat party with some frat *boy*.

College was about learning for Rebecca, not sex. Besides, she had promised her Aunt Willamena that she would be good. She, at least, owed her aunt that much for taking such loving care of her after her parents died.

She let out a sigh of relief as she closed the door of her dorm behind her. After kicking off her shoes, Rebecca plopped down on her bed and plucked a well-worn book from under her mattress. This book had *nothing* to do with business and everything to do with pure, unadulterated pleasure. She smiled, hoping Allie would be gone for most of the night.

"Turn in your tests as you leave," Professor Brundt announced in his booming voice. Rebecca jumped slightly at the sound and checked her watch. She had handed in her test twenty minutes ago and got caught up studying for the next one. She closed her textbook with a thud and started gathering her things.

"Rebecca? Please stay."

Rebecca looked up at the professor, making sure he was talking to her, and nodded. She checked her watch again. Thirty minutes to her next class. She could spare a few, even though she had no clue what Brundt could want from her.

"*Teacher's pet*," Allie muttered as she passed by.

Rebecca smiled sweetly, ignoring the jab. Whereas Allie was still miffed about the party, Rebecca had been relieved to get the entire weekend alone. Allie hadn't come back to their dorm until late Sunday afternoon which gave Rebecca ample time to study, take notes, read her trashy novels, and rest. It was perfect. She didn't even care when, as predicted, Allie asked for Rebecca's study notes. Being the dutiful roommate, Rebecca gave them to her knowing they probably wouldn't help anyway.

She turned her attention to her professor as the last student disappeared through the door. His course wasn't the most popular amongst the students. **Entrepreneurship Business Plan & Perspective** may not have been the most exciting subject. However, to someone with a mind for business like Rebecca, it was fascinating. "Is something wrong, Professor?"

The older man—likely in his mid-fifties if Rebecca guessed correctly—sat on the corner of his desk and waved a piece of paper in his hand. "You finished this test pretty quickly."

Rebecca shrugged. "I knew the material."

The professor shook his head. "It's more than that."

Rebecca tilted her head and studied her teacher. He was unassuming, perhaps a bit conservative with his sweater vests, tweed jackets, and khakis, but she couldn't deny he knew his stuff. And she was one of his best students. That wasn't her ego talking, just frankness based off of her grades. Surely, he wasn't suggesting she had cheated.

"I don't understand," she said carefully.

"I had a chance to grade your test while the others were finishing. It's perfect."

"I studied."

"Again, it's more than that, Miss Cuinn." He put the paper down behind him and picked up a folder. "These are just a few of your business proposals, though I've examined them all. They're brilliant."

"And, that's a problem?" Rebecca still had no idea why the professor had kept her after class. Not knowing all of the facts always made her a little nervous.

"On the contrary. It's extraordinary. Your innate ability to find multiple ways *any* business can turn a profit in a significantly abbreviated period of time is a commodity people will pay a fortune for. Which is why I've recommended you to a friend of mine."

All of the preposterous scenarios that ran through her mind evaporated at Brundt's words. "Wait, recommended me?"

"Precisely. My friend owns an exclusive business here in town. Their objective is to make major revisions; however, I've seen the books, and the place is bleeding money. What they need is someone to come in with a business plan that will not only bring the place back into the black and keep it upscale but give them the means to make these changes. I think you're that person."

"Me? But, I'm a student." She was flattered, of course. And the thought of putting more of her business solutions to the test real world was intoxicating. Was she ready? Hell, was she even qualified?

Professor Brundt shook his head. "You've done internships before, so I know you have more confidence than that, Miss Cuinn. You're about to graduate with your Bachelor's *and* Master's. Your work ethic is as exceptional as your work." He reached into the pocket of his tweed jacket and pulled out a business card. "If you are interested, call this number and make an appointment to meet with the owner. I implore you to do this, Rebecca. An opportunity like this doesn't come along very often. As you said, you're still a student. Imagine the work you will get with something like this under your belt."

Imagine what would happen to my reputation if I fail. Despite the negative thought, Rebecca stood and took the card from Brundt. The only thing on it was a number. No company name, no contact name.

"Who am I supposed to ask for?"

"Just tell them who you are. They'll know."

As confused as she was with the situation, she thanked him for the chance to prove herself.

SHE FLIPPED THE card over and over through her fingers. The anticipation of what came after a simple phone call had been enough of a distraction that she actually struggled to get through her last class. Something she didn't enjoy. Setting the card down on the table, Rebecca gave it a little spin. Of course, the intrigue was there. She'd be foolish not to be curious. Still, she had virtually zero information about who or what she would be working with.

It was meticulous research and preparation that made her good at what she did. How was she to do any of that when she hadn't a clue as to what type of business this place was? She didn't like being unprepared and here she was, being asked to go into one of the most important meetings of her young career, completely unprepared.

So, she did the only thing she could do at the moment. She picked up her Nokia and dialed.

"Hello?"

"Hey, Aunt Wills."

"Rebecca! What a surprise! Is something wrong?"

Rebecca chuckled at her aunt's ever-present need to be a therapist. "Nothing is wrong. Why do you always ask me that when I call you on an unscheduled day?"

"Because, you usually only call me on unscheduled days when something is wrong," her aunt countered with humor.

"Touché," Rebecca laughed. "To answer your question, *Dr.* Woodrow, nothing is really wrong. I simply need some advice."

"Ah, it just so happens that I have an incredibly expensive, highly distinguished degree that gives me the ability to do just that. And, I happen to be particularly good at it."

"I agree." It never ceased to amaze her how her Aunt Wills could always get a smile out of her. Even at a time when Rebecca thought she would never smile again, her aunt was there to make a devastating situation slightly more bearable. Aunt Willamena wasn't just a psychiatrist extraordinaire, she was the best aunt anyone could ever hope for. With that in mind, Rebecca described her current predicament.

"Rebecca," Aunt Wills began once Rebecca was finished. "Life is always going to be full of circumstances that you will not be able to control. I believe you know that better than most. It won't always be about how good you are at preparing for those events. Occasionally, you will need to discover how good you are at handling those unpredictable occurrences with grace. You are extraordinarily talented at what you do. Trust that. Trust yourself."

Rebecca remained silent for a moment, soaking up everything her aunt just told her. "Wow. That is one hell of a degree you must have."

"Eh, it's amazing what you can get out of a Cracker Jack box."

Rebecca laughed heartily. A rare occurrence when she wasn't speaking with her Aunt Wills. "You're crazy!"

"Ah, ah, ah. We shrinks do not approve of that word. Besides, we can't be the crazy ones when the crazy ones are calling us."

Rebecca shook her head at her aunt's shenanigans. The sense of humor was the same as her mother's and it reminded Rebecca of the times when she was a little kid watching the two women together. Fantastically wonderful memories that never failed to make Rebecca both happy and wistful. She could never allow herself to forget that she didn't just lose her mother, but Aunt Wills lost her sister.

"I love you, Aunt Wills," she said with quiet sincerity.

"I love you, too, my sweet girl. Now, make that call and knock 'em dead."

Rebecca hung up with her aunt and promptly made her next phone call. No one said life would be easy. She learned that the hard way ten years ago when her parents died suddenly and tragically in a car accident. She wouldn't tarnish their memory by easily giving up.

THE FOLLOWING DAY found Rebecca sitting straight in a large, leather chair, ankles crossed, and hands linked in front of her. Her portfolio rested nearby, and she waited. She had been waiting—in this position—for the past ten minutes.

Inside, she was fuming. If this was the way the owners of this establishment did business, she could see why they were in trouble. Outwardly, she remained poised and relaxed. She may be young, but she knew better than to show any sign of weakness.

The tick-tock of an antique clock that sat on the shelf of an ornate bookcase ticked off the seconds in a soothing rhythm. Rebecca tapped her fingers to the tempo as she counted, allowing it to help keep her calm. She was about to hit one hundred when the door finally opened.

Her eyes locked with an extremely alluring—and unexpected—woman in her mid-thirties and Rebecca was grateful for the ability to hide her emotions. The first thing that caught her attention was the height. The dark-haired woman must've had at least six inches on Rebecca's vertically challenged five-foot-two stature. Another prominent feature was how angular the woman was. Nose, chin, cheekbones. It was as though she were sculpted out of marble. She looked… hard, but it wasn't from a muscular build that Rebecca preferred.

Her lean body was attired smartly in black slacks and a blood-red button-up shirt that flared open at the collar. It somehow matched the edgy, androgynous hairstyle the woman sported. Despite the androgyny—which Rebecca had always preferred—the woman wasn't exactly Rebecca's type. Even so, there was definitely something about her that piqued Rebecca's interest.

She sat in her large, imposing chair and gave Rebecca a leering once-over and scoffed with an arrogant smirk. "You're the genius Jim sent me? How old are you, kid?"

Rebecca mentally patted herself on the back for maintaining her professional composure and not rolling her eyes. Her looks often got a reaction from men and women alike. Most, like Allie, thought beauty equaled stupidity. Especially if you were young. "I'm twenty-one." She tilted her head, keeping eye contact. "Forgive me, Ms.?"

"Pryce. Samantha Pryce," the woman responded. It would seem the smirk was going to be a permanent fixture on that angular face. Fantastic.

"Ms. Pryce. You don't strike me as a woman who would take a meeting with a stranger about your business without knowing everything there is to know about them. And, knowing Professor Brundt as I do, he would be completely upfront with you about who he's sending." Samantha's smirk turned to something resembling admiration, but Rebecca wasn't finished. She stood. "Perhaps this is a test to see if I would be intimidated by you. I'm not. You've kept me waiting and then you greet me with insults. If this is how you do business, Ms. Pryce, I'm not interested in getting involved."

"Well, well," Samantha grinned charmingly. "Jim was right. You are spirited."

"I prefer to think of myself as driven and professional," Rebecca countered. Ever the feminist, she wasn't about to let someone belittle her will to become successful. Especially another woman.

The woman threw her hands in the air in surrender and laughed. "Okay, okay. I apologize if I offended you."

Rebecca lifted a blonde brow. For some reason, she didn't think Samantha Pryce apologized very often. Hell, she wasn't even sure it was sincere.

"Do you know what it is that we do here, Miss Cuinn?" the older woman asked, proving to Rebecca that she knew exactly who she was.

"I don't," she admitted readily. "Though I imagine that's by design as well."

Samantha stood as well, accentuating the height difference. She looked down at Rebecca with that smirk of hers. "Some would consider your candor a challenge." She gestured to the door. "Come with me. I'll show you around and tell you what I'm looking to do."

Rebecca—momentarily thrown off by the "challenge" statement—followed dutifully. She blinked, waiting for her eyes to adjust to the sudden dimness they walked into. Through the low light, she saw exactly what she was getting herself into. The dark room—illuminated only by the soft lighting of multi-colored bulbs that lined the ceiling—was trimmed in plush, red velvet. High backed chairs and booths encircled a black, glossy stage. In the middle of that stage was a brass pole. A scantily clad, huge breasted woman strutted by as if conjured up by some spirit with a sense of humor. She gave Samantha a sexy grin and the evil eye to Rebecca.

"This is Rebecca Cuinn, Gigi. She's a VIP. Anything she wants, you get. Got me?"

"Yes, ma'am. Should I bring drinks?"

Samantha looked at Rebecca for an answer. When she received a negative shake of the head, she dismissed the young—man, she had big tits!—woman with a flick of the wrist.

"A strip club?" Rebecca asked haughtily. Surely, her skills were better than some titty bar!

Samantha frowned. "It's more than a strip club, Miss Cuinn. We're a "Gentlemen's Club" if you will. Though more than half of our clientele is women." She paused until Rebecca looked up at her. "Women who like women. Does that bother you?"

Another test, Rebecca thought with a mental eye roll. "Why should it?"

"You sounded relatively concerned about what goes on in our fine establishment. It's only natural to assume…"

"My *concern*, as you called it, Ms. Pryce, was more surprise. And, seeing as I'm a lesbian myself, it would be hypocritical of me to be bothered by it."

Samantha smiled. It was a smile that Rebecca could only define as predatory and her blood heated as it traveled south. She couldn't understand her reaction to the smug woman. It wasn't like Rebecca to mix business with pleasure. Her "pleasure" was a well thought out, successful business plan. Shit. Maybe she *was* boring.

"What exactly is it that *you* do for fun, Miss Cuinn?" Samantha asked, eerily paralleling Rebecca's inner thoughts.

"Is that relevant to this meeting?" she answered before thinking.

Samantha took a step closer making Rebecca feel slightly claustrophobic. And hot. "If I said it was?"

Rebecca tilted her head up and cleared her throat. "I'm working on a double degree, Ms. Pryce. There's a reason Professor Brundt sent me to you." Though, now that she thought about that, how in the hell did stodgy Professor Brundt know about a place like this? "I'm very good at what I do, despite my age. That means I don't have time for much else."

"Hmm."

That was the only response Samantha gave before turning and walking away. Rebecca wasn't sure if she should follow or if she had been dismissed. She erred on the side of caution and jogged to catch up with the taller woman's long strides. When Samantha came to an abrupt stop in front of a row of doors, Rebecca narrowly missed running into her.

"These," Samantha pivoted just in time to see Rebecca taking a step back. She smiled that predatory smile again and continued. "These are the rooms we use for private lap dances. I have a vision for them. I have a vision for this whole place. That's why you're here."

"I'm listening."

"I want to expand our horizons. Instead of just lap dances in here, I want to equip them for more… fun."

Despite Rebecca's uneasiness with where she thought this was headed, she pressed on. "Fun?"

"Yes. Each room," she pointed at them to emphasize her point, "will be a distinct color. Each color will represent the experience level of the occupants. Or, what they're willing to try."

"What exactly are we talking about, Ms. Pryce?"

"I'm talking about a sex club, Miss Cuinn. Specifically, a BDSM club." Samantha watched Rebecca closely. "Do you know what that is?"

Rebecca had never felt so naïve in her life. And completely out of her element. "I—I think Professor Brundt made a mistake. I'm not the right person for this job." She realized she didn't answer Samantha's question, but she already felt foolish. Admitting she had no idea what BDSM was too much for her bruised ego.

"I don't agree." Again, Samantha took a dangerous step closer to Rebecca. "I need someone with fresh… eyes. Someone who can be taught."

Rebecca backed up. "Miss Pryce…"

Samantha smirked. "If you don't have your own ideas about what to do here, Miss Cuinn, it means we're working with a clean slate. I don't have to justify my concepts, just explain them to you. You're here to help me make this possible monetarily. What's the harm in learning a little something while you're at it?" Another step. "It could be the fun you've been missing out on. One thing is certain, it won't be boring."

Rebecca prided herself on thriving during challenging situations. It was how she survived all these years with the void that was left in her soul. This was merely one more challenge.

"What did you mean by 'equip them'?" she asked, thankful that her voice was steady given Samantha's proximity.

"Does that mean you'll stick around?"

Rebecca nodded. "I'm willing to help if I can."

Samantha smiled. "I love women who are willing. Each specific room," she continued as though she didn't just say something that made Rebecca's pulse spike, "will be equipped according to experience and comfort levels. For instance, this room will be black." She opened the door and ushered Rebecca in. "Black will be our top level. Diverse types of whips, flogs, spreaders, clamps, restraints, and so on will be readily available for the dominant to do what they desire to their submissive."

Why in the hell did Rebecca's body respond to that? She swallowed hard, wishing she had taken the offer for that drink earlier.

"I, um, don't think I need all of the intricate details." Rebecca cringed inwardly at the waver in her voice.

Samantha turned her hard, brown eyes on Rebecca. "I disagree. I think the more you understand what my vision is for this place, the more… diligent you'll be in writing that proposal. I need it to be brilliant enough to win over every investor you approach."

"I approach? Ms. Pryce, my understanding was that I'm to write the proposal for you."

"No," Samantha interrupted abruptly. "I want you to work closely with me on this. You have the face and knowledge that investors, especially mine, will be extremely receptive to. And, you have the attitude and more that entices me to get to know you better."

Perhaps it was the way Samantha said the word "more" that made Rebecca sweat. Or, perhaps it was the implication of the words "know you better." Regardless of how she felt about the enigmatic Samantha Pryce, an opportunity like this would look incredible on Rebecca's resumé.

"If it helps your decision," Samantha said through Rebecca's continued silence. "I will talk to your professor about giving you credit for this in his class. What do you say, Miss Cuinn? Are you ready to learn?"

"Yes."

Chapter Two
REBECCA

The Pryce of Success – 1997

"I REFUSE TO work with that… that *woman* again!"

This was the sentiment of almost everyone Rebecca had spoken to since beginning her work with Samantha Pryce more than two months ago. Her answer was always the same.

"Then work with me. Look, Ronnie, I know Ms. Pryce can be difficult…"

"Difficult? She constantly complains about our markups and she's abusive to my employees. I will not tolerate that."

"Which is completely understandable. I know it's not an excuse, but Samantha is under a lot of pressure with this relaunch. And we couldn't do it without you. You're the best liquor distributor in the county."

Apparently, Rebecca wasn't above groveling a little to stay on track and on budget. Ronnie wasn't the best, but Samantha had already depleted most of their options *before* Rebecca even came on board. If they lost Ronnie, the club and its relaunch were going to fail.

"You pay 20% more markup and I'll think about it."

Rebecca closed her eyes and took a deep breath. "You know I can't do that," she said calmly. "We keep the current pricing and I guarantee that you and your employees deal with only me as long as I'm here."

It wasn't much of a deal, but it was all she had to bargain with. Samantha had given her autonomy and authority, but even in her brief time working with Samantha, Rebecca knew that there were limits. She also knew that Ronnie couldn't afford to lose their business any more than they could afford to lose his.

"Fine, Rebecca," Ronnie answered after a pause. "But I won't be so generous the next time."

"Understood. Thank you." She hung up the phone and sat back in her chair with a sigh. It seemed all she had been doing since agreeing to work for Samantha was putting out fires. How the woman stayed in business this long was a mystery. Personally, Rebecca found her to be charismatic, witty, and intelligent. Professionally, she was abrasive, arrogant, and callous.

There was a learning curve working with someone so mercurial. It was a whirlwind of information to take in. Luckily, Rebecca was a fast learner. The most sensitive subject was money. She quickly found that out when examining the books and making suggestions to stop frivolous spending. It seemed an easy decision for Rebecca. The club was swimming in the red, but even minor changes could only help. However, Samantha was repeatedly offended by Rebecca's advice and would continue spending as though the money was pouring in. Contrarily, when it came to the things they actually needed—like a liquor distributor and licenses—Samantha couldn't be bothered.

Thinking of licenses caused another sigh to escape from Rebecca's lips. She checked her watch, noting that she had a mere twenty minutes before the person she needed to speak with left for the day. Nothing like a bit of stress to keep her on her toes. With that in mind, she picked up the phone.

"Mr. Schumer, it's Rebecca Cuinn calling for Samantha Pryce," she said when a man answered the phone.

"Miss Cuinn, I'm heading out in a few minutes. So, unless you're calling to tell me you've come up with the past-due fees, there's nothing more to discuss."

Rebecca pinched the bridge of her nose. *Remain calm.* "Mr. Schumer, we're set to open in less than three months and you're threatening to revoke our zoning permit. This club has been selling alcohol in this area for over five years. You can't just pull the rug out from under us."

"I can, and I will. Blame your boss."

Oh, Rebecca *did* blame Samantha. But that wouldn't help her out of this situation. "Surely, we can find *some way* to settle this. I know that you and Ms. Pryce had found compromises before." Those compromises consisted of unlimited time in the private rooms of the club in exchange for extensions on liquor license fees. After doing her homework, she discovered that good old Mr. Schumer had a wife that would be none-too-pleased to learn of that arrangement.

"Are you trying to blackmail me, Miss Cuinn?"

"Of course not. I'm merely trying to find a solution that works for everyone."

"I cannot in good conscience keep this up, Miss Cuinn. Ms. Pryce has exhausted all of her extensions and owes in excess of $30,000 in fees and penalties."

Extensions of which you approved of and penalties you ignored for some kicks of your own, Rebecca thought with disgust.

"I understand that, Mr. Schumer. However, I have to assume that if you hadn't been so lenient before, she wouldn't be in this position. Were your arrangements approved by your superiors?" *Or your wife?*

"You're just as bad as her," he spat back.

"I'm sorry you feel that way. But, since we're trying to find a resolution before the relaunch, here's what I'm proposing. We will pay half of the back fees and penalties. In return, you will make the necessary adjustments to show that we are caught up and in good standing. I will then request a new representative. After that, we move on with a fresh start."

"What makes you think I'll agree to this and not just block you?"

"Video surveillance," Rebecca answered simply. Hell, she didn't actually know if the private rooms had video. It didn't matter if it was true if he believed it. Obviously, blackmail was another skill she had to learn quickly.

"Half," Mr. Schumer grunted. "By the end of the week." Click.

"Great. Now to find $15,000 in four days," Rebecca muttered to herself. It was going to be another long night. That was something Rebecca was getting used to. It wasn't easy. Not by any stretch of the imagination. She still had classes to attend. She couldn't let her work here negate everything she'd done in college. Especially with less than a semester left. Yeah, all of her free time was spent here, but it wasn't so bad. She had her own office, cramped as it was. And it wasn't like she had a personal life to ruin anyway. *This* was her life. For now. She opened the side drawer of her small desk and randomly grabbed a take-out menu.

"Rebecca!"

Rebecca banged her head on her desk. "So close yet so far away." Eating would have to wait. Again. She rose and made her way two doors down to Samantha's office. Instead of entering, she stood in the doorway. "Yes?"

"Come in here and sit down. There are things I want to discuss." Samantha absently waved towards the guest chair. "I have some changes that I need you to take to the contractor."

"Changes?" *She can't be serious. We barely have the money to do what we're doing now.*

Samantha looked up with a proud smile. "A cigar lounge."

"What?" The older woman pushed a piece of paper towards Rebecca. Yep. She had heard correctly. A cigar lounge. Complete with humidor cabinets and whiskey bar. "Samantha, this is impossible."

"I don't want to hear that. Just get it done."

"Please listen to me. Not only are you asking me to tack on thousands of dollars that we don't have, this will add at least another month to construction. We simply don't have the resources."

"This is what I hired you for, Rebecca. Call the investors and do what you need to do. Hell, fuck them if you have to. I want this room."

Rebecca was speechless. Groveling she could handle. Blackmail? That was fine, too. But, it would be a frigid day in hell before she offered her body.

"No."

"Excuse me?" Samantha's voice turned to ice at Rebecca's refusal.

"You hired me to help you and that's exactly what I've done. I have jumped through hoop after hoop and nailed the goddamn landing every time. But, you telling me to sell my body for something you don't need? That's bullshit! The plans were drawn up, sent to the city, and approved. This isn't just an investor problem. If you want to piss away your money you can do it without me."

They stared each other down for what seemed like an eternity. Surprisingly, Samantha was the one to break first. She gave Rebecca a tight smile. "Very well, Miss Cuinn. No changes."

Rebecca let out a sigh of relief. Well, she wasn't fired, and she won. This round at least. "Thank you."

"Don't thank me. I will get this room at some point. You better be *that* good. And, the next time you decide to speak to me in that manner… well, we will have to think of a good punishment."

A light knock sounded at the door and Rebecca looked over to see Gigi—scantily clad as always—standing there.

"You may go."

Samantha had dismissed Rebecca like a child. Unfortunately, Rebecca wasn't finished. She still needed to talk to Samantha about the money they needed by the end of the week.

"I need to discuss…"

"Unless you want to drop to your knees and suck my clit, you need to get out."

Rebecca stood abruptly, hating the fact that she tasted that now familiar bitterness of anger and jealousy. It wasn't the first time she was sent away, ousted by Gigi. It wouldn't be the last. If only she hadn't *wanted* to be the one to drop to her knees.

REBECCA PRESSED A hand to her stomach as it growled loudly. Once she had gotten back to her office after that disaster with Samantha, she got right to work. It was typical of her to forget to eat, even when she was starving. But, since Samantha would rather have a *playdate* than discuss business, it was up to Rebecca to figure out the impossible. In the grand scheme of things, fifteen grand should be the easy part. *And, it could be*, she told herself silently.

She jumped at the sound of a throat clearing and looked up to see Samantha leaning against the doorjamb. It would help matters enormously for Rebecca if she didn't find the woman sexy and intriguing.

"May I come in?" Rebecca nodded, and Samantha folded her long frame into the uncomfortable guest chair. "I wanted to apologize for earlier."

Blonde eyebrows shot up in surprise. She had been on the receiving end of Samantha's bad moods quite a few times. Never once had the woman apologized.

Samantha smirked. "I shouldn't have said what I said. It was inappropriate and rude."

"I'm not sure what to say."

"I think you said it all when you put me in my place," Samantha answered. She held her hand up when Rebecca opened her mouth. "If you're thinking of saying sorry, don't. I deserved it."

"All right." Truth was, Rebecca still wasn't sure what to say. She wasn't sorry for what she said, but perhaps she could have been a bit more tactful.

"I would like to make it up to you if you would allow me to."

"Samantha, there's no need."

"I insist," Samantha interrupted. "How about dinner?"

Rebecca tilted her head. "What would your girlfriend think about you taking me out?"

"Girlfriend? You mean Gigi?" Samantha laughed heartily. "Gigi is merely a means to an end. I'm in between… companions at the moment. Gigi assuages any needs I may have."

"I see." *I'm not jealous.* "Even so, I have class in the morning. I should have left more than an hour ago."

"Yet, you're still here. And, from the noise I heard coming from your stomach when I came in, you need to eat." Samantha leaned up in her seat. "Come to dinner with me, Rebecca."

Part of Rebecca begged her to say no. Another part, the one that was consistently intrigued by Samantha, begged her to say yes. Her stomach chose that moment to growl again and she made her decision.

"Okay."

In Retrospect - 2000

HINDSIGHT IS TWENTY-TWENTY. Isn't that what they say? There are those moments in life when you had to ask yourself; if you knew then what you know now, would you have done it all differently? Rebecca's answer was a resounding yes. If she *had* known then what her future would be, she never would have said yes to having dinner with Samantha that fateful night nearly a year ago. But she did. And that was something she now had to live with.

She couldn't remember now if it was the attention Samantha gave her? Or maybe it was the fear that she really was boring? Or perhaps it was the intrigue of letting go and giving herself over to someone completely? Had she been lonely and never realized it? Ever since Rebecca's parents died, she had pushed herself to be the person she thought they would be proud of. The demanding work never allowed for much of a social life, but Rebecca hadn't cared much about that.

Fact was, whenever Rebecca was feeling particularly horny, it was easy for her to take care of it herself. She didn't need anyone, and honestly, she thought that was the way she preferred it. From what she had observed around her, relationships were messy and falling in love couldn't be an option for her at this point in her career or life. However, that one dinner had changed everything. She told herself it was bound to happen eventually. Working so close with someone as sexual as Samantha had Rebecca yearning for more for the first time in her young life. How could she resist the pull she felt every time the woman was near?

God, how she had thought she fully understood what getting involved with Samantha would mean. She knew the sex would be anything but conventional. She knew that if she gave in she would be submitting to Samantha and everything she thought a lover should give. Having heard all that entailed on her first tour of the club, it was perhaps the one major element that had caused Rebecca's hesitation to get too close. She hadn't known if she had it in her to be a submissive. The thought of the pain that she was told came with pleasure was daunting. Nevertheless, in the end, the attraction was too strong to resist.

Eyes—once silver and bright, now dull—looked up and Rebecca stared at herself in the mirror. How had she ended up here? How did something that started off as incredibly erotic turn into something so sadistic? Rebecca untied her silk robe and gingerly peeled it away from her skin. She winced as the fabric caught on a fresh wound. Tossing the robe aside, she turned to see what the damage was this time. Angry red welts crisscrossed her back and a trickle of blood rolled down slowly. She followed its progress until the steam from the running shower fogged the mirror enough to obscure her view.

This was the worst it had ever been. In the beginning, the pain—as hurtful as it was—had been bearable because it was always followed up by incredible pleasure. As time went on, Samantha became increasingly stressed out about money and the club. The pain increased, and the pleasure stopped. It was as though torturing Rebecca somehow eased Samantha's anxiety. When Rebecca would beg for Samantha to stop, it would get worse.

In an attempt to save herself—save her soul—Rebecca did something drastic. Something she never thought she would do. She went to her aunt and asked for an advance in her inheritance. That wasn't an easy conversation. As things declined with Samantha, Rebecca's phone calls to her aunt declined as well. She was afraid her Aunt Wills would hear something in her voice that would give away what her life had become. Rebecca had to explain exactly what she wanted to do. That it was not only to help her girlfriend, but it would be beneficial to her career as well. It wasn't exactly a lie. She didn't have a hefty amount, but if she could just buy the club, bring it into the black, things would get better. They had to. She looked at her back again and thought about how wrong she was.

IN RETROSPECT, REBECCA probably should have discussed her plan with Samantha. Unfortunately, they didn't have that kind of relationship. Once they got involved physically, Samantha's respect for Rebecca and her abilities dwindled drastically. Every idea, whether it was made to save money or make money, was rejected as though some silly schoolgirl was making them. So, Rebecca kept her plan to herself, opting to surprise her lover once she could hand a thriving business back over to its rightful owner.

It was a good plan. At least it had been in Rebecca's mind. Regrettably, she neglected to take Samantha's ego into account. Of course, she knew it would be hard for Samantha to give up control. After all, that was the epitome of who Samantha is. But Rebecca made considerable effort to ensure the change of owners was private from the employees, and Samantha remained in charge as the manager. Nevertheless, the older woman saw losing ownership of her club as a failure. And Samantha's defeat meant Rebecca's agony. There were many times when Rebecca faltered and nearly confessed everything she had been fighting to do for Samantha. But, she couldn't do that without having something to show for her efforts or her pain. So, she waited. And endured.

It took more than two *excruciating* years for the club to start seeing a significant profit. It was during that time that Samantha began her love affair with heroin. A long-time patron had introduced her during a particularly stressful time. It didn't take much for Samantha to become as addicted to this new hobby as she was to being a Dominant. It soon overtook her love for practically everything else.

Of course, she justified her frequent using by arguing how it helped her get through the pain of losing the club. She also claimed sex became euphoric and more heightened, though Rebecca was never "allowed" to share in that experience—something she was secretly grateful for. The only thing that helped Rebecca in the bedroom was the charade that Samantha was solely responsible for all of the club's success. Stroking her ego was easily accomplished when Samantha was in an altered state.

It only helped marginally as soon as the drug use became a daily occurrence and Samantha became increasingly aggressive. Rebecca's appearance in the club had been reduced to nothing more than Samantha's stress reliever in the black room. Those times when Rebecca physically couldn't take more, Samantha would find other willing participants. Despite Samantha's vow to remain loyal, her unfaithfulness no longer fazed Rebecca. The reality of that depressed her. Perhaps she had been naïve to think whatever she and Samantha had would grow into something resembling love. Now, all she could hope for was mutual respect.

SHE LOOKED AT the stripes that marred her once smooth back again, and for the millionth time, she wondered why she stayed. What was this hold Samantha had on her? Did she feel indebted to the woman for giving her an opportunity? Did she feel bound as Samantha's sub because she knew no other way to be other than a slave to her lover's every wish?

Why did she keep trying to make things better? Why did she ever think anything she did would make a difference? These were the questions that swirled inside her head each time things got too excessive. Which is exactly what happened tonight. All she had wanted to do was make things better. She cooked a romantic dinner, dressed in something she knew Samantha would like and had the papers on hand to sign the club back over. She had hoped it would be a joyous occasion that would end in the two making love for the first time. Or, at the least, bring the pleasure back after the pain.

Hindsight is twenty-twenty. If only Rebecca had known Samantha had spent the day shooting up. If only she had grasped the extent of Samantha's ego. If only she hadn't tried so hard to win Samantha's love. But hindsight never helped anyone. The reality was dinner sat cold and untouched on the table. Candles were long ago burned out. And the contract was in shreds all over the dining room floor. Instead of the elation Rebecca had expected and hoped for, it was anger she was met with.

"Those are going to sting in the hot water."

Rebecca lifted pain-filled eyes and met a smirking Samantha. No longer did she see a charming, clever woman. Instead, she saw a vicious bully. Rebecca's weary eyes stayed with Samantha as the woman stepped closer. When Samantha leaned in, she felt that hot breath on her neck. It used to excite her. Now, it instilled fear inside her.

"*It'll teach you never to lie to me again.*" She bit Rebecca's ear painfully, but the younger woman remained quiet. She had learned earlier in the night that trying to explain only brought on more pain. Every "excuse" was met with another strike on her back. "Get in."

As much as Rebecca didn't want to get in the shower with Samantha watching, she didn't argue. All she needed to do was will herself not to react. If she cried from the pain, she would be giving the older woman exactly what she wanted. And Rebecca refused to be humiliated even more tonight. She felt a hard smack on her bare ass when she failed to move fast enough.

"I said, get in."

With her head held high, Rebecca walked over to the shower and took a breath. *Do not cry. Do not cry.* She kept that mantra in her head as she stepped in. The bite of the steaming water nearly caused Rebecca to gasp and her knees to buckle. Tears pooled in her eyes but they never fell. She knew Samantha was watching carefully. She could see her smiling at Rebecca's obvious discomfort. Once again, she wondered why she was still here. She even wondered how she was still alive.

"Hurry up. I'm hungry," Samantha said finally and walked out.

Rebecca released the breath she had been holding, and with that came the tears. Yet, she never stepped out of the spray of the shower. She welcomed the pain, knowing that each splash against her skin meant the blood of the night was being washed away. How fitting that she should feel as though it was her life circling the drain.

Please - 2001

"Rebecca!"

Samantha's agitated voice carried through the apartment, causing Rebecca's entire body to shake. She closed the book she was reading and set it aside. It had been months since Rebecca had told Samantha about buying the club. Since then, their relationship declined even further. Samantha stayed high more often than not. Her temper became out of control. The only fortunate thing was her memory was lapsing. Rebecca had gotten away with never mentioning the ownership of the club again. Fortunate because Rebecca couldn't imagine giving Samantha control in the state she was in.

"In the bedroom," Rebecca called out as calmly as she could. *Where I always am. Every night.* It was another lesson learned after that horrible night. The sight of Rebecca in the kitchen only served to piss Samantha off. The blonde had been all but banned from the club. And when Samantha came home, Rebecca was to be waiting in the bedroom for her, ready for whatever mood Samantha happened to be in.

"What the fuck are you doing in here?" Samantha staggered into the room, hitting her shoulder on the door jam. "Shit!"

"I was…"

"Shut up!"

Fantastic. Nights like these were the worst. Samantha would come home completely wasted and Rebecca would take the brunt of her wrath. The only good thing was there were times she was too wasted to do anything sexual. Words and insults were bad, but they were far better than the physical pain of the whips.

"Would you like me to run you a bath?" Rebecca suggested softly. If she could get Samantha to calm down, there was a chance the night would be short and painless. *Maybe she will fall asleep in the tub.* Rebecca cut off that line of thinking.

"No, I don't want a fucking bath." Samantha threw her small bag on the bed, hitting Rebecca's shin. "I want you naked." She unzipped the bag revealing needles, a tourniquet, and vials of black tar heroin.

In a ritual Rebecca had seen many times before, Samantha took out the tourniquet and wrapped it around her upper arm. She remained silent as she watched Samantha fill the syringe with a precise dose. With the state Samantha was in already, Rebecca could only hope that another shot would incapacitate her enough that Rebecca would get the night off.

"Did you hear me? Undress." With great care, Samantha stuck the needle in a plump vein. She closed her eyes, and Rebecca could only assume she was feeling whatever euphoria the drugs brought her.

"Samantha, maybe we could just relax tonight. It sounds like you've had a rough day. I think," Rebecca began. Pain exploded in her head when Samantha back-handed her.

"I don't want your goddamn opinion! You do what I say when I say." Samantha staggered towards the bathroom. "You had better be ready when I get out."

Rebecca wiped blood from her chin and slowly lifted her nightgown over her head. Every inch of her body still ached from the night before. If only she had called her aunt as she was desperate to do. If only Rebecca could find it within herself beg her aunt to convince her that she deserved more.

"Rebecca!"

Rebecca heard a crash coming from the bathroom and braced herself. She had no idea what had happened that day to make Samantha so angry, so she had no idea how to fix it. Rebecca scoffed silently. *Like I could fix it anyway. My mere presence pisses her off.* She quickly made her way to the bathroom and knocked timidly.

"Samantha? Are you okay?"

The door swung open violently. "What the fuck is this!"

She threw a toothbrush at Rebecca's face, narrowly missing her eye.

Rebecca frowned in confusion. "It's my toothbrush." She did all she could to stay calm as she was confronted with Samantha's unfounded wrath. "Is something wrong with it?" She wracked her brain, trying to remember if she had left the toothbrush out, or failed to put it back in its "rightful spot."

"Bullshit! Your toothbrush is not this color. Who the fuck has been here?"

Rebecca shook her head. "No one. I swear. I bought new brushes for us both the other day. Remember?"

Another backhand caught Rebecca off-guard.

"Don't fucking lie to me! Where is the bastard, you fucking whore!"

This time it was a punch that made contact with Rebecca's jaw, causing the young blonde to crumple to the floor in pain. She curled her naked body up as Samantha continued to wail on her. Each kick, each punch, was like being branded with a hot-iron. She wanted to argue, wanted to beg Samantha to stop, but she couldn't catch her breath and was pretty sure her jaw was broken. Temporary relief only came when Samantha turned her attention to destroying the room looking for the "bastard" Rebecca was cheating on her with.

Rebecca did her best to protect her stomach with the arm she could still move. The other arm lay limp at her side. It was tough to determine what was hurting worse. Her ribs ached so much she could barely breathe. There was a pain in her stomach that made her wonder if Samantha had caused internal bleeding with the multiple kicks to the area. Her left eye was swollen shut and the right had blood dripping into it.

This is it. She's finally going to kill me. I love you, Aunt Wills. I'm sorry. Maybe I'll be able to see mom and dad again. Please don't let them be disappointed in me.

"Who is it, huh?" Samantha grabbed Rebecca by the hair, yanking her head back. "One of the vendors? Maybe an investor? Is that how you get things done? By spreading your legs?" She wrapped a hand around Rebecca's throat and squeezed. "What? Nothing to say? You always had something to say. You know, the only reason I let myself be with you is because I wanted to punish you for thinking you could talk to me the way you did." Samantha let out an evil laugh when a blood-stained tear rolled down Rebecca's bruised cheek. "Did you think I really wanted you? That I could love someone as pathetic as you? Fuck no. I wanted you to know *exactly* who the boss is and always will be."

Regardless of what Samantha thought, Rebecca wasn't crying because of the words Samantha was spitting out at her. She couldn't deny she had had her suspicions lately as to why Samantha was with her. No, what was causing the tears was the inability to breathe. Samantha's large hand squeezed against her throat, cutting off her air supply.

"*Please*," Rebecca managed. She grabbed onto Samantha's wrist but didn't have the strength to fight off the bigger woman.

Samantha raised her free hand, poised to strike again. "That's right, beg me, bitch. Beg me to…"

All of a sudden, Samantha's grip loosened, and she stumbled backward. Her glassy eyes widened as she clutched at her chest. The exertion she had displayed by trashing the place already had her breathing hard, but this was different. This, to Rebecca, was more like the inability to catch her breath.

Rebecca scooted herself back as far and as fast as she could. Before she knew what was happening, Samantha began retching. It seemed as endless as the beating did. When Samantha started vomiting blood and convulsing, Rebecca instinctively reached for the phone. Adrenaline must have dulled the pain as she pulled herself up off the floor, and with her fingers poised to dial, Rebecca met Samantha's wild gaze.

"*Help me*," the older woman wheezed in between heaves.

Every hit, every whip, every kick, every slap, every bite, every harsh word that Samantha did to Rebecca came back with a vengeance. It was like reliving it all over again. Not to mention, Rebecca stood there bleeding and broken, contemplating helping the woman who did it to her. *Why should I?*

"*Rebecca.*"

For the first time, hearing her name come from Samantha's mouth didn't sound like a demand, but a plea. Rebecca held Samantha's frightened gaze as she lowered the phone.

"*No!*" Samantha gasped and doubled over, her hand beating weakly at her chest. "*Please!*"

Unable to stay standing, Rebecca sank onto the bed. There was an abundance of things going through her head that she wanted to say to Samantha. How saying please never helped her. How Samantha deserved what she was going through right now. How ironic it was that Rebecca was the one with unanswered pleas just moments before. Yet, she said none of those things. She simply sat there and watched as Samantha's eyes rolled back into her head. Rebecca exhaled softly as Samantha's last breath left her body.

Chapter Three
REBECCA

Taking Back Control – 2001

FEAR OR HOPE—possibly a combination of the two—had Rebecca's good eye riveted on Samantha's chest. She counted. One, two, three... all the way to fifty. There was not one rise or fall. Not one breath, not one beat. Samantha's eyes were open, but Rebecca could no longer see the hard, brown that seemed to always look right through her.

The phone felt heavy in her hand. Or perhaps that was the guilt weighing down on her. She should have called for help. She should have done *something*. Right? The problem was, it wasn't only guilt she felt. There was something else there. It was the unmistakable feeling of relief. Should she feel guilty about that as well?

A sharp, shooting pain caused Rebecca to gasp. Adrenaline began to wane, and agony set in. As the prickly fingers of unconsciousness began to pull her under, Rebecca quickly sent a text to the first person she thought could help.

Need help. 911. Home.

"REBECCA?"

Her head was pounding, her body felt as though she'd been run over by a car. Twice. All she wanted to do was sleep. But *someone* kept calling her name and touching her.

"Rebecca, can you hear me? I need you to wake up."

"*Don't want to.*"

"With the way you look, I bet you don't. Come on, sweetheart."

It took significant effort, but Rebecca managed to open one eye. Recognition of the familiar face in front of her took a moment.

"*Lou?*"

Detective Lou Chi. One of L.A.'s finest. And one of the club's most frequent guests. Rebecca had met the man more than a year ago when he stepped in the middle of one of the many arguments between her and Samantha. Of course, Samantha was high, and Lou threatened to bust her for possession. Rebecca, having noticed the man coming from inside the club, offered a deal instead. Look the other way and use of the club would be free. Sex is a powerful negotiating tool. Since then, he became a friend. He never made it a secret that he wasn't fond of Samantha or the way she treated Rebecca, but he promised to never interfere unless asked. Now, Rebecca was asking.

"Yeah, it's me. Can you sit up?" Rebecca shook her head. "Okay, that's okay. I'm going to call for an ambulance."

"No! Please, don't."

"Rebecca, you're bleeding. You were unconscious when I got here. I'm not a doctor, but I'm pretty sure you have some broken shit. What the hell happened here?"

"Is she dead?"

"Yeah, I checked on her when I got here. There was nothing I could do." He grabbed a pillow from the bed and gently lifted Rebecca's head. "That should help a little until the ambo gets here."

"They'll ask what happened."

"*I'm* asking what happened." He cut off her response, speaking quickly and precisely into his phone. "Help is on the way. Let's use this time to work things out. I know it hurts, Rebecca, but I need to know how to fix this."

It took most of her dwindling strength, but she told him everything that happened. Even the part where she didn't call for help.

"Okay." He scrubbed his face. "This is a clear-cut case of abuse and an overdose. You were unconscious, and therefore, unable to administer any type of aid."

"Texted you instead of calling 911," Rebecca countered weakly. Her breathing was becoming more labored, and the darkness lurked close by.

"You should have been a damn lawyer," he grumbled. "You did nothing wrong, Rebecca. You contacted me because you can trust me. I'm a cop. If you were trying to hide something, you'd call someone *not* involved with the police force."

Rebecca turned her head slightly in the direction of Samantha's body. Because her vision was compromised, she couldn't see her. But she knew she was there. The image was seared into her brain.

"I didn't help her."

"Judging by how much pain I'm positive you're in, you shouldn't have. Why didn't you tell me it was this bad, Rebecca? I would have helped you."

"Couldn't." She lost her battle with consciousness then, this time welcoming oblivion.

HER EYE FLUTTERED open and was met with bright fluorescent light. *Ow.* She could hear the beeping and whirring of machines around her. *I guess the ambulance showed up*, she thought, taking stock of what she could and couldn't feel. Loopy? Check. Pain? Eleven out of ten. She couldn't be sure because she couldn't move her head, but Rebecca was pretty certain she still had all of her limbs.

"Welcome back."

Rebecca's head automatically turned towards the smooth tone. An extremely attractive, kind-looking woman in a white coat stood close by. Her vision wasn't that great, but from what she could see, the woman had shockingly blue eyes.

"I'm Dr. Vale. Do you know where you are?" The woman asked softly as if she knew Rebecca's head was pounding.

"*Hospital.*"

"Good." The doctor wrote something on the chart she held. "Do you know your name?"

"*Rebecca.*"

Another note with a nod of the head. "Do you remember what happened to you?"

"*Beaten.*" Rebecca wished she could give more than one-word answers, but it hurt to speak. She had watched enough medical dramas to know the questions were important, especially with head injuries. Unfortunately, in real life, the pain was overwhelming.

Compassion filled the doctor's eyes. "A cop came in with you. Does that mean the bastard was caught?"

Rebecca closed her eye. "*She's dead.*"

She missed the shocked look directed at her. "Good."

One silver eye popped open. "*You're a doctor.*"

Dr. Vale held Rebecca's gaze unapologetically. "And, I have a patient with broken bones, bruises, and who just spent hours in surgery. Anyone who can do that to another human being deserves what they get."

"*Hours? What…?*"

"There was some internal bleeding. We had to go in and remove a couple of things. But, we'll talk more about that when you're a little more lucid."

When Rebecca reached up in an attempt to touch her face and access the damage, Dr. Vale stopped her with a gentle touch.

"Try not to move around too much or disturb the bandages."

"*Will I?*" *Will I be scarred for life? Will my face be maimed? Is this what I deserve?*

"The scars on your face will fade," Dr. Vale answered, correctly guessing Rebecca's concerns. "I'm *that* good," she smiled kindly. Her smile faded, and she looked at Rebecca seriously. "If you would like to talk about the scars on your back at a later date, we can."

Rebecca nodded slightly.

"Is there someone I can call for you?"

Rebecca scoffed. How the hell was she going to explain this to her aunt? "*Would you want anyone you loved to see you like this?*" She sighed tiredly. God, pain really took a lot out of you.

"I would want to be surrounded by people who loved me," the doctor answered with a gentleness Rebecca wasn't used to these days.

"*My fault. I stayed.*" Even though her voice was merely a rasp of a whisper, the defeat was clear.

The tall doctor gingerly sat on the edge of Rebecca's bed and took her hand. "Rebecca, abuse like this is *never* the victim's fault. Whether you stayed or not, *you* are not to blame. However, if you'd rather, I could call someone to evaluate your emotional state."

"*A shrink?*"

"A psychiatrist, yes."

Rebecca smiled for the first time. "*My aunt. Built-in shrink.*"

Dr. Vale chuckled. "Is she your emergency contact?" Rebecca nodded. The doctor reached over to grab the call cord. "I'll have Patty give her a call. She's the head nurse around here and runs a tight ship. If you need anything at all, just press this button and she'll be here. I'll be back during my rounds to check up on you."

"*Thank you, Dr. Vale.*"

"REBECCA, ARE YOU sure you're ready?" Dr. Willamena Woodrow paced around the hospital room. Her normally well-groomed chestnut hair was mussed, most likely due to being driven crazy by her head-strong niece.

Willamena was barely in her twenties when her older sister died, and Willamena was entrusted with the care of her young niece. Despite the closeness in age—just ten years—Willamena took Rebecca under her wing and raised her in a way she hoped her sister would be proud of. It wasn't always easy, and right now was one of those times.

"I'm sure. Hunter has cleared me, Aunt Wills." Rebecca continued to pack the things her aunt had brought her during her stay. She'd been cooped up in this place for almost two weeks and she was ready to get out. It wasn't all bad, of course. She had gotten to know Dr. Hunter Vale better, as well as Nurse Patty and her wife Mo (also a nurse). But, if she didn't get out of this room soon, she was going to go crazy. Though if she said those words to her aunt, she would get "the look."

"Maybe I should talk to this Hunter person. Why haven't I, by the way? Isn't she your doctor?"

"Yes. I think she's avoiding you," Rebecca answered truthfully with a touch of mirth. It was true, however. Whenever her aunt was around, Hunter tended to disappear. In the short amount of time Rebecca had known the doctor, she sensed there was something going on in her life that she may not be ready to face. Maybe Hunter was afraid Aunt Wills would see that and begin shrinking her. Rebecca chuckled silently at the thought.

"Story of my life," Willamena muttered playfully. "Fine, I realize I can't stop you from leaving." She ignored her niece's sarcastic "thank you," and continued. "But, please tell me you're not going back to that place." She had been horrified to learn what Rebecca had been going through. Guilt settled in all nice and cozy. She should have noticed something. She was a psychiatrist for chrissake. Once again, she sent up heartfelt apologies to her sister.

Rebecca's actions faltered slightly. "No. It was Samantha's place." And it was filled with ghosts of the past. "While being stuck in here with nothing to do, I was able to find a small bungalow to move into."

"I wish you would come home to New York with me." *So, I can keep an eye on you*, Willamena added silently.

"Aunt Wills," Rebecca warned softly. They had had this conversation countless times since her aunt showed up. She could see that her aunt felt the weight of responsibility on her shoulders, and that bothered her. Rebecca had done a remarkable job of hiding what was happening. Nothing that happened to her was her aunt's fault. "She can't hurt me anymore and I'm not running from a ghost. Besides, I still have the club."

Another subject of conflict. Wills wanted Rebecca to sell the club and be done with everything having to do with Samantha. Rebecca, on the other hand, had more than one reason to keep the club. None of which she wanted to discuss with her aunt at the moment.

"You are the most stubborn person. Your mother…"

"Would be proud?" Rebecca finished with a laugh. "You know I get it from her."

"I believe even she would have issues with this decision, Becca. Especially after all you've been through."

"Which is *exactly* why I have to stay and do this, Aunt Wills. If I run and hide, she wins anyway."

"There's no shame in taking some time to recuperate your body and soul, Becca. You've been on the go since, well since you were born. Take a sabbatical. Travel around the world. Do something for just you."

Rebecca sighed and sat down on the bed. She couldn't deny that what Aunt Wills was suggesting sounded wonderful. Especially since she could still feel the effects of the beating. On the one hand, she had been lucky enough that the only things broken were her nose, eye socket, and ribs. She had been afraid her arm was broken, but it had turned out to be a dislocated shoulder. Even so, she was still weak, and it took her a moment longer than normal to catch her breath due to the lung that had been punctured. Sutures from the surgery to remove her spleen—and mend other things inside—ached. Mentally, she was trying to come to terms with everything she had lost.

"The problem with that is it gives me time to think. If I think, I'll wonder why I wasn't strong enough to leave her." She held up her hand when Wills began to argue. "I know how you feel, okay. And, maybe one day I'll get there. I have a lot to learn about myself, but I think I need to do it in my own way. Not by traveling, but by taking back control of my life."

Wills studied her niece. Something told her she probably wasn't going to like what Rebecca had in mind, but she would stand by her nonetheless. In fact, she would do whatever it took to make up for not being there.

"How do you plan on doing that?"

"By doing things on my terms now. The club is mine and I intend to start doing things my way. Samantha's hold on that place—and me—is… over, Aunt Wills. I need to know I can do this."

Wills nodded. That was something she could understand. "Very well. I can take a couple more weeks off, stay here until you're set."

"Not necessary." Rebecca hopped off the bed and immediately regretted it. Her ribs still hurt like a bitch. She shook it off and walked over to her aunt, taking her hands. "I know you want to protect me, Aunt Wills. We can talk every day or email, but I have to do this myself. You have to let me do this myself."

"You're asking me to go against all of my training, and my instincts, Becca."

"I know."

Wills sighed. "All right. On *one* condition. I hear from you daily, at least in the beginning. And, *if* something like this happens again, you tell me immediately. And, I want weekly sessions with you."

Rebecca raised a blonde brow. "That's three conditions. Is it ethical to counsel a family member?"

"Screw semantics and ethics. I want to make sure you're okay. I know you, Becca. You won't go to another therapist, so you're stuck with me."

Rebecca laughed softly. "I agree with calling, texting, or emailing you daily. I won't allow anything like this to ever happen again." *I've learned my lesson.* "And, I only agree to weekly therapy sessions if I get the family discount."

Willamena's lips twitched. "You're quite the negotiator." She held her hand out to Rebecca. "Deal."

Rebecca took her aunt's hand, shook it once, and pulled her in for a hug. "Thank you."

Willamena pushed her back enough to frame her face with her hands and look her in the eyes. One iris was still red from the burst blood vessels, and both eyes were underlined by fading bruises. Even with the blemishes, Rebecca was beautiful and captivating.

"Please, don't shut me out again, Becca."

"I promise."

Becoming Mistress – Present

REBECCA SAT IN her newly renovated office. It was here that she dominated over everything she had re-built. The once small, semi-profitable club was now a two-story, high-end lounge where entrance was by application and invitation only. Yes, it still held much of Samantha's BDSM vision, but gone was the old staff, mediocre vendors, and greedy investors. In their place were professionals that were meticulously vetted by Rebecca before they were even brought in for an interview. She had strict rules, and if they were not adhered to, there were no second chances. None of them met the real Rebecca Cuinn. Instead, they encountered leather-clad, mask-wearing Mistress. It was a mystery to them who she really was, and that's exactly what Rebecca wanted.

Another major change was Rebecca's demeanor. Being a sub was buried with her past. Mistress—now a Dom—was born out of the necessity to take charge of her life again. She also had the idea to show subs in the BDSM world that what they may have thought of the lifestyle didn't have to be so black and white. It was why she chose the pink room as her personal room. Each person she had in that room—also carefully investigated before Mistress would allow them in—saw a different side of BDSM. A side where the Submissive had just as much power as the Dominant.

The main difference between Mistress and the other Doms in the club was Mistress never had sex with her clients. Sex certainly wasn't something she wanted to be paid for. Not to mention, she didn't feel sexy underneath the leather. Underneath the mask. Scars still branded her back, and though the scars on her face were gone, she felt them nevertheless. Even without the sex, Mistress was the most sought-after Dominant in the club. They all wanted to be whipped, bound, and punished by Mistress. Just having her in the room was enough of a sexual experience for them.

It was enough for Rebecca to get her confidence back. Not just the dominance over others, but the success of the club. Samantha had worn her down so much, told her she was stupid so often, that she wasn't sure she had the same business mind anymore. But with Samantha gone, everything that Rebecca touched seemed to turn to gold. That's not to say she didn't have problems. She most certainly did. At times it took double therapy sessions with her aunt just to pause the nightmares.

As the years wore on, Rebecca became tired of the tedium of her life. Time in the pink room did nothing for her anymore. She merely went through the motions with clients who never lost the novelty of being dominated by the small woman. The effect on her, though, wasn't the same as it was before. With her confidence high, sexless domination over her clients got… boring. Unfortunately, as of yet, no one had intrigued her enough to go down that road again. Or, perhaps, she was lying to herself about being too scared to bring sex into it. What if she found out that she would be just as bad as Samantha if she let herself go?

In order to suppress temptation, Mistress closed the pink room, indefinitely. Clients and staff both were disappointed in the decision, but her staff was astute enough not to argue with Mistress. Clients begged, threatened, and begged some more for Mistress to keep seeing them. However, per their binding contract, they had no choice but to let her go. They were more than welcome, however, to choose a new Dom if they wanted to continue their patronage at the club.

These days, Mistress stayed in her office, high above the action, watching. She was getting pretty good at determining which room clients would request. There had been only one time she had been surprised by the gender choice of one sub, but fine-tuning her observance was easy enough. Mistress knew every name, every career, every fetish, every family member of every single person that stepped foot in her building. She refused married people, but allowed couples. She wasn't in the business of tearing families apart. Mistress preferred showing them exactly what they had with each other.

Mistress picked up a file and flipped it open. The club was hosting a bachelorette party—she checked the clock—starting about now. She had dossiers on everyone attending that party. Each had to sign non-disclosure contracts, fill out applications, and give two forms of ID. It was an arduous task, but it helped Mistress filter out those who weren't serious about the lifestyle or who wanted to use it as a way to hurt others.

She plucked a sheet from the file. Miranda Loring, bride-to-be—and frequent customer with her fiancé—had submitted a request for time with someone other than her groom and vice-versa. *That won't do*, Mistress concluded. *They just need a push in the right direction.* In lieu of a surrogate, she arranged for the couple to be placed together without them knowing. Blindfolds were wonderful tools if used correctly.

She stood and walked to the window that overlooked the main room and VIP section. One change Mistress loved after her takeover was how diverse the group always was. Yes, they had rules, but in the end, every type of person you could think of could be here at any given time. As long as you followed the guidelines, your race, gender, sexuality, body type, didn't matter.

Her breath caught, and her chest tightened when she saw one particular club-goer. This was someone she had never seen before, and part of her wished she had missed seeing the tall woman now. Her body's response was too intense to be good for her. With a shaking hand, she pressed the intercom button on the wall next to her.

"Yes, Mistress?"

"Bring me the files on the entire Loring party." At least her voice hadn't betrayed the chaos she felt inside. Less than a minute later, there was a knock at her door. "Enter."

"The files, Mistress."

"Thank you, Carlie." Once she was alone again, she began sifting through the files. *"You shouldn't be doing this,"* she told herself. It didn't stop her. Nothing stopped her until she came to the one photo she was looking for. A scan of the attached copy of the driver's license gave her the information she was looking for. "Cassidy Giles. Oh God, she's only twenty-five!"

Mistress tossed the file aside, determined to forget about the incredibly hot, tall, androgynous woman. She couldn't care less how the black jeans made that ass look. Or how the crisp, white button-up shirt was unbuttoned dangerously low. And, she certainly wasn't thinking about fisting her hands in that short, dark hair. Nope.

"She's too young, Rebecca," she said aloud in an attempt to remind herself to get the gorgeously handsome… "Stop!" *Too young. Too young. Too young.* She groaned in frustration when that wasn't working. She walked away from the window, paced for a moment, before sitting back at her desk. She tapped her pale pink tipped nails on the surface, then let curiosity get the best of her.

Mistress activated the monitors in front of her. She had a view of almost every single inch of the club. Except for the private rooms, of course. Those sessions were recorded on an encrypted server that purged itself every forty-eight hours unless a specific order came from the

Mistress herself. As with all the cameras around the place, it was purely a safety measure.

But, what she was looking for right now, had nothing to do with safety and everything to do with her aroused libido. "You're playing with fire," she told herself, wondering when she started talking to herself. She scanned the area, stopping at the VIP section. "Ah, there you are, Cassidy Giles." A couple of clicks from the mouse had the camera zooming in on that exquisite face. "Jesus, you're gorgeous."

She sat back in her chair with a huff. "Carlie!"

"Yes, Mistress?"

Good lord, does she stand right outside my door?

"Send a shot of Fireball to table one in the VIP section. From me."

"Yes, Mistress."

The sprite of a woman disappeared as fast as she appeared, and Mistress shook her head. "Okay, so you sent her a drink. That's it. Your room is closed, and you will *not* open it for someone who is young enough to be your..." She stopped talking and banged her head on her desk. "Anyone who makes you talk to yourself should not be messed with," she muttered.

As if it were on a string, her head lifted in time to see Cassidy Giles look around, raise the glass in salute, then slam back the amber liquid. Consequences be damned, Mistress opened her desk drawer and took out the one thing she never thought she would use again.

Chapter Four
REBECCA

Giving in to desires

MISTRESS BARELY RESISTED making a fool out of herself by touching Cassidy's hair as she passed by. In her defense, she only wanted to know if it was a soft as it looked. She managed to stick to her task of putting her pink card on the table, bringing attention to it with a tap of her fingertip and walking away. She never looked back to see if Cassidy followed her. Truth be told, part of her hoped she didn't. A much bigger, more horny part, was desperate that she did. That she was considering actually having sex with this woman surprised the hell out of Mistress. She *never* wanted to have sex with paying clients. *Technically, Miranda Loring is paying.* It was a thin technicality, but one Mistress held on to.

She entered the room painted in a soft pink hue for the first time in months. Since no one was allowed in here, nothing had changed. It was minimally but tastefully decorated with the finest furniture, carpet, and accessories. Mistress wanted the ambiance to portray safety and peacefulness. Some may say that was ironic, but she thought it made perfect sense.

Once inside the room, you found two high-back, pink chairs that faced each other. A door on the left led you into a full bathroom complete with a shower and soaking tub. Further in the room was the pièce de résistance. A colossal California King four poster bed. It was perfect for bondage. Not far from the bed stood an armoire full of implements of pleasure and pain. Mistress's heart rate spiked when she thought of using those things on Cassidy Giles. *If* she showed up.

Determined not to get her hopes up, Mistress sat in one of the chairs that faced the doorway. Her posture—straight back, feet crossed at the ankles, and hands clasped together in her lap—gave off a relaxed, yet commanding, vibe. Inside, she was anxious and aroused. A feeling she deliberately avoided for years. It left her feeling a bit off-kilter.

She wasn't sure how much time had passed since she laid that card down on Cassidy's table, but it seemed like hours. Just as she was about to give up, there was a knock at the door. For the first time, Mistress was speechless. She opened her mouth to say something and nothing happened. Apparently—luckily—that didn't stop Cassidy from entering.

If Mistress thought Cassidy was hot from afar, being so close nearly caused her to gasp. Lust coursed through every vein in her body, and it took her a moment for her brain to function.

"Come," Mistress commanded softly. Cassidy merely stood there, staring, so Mistress tried again. "Sit." Her eyes glanced at the chair in front of her. When Cassidy still remained close to the door, Mistress tilted her head and studied her. Defiant. Strong-willed. Someone who could be difficult, yet oh so fun, to dominate. "You don't like being told what to do."

This is a waste of time, Mistress thought dejectedly. She had taken a chance by reopening her room for someone too young for her, and got what she perceived as rejection. Having had enough humiliation in her life, Mistress began to rise.

"Wait!" Cassidy moved to the chair quickly and sat.

"Why are you here?" Mistress asked as she resumed her position.

"I'm here in support of my friend." She rolled her eyes slightly. "Of course, I haven't seen her since."

Mistress nodded. "Miranda. She and her friends are being well taken care of. You didn't join in the fun." *Thank you for not joining in with someone else.*

"Not my scene."

Judging by Cassidy's distasteful look, Mistress wondered if she would leave this room unsatisfied.

"You don't approve."

Cassidy shrugged. "Who am I to judge? I'm sure you get a lot of cheaters in here. Part of the reason I could never get into this lifestyle. What if I did something wrong? Forgot to obey? My 'Dom' would just find someone who would, right?"

There is definitely something deeper there, Mistress thought. People with that much passion, good or bad, usually had a reason for being that way. Cassidy had a point. There were Doms out there that did exactly what she described. Mistress knew that better than most. But that's not what it was truly about. Especially here for Mistress.

"You have no idea what this lifestyle is about, do you?" Cassidy shook her head. "Would it make you feel better if I told you that Connor is with Miranda?"

Cassidy frowned in confusion and Mistress explained.

"They don't know it's each other. They wanted a different experience, so we're giving them one. They'll see that all they really need is each other at the end of the night. The purpose of this place is not to tear people apart, Cassidy. It's to bring fire to the relationship. To give them something more than what they have right now. It's not for everyone. But for those who enjoy it, it does not make them bad people."

"How did you know my name?"

Mistress smiled. *All of that I said, and she focuses on that.* "This is my club. I make it my business to know what goes on in here. Do you feel better about Miranda now?"

Cassidy shrugged again. Mistress could tell she was still uneasy about everything that went on in this establishment. Especially when it came to her friend. She wanted to show Cassidy that what happened here could be incredible.

"Would you like to learn more about what we do here, Cassidy?" Mistress titled her head again at Cassidy's hesitation. It almost scared her that Cassidy would say no. It was a very vulnerable way to feel.

"Yes."

That one small tremble in Cassidy's voice caused desire to explode inside Mistress. She had never wanted to be with someone as much as she did at this moment. With this woman. It was enough to make her ignore the warning bells.

"Let me bind your hands."

Cassidy's eyes, that had been trained on Mistress's cleavage, snapped up at the demand. "Take off your mask."

The request took Mistress by surprise. No one had ever questioned her, countered her, or asked for anything more than what she was willing to give. Until now.

"No. If you can't comply, Cassidy, we're wasting our time here."

"You mean submit."

Mistress set her desire aside. She became a dominant because it was what she needed in her life. Control. It didn't do to have someone demanding things from her at this point in her life.

"I admit that I don't know much about this… stuff," Cassidy said quickly. "But I'm pretty sure that trust is a big thing, right? Don't I need to trust whoever is going to be causing me pain?

Mistress caught the slight shiver that ran through Cassidy and felt compassion. "I don't want to cause you pain, Cassidy."

"Cass. Remove the mask. Please?"

"Since this is your first time, I'll compromise with you." *You'll what?* She couldn't believe she just said that. Mistress did not compromise. *What the hell? I seem to want to do a lot of things with Cassidy that I haven't before.* With a confidence she didn't fully feel, Mistress looked Cassidy in the eyes. *Extraordinary eyes.* "Let me bind you, and I will take off the mask."

"Take the mask off first."

Ah, yes, you are a defiant one. That will have to be dealt with. With a stern but delicate hand, of course.

"You don't like authority. If you want to learn, *Cassidy,* you're going to have to knock that chip off your shoulder. Or I can do it for you." Mistress made sure to emphasize Cassidy's full name. It was clear that Cassidy was used to getting her way. She would have to learn that not everything is negotiable.

Cassidy slowly put her arms behind her back and, essentially submitted to Mistress. It was a small victory, but it definitely had the desire coming back ten-fold. Mistress stood and walked behind Cassidy's chair. She slipped a long piece of silk out of her cleavage and bound Cassidy's hands together. She made sure the silk would hold, but not hurt. Too much.

Mistress leaned close to Cassidy's ear. "That wasn't so hard now, was it?" she whispered. She closed her eyes and silently breathed in the handsome woman's scent. It was a woody/citrus combination that ramped up Mistress's arousal even more. Cassidy turned her head and Mistress nearly kissed her. Unnerved, she moved away quickly and sat down.

"Now the mask."

The husky, low octave of Cassidy's voice made Mistress want to give into anything she asked. Even take off her mask. She lifted her blonde hair away from her neck and grabbed the ribbon that kept the mask in place. Holding the mask to her face, she pulls the ribbon to untie it. She closed her eyes and thought about what she was about to do. Not even her staff had seen her without a mask firmly in place. What was it about this woman that made her give in to her desires so easily? With both hands, she lowered the mask from her face.

There was a small gasp in the room. When silver eyes met bicolored ones, Mistress could see the hunger in Cassidy's gaze. It filled her with a confidence she had lacked behind the mask. With the mask, clients had to use their imagination as to what Mistress looked like. She could be anyone they wanted her to be. Most importantly, she didn't have to be herself. As beautiful as people always told her she was, years with Samantha had chipped away at her self-esteem. She no longer saw the beauty everyone else did. Refuge behind the mask became her salvation.

"Are you ready for your next lesson?"

"What's your name?"

"You may call me Mistress."

"You know my name."

Mistress wasn't sure whether to laugh or leave. Cassidy was perilously close to whining, and the pout was beyond cute. But this was a lesson. If Mistress was going to keep any semblance of control, she would have to make Cassidy understand who the boss was.

"I've given you the mask, Cassidy. That's all I'm willing to give you. Stand." Cassidy didn't hesitate this time, and Mistress smiled. *Progress. God, she's tall. And, oh so damned sexy,* she thought as she stood as well. "Walk to the edge of the bed." When Cassidy reached her destination, Mistress spoke again. "Face me, Cassidy."

The sexual tension in the room was palpable. There was an animalistic magnetism between the two that had them leaning into each other. *No kissing!* It was Mistress's one unbreakable rule. Kissing meant emotions. Emotions meant the possibility of heartache. *Not to mention, she's way too young for you! Play and then step away.* She pressed a hand firmly to Cassidy's chest.

"No touching. Not with your hands, not with your mouth." Mistress started to unbutton Cassidy's shirt. "What's your favorite word, Cassidy?"

Mistress stopped her task when Cassidy didn't answer. Her lips twitched as she realized Cassidy was focused on her breasts. She waited until cheeky woman realized she seriously wanted to know the answer.

"Um. Platypus."

The answer was so out of left field, it caused Mistress to laugh. "Platypus?" Cassidy nodded earnestly. *Cute.* "All right then. That is your safe word. Should be easy for you to remember. If I do anything that you're not comfortable with, or you want me to stop, all you have to say is your safe word. I will stop without hesitation. Without question. Understand?"

Cassidy nodded again. Mistress found the speechlessness endearing. In a move purely born out of a need to feel Cassidy's body, Mistress wrapped her arms around her. Of course, she could have used a different tactic to untether Cassidy's hands, but where was the fun in that? Once her task was done, she stepped back.

"Remove your shirt." Interest turned into surprise when it was revealed that Cassidy wasn't wearing a bra. *Nice*. Mistress allowed her eyes to roam further down. The six-pack abs caused her sex to clench almost painfully. *Very nice!* She couldn't resist feathering her fingers down that hard stomach.

Hell, if she didn't get Cassidy inside her soon, she may just implode. Such a visceral reaction nearly brought Mistress to her knees.

"Unbutton your jeans, but leave them on." *If you take them off right now, I may lose control.* Cassidy did as she was told, and Mistress continued. "Now get on the bed. Lay down in the middle, with your hands above your head."

Cassidy hopped up on the bed—not quite the arduous task as it was for Mistress—and assumed the position. Mistress's hands itched to touch Cassidy. Everywhere. She forced herself to maintain control. To stretch this experience out for both of them.

"Grab ahold of this bar," Mistress demanded, pleased when Cassidy obliged. She wrapped the attached ropes around Cassidy's wrists, again making them tight enough to feel the bite of the rope on the skin. After completing her task on both hands, Mistress allowed herself a moment to take in all that was Cassidy Giles, bound and at her mercy. As marvelous as the view was, she needed to see the rest. Hooking her fingers into the waistband of Cassidy's jeans and boxer briefs, she tugged.

"Lift."

Cassidy complied and grinned when Mistress hit a "snag." She let out a small gasp when she saw what had impeded her progress. There, in all its wonderful glory, was an impressive dildo. Cassidy Giles packs and that made Mistress *very* happy. She had used them on herself in the past. A very enjoyable experience. One that Samantha never gave her. She was all about using instruments to torture Rebecca, but never that. If Rebecca wanted a dick, she could find a man. It looked as though Cassidy didn't have the same hang-ups.

She lifted a brow at Cassidy's arrogant smirk. It's not often she was surprised by people these days. This surprise had her mouth watering. As did the multitude of tattoos that painted Cassidy's body. Tiny works of art that Mistress would love to trace with her tongue. She licked her lips at the thought.

"Spread your legs."

Mistress was mesmerized by the delicious sight of Cassidy's glistening sex. If she were ever ambivalent about being a lesbian, this sight cured her of that rather quickly. *More!*

"More, Cassidy!" she echoed her needy thought. There was hesitation this time. One that Mistress could understand. It wasn't easy opening yourself up—literally—to someone. Particularly someone you didn't know. She waited semi-patiently—despite the tapping of her nail on the bedpost—to see if Cassidy could do it. Finally, Cassidy chose to trust Mistress and spread her legs. "Good girl."

She tied Cassidy's ankles in the same fashion as her wrists, patted her on the calf and made her way to the armoire. She swung the doors open and pondered her options. This was Cassidy's first experience. Mistress wanted to make it memorable, yet adventurous. She didn't want to go overboard on the pain. But she also knew that the combination of powerful pleasure with the sharp sting of a whip was intoxicating. *Ah, a whip. Perfect.*

Mistress chose a fringed whip for maximum pleasure. She slapped her palm a couple of times. Partly out of the need to feel the leather on her skin. Partly to get a reaction out of her Sub. It worked as each sound of the snap caused Cassidy to jump. Mistress used the fringe to tickle

Cassidy's ribcage, knowing the sensation would amplify her next move. With a flick of her wrist, she slapped the whip against Cassidy's side, who immediately hissed through clenched teeth.

"Do you always wear that?" Mistress asked, nodding towards the dildo. When Cassidy failed to respond audibly, Mistress slapped the whip across her nipple. "Answer me!"

"Yes."

Another slap, another hiss. Mistress noticed the small movement away from her, but she had other things to deal with at the moment.

"Yes, what?"

More hesitation. She knew Cassidy would have a problem with this. Hell, it was something Rebecca herself had issues with. All Cassidy needed to do was say her safe word and this would be over. She almost expected it.

"Yes, Mistress."

More progress. "And do you use that often?" Cassidy shrugged and received two stinging snaps from Mistress. "Tell me the truth, Cassidy." *Even if I don't want to hear how others have enjoyed you.* The unbidden thought shook her.

"I used to, Mistress. Not so much these days."

Mistress wondered if Cassidy revealed so much because she was scared of getting punished again, or she was just that open. *Let's see how much she will tell me.*

"Why?"

"I haven't found anyone that holds my attention lately, Mistress."

A young, handsome, obviously passionate woman such as Cassidy didn't seem like she'd have a challenging time finding *anyone* that would fight to hold her attention.

"Do I hold your attention, Cassidy?"

"Yes, Mistress. Very much so."

The vulnerability and honesty in Cassidy's gaze took Mistress's breath away. As a reward for her candor, Mistress fanned the fringe of the whip softly over Cassidy's breasts. She could practically see the tension flowing out of Cassidy's body, though her hands still held tightly to the headboard.

"I don't want to hurt you, Cassidy. That's not what this is about." She ran her fingers up her captive's arm and tapped the firm grip. "Relax. Loosen your grip. Your brain is anticipating the pain, your body bracing for it. So much so that you can't feel the pleasure that being like this can give you."

"Easy for you to say. Why don't you lay here all tied up, and let me hit you. See if you like it."

Pain of a different kind rushed through Mistress causing her to frown. She forced herself to erase the images of her past before they took over.

"Say your safe word, Cassidy." The woman's mouth clamped shut, and Mistress could see the contrition in that handsome face. "I know what it's like to be hit. The kind of hitting that *doesn't* come with pleasure at the end of it." *Stop talking! You're getting too personal, Rebecca.*

"I'll kill them!"

As though surprised by her outburst, Cassidy quickly looked away. Mistress, on the other hand, was touched by the ferocity and protectiveness she heard. With her fingertips, she brought Cassidy's gaze to hers.

"You're sweet." Mistress smiled at the cute little blush that graced Cassidy's face. It tugged at her heartstrings. *Time to get back to business*, she thought with conviction. *She's not your lover or your girlfriend. She's a client. A Sub.* Not thoroughly convinced, Mistress called on all of the disciplines she had built up over the years.

"You're associating the feel of this," she whipped Cassidy on the side, "with pain and humility. It doesn't have to be like that." Mistress took Cassidy's "cock" in her hand. She realized then that it was double-sided, and one side was snugly inside her Sub. *Perfect.* "I want you to associate this, with this." With deliberate movements, Mistress jerked Cassidy's cock while flicking her nipples smartly with the whip.

"Fuck!"

Mistress leaned in close. "Did your pussy contract when I did that?"

"Yes, Mistress," Cassidy panted.

She's beginning to understand. Mistress continued to stroke in slow, torturous strokes as she kept the whip moving sensually across Cassidy's nipples. Cassidy's hip began to move in rhythm sending electric currents to already aching parts of Mistress's body. As Cassidy's breathing became erratic, Mistress knew she was close. She increased the speed of her strokes, and at just the right moment, she snapped the whip, hard, across Cassidy's breasts.

Cassidy yelled and thrashed. Legs tried to close but were held open by ropes. The vision proved to be Mistress's breaking point. She *needed* to be fucked by Cassidy or she would explode. And, not in the good way. Her eyes were trained on that cock that she could practically feel inside of her right now and she licked her lips in anticipation.

"In my opinion," Mistress began, warring with herself to give in to everything she wanted. "People have it all wrong. Even those who are deeply *into* this stuff." Cassidy had a charmingly confused look on her face, so Mistress explained. "This Dom/Sub lifestyle. Everyone assumes that the Sub is weak and that it is the Dom that is in control."

She chuckled lightly when Cassidy looked pointedly at her wrists and ankles and raised a brow. She gave her a playful flick of the whip but located it very precisely. Cassidy moaned with pleasure as the fringe caught her clit.

"One word, Cassidy. That's all it takes from you that could stop all of this. *You* have the power to leave me wanting. And, oh god, do I want you. If you could only feel how wet I am for you." Another groan from Cassidy nearly had Mistress fidgeting. "If you break the rules, you get punished, but there's always a reward for you at the end. If *I* do something you don't like, one word and it's over for me. No rewards. So, you see? *You* have the power here. *You* are allowing me to do these things to you. I wouldn't be able to do them without your permission."

Mistress started unfastening her corset. There was no denying what she wanted from Cassidy. She made the rules. If she wanted to fuck someone, that was her right. She didn't think Cassidy would object. The corset comes off and her full breasts spill out, captivating Cassidy. Of course, Mistress didn't mind having her rosy-tipped nipples stared at by this woman. It made her feel wanted. Yet, even though *she* made the rules, there were still rules. She paused in taking off her leather pants until Cassidy finally looked up at her.

"Paying attention?" she smirked.

"Yes, Mistress."

"You're not to move. If you move your hips, I will stop. Do you understand?"

"Yes, Mistress," Cassidy responded after a second's hesitation.

That was as convincing as my understanding of what's happening here, Mistress thought sardonically. Nevertheless, she continued to undress until she stood in front of Cassidy completely naked. It was the first time since Samantha since anyone had seen her like this. That would have been more daunting if Cassidy didn't look as though she could start drooling at any moment. Mistress never stopped taking care of her body and was proud of her femininity. As long as Cassidy didn't focus on Mistress's back, things would be okay. She was quite confident she could keep Cassidy's attention elsewhere.

Mistress crawled up on the bed until she was straddling Cassidy. She knew the woman beneath her could feel the heat radiating from her center, and praised her silently for her control.

A soft touch started on Cassidy's cheek and moved down her neck. She tweaked Cassidy's nipples hard, before moving her hand down between them. Taking the 'cock' in her hand, she guided it to her opening.

"Don't move," she reminded Cassidy before sinking down onto her. She's so wet the dildo slid in easily, and she moaned in ecstasy. Cassidy moaned in response but still managed not to move. *Impressive.*

Unable to keep her own body from moving, Mistress lifted her hips and impaled herself on Cassidy once again. Being watched with such intensity only heightened her passion as she moved her hips back and forth, her clit rubbing against Cassidy's chiseled stomach with each stroke. Her breasts bounced in rhythm with the thrusts, effectively holding

Cassidy's enraptured attention.

"Don't come until I tell you," Mistress rasped, hearing the change in Cassidy's breathing. It was a lot to ask for, she knew, if Cassidy was feeling even a fraction of what Mistress felt. Her hand clutched at Cassidy, and she dug her fingernails digging into her stomach as her breath hitched. *So close.*

She fell forward, enticing Cassidy with her swaying tits. When she felt Cassidy's hot mouth suck in one of her nipples, she gasped loudly. Using her left hand to hold herself up, she tangled her right hand in Cassidy's hair and pulled her closer. She needed more, and Cassidy responded by biting her nipple hard. That sensation of that pain with the pleasure that she was feeling having Cassidy inside her had a strikingly fierce orgasm racing to be released. She bucked wildly and slammed her body down on Cassidy's hard and fast.

"Move!" she cried out. "Fuck me!"

There was absolutely no hesitation in Cassidy as she brought her hips up with strong thrusts, giving Mistress everything she needed. Flesh slapped against flesh, rough and fast, and the sound was intoxicating.

"Now! Come with me!"

Cassidy let go with a roar that reverberated through Mistress, causing her to come hard. She squeezed Cassidy's breasts as she rode out the last waves of an orgasm that was unlike anything she had ever felt before. Something else happened that she had never felt before. A warmth flowed from her and washed over Cassidy. Mistress had a moment of embarrassment until she realized Cassidy climaxed again.

Depleted—literally—by the power of what just happened, Mistress collapsed on top of an awfully triumphant Sub. She let out a small sigh and weakly reached up to release Cassidy's hands. She tensed almost involuntarily when Cassidy immediately wrapped her arms around her. She would have loved to lay there and be held by her incredible lover… she sighed silently. *She's not your lover. This is your job.* It was an ugly thought, especially since what just happened between them felt *nothing* like a job. It felt… real.

Gingerly she dislodged herself from the woman beneath her, and rolled off the bed and shuffled to the bathroom. The least she could do was clean up the mess she left behind. Armed with a warm, wet washcloth, she came back into the room. She was surprised to see Cassidy's ankles still shackled to the bed. *Maybe she was afraid to untie herself.* Mistress didn't like the idea that Cassidy could be afraid of her. She placed the washcloth on Cassidy's tummy and proceeded to untie her, gently rubbing the redness that was left behind on her skin.

Once that was finished, she began wiping Cassidy clean. "I got you all messy," she said quietly. It still surprised and embarrassed her that she had that reaction. She hadn't known her body was even capable of that.

"That's quite all right. I enjoyed it immensely." Cassidy grinned sincerely.

"So did I," Mistress answered just as honestly. She brushed the washcloth over the small, red welts left behind by the whip. Had she been too harsh? The thought of hurting Cassidy made her unbelievably sad.

"Kiss me," Cassidy whispered.

Her hand stilled. She wanted to. Oh, God, she wanted to so badly. But she couldn't let herself get emotionally involved.

"I can't."

"Against the rules?"

The disappointment in Cassidy's voice was enough for Mistress to bring the emotional shutters down.

"Something like that," she responded evenly and turned away.

"So, no name and no kissing. What else should I know?"

"Perhaps this lifestyle isn't for you, Cassidy." Mistress knelt to pick up Cassidy's clothes and tossed them at her. "Get dressed."

She started to get dressed, disappointed that such an awe-inspiring time was ending this way.

"I'm sorry."

Mistress paused but said nothing.

"Please, Mistress. I didn't mean to upset you."

She noticed from the corner of her eye that Cassidy was not getting dressed. That immaculate body made her want to start all over again. But, she couldn't.

"It's okay, Cassidy. Not all of us are made for this."

"I am! With you. May I see you again?"

Mistress contemplated the ramifications of seeing Cassidy again. She had already stepped out of bounds.

"I don't think…"

"Please! I have more to learn. I *want* to learn. With you."

Mistress finished dressing and reached for her mask. "Okay."

"When?"

"You have an open invitation, Cassidy. Come whenever you desire." They both smile at Mistress's play on words.

"How will I know you're here?"

"You'll know."

"It'll be you, right? I don't want anyone else, Mistress."

Mistress nodded. "It'll be me. Now, you should get dressed and join your friends."

"I'd rather stay with you."

I'd rather stay with you, too. Mistress secured the mask, hopefully hiding what she was feeling inside, and stepped to Cassidy. "You've learned enough for tonight, Cassidy. I'm sure by now Rand is finished with her 'conquest.' Celebrate with her."

"Promise you'll be here again?"

Mistress, unfortunately, felt the neediness she heard coming from Cassidy. *Not good. Do not promise!* "Yes." She relaxed minimally when Cassidy seemed to accept that answer and slipped on her shirt. "You're welcome to stay here as long as you need to. There's a full bathroom through that door," she informed her guest.

"Won't someone else need the room?"

There was no mistaking the real question, and Mistress answered honestly. "This is my personal room. No one is allowed in here without me. I won't be needing it anymore tonight."

Cassidy caught Mistress's hand as she walked by and brought it to her lips, kissing it lightly.

"Thank you," she whispered.

The gesture touched Mistress deeply. *This was a mistake. You should have left her alone.* She caressed Cassidy's cheek and smiled softly before walking away.

Chapter Five
REBECCA

Trouble

SHE WAS A coward. She freely admitted that. Being with Cassidy that night brought up hopes she didn't want to feel. Because of her cowardice, Rebecca didn't hesitate when a friend called her for help with a business venture. She could have refused, but she hoped by going away for a bit, she could get Cassidy out of her system. Or at least put her feelings in perspective. It didn't work.

When she arrived at the club that night, she was informed that Cassidy had been there every night. She was also informed that she had been propositioned many times. And refused. As much as Mistress didn't deserve to feel relieved, she did. She wasn't sure how she would have handled Cassidy being in someone else's room in *her* club.

Mistress's step faltered when she saw Cassidy toying with the black card that had been left on her table. She seriously considered firing every single Dom that worked here if Cassidy accepted. The relief when Cassidy pushed the card away was remarkable. *I'm in so much trouble.* Of course, that relief was short-lived when she saw how sad Cassidy looked. The passionate woman she remembered was now laying her head back on the couch with those peculiar eyes closed.

She wanted to comfort her. To hold her in her arms and apologize for not being here. *Rules!* With a sigh, Mistress carefully placed her card on Cassidy's table, caressing her cheek briefly before walking away. Just as she was closing the door, she heard Cassidy call out to her.

"Where the hell have you been?"

Oh, hell no. No one talked like that to her now. *She* was the boss. *She* was in control. She closed the door with a distinct click.

"Go to the foot of the bed and strip."

Cassidy didn't move. "Where have you been?" She repeated with irritation. "You said you'd be here. You lied!"

Anger filled Mistress. "I'm here now. And, I will not tolerate you speaking to me in this way. Say your safe word, Cassidy, and leave. Otherwise, do as you are told, and go to the foot of the bed and strip."

It was like a switch had been thrown. Cassidy, who had just been fired up with resentment, now hung her head in defeat. Perhaps it was fitting that they were both dressed in black tonight with the way this was starting.

"Face me," Mistress ordered. She watched as Cassidy disrobed, never once lifting her head. "Look at me."

Her heart broke as a single tear rolled down Cassidy's cheek and her eyes fluttered closed to block out the image. Or, maybe it was to remember this feeling of regret so she wouldn't do it again. She reached up and removed her mask, tossing it aside. Whether it was Mistress or Rebecca that gently wiped the tear from Cassidy's cheek, she didn't know.

"Turn towards the bed." Mistress stood close enough that her corset scraped against her tanned back. Placing a hand on Cassidy's left shoulder blade, she hoped she could convey her remorse. "I was called out of town on business," she explained quietly. "It was sudden, and I didn't have time to get word to you. I'm sorry."

She never saw the second tear.

Emotions weren't her forte. The best way she could make it up to Cassidy is by rocking her world. And that's exactly what she intended to do. If she got lucky, she would get the same results as the last time they were together. "Kneel on the edge of the bed. Hold on to the bedposts."

The muscles in Cassidy's back stretched as she obeyed. She had so much strength, and yet, someone as small as Mistress could bring her to tears. It nearly felt like too much control for Mistress, until she had to bring out the step-stool in order to reach up and tie Cassidy's hands. She tied them a little tighter than usual, then dipped her head close to Cassidy's ear.

"Don't fall in love with me," Mistress whispered. It was a desperate plea to Cassidy and to herself. Either way, it tore her apart to say them. In order to give her some time to gather herself, she stepped down and went to her armoire. Tonight deserved something more advanced. A riding crop would do. For now.

She took that crop and traced those spectacular muscles and colorful tattoos before moving lower. The slap of the crop against Cassidy's ass rang out in the silence of the room.

"That's for speaking to me the way you did."

It didn't surprise her that Cassidy pushed her ass towards her, silently asking for more. Emotions could do that. They could make you crave the physical pain over the emotional.

"Did you get other cards while I was away, Cassidy?" Mistress asked, knowing full well the answer.

"No, Mistress."

She wants the pain. Mistress made sure to hit the same place for an extra sting. "Don't lie to me! Did you receive invitations?"

"Yes, Mistress," Cassidy panted.

"Did you follow through with them?" Mistress slipped the crop between Cassidy's legs and caressed her soaked pussy lips with it.

"No, Mistress."

Mistress moved the crop when Cassidy began moving her hips, effectively depriving her of finding more pleasure.

"Did you want to?" She asked. She dipped the crop into the crack of Cassidy's ass, eliciting a gasp from the bound woman.

"No, Mistress."

The vision of Cassidy toying with that black card flashed through Mistress's mind and she spanked Cassidy harder than she had dared to before.

"Don't lie to me, Cassidy. One more lie and this is over." It wasn't the rules, but she wouldn't condone being lied to.

"Tonight was the first time I considered it," Cassidy confessed in a hurry. "I thought you lied to me. I thought you never wanted to see me again. I thought I had done something wrong to drive you away. I waited for you every day. When you didn't show up it…" The pause spoke volumes. "I considered it, but I couldn't do it. I don't want to do this without you. I don't care about the lifestyle if it's not with you, Mistress."

Speechless and sorrowful at what could never be, it was Mistress who shed a tear this time. "Don't turn around," she commanded, her voice rough with emotion. Her need for this woman was dangerous and thrilling. And, she was coming to find, addictive. Her pussy ached to be filled by Cassidy. To feel her pounding deep inside her, making her forget how bad it used to be. Suddenly, her clothes were too restricting, and she peeled them off as quickly as she could. "Stay facing forward. Understand?"

"Yes, Mistress."

Cassidy's voice cracked as Mistress pressed her breasts into Cassidy's back. Nipples hardened achingly as she reached around Cassidy to stroke her cock. Mistress had been more than pleased to see her Sub had come prepared again tonight. She jerked Cassidy off as the trussed woman watched. Wanting to watch herself, Mistress pressed a hidden button, revealing a mirror directly in front of them.

"Watch me jerk you off," she commanded, barely recognizing the hunger in her voice. She teased Cassidy by nearly pulling it out completely until Cassidy was stretched by the thick knob of the double-sided dildo. She would then thrust it back in harshly, causing Cassidy to lose her breath. With her free hand, she caressed her Sub's rock-hard nipples with the crop. She knew the simultaneous friction was creating havoc with Cassidy's body, and she wanted to hear the words. She wanted to know for sure the pain was going to be welcomed.

"Tell me, Cassidy. Tell me you want it."

"I want it, Mistress. Please."

Mistress's nostrils flared with desire, and she slammed the dildo inside Cassidy, grinding her clit with the base. She waited until the precise moment, the intense beginning of the orgasm, to whip the crop across Cassidy's nipple. A guttural response came from the bound woman before she slumped forward as much as her tied limbs would allow.

"Are you okay?" Mistress could have sworn that Cassidy lost consciousness there for a second.

"Yes, Mistress."

Mistress smiled at how easy those words seem to come from Cassidy now. She patted her on the ass and moved to the armoire for something a little more aggressive. After picking out her carefully selected choice, she used the stepstool to climb up onto the bed. She shook her head with mirth when Cassidy's eyes never left her tits. Using a fingertip, she raised Cassidy's chin until their eyes locked.

"Can you handle more, Cassidy?" she asked, genuinely concerned about giving the newbie too much to handle.

"Yes, Mistress."

With a nod, Mistress eased the dildo out of Cassidy. What she had in mind had the smaller woman sliding off the bed to stand behind her Sub. She scraped a fingernail across the tattooed back, loving the feeling of rippling muscles as she went. *I hope you're ready for this, Cassidy.* She pushed the taller woman lightly until she was bent forward as much as her binds would allow. The same finger that journeyed down Cassidy's back tracked lower, finding its destination.

"Have you done this before, Cassidy?" Mistress asked when Cassidy gasped. She carefully watched the reaction in the mirror.

Cassidy shook her head. The trepidation was evident, and Mistress wondered if she would say her safe word.

"I've never trusted anyone that much," the young woman answered with a trembling voice.

Stirred by Cassidy's faith in her, Mistress vowed silently to be as gentle as she could. She reached over and picked up the anal beads she had a sneaky suspicion Cassidy hadn't noticed yet and began coating them with Cassidy's wetness.

"Do you trust me?" Mistress asked, holding Cassidy's gaze in the mirror.

"Yes, Mistress," Cassidy whispered.

"You can tell me to stop, Cassidy. I will go slow, one bead at a time. If it hurts or makes you uncomfortable, please let me know." Cassidy merely nodded as Mistress slipped the first small bead into uncharted territory. "Relax," she coaxed.

Cassidy took a deep breath, and Mistress could feel a slight loosening. In an effort to help calm Cassidy, Mistress started rubbing small circles on her smooth ass cheek. Once the first bead was securely in place with no complaint, Mistress proceeded to slip the slightly larger second bead in. Cassidy pressed her ass back, offering herself even more. Mistress approved, and slipped the third, even larger, bead in.

"Enough," Cassidy groaned huskily, and Mistress immediately stopped the pressure.

"Do you want me to pull out, Cassidy?"

"No, Mistress. Just give me a minute, please."

"Of course." She increased the breadth of her strokes, rubbing hypnotic circles on Cassidy's ass and back. She waited patiently for Cassidy to get used to the sensation.

"I'm okay," the younger woman finally pronounced.

"Are you sure?"

"I'm sure, Mistress."

Perfect. Mistress smiled and climbed back up onto the bed in front of

Cassidy. "Do you remember your safe word?"

"Yes, Mistress, but I don't need it."

"Just in case, Cassidy."

Now for the big guns. This is going to be fun. Mistress picked up a large, triple-pronged dildo. She laughed lightly at the expression of fear mixed with excitement on Cassidy's face.

"This fits inside you, like yours," she explained. "The other parts are for me. Okay?"

Cassidy nodded with enthusiasm. *She likes the idea of doing to me what I'm doing to her.* Mistress had been told multiple times that her ass was fuckable. When Samantha forced her to do things like this, it had been painful. So, when she chose to do this with Cassidy without much thought, it had surprised her. Not only was she doing something she hadn't necessarily enjoyed with Samantha, it meant exposing her back. But it seemed as though her body had cravings that only Cassidy could feed. She could only hope that her scars would be the last thing Cassidy was looking at.

"Ready?" Mistress asked, amused by Cassidy's enthrallment with the dildo.

"Ready."

It was relatively easy to slip Cassidy's part inside of her due to her abundance of wetness. Mistress was pretty sure the same would be true for her. Not yet finished, Mistress leaned over to get one more gadget. She let the delicate chain drape through her fingers. *Can you handle this, Cassidy? Let's test it.* She cupped Cassidy's modest breasts and pinched her nipples. That beautiful, powerful body jerked beneath her touch.

Mistress squeezed the small clamp open, hearing an audible gulp from Cassidy. The temptation was too great, and instead of immediately using the implement, she bent her head to suck Cassidy's nipple into her mouth. She had no doubt that what she was doing affected Cassidy by the way her hips bucked wildly.

Cassidy moaned from somewhere deep inside her, causing Mistress to moan in return. She brought her gaze up, making sure Cassidy was paying attention. Those magnificent eyes were vibrant with excitement. Cassidy was close, and Mistress knew just what to do to push her over that threshold. Her pink tongue came out to circle the tip before taking it between her teeth and biting. Hard.

"Fuck!"

As soon as Cassidy threw her head back in total euphoria, Mistress fastened the nipple clamps to nipples she knew had to be incredibly sensitive. The taut body spasmed again with another orgasm much to Mistress's delight.

"Don't move!" Mistress whispered harshly. She couldn't hold back any longer. She *needed* Cassidy inside her, now! She got on her hands and knees in front of Cassidy, backing up until she was positioned just right. She reached back to arrange the dildo, then filled herself by pushing back with force. As wet and turned on as she was, the pain never came. Only unimaginable pleasure.

Cassidy is a quick learner. The tall woman merely braced herself as Mistress increased her speed. She brought a hand between her own legs and stroked her throbbing clit. It wasn't going to take much after seeing Cassidy come twice already.

"Oh, Cassidy!"

"Please!" Cassidy begged.

"Fuck me, Cassidy! Hard!" Mistress commanded.

There wasn't even a second's hesitation from Cassidy. With hard, fast thrusts, Cassidy quickly drove Mistress to the edge of a violent orgasm.

"I'm coming, Cassidy!"

"Me, too!"

Both women cried out simultaneously. They were loud, and at the moment, Mistress couldn't care less if anyone heard them. In fact, the possibility that someone could hear them spurred Mistress on. She wasn't even close to being done. She slid Cassidy out of her, then relieved the slightly exhausted woman of the dildo as well, and tossed it aside. She then released Cassidy's nipples from the clamps, causing her to hiss, and untied her wrists.

"Keep your hands there until I tell you to move them. Understand?" she panted, yet her authority was still loud and clear.

"Yes, Mistress."

Satisfied that Cassidy would do as told, she picked up the dildo Cassidy wore to the club and spread herself out in front of Cassidy. It was the first time she had ever willingly exposed this much of herself to someone. The first time she ever wanted to do what she was about to do. She watched Cassidy's reaction as she began fucking herself with the dildo.

"Mmm. Fuck yourself for me."

Mistress hadn't expected Cassidy to say anything. When those words came out of her mouth, her pussy clenched, and a thrill ran through her body. She watched as Cassidy's body bucked in time with her as though she was the one fucking Mistress. Watched as Cassidy licked her lips as the dildo was thrust in and out of Mistress's wet pussy. She wanted that tongue inside her. With only slight reluctance, she pulled the dildo out.

"Eat me, Cassidy!" It was like Cassidy had been waiting for Mistress to free her. She dove at Mistress as though she had been parched for weeks. The way Cassidy sucked in her clit, then batted it with her tongue, drove Mistress crazy. *More.* "Use your fingers, Cassidy!"

Cassidy buried three fingers inside her, and Mistress lifted her hips, helping her go deeper. Teeth got in on the act, and when Cassidy curled her fingers, hitting that elusive spot, Mistress knew she was about to explode.

"Cassidy!"

"Come for me like I know you can. Let me drink you."

Oh, God! It was Rebecca—not Mistress—who screamed, arched her back off the bed, and gave Cassidy exactly what she commanded from her.

Doing what's best.

AM I ALIVE? If she wasn't, Mistress couldn't think of a better way to die. That orgasm was so unreal, she still hadn't caught her breath. Cassidy had yet to move, though that could have been because Mistress had a firm hold of her hair. She couldn't say she didn't enjoy feeling Cassidy's hot breath on her *extremely* sensitive sex. She would love to stay this way forever.

That thought, coupled with the small kiss she felt Cassidy place on her mound, scared the hell out of Mistress. She extracted her fist from Cassidy's hair, but even fear didn't stop her from giving the woman a light, affectionate scratch on her head.

"Go into the bathroom and start the shower for us," she ordered softly. She had given up trying to figure out why she was treating Cassidy so different than any other client. *Not client.* No money had been exchanged between the two of them. That, at least, was something Mistress could be happy about.

"Um, Mistress?"

Mistress was brought out of her thoughts by Cassidy timidly calling out for her attention. *Does she not want to shower with me? Is that too personal? And, why the hell am I disappointed by that when getting too personal is something I really* don't *need?*

Cassidy sheepishly looked behind her. Not understanding, Mistress frowned. That is until she remembered what was causing Cassidy to hesitate.

"Oh!" Her lips twitched, but she somehow managed not to laugh. She scooted out from under the younger woman. "Sorry, Cassidy." *Do not laugh. Do not laugh. Do not laugh.* This had to be uncomfortable for Cassidy, so Mistress patted her butt cheek and told her to relax. Which, apparently, was not working.

"Cassidy, this is going to hurt if you don't… let go." *Well, this is awkward.* Yet, Mistress felt a certain intimacy had been formed. She didn't have time to explore that feeling as Cassidy took a deep breath and finally let go. As delicately as she could, Mistress relieved Cassidy of the anal beads.

She frowned when Cassidy didn't get up right away. Fear that she had hurt her made Mistress's heart hurt. "Are you okay?"

"Yes, Mistress." The reply was muffled because of the pillow Cassidy had her face buried in.

"Come here, Cassidy." There was only a small hesitation before she obeyed. "Are you sure you're okay? I'm sorry about that."

Cassidy didn't answer. Instead, she leaned down, coming close to kissing her. Mistress couldn't allow that. As much as she wanted it—God, how she wanted it—she couldn't allow that kind of closeness. She braced a hand on Cassidy's chest, keeping the distance between them.

"*Cassidy,*" she breathed. The taller woman lowered her head and sighed, not bothering to hide her disappointment. *This hurt—hers and yours—is exactly why you shouldn't be involved with anyone.* "Start the shower. I'll be right in." She hoped Cassidy didn't notice the hitch in her voice.

"Yes, Mistress."

When Cassidy disappeared into the bathroom, Rebecca gripped the bedpost and pressed her forehead to the cool wood. *You shouldn't want what you can't have. You should have left her alone. You know a relationship is impossible.* She sniffled quietly, telling herself to get over it. The sex was incredible, but that's all it could be.

"It's ready, Mistress!" Cassidy called out from the bathroom.

Mistress wiped away any errant tears and squared her shoulders. *Just sex, nothing more.*

"Thank you," she said as she walked in, curiously startling Cassidy.

"Yes, Mistress."

Mistress swept her hair up into a messy bun and grabbed Cassidy's hand as she walked by her. She let the water wash over her, wash away the depression that wanted to take over. She picked up a loofah, dolloped it with her favorite lavender and chamomile body wash, and handed it to Cassidy.

"Wash me," she commanded, hoping that having Cassidy's hands on her would help. Cassidy complied, her eyes never leaving Mistress's, as she bathed her tenderly. It was all Rebecca had ever wanted. What she had craved all those years ago with Samantha. Something she had never received. Her heart rate and breathing became erratic when Cassidy moved closer.

Mistress moaned softly but didn't move, when Cassidy progressed lower and cupped Mistress's sex. She wanted to see how far Cassidy would go in a situation such as this. Her palm rubbed against Mistress's clit and she closed her eyes to the sensation. The next thing she felt was Cassidy's lips on her neck. *God, that feels incredible.* She moaned louder, pressing herself even closer to Cassidy. But, when Cassidy's lips started to make a path to her lips…

"Cassidy, no." She pushed Cassidy away and turned around to rinse her body.

"Why?"

Mistress stiffened when Cassidy put her hands on her shoulders.

"Mistress?"

Mistress knelt to pick up the loofah that Cassidy dropped earlier. "Finish in here, and then join me in the room."

Why? Why did she have to make this so difficult? Why couldn't she just want sex like everyone else? Mistress snapped a towel off the rod, pissed that she didn't know which one of them she was questioning. *This has to end. It's what's best for both of us.* She kept telling herself that, hoping she would believe it, as she dressed. Once she was fully dressed, she picked up her mask. *This is who you are. Cassidy could never love who you were. You're broken. You're too old.* She shook her head sadly before putting the mask on.

She sat in the chair, in the same position she had been in when Cassidy first came into this room. And she waited.

"Mistress?"

The waver in Cassidy's voice shook Mistress's resolve. *Do it. For her.* She couldn't bring herself to look at Cassidy. If she did, she may not be able to go through with this.

"Get dressed and sit, Cassidy." Cassidy dressed but didn't sit. "Please."

"What's with the mask?"

"This will be our last session, Cassidy." Though it hurt her to say those words, Mistress kept her tone even as to not give up any emotion.

"What? Why? What did I do? If this is because I kissed your…"

"It's not that," Mistress interrupted. The pain, fear, and anger in Cassidy's voice were like torture. So, she did the only thing she could think of to make this marginally easier on both of them. She lied. "The business that I was called away for? I'm opening a new club. I'll be going there to get it up and running."

"No. We—we just started. You told me you would teach me."

It was unfortunate that Mistress, no that Rebecca, felt the same desperation she could see in Cassidy. Yet, she continued.

"This is for the best, Cassidy."

"For who? You? Am I that bad? You can't tell me you didn't get off on all of this!" Cassidy gestured angrily towards the bed.

It took everything in her not to flinch at Cassidy's anger. She didn't believe Cassidy would do anything to hurt her, but anger never bodes well for her.

"It's normal for a Sub to get attached…"

"Don't! Don't fucking do that!" Cassidy stood abruptly. "I didn't get attached to my *Dom*! It's more than that. You *know* it!"

A small trickle of fear made it past Mistress's defenses as Cassidy towered over her. She looked up at her, genuinely apologetic for causing this animosity between them. "I'm sorry."

"Where?"

"What?"

"Where are you going? My job is flexible."

Though she knew that to be true, Mistress had nothing to offer her. Besides, there was no 'other club.' "Cassidy, you can't leave your home here."

"I'm pretty sure I can do whatever I want. Except in this fucking room." Unable to hold her gaze, Mistress lowered her eyes. Apparently, that only managed to piss Cassidy off more. "Ah, I get it. It's time for you to move on, right? What's the matter, *Mistress*? Run out of conquests here? You successfully recruited me, and now you have to find more?"

Those words hurt as much as any blow to her. But, Mistress couldn't—*wouldn't*—allow anyone to hurt her like that ever again. Her shutters came down with force.

"You are welcome here at the club anytime you want," Mistress said evenly, hoping that Cassidy would never show up here again. She just couldn't fathom thinking of her with someone else here. "But this room will be closed. Indefinitely."

"Please, Mistress. Please don't go. Please don't leave me."

Mistress stood immediately as this beautiful, strong, proud woman fell to her knees and begged. It was something Mistress never expected. And something she never wanted to see. She wasn't worth it. No one was.

"Get up, Cassidy." She grabbed Cassidy's shoulders when she didn't move. "Please get up. You don't deserve this. Get off your knees." She pulled Cassidy desperately. "This world isn't for you."

"Have I not done everything you've asked of me? I may have had some issues, but I got over them. All I want is to be… is to be a good Sub for you."

Cassidy's tears brought Mistress to her knees. Kneeling in front of her, she took Cassidy's face in her hands "God, Cassidy, you are so much more than this. I'm leaving because it's what's healthiest. For both of us." She wiped Cassidy's tears with her thumbs, fighting to keep her own tears from falling. "*I should have left you alone,*" she whispered, then leaned in to feather a kiss on Cassidy's cheek. "*I was selfish, and I'm sorry. I'll never forget you, Cassidy.*"

She rose quickly and left before she didn't have the strength to. It was one of the hardest things she had ever had to do. With all that she had been through, she found it curious that a woman she had just met could affect her so profoundly. And wondered if she had the power to move on this time.

Chapter Six
REBECCA

Mistakes

"How long am I going to have to apologize for this, Hunter?" Rebecca tapped her fingernails on the table as she talked to her old friend on the phone.

"Until I decide to forgive you for disappearing," Hunter replied with mirth.

"I didn't just disappear. I had business to take care of," Rebecca explained once again. It was the truth.

"You didn't say goodbye, Becca. And, you've been gone for quite a while. Do you expect me to believe that something else wasn't involved?"

Rebecca sighed because that was the truth, too. "You're right. There are things I need to work out."

"Things that you couldn't have talked to me about?"

"It's… complicated. I think I just needed to be near my aunt for a bit."

"Yeah, okay. How much longer do you think you will be?"

It seemed the only time she genuinely smiled these days is when she talked to Hunter. The doctor who saved her that night so long ago continued to save her as her best friend. Though she found the doctor charming and beautiful, the two never became intimate. A fact that Rebecca was truly thankful for. Hunter's friendship meant the world to her, and she wouldn't dream of ruining that with sex. Besides, as Rebecca found out during one of their late-night conversations, Hunter was dealing with her own complicated situation.

"I don't know, babe." The reality was, Rebecca was getting restless. She didn't know how long she could keep running away from what she was feeling. "I promise to let you know the minute I'm on my way back."

"Do that. I'll be visiting my folks this weekend, but I'm always available. You know that."

Rebecca always had a bit of anxiety when Hunter went to visit her parents. Her "complicated situation" came in the form of a woman there that was no good for Hunter. She had no idea how deep those complications were. But seeing how much it hurt Hunter, Rebecca wished she could convince her friend to get rid of the problem permanently. But who was she to give relationship advice when she couldn't handle her own shit? Even so, she kept trying. "I do. And, Hunter? Please try to stay away from Susan."

There was a slight hesitation on the other end. "It's been three months, Becca. I'm doing my best, I swear."

That was all Rebecca could ask for. They said their goodbyes and Rebecca put her phone away just as a cup of tea was set in front of her.

"Thank you."

"You're welcome. Problems?" Rebecca's companion took a seat next to her and sipped from her own tea.

"My weekly guilt-trip from a friend back in LA. She wonders why I'm here and when I'm coming home."

"Hmm. Not that I don't enjoy your company, but why are you here?"

Rebecca cautiously took a drink of her tea. "If I recall, Eve, you asked for my help."

Eve Sumptor-Riley was one of those women you either love or hate. Rebecca found herself on the side of the former when, after a consulting job a few years ago, they formed a working relationship. Over time, that turned into a lasting friendship. Yes, their analytical minds caused occasional head-butting, but all-in-all, the two women got along beautifully. So, when Eve called her to help out with a new art gallery she was opening in LA, Rebecca didn't hesitate to say yes.

It was the reason she had left Cassidy the first time. Rebecca flew to New York to meet with Eve and ultimately agreed to assist her with a business plan and vet new employees. With Eve being a savvy businesswoman herself, Rebecca reveled in the challenge. While she did most of the heavy lifting on the business end, Eve and her associate Lainey were able to focus on the talent that would fill the gallery.

"I did," Eve acknowledged with a smile. "However, when you came here that first time weeks ago, we had determined that you being in LA near the gallery would be more beneficial."

"I can do the job from anywhere." Rebecca pushed a file towards Eve as evidence. "I found your curator, didn't I?"

Eve chuckled. "Lauren sounds perfect and I can't wait to meet her. But, that doesn't answer my question. I know you, Rebecca. You haven't been yourself since you've been here."

Rebecca breathed in the crisp New York air. They sat at a small café near Sumptor Gallery, NY, in a rare quiet moment. Though Eve was inundated with opening a new gallery, running multiple businesses, and even her own personal turmoil, she remained perceptive of everything going on around her. If Rebecca thought she could get anything past the astute woman, she was severely mistaken.

"I made a mistake, Eve."

Eve leaned forward, giving Rebecca her full attention. The absolute beauty and power that radiated from the woman never ceased to amaze Rebecca. Or catch her off-guard at the oddest of moments. The one thing that kept Rebecca from ever being attracted to Eve was the fact that everyone thought they were sisters. Well, that and Eve was completely in love with someone else.

"I'm listening."

Rebecca took a breath, letting it out slowly. It was a pathetic stall for time, but it allowed her to find the words.

"I met someone. She walked into my club, and no matter how hard I tried to resist her," she paused, thinking of how her body seemed to act of its own accord when it came to Cassidy. "I gave her a card. An invitation to my room."

Eve's eyebrows raised slightly. "I thought you had given that up."

"I had. *Have*. But, I needed to be near her."

"I can understand that feeling," Eve said with a touch of melancholy.

"I know you can. I wish that…"

"No, Rebecca. Don't try to distract me with my own problems. I do that enough these days. Go on. This woman accepted your invitation, I presume."

Damn it, Rebecca sighed. "Yes, unfortunately. Or, fortunately depending on how you look at it."

"And, how do *you* look at it?"

"I don't know," Rebecca answered honestly. "On the one hand, it was the most incredible sex I've ever had."

"Sex?" Eve interrupted with surprise. "I was under the impression that sex was never an option in that room."

"Your impression is right. It isn't."

"But with this woman everything is different," Eve guessed.

"Yes."

"And, on the other hand?" Eve prompted when Rebecca remained quiet.

"Hmm? Oh, right. The unfortunate part." Rebecca absent-mindedly turned her teacup in circles on the table. "She's young. *Very* young. I should have left her alone." The last part was said quietly, almost to herself.

"How young are we talking?" Eve asked.

"Twenty-five."

Eve hummed and sat back in her chair. "That is young. However, she's old enough to know what she's doing."

"I could be her mother, Eve."

Eve chuckled. "Perhaps. If you started early enough. But is age really the biggest factor here? I can't see you being this troubled by someone who is immature."

"She's not. It's not that." She groaned in frustration. "It's the combination of that, the sex, the emotions. It's too much."

"So, you ran."

Rebecca couldn't be upset with the truth, and the fact that Eve's eyes held compassion told her that Eve wasn't judging her.

"I ran."

"May I ask, which one of those things was the mistake? The invitation, the sex, the emotions, or the running?"

Rebecca let out a mirthless laugh. "All of the above?"

"Are you asking or telling?"

"I should have left her alone."

"So you've said. What I would like to know is why you feel that way."

Rebecca closed her eyes. This was what she was trying to figure out in her head. In her heart. Why it hurt so much to be with Cassidy. And why it hurt, even more, to be away. She had been with the woman twice. It shouldn't be like this. Walking away should have been easy and painless. Yet, here she was.

"She wasn't a fan of the lifestyle," Rebecca began. "She doesn't like being told what to do."

"I'm guessing you changed her mind."

Distraught eyes looked up at Eve. "She's young. Impressionable. Just like I was."

Comprehension lit in Eve's eyes. "With Samantha."

Rebecca nodded. "Cassidy is not immature, but there's a naiveté to her. She deserves more."

"More than what? You?"

"Yes. What if I turn out to be like her, Eve?"

"Like Samantha?" Rebecca nodded again, and Eve reached out to take her hands in hers. "Oh, honey, *that's* what this is about? You are *nothing* like that monster. You must know that."

"I convinced Cassidy to do things, Eve. Things even I have never done before."

"Convinced her or offered and she said yes? You are projecting your fears from your past onto your present."

"You sound like my aunt," Rebecca muttered.

"Well, she is a good therapist. Perhaps you should think about having some sessions with her."

"I do. Once, sometimes twice a week," she smirked.

"Show-off," Eve laughed.

"To be honest, I haven't told her that, yet. I've been trying to work things out in my head before I get her involved. She knows about Cassidy and how old she is, but that's about it." She eyed Eve with a smirk. "She says hi, by the way. And that she misses you."

Eve rolled her eyes playfully. "I don't know if it's a blessing or a curse having a friend whose aunt is my therapist."

"A blessing, of course," Rebecca winked.

"Mmhmm. It has only been a couple of weeks, but I will go see her. Soon." Eve studied Rebecca silently for a moment. "May I ask you something?"

"Of course."

"Have you thought of this Cassidy since you've been here?"

"Only every day," Rebecca answered honestly.

"Do you miss her?"

"*Only every day*," she whispered.

"Then go home, Rebecca."

"What's the point, Eve? We spent two days together. No, mere hours.

It's ridiculous that I even feel this way. We don't even know each other. Besides, she's probably forgotten about me and moved on. As she should."

"First, I know *you*, Rebecca. No one steps into your club without you learning everything there is to learn about them. And, second, knowing you as I do, it's safe to say you affected her as much as she affected you."

Rebecca shook her head even as she hoped that what Eve said was true. Believing that Cassidy still thought about her gave her hope. And anxiety. *Wow. I could do with a session right now.* "I don't know about that. And Cassidy was a guest of another member. I didn't do a full workup on her. Her age, her finances, her friends. Basic information that doesn't tell me what she likes or dislikes. It doesn't tell me if we're compatible anywhere other than in bed. Don't you think that's important?"

"What I think is important is that you found someone who made you feel something pretty remarkable after everything you've been through," Eve answered gently. "It doesn't have to take weeks, months, or years to recognize that." She looked away, a wistfulness in her eyes. "Regret is a bitter pill to swallow, Rebecca. Fear causes you to make extremely regrettable decisions. Even if you think you're doing the right thing."

This time it was Rebecca who reached for Eve's hand in compassion. She knew of Eve's past. The horrors that she had been through. She also knew that Eve gave up the one person she was in love with in order to "do the right thing." If Rebecca felt this despondent about a woman she barely knew, she could only imagine what Eve was feeling.

"You can change things, Eve."

Eve brought her gaze back to Rebecca. "You have no idea how much I wish that were true. There are too many obstacles. Too many lives that can be destroyed."

"So, you sacrifice your own happiness?"

Eve shrugged. "It was the choice I made. One I have to live with until…" She cleared her throat, obviously not comfortable with where the conversation was going. "This thing you feel for Cassidy? Go home and explore it while you have a chance. While there are no other obstacles standing in your path. I understand your fears, Rebecca, more than anyone. But the 'what-ifs' will be even worse. I promise you that."

From her peripheral, Rebecca saw the object of Eve's happiness and sorrow. Judging by the not-so-happy look that was being directed at her, the fact that Rebecca was holding Eve's hand was not appreciated. Rebecca squeezed the hand in hers before letting it go and standing up.

"Lainey," Rebecca smiled, going in for a hug that was readily returned. She and Lainey had gotten to know each other much better over the past couple of years. The quiet woman was kind, intelligent, beautiful, talented… and married with children. She was also just as in love with Eve as Eve was with her. It made her situation feel tame in comparison.

"Hello, Rebecca."

Lainey smiled warmly, though Rebecca could see the tension behind those green eyes.

"Please, take my seat. I was just leaving."

"Not on my account, I hope."

"Of course not," Rebecca smiled at both of her friends. "I need to make arrangements to go back home. Of course, that means breaking the news to my aunt. She's gotten pretty used to me being here."

Lainey laughed as she took the seat Rebecca vacated. "You have your work cut out for you." She absently picked up Eve's tea and lifted it in a salute. "Here's hoping she doesn't bring out her notebook."

Rebecca watched as Lainey sipped from Eve's cup. She was sure it was as second nature to her as breathing. But Rebecca found something acutely intimate about the gesture.

"Take the jet," Eve offered as she smiled at Lainey.

"It really is nice having a friend with a private plane," Rebecca chuckled. Actually, it was an offer Rebecca rarely refused. Anytime she could fly in style was an enjoyable time. *And, now I'm thinking about Cassidy being in that jet with me. Great.*

"Yes, it is."

Rebecca was sure Lainey's thoughts of being in a private jet with Eve were along the lines of hers with Cassidy. She wished she could do something to help her friends. Unfortunately, she didn't even know what to do to help herself.

"Thank you for the kick in the ass," she said to Eve. Noticing Lainey's confused look, she added, "I'm sure Eve will fill you in when I leave."

"Only with your permission," Eve assured.

"You have it."

"Are you going to take my advice?"

Rebecca thought for a moment. "I don't know. But, at least I'm taking the first step."

Eve nodded her approval. "If you need anything, you know where to find me." She laid her hand on the folder Rebecca had given her earlier. "Thank you for this and everything else you've done for Sumptor Galleries."

"It's been a welcome distraction. I'll see you both in LA before the opening, I'm sure."

"Absolutely. Good luck, Rebecca."

Confessions of a Mistress

REBECCA WALKED ALONG the sidewalk, occasionally stopping to look at the cute merchandise the outdoor marketers were hawking. It was the first time she had actually been out since moving back home two weeks ago. Yes, she knew full well that she was being a coward—again—but she couldn't bring herself to go to the club just yet. Fear of not seeing Cassidy there was just as bad as the fear she would.

What would she say? How would she act? Would Cassidy even want anything to do with her anymore? Then there was the fact that Rebecca still didn't feel worthy without the mask. As intelligent and successful as Rebecca was, she felt incredibly inept when it came to matters of the heart. *Why do I feel this way about someone I barely know? What is it about Cassidy Giles that makes me want more?*

Rebecca was so completely preoccupied with her thoughts that she didn't see the other person coming right towards her. When they collided, Rebecca immediately began to apologize for being distracted.

"I'm so sorry, I wasn't…"

"I'm sorry…" Rebecca gasped when she looked up into the bicolored eyes she had thought about so often. "*Cassidy.*" *No! I'm not ready! Not like this! Not as Rebecca!*

"M—um. You're back."

Cassidy looked as shocked as Rebecca felt. *She probably hates me.* "Y-yes."

"How long?"

Two weeks, but I've been too much of a coward to seek you out. Rebecca shrugged apprehensively. *I wish I had dressed more appropriately.* She almost laughed out loud at the thought. How could she have known that she'd run into the one person that could bring her to her knees? What was she supposed to do? Wear a bustier and mask everywhere?

"I've been back to the club a few times."

Jealousy coursed through Rebecca. She forced herself not to ask about… clients while she had been away. There were just some things she didn't want to know. Now, as Cassidy stood in front of her looking amazingly sexy in dark, ripped blue jeans and a low-cut V-neck tee, Rebecca *needed* to know. She lifted a brow.

"Find someone that will give you what you need?" Okay, that came out a little more resentful than Rebecca meant.

"No. You weren't there. I looked for you. Hoped you would come back."

Rebecca's heart ached at Cassidy's honesty. "I should go."

"What is your name?" Cassidy asked quickly. Sounding almost desperate.

Rebecca looked away. Giving her name meant she would have to step out from behind the mask completely. Insecurities embedded so deep in her psyche bubbled up, making it impossible to answer.

"Did I mean anything to you at all?"

So much more than you know. More than should be possible.

"You know," Cassidy continued angrily, "when you told me not to fall in love with you? There was only one problem with that, *Mistress*. You said it a little too late."

Rebecca was stunned. She knew Cassidy was attracted to her. She *knew* that there was more going on than just sex in the Pink room. But, falling in love? So quickly? *Don't pretend you don't know what she's talking about*, Rebecca scolded herself silently. *You know what you feel is more than just physical attraction. You don't have to understand it, but you damn well need to own it.*

"Rebecca," she called out timidly as Cassidy marched away. The younger woman stopped but didn't turn to face Rebecca.

"What?"

"My name is Rebecca."

Slowly, Cassidy finally turned to face her, speechless.

"Not what you were expecting, is it?" Rebecca asked sardonically. It wasn't exotic. It wasn't a name that fit Mistress's persona. However, right here and now? It's who she was.

"It's beautiful," Cassidy says sincerely as she took a step towards Rebecca.

"It's normal."

Cassidy frowned. "It suits you."

"Not when I'm behind the mask. People assume I have some erotic name that goes with that persona. I don't."

"I'm glad you don't."

For some reason, Rebecca believed Cassidy.

"Why?"

Rebecca frowned this time, tilting her head in question.

"Why the club? The mask?"

"That's a long story, Cassidy." *And one that will surely scare you away.*

"I have all the time in the world. Rebecca."

Rebecca's breath hitched hearing her name come from Cassidy's lips.

There was no demand, no plea. Just a quiet offering to listen.

Cassidy gestured to a bench across the way. "Sit with me?"

If you sit with her, you have to tell her the truth, Rebecca. All of it. Are you ready for that? Perhaps this was her out. Cassidy could never love someone who did what Rebecca had done. With a heavy sigh full of dread, Rebecca nodded. She followed Cassidy, and settled in on the bench, tucking one leg under her.

"What do you want to know?" she asked warily.

Cassidy faced her. "Everything."

Rebecca shook her head. *Everything. Be careful what you wish for, Cassidy Giles. You may regret this. So could I.*

"I used to be a Sub," she began quietly. Rebecca then did something she wished she didn't have to do. If she had any hope at all of getting to know Cassidy better—as Rebecca—she would have to tell Cassidy about her past. About Samantha, about the club, about how she stayed despite the pain, about the drug use. But could Rebecca have the courage to tell Cassidy *everything*?

Cassidy listened intently, only leaving once to get them both something to drink. *Well, at least she came back.* Cassidy asked questions, made comments, but never once judged. It was better than Rebecca could have hoped for.

"Where is she now?"

"Dead." Rebecca's tone was emotionless, and she noticed the shock on Cassidy's face. "You're wondering if I killed her. I can see the question written all over your face, Cassidy. Do you think I'm capable of that?"

"I think everyone is capable if pushed to their limit, Rebecca. But I didn't think... I mean, I just..."

Rebecca smiled at a flustered Cassidy. *She's cute when she's flustered.* "I know. The thing is, I'm not sure if I can say I didn't kill her."

Cassidy frowned. "I don't understand."

"The official cause of death was an overdose. Samantha liked to party. Hard. Everything she did was over the top. Drinking, drugs... me." She fidgeted, hating that she had to think about all of this.

"Did she make you?"

Cassidy didn't finish her question, but Rebecca understood what she was asking. "I never did drugs, Cassidy. That's one thing I could be grateful for. Samantha was a very selfish person, especially with things that gave her pleasure. That night was no different than any other. She came home already high and wanting more. She liked having me watch her shoot up. It made her feel powerful to let me know that I was not 'worthy enough' to participate."

"Do you think that by watching, you killed her?"

Rebecca was impressed with Cassidy's intuition. "I felt nothing when she died. There was no remorse." She swirled the water in her bottle and was mesmerized by the tiny twister that formed. *You've been honest so far, may as well keep going.* "Actually, that's not true. I did feel one thing. Relief."

It didn't quite answer Cassidy's question, but at least it was the truth.

"With everything she put you through, I think that's normal."

"Is it normal to sit there and watch her take her last breath?" Rebecca asked quietly. She took a chance and looked up at Cassidy. "After she took that last hit, she became more and more agitated, which she took out on me. She kept screaming at me that I was cheating on her, that there was someone hiding in our bedroom. If she wasn't searching, she was hitting me. Then it all just stopped. Samantha raised her hand to hit me again and just froze. Convulsions started, she began to get sick."

Rebecca shuddered at the memory. Then she felt the warmth of Cassidy's touch on her arm. That simple touch felt like a balm on her soul and gave her the bravery to continue.

"I could have called the ambulance, Cassidy. I could have called 911, and maybe she would still be alive. But, I stood there, bloodied, watching her suffer, and I couldn't."

"I don't blame you, Rebecca. She did this to herself. She doesn't deserve your guilt."

It wasn't just blithe comments. They were an absolution to Rebecca. Perhaps one that she didn't deserve.

"Those are easy words to say, Cassidy."

"I know, but it's true."

Rebecca gave Cassidy a small shrug. "Fortunately for me, you weren't the only one that feels that way."

"You found someone you were able to trust?"

As steady as Cassidy's voice was, Rebecca thought she detected a note of jealousy. Or, perhaps she was just hoping that Cassidy would care enough to have wanted to be the one to save her. It was a silly notion, of course.

"I don't know about trust, but he's a cop. And he knew Samantha did drugs. He always looked the other way because she gave him free access to the club." She didn't know why she didn't tell the exact truth then. Maybe she didn't want Cassidy to know that it was Rebecca that gave him a free pass. That would be admitting that she let Samantha get away with so much more.

"Wait, he's a cop and he didn't protect you?" Cassidy asked angrily.

"He didn't know about that, Cassidy. I never said anything. Not until that night, and then it was only because there was no way for me to hide it from him. Not after what she did to me. It's why he agreed to help me and wrote in the report that I had called him, but he was unable to resuscitate Samantha when he arrived."

Cassidy shook her head. "But that's all true from what you're telling me. She overdosed, you called him, she was already gone. Clear case."

Rebecca tilted her head, eyeing Cassidy. "Are you a lawyer?"

Cassidy's chuckle was a much-needed sound after the conversation they were having. "No, but my dad is. I've listened to him discuss cases enough to know the basics."

"I see. And, what do you do?" Rebecca asked, hoping to veer the conversation in a different direction.

Cassidy's eyebrow flinched, and Rebecca suspected Cassidy saw right through her little ruse.

"We can discuss that later. We were talking about you."

Though the thought of spending more time with Cassidy was tempting, Rebecca became weary of discussing more of her problems.

Surely, they would be too much at some point. "Aren't you tired of hearing my problems?"

"I could never be tired of you."

Cassidy continued to surprise Rebecca. "I don't know about that, Cassidy. I'm pretty boring behind the mask."

Cassidy leaned closer. "You took the mask off for me. There was *nothing* boring about you, Rebecca. Or do you not remember our time together?"

Rebecca closed her eyes and breathed in deeply. Every single second of their time together was burned into her brain. Her body could never forget the things Cassidy did. The memory of *that* brought tears to her eyes.

"I remember."

Chapter Seven
REBECCA

Taking Chances

THE CONVERSATION SHIFTED back to the club, and Rebecca explained to Cassidy how she came to own it. It was almost funny how, looking back, she could see all of the mistakes she made. And, how she fought to correct those mistakes in the years that followed. Perhaps it was a bit extreme to hide her true identity from those who worked for her. Or to vet the patrons of her club so diligently. However, when you come close to losing your life to someone you thought you could trust, trust becomes a rare commodity.

"Why, Rebecca? Why did you stay?" Cassidy asked after Rebecca alluded to being beaten after Samantha found out she had bought the club. "I'm sorry…"

"Don't be," Rebecca interrupted. "It's a legitimate question. I obviously had the means," she shrugged. It was a question she knew would come eventually. One she had asked herself many times. One she didn't know if she actually had an answer to.

"You loved her."

Rebecca laughed joylessly. "No. I hated her. At least I did at the end. If anything, I was infatuated with her at the most. Her strength and control intrigued me. She introduced me to this lifestyle and I became addicted. It wasn't bad in the beginning, Cassidy."

"And when it turned bad?"

"By that point, she had it ingrained in my head that it was my duty as her Sub to do as she commands. Like I said before, I was so naïve and impressionable that she convinced me what she did to me was normal for those who practice this type of relationship. I hate to use that as an excuse, but I really didn't know that her version of this way of life was extreme. I know that's probably hard for you to understand."

"Not really. I did things with you I never thought I would do without questioning it."

Rebecca frowned. "That's exactly what I wanted to avoid when I took over the club."

"I didn't mean that in a bad way, Rebecca," Cassidy said quickly. "You're nothing like her."

I hope that's true. "I never want to be," she said softly. "The moment she took her last breath I stopped being a Sub. Unfortunately, that also meant I was lost. It took the staff fighting over who should take control of the club that snapped me out of it. I took over the club, fired *everyone*, exhaustively vetted a new staff, and donned the mask."

"And became Mistress?"

"Yes. Even my staff knows me only as Mistress. They don't know Rebecca. I needed my control back, and that was the start. Becoming a true Dom was the next." Rebecca glanced at Cassidy, debating her next words. "Every person I brought into that room was carefully selected in order to build myself up. I know that sounds callous, but I made sure that they all left feeling that everything they did in that room was their decision."

"Is it normal for a Sub to become a Dom?" Cassidy asked, sounding a bit dejected.

"For some. Some are very set in their roles. Others use the experience as a stepping stone." She tilted her head again, and her eyebrows furrowed. *Why are you so sad, Cassidy? Do you really want to be a Dom? How could I ever go back to being a Sub?*

"Why me?"

She let out a sharp laugh. "Believe me, Cassidy, I tried to stay away from you." The defeat she heard in Cassidy's voice now showed on her face. Without much thought, she softly touched the back of Cassidy's hand. "I didn't mean that the way it sounded. Before you walked into my club, I had decided I was done. I was getting nothing from it anymore. In fact, there hadn't been anyone in my room for months."

"A myth."

"Excuse me?"

Cassidy looked up from tracing little patterns on the bench. "My waitress that night. When I asked her about the card, she said she thought that it was a myth."

Rebecca nodded with a little smile. "It had been a long time. But when I saw you walk in with Miranda, I wanted you."

Cassidy shivered at Rebecca's words causing Rebecca to feel that familiar hint of desire she now associated with only Cassidy.

"I fought with myself, telling myself to leave you alone," she continued before Cassidy could say anything. "Next thing I knew, I was buying you a drink. No matter how hard I tried to stay clear of you, my body had other ideas."

"What was so wrong with me that you tried to avoid me?"

Oh, Cassidy. You have it all wrong. "*Nothing* is wrong with you. I tried to stay away for many reasons. The biggest one being that I *knew* things would be different with you in that room." Rebecca pinched the bridge of her nose. It was as though her mouth had a mind of its own. It was bound and determined to tell Cassidy *anything* and *everything*. "I know what you think happened with the others, but you're wrong. None of them ever saw me without my mask. None of them ever saw me naked. *You* did."

Cassidy frowned in confusion.

"I never had sex with any of them, Cassidy."

"But," Cassidy shook her head as though she were trying to find the right words. Or any words for that matter. "I… we…"

Yep. So very cute when she's flustered. "It was never about sex. It was about control. For both parties. That's what I meant when I said I chose them carefully. They were more interested in just giving their bodies over to the pleasure of the pain. *That's* what they got off on. I never touched them without some sort of instrument of torture. Touching me was off limits. No exceptions. Until you. I broke all of my rules with you."

"Not all of them," Cassidy muttered. "Did you feel *anything* for me, Rebecca?"

"Oh, Cassidy." Rebecca scooted closer to her companion and touched her face gently. "I felt *too* much. It's why I had to leave. It's why I should leave now." She dropped her hand and stood.

"Oh no!" Cassidy grabbed both of Rebecca's hands and turned her until they were facing each other. Her grip was tight, but not painful. As though she were afraid Rebecca would run if her grip loosened. "I'm not letting you walk away again, Rebecca. You said it was for the best, but didn't say why. You said it was what was healthiest, but still no reason. I *need* a reason. A *legitimate*, concrete reason."

Rebecca didn't know whether to be irritated or terrified. Irritated that Cassidy was demanding something of her, and she was considering giving her the reasons. Terrified because… she was considering giving her *all* the reasons.

"I don't know how to have a real relationship, Cassidy."

"I've never been in a serious relationship, either. So we'll learn. Together."

Rebecca shook her head a little. "I'm damaged. Why would you want to get involved with that?"

"We all have our demons, Rebecca. Yours may be a bit more complicated, but I don't care. I want to be there for you."

"You don't even know me."

"I'm *trying* to! And, so far, your excuses are feeble. Give me a *real* reason!"

Rebecca let out an exasperated breath. *She's really going to make me say it.* "Fine. You want a real reason? I am technically old enough to be your mother, Cassidy!"

"Bullshit! You know I'm twenty-five, right? You can't be more than five years older than me."

"It's not nice to lie to your Mistress, Cassidy." *Shit! I just called myself her Mistress!* Any hope that Cassidy missed that little slip was dashed when her nose flared with a desire that most likely mirrored Rebecca's.

"I have no reason to lie to you. The *most* you can be is ten years older than me. And that's pushing it. Besides my mom is like that much older than my dad."

Rebecca threw her head back and groaned. Determined to make Cassidy understand that they were probably doomed from the start, she locked gazes with her.

"Cassidy, I'm sixteen years older than you."

"Bullshit!" Cassidy snickered at herself as Rebecca rolled her eyes a little at the unimaginative outburst. "Damn!"

"Exactly." *Now she gets it.* Yeah, it hurt, but what else did she expect? That Cassidy would say 'fuck our ages' and whisk her away?

"Uh-uh, nope. You're not going anywhere." She spread their linked hands and leered at her Rebecca in a way that made her feel much younger. And aroused. "Well, shit. I just figured out what my problem has been all along. I've been dating down when I should be dating up! If this is what forty-one looks like, sign me up!"

Rebecca couldn't stop the smile if she tried, but it faded as quickly as it appeared. "And when we have nothing in common?" she asked.

"More to talk about."

Another smile tugged at Rebecca's lips. "Mmhmm. And when your parents and friends disapprove?"

Cassidy shrugged a shoulder. "I'm an adult, Rebecca. I've been making my own decisions for a while now. Besides, like I said, mom is older than dad."

"Cassidy! I'm probably closer to *their* age than I am yours." *Ugh! I hate saying that!* Her nose wrinkled in distaste.

"I don't care. It's my life, and I want you in it, Rebecca."

She's relentless! "Okay. How about when you're thirty-five and I'm fifty-one?" Again, her nose crinkled. Must be a side-effect of their age gap. Or perhaps just her age. She was not a young, naïve woman anymore.

"Then I hope I can keep up with you."

"You have an answer for everything, don't you?"

"When something is important to me, yes," Cassidy answered, squeezing Rebecca's hands lightly. "Rebecca, you're afraid you don't know how to have a real relationship because you've never had one. But even if you had, all relationships are different. There's no magic recipe. We work at it, and we find our own way. Nothing is a guarantee. Hell, you could wake up next week, and figure out I'm some immature idiot. It would devastate me, but at least I'll know that I was courageous enough to give it a try. I've learned enough in the times I've been with you to know that I'm willing to take a risk. I know you're scared, Rebecca. I'm scared, too. But, please, let me be the risk you take."

They were all the right words. Everything she had wished she could have heard years ago. Yet, if she had, they wouldn't mean as much as they did today. Rebecca searched for any signs of malice or dishonesty. She didn't think Cassidy had it in her to be that cruel. Trust didn't come easy for Rebecca, but for some reason, she trusted this woman. A woman she barely knew. A woman she had the overwhelming desire to…

"God, why can't I stay away from you?" She pulled her hands from Cassidy's and wrapped them around her neck. Taking a chance, she lowered her lips to Cassidy's and kissed her.

REBECCA SAT IN her Mercedes trying not to hyperventilate. After kissing Cassidy, she agreed to come back to Cassidy's place. Now, as she sat in front of the cute house, she wondered if she could go through with what Cassidy proposed.

"Go somewhere with me," Cassidy murmured against Rebecca's lips.

"Where?" God, it felt wonderful when Cassidy continued to feather kisses across her lips and cheeks.

"My place. Yours. Anywhere but the Pink Room." She cupped Rebecca's cheek. "I want to know what it's like with you outside of that room, Rebecca. I want to make love with you."

"I don't know how," Rebecca whispered with trepidation.

"Would you like to learn?" Cassidy asked, reminding Rebecca of their first time together. "We could teach each other."

"Yes."

Make love. How in the hell was she supposed to know how to do that? She was a virgin when she met Samantha. Lord knows the two of them never did anything that was anywhere close to loving. Making love to Cassidy meant shedding every defense she had. There was no mask, no control, no lifestyle to hide behind. Just her and Cassidy. *Shit.* Rebecca closed her eyes and took a deep breath. *She trusted you, now it's your turn to trust her.*

She stepped out of the car, grateful that Cassidy hadn't hovered or pressured her. The younger woman simply waited, then held her hand out to Rebecca when she was ready. Rebecca took Cassidy's hand and squeezed it lightly. A silent thank you. The fact that Cassidy was trembling just as much as she was, made Rebecca feel a little better.

"This is a beautiful home." She said it to get their minds off of why they were there. But, it was true. The modern design seemed to suit Cassidy, though it was much bigger than Rebecca expected from someone so young. *No biased ideas, Rebecca. Go into this with an open mind. And heart.*

Cassidy shrugged, still trying to get the door open. "It's not much…"

"Cassidy, it's beautiful," Rebecca repeated forcefully. She never wanted Cassidy to be anything but proud of what she had and who she was.

"Thank you." Cassidy finally got the door open and ushered Rebecca inside. "Would you, um, like something to drink?"

"Water is good," Rebecca answered, taking in her surroundings. The main living area was open and airy. Filled with natural light from the oversized sliding glass doors that led to a private patio. *Nice. And clean.* She didn't know why that surprised her.

"I have something stronger if you like."

Oh, yeah. She's definitely nervous, too. Time to be an adult. Rebecca smiled and traced a finger down Cassidy's jaw. "I want to be completely sober for this, Cassidy." She kissed Cassidy softly and stepped back.

"Be right back." Cassidy gestured around them. "Make yourself at home."

Rebecca took that as an invitation to snoop a bit but was completely distracted by the mural on the far wall. It was mesmerizing and impeccably done. The beach scene featured a mermaid in the crest of a wave. She walked up to the wall, feeling compelled to touch the creation. As she drew closer, she realized that the mermaid was faceless.

"It's not quite done. I—I just couldn't find my muse for the mermaid."

"You did this?" Rebecca asked in awe.

"Yeah." Cassidy smiled proudly and handed a bottle of water to her guest. "I do murals all around the city. You know, hospitals and stuff. And, my friend's an interior decorator. If her clients want something a little special, she calls me." Another shrug. "Drives my parents insane, but it pays the bills and I love it."

"You're an artist." When her preliminary report came back on Cassidy, it said she was a painter. Rebecca hadn't known that meant an artist. "This is amazing, Cassidy." She followed each brush stroke with her eyes and almost felt as though she were in that wave. "Freehand?"

"Yeah. I see a picture in my mind, and just paint."

"Are you in galleries?" Eve needed to see this woman's work, Rebecca decided. Cassidy laughed but stopped when Rebecca didn't join in. She wasn't kidding.

"I have a few canvases, but I don't think I'm gallery caliber. It's okay. I like doing murals."

"This is definitely worthy of being displayed or sold as prints, Cassidy. I have a friend who's opening a gallery here soon." She downplayed the significance of the gallery and owner for Cassidy's sake. If Cassidy knew anything about the art world, she would know who Eve Sumptor was. Rebecca wanted to be sure Cassidy was willing, first. "Would you like for me to talk to her?"

"Um, what kind of friend?"

Ouch. Rebecca smiled sadly. "You should know I don't become friends with people who have been in my room. Just one more rule I broke with you. Besides, I don't think there's a human being alive who could dominate Eve." *Except maybe one.*

"You don't have to do that."

"I know. I want to."

Cassidy looked a tad uncomfortable. "Okay." She cleared her throat. "Would you, um, like a tour?"

Okay, we're going to have to do something to get her over this nervousness. And hopefully, it'll help me, too. Rebecca took the water bottle from Cassidy and set them aside. "Maybe later," she said, pulling Cassidy to her. "Right now, I just want you."

The kiss they shared was the most passionate kiss Rebecca had ever experienced. Cassidy began unbuttoning Rebecca's shirt and slipped it off her shoulders. Her hard nipples strained against her satin bra, needing to be touched.

"You're so beautiful," Cassidy murmured as Rebecca's bra joined her shirt on the floor.

Rebecca's eyes teared up with emotion. All of her life, people have told her she was beautiful. But no one had ever sounded so sincere, so tender. Cassidy sunk to her knees in front of her and began unbuttoning her jeans. She whimpered when Cassidy took her bellybutton piercing between her teeth and tugged gently.

Cassidy hooked her fingertips into the waistband of Rebecca's jeans and panties. Before she knew it, she was naked in front of a very attentive Cassidy. Her tummy muscles contracted when Cassidy traced her tattoo with a blunt nail.

"I got it after," Rebecca hesitated. The bird in flight on her hip had significant meaning to her. It took Rebecca a long time before she felt she was worthy of it. "When I became free."

Cassidy kissed the tattoo tenderly. An act that spoke louder than any words that could ever be said. Rebecca ran her hands through Cassidy's hair, lost in the way she peered up at her. She didn't understand how or why this connection with Cassidy happened. But, at the moment, all she wanted to do was bask in the way Cassidy made her feel.

Rebecca's knees buckled, and she grasped Cassidy's shoulders when Cassidy's nose grazed her clit as she breathed Rebecca in. She gasped, digging her fingers into those shoulders when she felt Cassidy's tongue tasting her. Teasing her.

"I'm going to fall, Cassidy."

Cassidy responded by gripping Rebecca's ass. "I won't let you," she purred against Rebecca's extremely wet pussy. Her tongue dipped further inside and dual guttural moans filled the air.

"Baby, please." *Whoa. I've never called anyone that, before. I like it. I like her.* Cassidy stood, grasping the back of Rebecca's thighs. When she found herself in Cassidy's arms, her legs wrapped around Cassidy's waist, Rebecca's arousal tripled. Hell, it went through the fucking roof.

She supposed she could have made it easier for Cassidy to carry her up the stairs by not having her mouth glued to Cassidy's. But, she couldn't help herself. She was being carried by a very muscular, very androgynous, very gorgeous woman. Rebecca was a woman who knew her weaknesses.

"I'm, uh, sorry about the mess. Maid's day off," Cassidy said as she gently let Rebecca down. "But, um, the sheets are clean. I just changed them."

Rebecca frowned. She had no right to feel jealous, yet color her green.

"Not sure I want to think about why at this point."

Cassidy's eyes widened. "No! I just meant it was time. Rebecca, I haven't been with anyone since… well, since I met you."

As surprising as that was, it made Rebecca feel special. And much better than she did just moments before. "Neither have I. Even before, Cassidy."

"No one wherever you went? You know, breaking in the new club?"

Rebecca sighed. "No." She could feel Cassidy's apology in the warmth of her arms as she embraced her. *Tell her the truth, Rebecca. Put her out of her misery.* "I didn't lie to you when I said I was leaving for business. But it wasn't for another club like the one here. I was consulting on a business venture. I just wasn't able to concentrate."

"Why?"

"I couldn't stop thinking about you." *Great. Geez, what is it about her that makes you spill your guts.*

"Is that why you came back?"

Cassidy looked so hopeful, it almost made Rebecca smile. Then she remembered she was completely naked and just moments before they were locked in a heated kiss ready to let their bodies talk for them.

"Cassidy, I'm feeling very vulnerable here."

It literally took Cassidy two seconds to get as naked as Rebecca was, causing Rebecca to chuckle. Of course, that turned into a gasp when Cassidy pulled her close and their bodies touched. Cassidy's warm skin on hers was thrilling, but there was something missing. "You're not wearing it."

She shrugged sheepishly. "I haven't had the urge to wear it lately. Since you left, actually. With the way I was feeling, I didn't need it. I spent most of my time in here, but alone. I missed you. I didn't want to do anything but sleep. At least then I could dream about you. I had no idea where to find you, or if you were even still in the country. I didn't even know your name. But I missed you so much that I was dying inside."

Cassidy didn't just shed her clothes for Rebecca. She stood before Rebecca, tears running unchecked down her cheeks, and exposed her soul. Rebecca, who fought her own tears, reached up captured Cassidy's tears with the pads of her thumbs.

"I missed you, too. It felt so wrong in my head to want you, but my heart ached. I couldn't stand being so far away from you anymore. I didn't think I'd ever see you again, but I needed to be closer to you. You were here, I needed to be here, too."

"Rebecca." Cassidy rested her forehead against Rebecca's.

The two women just let the emotions envelop them. There are just some things in life that can't be explained. Rebecca, in this moment, had given up trying to explain why this felt so incredibly right.

"Make love to me, Cassidy," she breathed.

"Do you want me to get…"

Rebecca placed her fingertips on Cassidy's lips. "No. I want to feel you."

This is what she wanted. What she had always wanted. Someone who treated her as though she were a gift. Someone who would touch her as though she meant the world to them. So, the fear that crept up when Cassidy nudged her back on the bed and began lowering herself on top of her surprised her. She couldn't stop herself from pushing Cassidy away even though that was the *last* thing she wanted to do.

"What's wrong?"

How do I explain that this position has always been one of pain and submission for me? "I'm sorry. I…"

"Does this scare you?" Cassidy asked gently.

Rebecca looked away, full of shame, and nodded. *She doesn't need this burden.*

"Oh, baby, you have nothing to be ashamed of. We can try this another way, it's okay. I just need you to know I would never hurt you. Never, Rebecca."

The passion in Cassidy's voice calmed Rebecca. *This is not like it was with Samantha.* "Wait, please," Rebecca pleaded when Cassidy began to move off of her. "I want to feel you on top of me."

"I never want to do anything that makes you uncomfortable. We can try this another time."

"I'm okay. I want this, baby. I just panicked for a minute." She wrapped her arms around Cassidy's neck, holding her in place. "I'll tell you if it's too much. I promise."

Cassidy hesitated, so Rebecca made the decision for her by pulling her down on top of her. They both moaned at the contact of their bodies. Accelerated breathing and soft whimpers filled the air as Cassidy kissed Rebecca's neck. The sounds of ecstasy got louder when Cassidy took Rebecca's nipple in her mouth, and her body moved sensually on hers. All of the earlier fear disappeared without another single thought.

Rebecca's body writhed under Cassidy. Her hips lifted, pushing her wet, hot center against Cassidy's thigh. Then she lifted her knee, and her smooth, strong thigh came in contact with Cassidy's clit. They were both soaked and the sound of them together filled the room with an undeniable erotic charge.

"Touch me, Cassidy," Rebecca breathed close to Cassidy's ear. She felt the tremors throughout Cassidy's body and felt a surge of power in her own body. Even in this position, she could have control. Even when giving it up, she could feel safe.

Cassidy slipped a hand between them, and for the first time in two months, Rebecca felt… whole.

"Mmm, you feel so good," Cassidy moaned.

Rebecca's fingers clamped onto Cassidy's ass, squeezing and pulling at the same time. She almost came immediately when Cassidy slipped two fingers inside her and curled them, hitting a particularly sensitive spot.

"I need to touch you." Truth was, Rebecca had been dreaming of touching Cassidy since that first night they shared together. She couldn't allow herself before. Touching was as intimate as kissing. Now? Oh, now all bets were off.

Cassidy didn't hesitate to oblige. She shifted slightly, staying inside Rebecca while she got to her knees. Rebecca scraped her fingernails down Cassidy's ribs, then dipped her fingers between the lips of her lover's sex. The moan that came from her was hoarse and needy when she felt how wet Cassidy was for her.

"I've wanted to do this since I saw you walk into my club," Rebecca confessed her earlier thoughts before slipping two fingers inside Cassidy.

"Oh god!" Cassidy's hips bucked, drawing Rebecca deeper inside.

Cassidy pumped her hand faster and Rebecca matched each stroke with a stroke of her own. As if by some unspoken agreement, they each slipped another finger inside and the cries of ecstasy continued to get louder as they drew closer to that peak. Rebecca gripped Cassidy's hair with her free hand, their hips pumped passionately in unison. She felt Cassidy tighten around her fingers and there was no holding back any longer.

"Cassidy!"

"Rebecca!"

The rough sound that came from deep within Rebecca came from years of pent-up need. A need for passion. For something other than pain. For something incredible with someone who she felt cared about her. A need for someone like Cassidy. As the climax took a hold of her, Rebecca pulled Cassidy's hair as she came. She felt Cassidy's sex clamp around her fingers, tight and hot. And, oh so wet. It was fucking mind-blowing.

"It was you," Cassidy breathed with amazement.

Panting, Rebecca looked up at her. "What?"

"It wasn't what we did in that room. It's *you* who makes me feel this way, Rebecca."

It was as if the words turned on a faucet inside Rebecca. Emotions flowed out of her—literally—as she came again. Hard. She may have felt a little self-conscious about that if Cassidy hadn't followed with another orgasm right along with her. At this point, they were going to need to replenish their fluids if they were going to continue this way.

"You're the only one that's ever made me do that," Rebecca revealed almost bashfully. Of course, that bashfulness turned into a soft laugh when Cassidy gives her a cocky, prideful grin.

Let's see how long you keep that cocky grin, Rebecca thought, relying solely on her instincts when it came to what to do next. Though she had never had a normal sex life, her imagination never suffered. In fact, it flourished in those times when she had to endure the pain or humiliation. There were so many things she had wanted to try. It should have amazed her that she felt safe enough with Cassidy to do exactly what she'd always wanted.

Cassidy's cocky grin turned into a whimper as Rebecca pulled her fingers out. Disappointment flashed in Cassidy's eyes as she pulled out of Rebecca, but that would soon disappear, too. Once she was sure she had Cassidy's full attention, she plunged her fingers – still soaked from Cassidy – inside herself. Making sure her fingers were nicely coated with both of their juices, Rebecca promptly thrust them back into Cassidy's greedy pussy.

Cassidy groaned and rotated her hips, but Rebecca didn't linger for long. She had more in mind. She needed more. She pulled her dripping fingers out, brought them to her mouth, and licked, tasting *both* of them. She hummed her approval. *So good.*

Obviously feeling a bit left out, Cassidy dipped her head and sucked Rebecca's fingers into her mouth, and licked those fingers clean.

When she was done, Cassidy collapsed beside Rebecca with a big, happy smile. "That was incredible," she gasped.

Rebecca rolled on top of Cassidy and smiled. "Yes, it was." She gave her a quick peck. "How's your stamina? Because I'm not even close to being done."

"Oh, I can do this *all* night long, baby."

Oh, this is going to be so much fun! "Good to hear. Why don't you get your little friend?"

Chapter Eight
REBECCA

Getting to Know You

TURNS OUT, THE body needs a bit of rest after being depleted of fluids for hours on end.

"Tell me about yourself, Cassidy." Rebecca took a sip of water, then passed the bottle over. It may have been an odd time to begin a conversation. They were both naked, sweaty, and not even close to being done with their marathon sex. But since they were currently on a break, why not get to know the person that was fucking her brains out?

"Not much to tell," Cassidy shrugged.

"Come on. I've bared my soul to you. Literally. What is it you don't want me to know?"

Cassidy's eyes widened. "Nothing, I swear. It's just…"

"Just?"

"There's no story, Rebecca."

"What do you mean?"

"I mean, I grew up with a great family and never really had anything bad happen to me."

The way Cassidy explained that made it seem like she was apologizing. "Cassidy, why on earth would you feel sorry about that?"

"I don't. Not really. I mean…" Cassidy grunted with frustration.

Rebecca reached out and caressed Cassidy's cheek. "Never feel guilty about having a good life, baby. Be happy. Hell, be proud of that fact."

Cassidy brought Rebecca's hand to her lips and pressed a kiss to her palm. "I'm so sorry for everything you've been through."

"You're sweet. Now, tell me about Cassidy Giles."

Cassidy's charming smile turned confused. "How did you know my last name?"

Rebecca chuckled. "The same way I knew your first name. If people enter my club, I know about them."

"Does that mean you did a background check on me?"

There was no bitterness in Cassidy's question, just pure curiosity.

"Actually, you were a guest of a member. So, only the basics were done. Nothing too invasive," Rebecca winked.

"Were you tempted? I mean, after we, you know, in the Pink room?"

"I'm interested now, baby. I'm asking *you* to tell me about you. I don't want to read some report. I want to hear your voice telling me what you were like as a child."

Cassidy gave her a toothy smile. "I don't know. I was a tomboy. I guess I still am," she shrugged sheepishly. "I used to walk around without a shirt." She looked down at her small tits. "Guess I could still do that now."

"Um, no, you can't. I don't want to have to bitch slap every woman that looks at you," Rebecca joked.

Cassidy grinned again. "I may like watching that."

Rebecca rolled her eyes. "Tell me more."

"Okay, let's see." Cassidy repositioned herself and laid her head on Rebecca's naked thigh. "I used to love helping my dad whenever he was cutting wood or fixing the cars."

"I thought your dad was a lawyer."

Cassidy looked up at her with those bicolored eyes. "He is. But he always made it a point to be with us. He wasn't interested in making the big money. He was more interested in helping those who didn't have as much. Family was important to him and my mom. We spent a lot of time together. Of course, as a teenager, I thought it was lame. But, now, I'm grateful that they made us do that."

"That's beautiful." It was something Rebecca wished she could have had. Before their death, her parents were always present and loving. She wondered if she would have been resentful of having to spend so much time with them had they lived. "Do you have siblings?"

"Yeah, I have a big brother. We don't see each other much. He lives in the midwest now of all places. He's busy with his life. Has a wife and kids and I get that. At least I get to see him and my niece and nephew on the holidays when they come to mom and dad's place." She tinkered with Rebecca's bellyring. "What about you? Have any brothers or sisters?"

"No, I'm an only child." Rebecca ran her fingers through Cassidy's soft hair. "When did you know you were gay?" She was changing the subject and knew Cassidy accepted that when she smiled and answered without question.

"I'm pretty sure I've known since I was a little sperm swimming around looking for a place to dock."

Rebecca laughed. "Oh, God. You're a nut!"

"I'm serious!" Cassidy joined in on the laughter. "I've always known. I never felt *different* or anything. I just knew that I liked girls. I mean, I knew girls who like boys, girls who liked girls, boys who liked girls, boys who liked boys. It was all normal to me."

"Different generation," Rebecca mumbled.

Cassidy leaned over and kissed Rebecca's tummy. "Maybe. I guess it's easier to accept these days."

"Easier to understand," Rebecca corrected. "There are still people out there that don't approve."

"Who the fuck cares about anyone who doesn't approve? I don't live my life for those people."

"I take it your parents approve."

"Yeah, they're cool. When I told them, my mom swore she knew before I did. Of course, I told her my sperm theory to set her straight."

Rebecca shook her head. She loved Cassidy's playfulness. Samantha was never like this. Hell, moments like this were unheard of. It was sex. And, of course, control.

"So, no awkward experimentations in college for you?"

"Uh." Cassidy rubbed the back of her neck. "I didn't go to college."

"You seem embarrassed about that."

"You're just so smart. Academics were never my specialty, Rebecca. Art was. And I didn't feel like I could learn how to hone my skills in a classroom learning math and shit. My dad hoped I'd be a lawyer, but my brother did that. My mom wanted me to do something that made me happy. And even though she didn't agree with me not going to college, she knows my art makes me happy."

"What you do with a paintbrush is magical, baby. You deserve to be in galleries." Rebecca slapped her playfully when Cassidy made a face. "Stop. You're more talented than occasional murals."

Clearly uncomfortable with the compliments, Cassidy returned to what they were discussing before. "So, um, what about you, Rebecca?"

"Cuinn," Rebecca offered.

"Cuinn. I like that. Rebecca Cuinn." She said Rebecca's full name as though she were rolling it around in her mouth like a fine wine. Then she cleared her throat when she saw Rebecca looking at her funny. "When did you know you were gay? Any sordid affairs in college?"

"Hmm, I think, like you, I always knew. Only, it wasn't as talked about back when I was a teen so I *did* feel different." She crinkled her nose at the thought. She didn't enjoy the age difference between them, but it was something she would have to get over. "When I was in college I was too busy getting a double degree to explore anything. And, then, in my senior year, I met… Samantha."

Cassidy averted her eyes and frowned. "She was your first?"

"Yes."

There was a moment of uncomfortable silence. "What about your parents? Are they supportive?" Cassidy asked, changing the subject.

Unfortunately, that was also an uncomfortable subject. "They, um, died when I was ten. They never knew, but I think I knew them well enough to believe they would be supportive."

Cassidy sat up and took Rebecca in her arms. "Jesus, Rebecca. I'm so sorry. How?" She cringed and shook her head. "I'm sorry," she apologized again.

"It's okay, Cassidy." She touched the younger woman's cheek. "It was a drunk driver. Apparently, it was over in seconds. The police always think that it's a comfort to say it was instant and they didn't suffer. Unfortunately, to a ten-year-old, that doesn't ease the pain."

"Where did you go, you know, after?"

"My aunt, my mom's sister, took me in. Listen, Cassidy, I know there are things in my life that have been horrible. But, it wasn't all bad. I had a good life with my aunt. It helps that she's a psychiatrist. I still talk to her as a therapist on a regular basis. Does that bother you?"

"Of course not! I think you're the strongest, bravest woman I've ever met."

"I don't know if I'd say that..."

"I said it. And I mean it." She leaned in and kissed Rebecca's lips briefly. "Anyone who can go through what you went through and come out so incredible has to be strong."

"You barely know me, Cassidy."

"I know enough, Rebecca. You're courageous, successful, intelligent. I mean, shit, you were getting a double degree while in college. You're beautiful as fuck and you have an ass to die for."

"Ah, yes. A quality to be proud of," Rebecca laughed.

"You *should* be proud of that ass, baby! You know, your ass is the first thing I saw after you left your card on my table. I sure as shit didn't want to be at that club that night. Thought I hated what that lifestyle stood for.

But I would have followed that ass to the depths of hell if I thought I had a chance of fucking it."

Rebecca lifted an eyebrow playfully. "And you did fuck it." She kissed Cassidy a little deeper. *"You can fuck it anytime you want, baby."*

"Hell, yeah." Cassidy pushed Rebecca back into a prone position and laid on top of her. "This okay?" she asked softly.

Rebecca touched Cassidy's lips with her fingertip. "I trust you, Cassidy."

She showed Cassidy how much she trusted her many, many more times that night. And well into the morning.

REBECCA WOKE UP to the strange sensation of a warm body next to hers. And by next to hers, she clearly meant she was wrapped around that warm body like an octopus. She knew exactly where she was and what they had done just a few hours before. The "strange" part was waking up to someone for the first time. Samantha had *her* side of the bed and that had been fine with Rebecca. Rebecca was never quite in the mood to snuggle with the woman who took pleasure in hurting her.

What she found with Cassidy was so different. Making love was an epiphany to Rebecca. She had thought, so long ago, that her life needed adventure. She had been so afraid of being the "boring" person everyone assumed she was that she allowed herself to be with someone that was toxic. If she had known then what Cassidy had taught her in mere hours, Samantha would never have happened. Or, perhaps Samantha had to happen in order for Rebecca to see how special someone like Cassidy was. If that was the case, Rebecca wouldn't have changed a thing if it meant ending up right here, right now, with Cassidy.

Rebecca could tell from Cassidy's breathing that she was awake. Cassidy's heart was beating fast beneath her cheek, and Rebecca wondered what she was thinking about. Or if she was uncomfortable in any way having Rebecca there. Hoping that wasn't the case, Rebecca took Cassidy's taut nipple into her mouth and hummed with approval. Cassidy's small gasp and the tightening of her arms around Rebecca was a good sign.

Rebecca released the nipple with a light pop and looked up at her companion with a smile. "Good morning."

"The best," Cassidy replied with a smile. She tenderly pushed a strand of hair off of Rebecca's face. "How did you sleep?"

"Like a baby." *For the first time ever. No dreams, no fears. Nothing but peaceful rest.* "You?"

"Never better." She kissed Rebecca's forehead so gently that it was just a feather of a touch.

Rebecca enjoyed the feeling almost as much as she was enjoying rolling Cassidy's nipple between her fingers. "How long have you been awake?"

"Um." There was a minuscule pause as though Cassidy was trying to think of a satisfactory answer. "Not long."

She hissed when Rebecca pinched her nipple hard. Rebecca had been awake for a little while herself and knew Cassidy wasn't being completely honest. "Mmhmm. Try again."

Cassidy laughed. "About fifteen minutes or so."

Or longer, Rebecca thought, but let Cassidy get away with her answer. Besides, she had more questions. Like what was making Cassidy's heart beat so fast. "What were you thinking about?"

"Um."

Note to self; Cassidy starts with 'um' when she's scared or nervous.

"Can I ask you a question?" Cassidy asked timidly.

Rebecca chuckled. Of course, she knew exactly what Cassidy was doing, but what could Cassidy possibly ask after their talk last night? During their breaks, they talked even more. They stayed away from anything particularly heavy after their first conversation, focusing more on likes and dislikes. Rebecca was surprised to find that they had a lot more in common than she thought they would.

"You didn't learn enough last night?"

"I could never learn enough. The more I discover, the more I need to know, Rebecca."

There was no mirth in Cassidy's words and the sincerity caused Rebecca to blush. She cleared her throat and fidgeted under Cassidy's intense stare.

"What's your question, Cassidy."

Cassidy's eyes widened a little. "Do you…?" She visibly gulped before trying again. "Do you…?"

Rebecca leaned back, amused by Cassidy's inability to get her question out. "You're cute when you're flustered."

Cassidy raised a brow. "I am not flustered."

She was sure Cassidy was trying to sound offended, but it didn't quite reach her eyes. So, Rebecca tweaked Cassidy's nipple again causing more laughter from Cassidy.

"What are you? A lie detector test?"

"Yes. You'd be wise to remember that," Rebecca teased with a smirk. "Now, what's your question?"

Another pause. "Do you…?"

"I got that part," Rebecca laughed. "Try different words."

"Do you think you could fall in love with me?"

Cassidy said the words so fast that they ran together, and it took Rebecca a minute to decipher what was said. When it all came together in her brain, she smiled brightly. Mostly for Cassidy's courage, but also because she was so cute about it.

"Yes," she said finally when Cassidy peeked down at her with anticipation.

Cassidy was now sporting that toothy, goofy grin of hers that Rebecca found irresistible.

"Do you think you've already started falling?"

Cassidy's mouth slammed shut. *She didn't mean to say that*, Rebecca surmised by the look of pure fear in Cassidy's eyes. A fear that Rebecca felt as well. She didn't know how it was possible, but it *did* feel like she was falling. That had to be what this feeling was. Since it felt good, *Cassidy* felt good, Rebecca allowed herself to be honest.

She caressed Cassidy's cheek and whispered, "*Yes.*" It was frightening how true that was. She was definitely going to have to talk to Aunt Wills about this. Was it even possible to fall this quickly for someone? She nearly squealed with surprise when she suddenly found herself pinned beneath a very happy Cassidy.

"You know, we *are* lesbians."

Rebecca laughed. "Really? What tipped you off?"

"Cute. What I mean is, we should take advantage of this stereotype we have. We've had three dates, that means a U-Haul is totally acceptable."

Oh shit. Okay, the possibility of falling fast for someone is one thing. Moving in is a whole other animal altogether. The last person Rebecca lived with almost killed her. She meant it when she said she trusted Cassidy, but did she trust herself? Did she trust her instincts? Hell, did she trust that *she* wouldn't become exactly like Samantha? *Be calm about this, Rebecca.*

"We have not had three dates," she said playfully. She certainly didn't want to scare Cassidy off. But she would need to make it clear that no matter how fast she was falling, they needed to take it slow.

"Sure, we have. The first two times at the club, and now. Or last night. If we make love right now, that'll be four. Which, if you need four dates, I'm totally willing to sacrifice," Cassidy grinned.

One thing was certain. Rebecca was going to laugh a lot in this relationship. She shook her head. "Sex? Sex is what constitutes a date for you?" Cassidy shrugged as if Rebecca just asked her the silliest question. "There was no food involved."

"Food? That's a date for you? Food?"

Well, it's a start, Rebecca thought. This was probably a significant difference in their age gap. Truth was, Rebecca had no clue how to date these days. She had avoided it like the plague. Maybe sex was all it took for this generation. But that's not how she wanted things with Cassidy. As phenomenal as the sex was, she wanted something deeper between them.

"For starters, yes," Rebecca chuckled and caught Cassidy by the ass cheek as she tried to get up. "Where are you going?"

"To see what I have in the fridge. I'm going to make you breakfast, lunch, and dinner." She frowned. "I think maybe I have some eggs. I know I have some beer."

"Such a bachelor," Rebecca mumbled blithely.

"Not anymore."

God, the way Cassidy looked at her, so cheerful and honest, it made Rebecca think things would actually work if she were to agree to move in right this second. Nevertheless, Rebecca Cuinn was a realist. She caught Cassidy again before she could get up.

"Cassidy. Don't rush this." She felt bad when Cassidy looked as though Rebecca just popped her perfect bubble.

"I'm not trying to, Rebecca. It's just…"

Cassidy hesitated, and Rebecca filled in the blanks. It was easy to do when the fear was quite apparent. "You're afraid I'll run again." Cassidy shrugged. "And, I'm afraid you'll find someone younger and more beautiful."

"Never," Cassidy said without uncertainty.

"I could say the same thing to you. I'll never leave again. I told you we would try this, and we will." Cassidy's long bangs fell into her worried eyes as she bowed her head slightly. Rebecca reached up and tucked them behind a multi-pierced ear. "But we're going to have to prove it to each other. If we're going to trust each other together, we're going to have to trust each other when we're apart."

Oh, Aunt Wills would be proud of that one. Perhaps Rebecca was learning more from these therapy sessions than she realized.

Cassidy let out an over-exaggerated sigh. "I know. But you'll stay sometimes, right?"

"Of course. We're in our honeymoon stage," Rebecca waggled her eyebrows at Cassidy causing her to chuckle. Her heart felt lighter now that this first hurdle was cleared. She knew there would be more. That's life. But if they could face them together like this, they would be fine. "We'll be together more than we're apart, Cassidy. We just need to know we *can* be apart without *falling* apart."

Somehow that would sound more convincing coming from someone other than Rebecca who had no clue what she was doing. But whether she was trying to convince herself or Cassidy, it didn't matter. Truth was truth.

"No problem. We totally got this."

Rebecca moaned softly when Cassidy kissed her firmly. "Totally," she murmured against Cassidy's lips before deepening the kiss even more. Unfortunately, she wasn't prepared for the angry sound coming from Cassidy's belly and began laughing just as things were getting heated.

"Hungry?" Rebecca managed between snickers.

"I missed dinner last night," Cassidy pouted and looking very cute doing so.

"Aww, poor baby." Rebecca was starving herself, but she wouldn't give Cassidy the satisfaction of knowing that. Instead, she patted Cassidy's ass and gave it a little squeeze. "Up. Let's get some food inside of you."

"I'd rather have *you* inside of me."

That would have worked wonders on Rebecca if Cassidy's stomach hadn't picked that moment to growl loudly again. *She's definitely cute when she blushes*, Rebecca thought with amusement.

"You'll have me. But you need some sustenance. I think your stamina needs a bit of a boost." *So does mine.*

"Fine. Can you cook?"

"I have many talents," Rebecca answered saucily with a wink. That confidence was only on the surface. Not that she wasn't a great cook. She was. She just hoped she could cook for Cassidy without having flashbacks or a fucking panic attack. "However, I think even my abilities won't be enough for possibly expired eggs and beer."

A sheepish grin told Rebecca she was probably right about the eggs. She scooted out from under Cassidy, knowing that if she stayed there much longer, they were never going to get up.

Cassidy propped herself up on her elbow, not bothering to cover up her glorious nakedness. *Yummy*.

"Want me to go pick something up?" Cassidy asked as her eyes followed Rebecca's every move.

After a quick scan of the bedroom floor, Rebecca remembered her clothes were downstairs decorating the living room floor. She bent over and picked up Cassidy's shirt and slipped it on. It dwarfed her, but noticing Cassidy's reaction, she'd say the shirt was perfect.

"No. I know of this great little diner not too far from here. Plus, it's close to the gallery I was telling you about." She padded to the bathroom, determined not to let the sexy way Cassidy was looking at her interfere with her plans for food. "It can be our first date."

"Rebecca?"

Rebecca paused, a small smile playing on her lips. She loved hearing Cassidy say her name. It made her feel… real.

"Yes?"

"Will you still teach me?"

Surprise wasn't a strong enough word for what Rebecca felt. She knew Cassidy didn't like authority. She knew that lifestyle wasn't something Cassidy really wanted. So, for her to ask Rebecca to teach her was completely unexpected.

"You still want to do that?"

"Yes. Only with you."

Rebecca's nose flared with desire. While she hadn't had time to think about how a relationship with Cassidy would affect her life as Mistress, Rebecca knew that would always be a part of her. Would she have been willing to give her up for Cassidy? With this request, maybe she wouldn't have to.

"Lay down and spread your legs, Cassidy."

A small smirk formed on Cassidy's lips. "Yes, Mistress."

Rebecca unbuttoned the shirt she just put on and stalked towards her Sub. She tamped down the fear that she would allow her dominant side to overpower her. There was a substantial difference between what she had with Samantha and what this was with Cassidy. That difference was, Rebecca cared.

She watched as Cassidy automatically placed her arms above her head and clasped onto the headboard. Her heart rate tripled when Cassidy spread her legs wide, exposing everything to Mistress. Oh, yeah. Having Cassidy as a girlfriend was going to be *very* fun.

Chapter Nine
REBECCA & CASS

Changing

IT FELT FOREIGN for Rebecca being back in her office at the club. She hadn't been back since she left Cassidy that night a little more than two months ago. So many things have changed since then. Within her life as well as within herself. She didn't feel that overwhelming feeling of obligation anymore. Of course, the guilt was still present. But the burden had lessened. Whether that was because of Cassidy or therapy, Rebecca wasn't sure. Perhaps it was a bit of both.

"Mistress?"

It took a moment for Rebecca to realize her assistant was calling for her attention. She blinked, putting her mental mask back into place behind the physical mask she still wore. Revealing herself to Cassidy, in more ways than one, made wearing a mask here a little more tedious. Maybe it was time to make some changes.

"Yes, Carlie?"

"Your appointment has arrived. Would you like me to set up your room?"

Rebecca looked up from the spreadsheets she had been *trying* to study since she got in.

"Excuse me?"

Rebecca could only imagine what Carlie saw as she stared back. A soft pink bustier was hidden behind a power suit in a darker shade. Mistress's mask was also pink today and hid most of her face. But she didn't think there was a mask big enough to hide the absolute confusion in her eyes. Carlie had been with her for a couple of years but had never seen Mistress as anything but confident and in control. That was something Mistress made sure of.

"Um." It was a rare moment of uncertainty from the normally efficient assistant. "Your appointment."

"This is my first day back. I don't have any appointments." Rebecca started flipping through her calendar. Rebecca was one who needed every "I" dotted, every "T" crossed. Which is why she had taken care of everything of importance regarding the club before she left. And, why she insisted on going over every line of the club's profit/loss reports herself. At this point, the club could practically run itself. As such, there'd be no way she would have set up any appointments on her first day back.

"Oh, well, Mr. Abrams came in and requested…"

"You booked a client? With me?"

"Yes, ma'am."

"Carlie, you know that I don't do that any longer. I haven't taken clients for almost a year now. Why did you book my room?"

"Well, um." Carlie shuffled her feet. It wasn't often Mistress got upset with her. "You had a client before you left, Mistress. I just assumed…"

"Never assume, Carlie," Mistress said harshly. She forced herself not to say Cassidy's name. Or to tell her assistant—who knew *nothing* about her personal life—that Cassidy was much more than a client. That she was *never* a client. "Cancel."

"But, Mistress." Carlie's mouth clamped shut when Mistress looked up at her sternly. "It's just, he's been calling every other week. He's paying triple your rate."

"I don't care." Mistress's voice turned icy. No matter how different she felt inside, she was still in control. Having Carlie go behind her back and take on a client for her without her permission was unacceptable. "Cancel. And, don't ever do this again. I am no longer taking clients. Understood?"

"Yes, Mistress. What should I tell Mr. Abrams?"

Mistress lifted a brow, but the effect was lost behind the mask. "You made the appointment, figure it out." She sighed when Carlie merely stood there. "Find him someone else, or tell him that under no circumstances will I be seeing him or anyone again. I've… retired." *Ugh, way to make yourself feel old.*

Rebecca's cell phone rang cutting off any further conversation between her and her assistant. She waved her out of the office before picking up her phone. A genuine—and relieved—smile graced her face when she saw Cassidy's name on her screen.

"Hey," she answered softly.

"Hey, baby. Is it okay that I called?"

They had been taking advantage of their "honeymoon stage" for the past week and it had been absolute bliss. Rebecca made good on her guarantee that they would spend more time together than apart. And, Cassidy made good on… well, everything she did to Rebecca. This was actually the first night they would be spending the night separately.

"Of course, it is. I'm actually glad to hear your voice."

"Everything okay?" Cass heard a slight edge to Rebecca's tone and was immediately alert.

Rebecca sighed. "Yes. My assistant somehow got it in her head that I'm taking clients again. She just told me I had an appointment."

Well, shit. Didn't see that one coming. Cassidy was eerily quiet for a second. "I see. I guess this is a bad time then. I'll let you go," she said flatly.

Amazingly, Rebecca kept her cool. Oddly enough, she understood Cassidy's confused jealousy. "Cassidy, I'm not taking any clients."

"Oh. I thought you said…"

"I said my assistant made the appointment. Not me. Apparently, since I had you in my room, she thought I was back in the game. I'm not. She'll have to tell Mr. Abrams to find someone else."

Cassidy blew out a breath of absolute relief. "Good. I mean, you know, if that's what you want." *Smooth, Cass.*

Rebecca chuckled at Cassidy's attempt at nonchalance. "It's what I want."

"So, I called… wait." Cass paused as something Rebecca said hit her brain. "*Mr.* Abrams? You had men clients?"

Uh oh. This was one topic they hadn't discussed. Yet. Maybe Cassidy had been purposefully avoiding the subject. Hell, maybe Rebecca was, too. It wasn't exactly sexy to talk about their time with other people. Even if it wasn't about sex.

"Yes," Rebecca answered carefully.

"But, you're a lesbian."

"I'm well aware of that fact, Cassidy."

"I don't understand."

"I told you it wasn't about sex in my room. Not until you. It was about control. And, for my clients, giving that control up. I didn't discriminate who I wielded that control on. In fact, men served me a great deal when it came to becoming stronger after Samantha. If I could control them, I could control anyone."

Rebecca could practically hear the wheels turning in Cassidy's head. Their time together had given her great insight into the inner workings of Cassidy's mind. She wasn't particularly analytical, but she had street smarts. When Cassidy was stuck on a specific issue, she would become quiet, working out the situation in her head. It was quite the interesting process to watch.

"I guess I get that," Cass said finally. And, she did. She didn't like it, but she understood it.

"But, you don't like it," Rebecca guessed correctly.

"I don't like thinking of anyone in that room with you, whether it was sexual or not," Cass confessed. "I know that's stupid, but all I think about when I think about the Pink room is what happened between us."

"You believe me when I tell you that it wasn't like that with anyone else, right?"

"Yeah, babe, of course, I do. But, that's the image in my head, you know? So, it takes me a minute to push that aside."

"Duly noted," Rebecca smiled. "Now, you were about to tell me why you called before we both got sidetracked. Not that you need a reason."

"Huh? Oh! Right."

Cassidy laughed at herself—another thing Rebecca learned was a frequent occurrence. Cassidy didn't take herself or life too seriously. And she rarely had a filter. Whatever she thought, she usually ended up saying. It was something Rebecca was learning to appreciate. There was no pretense with Cassidy. What you saw was what you got. And Rebecca undeniably liked what she saw. Very much.

"I, uh, know you said that you were staying at your place tonight. I totally get it," she said quickly. "I was just wondering if maybe I could take you to dinner first? Or, you know, come over with takeout and stuff?"

"Takeout and stuff," Rebecca repeated with amusement. "And, would 'stuff' include sex?"

"I didn't say that."

Cassidy's response was comically innocent.

"Mmhmm. And, after 'stuff' were you hoping I'd ask you to stay because we'd both be too exhausted to move?"

"I don't know where you're coming up with this, but I'm digging what you're suggesting, baby."

Rebecca heard the smile in Cassidy's voice and laughed. "You're a nut. You know that, right?"

"As long as I'm your nut, I'm good with that," Cass replied, unknowingly causing Rebecca to shiver at the thought.

"How are we ever going to know if we can be apart if we never are?" Rebecca asked lightly.

"We're apart right now," Cass pointed out. *And, I'm willing to forgo that experiment. I don't need to be apart from you.* For once, her mouth didn't bite her in the ass by saying that out loud.

"And, talking on the phone about being together later," Rebecca countered merrily.

"Hey, can I help it that my girlfriend is devastatingly sexy and my body aches for her every second she's not with me?"

Wow. "Whoa. If you could feel what your words just did to me," Rebecca said softly and heard a small groan from Cassidy.

"It's all true, baby." They have had sex every night since Rebecca came back into Cass's life. And, still, it wasn't enough. It wasn't just about the sex either. She truly enjoyed being in Rebecca's presence. Something about the woman made Cass feel… whole. And, exceedingly happy.

"Takeout. My place," Rebecca demanded. "Be there at seven. I'll try to be out of here early. And, Cassidy?"

"Yes, Mistress?"

Obviously, Cassidy was learning Rebecca's moods.

"Bring your friend and extra clothes."

"Yes, Mistress!"

"CAN I ASK you something?" Cassidy dug her chopsticks into the Chinese takeout box, coming up with a piece of beef dripping with brown sauce. She plopped it in her mouth as she waited for Rebecca's permission to go on.

"Just did," Rebecca joked. She twisted a good amount of Lo Mein noodles onto her chopsticks. "Go ahead," she said before taking her bite.

"Why did you keep the club? Was it just to become a Dom?"

Rebecca managed not to choke on her food, chewing carefully while trying to think of a way to explain. They were sitting in Rebecca's elegantly decorated living room. At first, Cassidy had been reluctant to sit on the cream-colored sofa and eat. It wasn't until Rebecca sat, cross-legged, at the coffee table, digging into the food that Cassidy acquiesced.

"Should I not have asked that?" Cass continued before Rebecca could answer.

"You can ask anything you want. Having a relationship means not keeping things from each other, right?"

Cassidy grinned as she leaned over and fed Rebecca a piece of broccoli. "Right."

"You know, you need to eat more vegetables," Rebecca said around the big piece Cassidy fed her.

"Yeah, yeah." Cassidy picked up a baby corn and made a show of eating it. "Is this your way of avoiding my question?"

Rebecca put her chopsticks to the side and sighed. "I'm not avoiding. I'm trying to figure out a way to explain it that makes sense."

Cassidy nodded and kept eating quietly. The woman must have had a bottomless pit for a stomach.

"Obligation," Rebecca said quietly.

"Obligation?" Cassidy repeated with a mouth full of food.

Rebecca passed her girlfriend a napkin. "Yes. That was the main reason I kept the club open. After what I did, I felt I owed it to Samantha to keep her dream going."

Cass frowned and pushed her food to the side. *Fucking Samantha.* She'd always been taught to not hate anyone. But, she was sure her mom would forgive her for this one. "You don't owe that bitch anything!"

Rebecca shook her head. "You don't understand..."

"You're right. I don't. She abused you. She tried to *kill* you. Why would you think you owed her anything?"

"I watched her die, Cassidy."

"Of her own doing! You didn't kill her."

"Didn't I?" Rebecca asked hotly. "I could have done something! I could have called for help! But, I did *nothing*. Nothing!"

Cassidy scooted closer and took Rebecca's trembling hand. "Tell me something. What were your injuries that night?"

Rebecca closed her eyes. She could still feel the pain from that beating. It was ingrained deep in her bones and memory. "It doesn't matter," she murmured.

"It matters to me, baby. Let me help you."

Rebecca nearly scoffed. If years of therapy with her aunt hadn't worked, what made Cassidy think she could help? She immediately felt bad for that thought. Maybe Cassidy was exactly what Rebecca needed.

"Broken ribs, nose, and eye socket, dislocated arm, perforated spleen, and a few other internal things," she answered as though she were reading words out of a dictionary.

"Jesus," Cassidy muttered. Her heart ached for Rebecca. And her blood boiled at the thought of what she had to endure. "After all of that, why can't you see why you owe her nothing? She deserved what she got after what she did to you."

"She begged me, Cassidy. Begged me to help her."

"Did you beg her to stop hurting you?" Cassidy asked carefully. Rebecca nodded. "And, did she?"

Rebecca looked up at Cassidy. "That makes me no better than she was."

"That's not true. Baby, what she did, she did because she was a fucking monster. *You* did what you had to do to survive. No one would blame you for that."

Except me, Rebecca thought miserably. "Obligation wasn't the only reason." She didn't agree with Cassidy, but it was time to move on.

"Okay." Cass was disappointed with the change, but she didn't show it. If Rebecca needed to move on, that's what they would do. Cass had hope that she would have years to convince Rebecca that what happened wasn't her fault. She would say it every day if she had to. But, for now, she sat with her back against the couch and pulled Rebecca to her. Gentle, yet strong arms surrounded the smaller woman like a safe cocoon. "I'm listening."

"By the time Samantha… passed away, she had taken everything from me. My job, my freedom, my confidence. I questioned myself on everything. I was top of my class, Cassidy. Major companies came to me—a college student—to bail out their business. And I was able to do it with ease. Hearing how inept I was day after day for years? It broke me. What was once easy for me seemed unfamiliar. It was like picking up a pencil and not knowing how to write anymore.

"So, once Samantha's voice was gone, and I was back on my feet, I had an opportunity to prove to myself that I still had the ability to… to be me. And more. I needed to take my control back. The club was perfect for me. I knew the ins and outs and had the opportunity to work on turning it into what it is today. And, the exclusivity offered the privacy I needed to get my control back by becoming the dominant one. I hid the weak Rebecca behind a mask and became Mistress. No one questions a dominatrix in a BDSM club about wearing a mask."

It was the most in-depth look at the time Rebecca spent from the night she almost died until now that Cass had received. She couldn't imagine what it had been like, but she thought she could grasp the reasoning behind everything Rebecca did. "I guess it worked. You certainly found your control."

Rebecca missed the little smirk on Cassidy's lips.

"It did. For a while."

"What changed?"

Rebecca shrugged. "It was a challenge for me at first. Becoming Mistress. Letting go of every doubt Samantha put in my head. Finding the strength within myself to be the one in command and pretend I knew what the hell I was doing until I actually did. In time, I became very good at what I do, and I had clients paying triple just to be in my room."

Cass grunted. She hadn't meant to, but as she told Rebecca earlier, the images from that room always came to her. Only, when they were speaking of Rebecca's clients, Cass's face became faceless strangers.

Rebecca nimbly got to her knees and straddled Cassidy's lap. "No sex," she reiterated.

"I know, I know. I'm working on it." Cass patted Rebecca's ass lightly. "Ignore my childishness and continue, please."

"It's not childish. It's human." Rebecca kissed Cassidy lightly. "What changed was me, I suppose. After fifteen plus years, it started to become laborious. I wasn't getting out of it what I was before."

"You outgrew it?" Cass suggested, and Rebecca nodded. "When I came in, were you looking for another challenge?" She hated asking the question, but she needed to know she was more than that to Rebecca.

"I wasn't looking for anything, Cassidy. Especially not someone as young as you."

Cass smirked. "You need someone as young as me to keep up with you, baby. Even I have trouble."

"You finally admit it!" Rebecca laughed, then caressed Cassidy's cheek. "You're not a challenge to me, Cassidy."

"Thank you for not getting pissed at me for asking that, baby."

"Were you afraid I would?"

Cass shrugged. "It was kinda insensitive. Okay, it was totally insensitive, and I regretted it the moment it left my traitorous mouth."

Rebecca laughed softly. "I love that you say what you're thinking and ask what you want to know. I never have to guess what's going on with you. It's refreshing."

You may regret saying that, Cass thought. She knew her damn mouth was about to spew out the one question that has been plaguing her brain for days now. "I hope you still feel that way after my next question."

Rebecca raised a brow. "What could you possibly ask that's any worse than what I've already told you?"

"Um, it's about sex."

"What about it?"

"Well..." If Cass could move her legs, they'd both be shaking with adrenaline and nerves right now. *You don't need to know this.* Of course, that didn't stop her from asking. "Have you, um, been, you know, celibate this whole time?"

"Oh!" Rebecca's eyebrows shot up. *Wasn't expecting that.* "I, uh." She laughed nervously. "Do you really want to talk about this?"

"No," Cass answered truthfully. "And, yes. I mean, whatever is in my head is probably ten times worse than the truth. I guess that's why I ask things all the time. Knowing the truth is better than imagining the worst, right?" She shrugged. "Look, I've been with many women."

"Many," Rebecca muttered and received a squeeze on her ass.

"Relatively. It's not something I'm proud of, but it's not something I'm ashamed of either. It's just a fact. I'd go to a bar, pick someone up. Maybe it would turn out to be something that lasted a week or so. Most of the time, it wasn't. My point is," she continued when Rebecca continued to frown. "It's unrealistic to think that the person we've, uh, fallen for has abstained for us. We've both lived. Maybe I just need to know what I'm up against?"

Rebecca rolled her eyes. "First of all, I'm going to need a roundabout number." *You're only twenty-five. How many women could you have slept with??* "And, where I stand in all of those women."

Cass snorted. "Less than twenty? And, you stand above all of them. I've never felt for any of them what I feel for you."

Though twenty was a high number for Rebecca, it was manageable. Hell, she had way more than that in her room over the years. Even if it were different circumstances. "Thank you."

Cass stared at Rebecca, silently urging her to answer Cass's original question. Rebecca finally relented under the scrutiny.

"No, I wasn't celibate. But," she continued hastily. "Ugh, this is going to make me sound terrible."

"Doubtful."

"Ha!" *Just wait.* "If I had nights where I needed something *more* than what a vibrator could give me, I would go to a lesbian club. At the risk of sounding conceited, it was easy for me to find someone to, um, service me. It was quick and easy, and saved me from having to deal with the mess of dating."

"Service you?" *Oh, sure, Cass. Get stuck on that part.*

"Cassidy. Do you really want me to spell it out?"

"Kinda." Cass tapped her temple. "All kinds of thoughts going on here."

Rebecca sighed. "They would go down on me. I didn't reciprocate, and again, it wasn't about sex for me. It was merely a way for me to get off quickly and painlessly."

"Sounds very… boring."

Rebecca barked out a laugh. "It wasn't meant to be mind-blowing. I didn't think that existed, actually, until I met you and you proved me wrong."

Cass grinned. "You're just trying to get my mind off of strange women going down on my girlfriend."

"Is it working?"

"Fuck, yeah, it is. I want to blow your mind right now."

"Yeah?" Rebecca undulated her hips, and kissed Cassidy deeply, nipping her lip before letting it go. "Do you want to go down on me?" she asked, her voice husky with need.

"*Yes, Mistress,*" Cass managed to whisper.

"Rebecca. Right now, I just want to be me with you. Is that okay?"

Cass peered deep into Rebecca's eyes. "It's perfect." She easily lifted Rebecca from her lap. "Take your jeans off and sit on the couch, baby. Open yourself up to me."

Fuck me. Rebecca was learning that Cassidy was great at many things. One of those things just happened to be turning Rebecca on so much that she wondered how her panties didn't disintegrate from the heat coming from between her legs. She did as Cassidy asked, sitting at the edge of the couch, her legs opened wide enough to accommodate Cassidy. As much as she needed that mouth on her, Rebecca placed a hand on Cassidy's shoulder while she could still think coherently.

"Perhaps we should get a couple of towels. You know what you do to me."

Cass groaned. "You're killing me, baby. You stay here, I'll get them.

Just tell me where to go."

"Down the hall, third door on your left. Hurry, Cassidy."

"I'm on it!"

Cass jumped up and did a speed walk down the hall, causing Rebecca to laugh. Something she's done more of in the past week than she had her entire life. Being with Cassidy was the best of both worlds for Rebecca. She was young enough to keep Rebecca feeling youthful. But, as cliché as it sounded, Cassidy had an old soul. Rebecca knew there was a huge gap in their ages, but Cassidy never made her feel it.

"Cassidy?" Rebecca called out as she took the rest of her clothes off. Her lover should have been back by now. What the hell was she doing? Getting all of the towels she could find in the house?

"Coming, babe!"

"Not yet, but both of us will be soon," Rebecca promised. Then all thoughts that didn't involve an abundance of imaginative sex with Cass left her as the tall, beautifully muscled woman stood before her in all her naked glory. Unless you counted the dildo that stood proudly between her legs. "Oh," Rebecca breathed.

Cassidy smirked. "Brought you those towels." She got to her knees in front of an ogling Rebecca. "Lift that beautiful ass, baby." She slid the towel into place when Rebecca lifted her hips. The scent of Rebecca's arousal hit her nostrils and she was sure she would start drooling if she didn't get a taste. Very soon. Even so, she took a moment to just appreciate the perfection that was Rebecca Cuinn. "You're incredible, Rebecca."

Rebecca's pulse spiked, her arousal heightened, and her heart melted. Unable to trust her voice, she simply pulled Cassidy's mouth down to her waiting sex.

They were both so ready for each other that Cass didn't bother wasting time teasing Rebecca. She needed that sweet nectar that only Rebecca could give her like she needed breath. Rebecca's hips jumped when Cass sucked in her hard, aroused clit. Knowing just what she liked, Cass used the tip of her tongue, flicking it across the velvety nub at a fast pace.

Rebecca's hand fisted in Cassidy's short hair. She didn't know whether to pull her closer or push her away. That's how intense Cassidy made her feel. No experience she had ever had even came close to this sensation. The hard, hot tip of Cassidy's tongue worked its magic, sending shockwaves through Rebecca's entire body.

"*Cassidy*!" Rebecca lifted her hips, deciding that pulling Cassidy closer was the right thing to do at this particular moment. Cassidy accommodated her by slipping her tongue deep inside her. Being filled with that hot, wet tongue, and having Cassidy's nose hitting her in just the right spot had Rebecca hurtling towards that ultimate peak. She wondered if it would always astound her how fast Cassidy could bring her to orgasm.

"Cassidy, I'm coming!"

Cass moaned but didn't let up on her assault. She was now alternating between sucking, fucking, and licking Rebecca's glorious pussy. As Rebecca's hips bucked, Cass became determined to make Rebecca forget there had ever been anyone else between these legs before. The way Cass forgot anyone before Rebecca. She knew Rebecca wanted to take things slow, but for Cass, life could now be described in two ways. Life before Rebecca and life after Rebecca.

Cass joyfully immersed herself in Rebecca's explosive orgasm. Having that effect on someone like Rebecca was fulfilling a fantasy Cass didn't even know she had. Yeah, she had always enjoyed sex. Who didn't like getting off? But sex with Rebecca was a spiritual revelation. Every. Time.

"*Jesus*!" Rebecca panted. Thankfully, her couch was large enough that she could lay back and try to catch her breath.

Cass had other things in mind. And giving Rebecca time to get over that orgasm was not one of them. She wrapped her upper arms around the outside of Rebecca's thighs, holding her steady as she thrust her hips forward. Hard.

Rebecca gasped. She was tight from the orgasm and when Cassidy slammed inside of her with the dildo, the feeling was profound. That bite of pain accompanied by the vivid pleasure of having Cassidy pumping inside her was almost more than Rebecca could bear. She sat up and wrapped her arms around her lover, holding her close as they moved together.

"Cassidy." Rebecca kissed Cassidy passionately. It was moments like these that made her wish they could stay this way forever. Just lock out the rest of the world.

Cass broke away from the kiss, breathing hard. "Rebecca! Oh, fuck!" She drew out of Rebecca, then gripped the dildo and pulled it from herself. Her entire body shook from the violent orgasm that ripped through her. "Shit," she exhaled. "That was… that."

Rebecca chuckled. "Yes, it was. Are you okay?"

Cass looked up at Rebecca and grinned. "Never been better. Probably should have brought more towels, though. Sorry about that."

"I'm not." Rebecca reached down, dragging her finger through Cassidy's wealth of wetness. She brought that glistening finger up to her lips, licking it clean. "Now I know why you always look so proud after that happens to me," she winked.

"Well, now that we've christened this room, what do you say about moving on to others?" Cass suggested with a sly smile.

Rebecca actually squealed when Cassidy flung her over her shoulder and headed for the kitchen.

"I have a bed!" Rebecca laughed.

"Great! That'll be awesome for when we're ready to sleep. The real question is; do you have whipped cream in the fridge?"

Chapter Ten
REBECCA & CASS

Feelings

CASS LEANED BACK carefully on the ladder to check her work. Ever since Rebecca told her Eve Sumptor-Riley was willing to look at her paintings, Cass had become more critical. Anyone who's anyone in the art industry knew Sumptor Galleries and the prestige they offered. Cass thought of herself as a street artist more than anything else. She painted murals around the city for store owners or city officials. She didn't think she was good enough to be in one of the most renowned galleries. But Rebecca believed in her and that was enough for Cass.

She had been trying to work on a few canvases for Eve's next visit, and she was a bit stressed out about it. But, of course, Cass could never say that to Rebecca. She would make Rebecca proud, however, right now she had a mural to finish. And, unless she wanted to keep making every female she painted to look like Rebecca, she needed to stay focused.

Cass chuckled at herself. It'd been a solid three weeks since she and Rebecca got together. The longest relationship she had ever been in. Cass had no clue how long that "honeymoon stage" lasted, but she was definitely still in it. And, if Rebecca's actions were anything to go by, she was still in it, too. In fact, just that morning…

"Hey!"

"Shit!" Cass dropped her paintbrush and gripped the ladder for dear life. She peered down with a frown and began climbing down. "You scared the hell out of me. What are you doing here?"

Miranda pushed a strand of red hair out of her face. "Nice way to talk to your best friend."

"Sorry. You startled me." Cass stooped to pick up her paintbrush. She grumbled at the dirt that now coated the paint covered bristles and tossed it aside. Taking a rag out of her back pocket, she wiped her hands as she glanced at Miranda. "How did you know where I was?"

Miranda put her hands on her hips. "It's not hard to find someone painting a huge mural."

"Fair enough. What's up?"

"I came to take you to lunch."

"Oh, um, that's nice, but I already ate." Cass gestured to her lunchbox. Rebecca had surprised her by making her an awesome roast beef sandwich, some of her favorite chips, and even a pickle. Best. Lunch. Ever.

"Oh, come on, Cass."

Cass frowned. "Sorry, but it's," she checked her watch, "quarter after one and I was hungry. I had no idea you'd be here."

"What's going on with you? You've been avoiding me for weeks."

"No, I haven't." At least, she didn't think she was. Though, if she were being honest with herself, Cass hadn't thought about Rand—or anything else—in the past three weeks. Her mind, body, and soul have been preoccupied with the beautiful woman that she was falling deeply in love with. Maybe that made her selfish, but what could she say? "We talked a few weeks ago. Besides, you're a newlywed. I was respecting your time with Connor. And, the phone works both ways, Rand. You haven't exactly contacted me, either."

Miranda snorted. "Respecting my time with Connor. Since when? And, anyway, I thought you were upset, so I waited for you to make the first move."

"That's not fair, Rand. I've always been supportive and respectful. The one who hasn't is Connor. He never liked that you have a lesbian friend."

"That's not true."

Cass resisted rolling her eyes. Rand had a bad habit of seeing things the way *she* wanted to see them. Rose colored glasses. There was nothing Cass could say or do to change her mind, so she didn't even try. "What was I supposed to be upset about?" she asked, steering the conversation back on track.

"I don't know. You've been different ever since my bachelorette party. I know you don't agree with what I did that night…"

Cass held up a hand, cutting Miranda off. "I'm not upset about that. It's your life, Rand." She was right about one thing. Cass had been changed that night. But not for the reasons Miranda thought.

"Okay, fine. You're not upset. So, let's go out then. We can go clubbing. It feels like ages since we've done that. We can dance and get stupid drunk. It'll be like old times. Maybe I can even crash at your place since Connor doesn't really like it when I drink that much." Miranda punched Cass lightly on the arm. "What do you say?"

Cass studied Miranda. There must be trouble in paradise if she was proposing to stay over at Cass's place. The only reason she would do that is to piss Connor off. According to Rand's social media, she'd been out plenty of times with her straight friends. It ticked her off a bit to know she was probably being used. "I can't. I don't do that anymore."

Miranda laughed. "What do you mean you don't do that anymore? Don't tell me you met someone."

Why is that funny? "I did, actually. But…"

"So, I should wait a week and then you'll be ready for something new?" Miranda joked.

Ouch. As much as it hurt to hear Rand say something like that, Cass couldn't exactly dispute it. "Rand, I've told you before that I was fed up with all that. Even before this relationship. Which, for your information, has been going strong for three weeks now."

"Wow, three weeks. You're usually bored after one."

"Are you going for some kind of record for insulting your 'best friend'?" Cass asked dryly.

"I'm kidding! Damn, girl, you used to be able to take a joke. Even though I'm totally right."

"I didn't get bored, Rand." This time she did roll her eyes when Miranda just stared at her. "Fine. *If* I did, it was because I was picking the wrong woman. I've found the right one, now."

"Right one as in *right* one? Why am I just hearing about this now?"

Cass shrugged. "Honestly, I haven't really told anyone." She knew Rebecca had told her aunt about them, but she was pretty sure that was because her aunt is also her therapist. If she didn't understand that Rebecca still had a tiny issue with their age gap, Cass would have been bothered by that. Then again, neither of them had suggested introducing each other to the important people in their lives. Maybe that was something to be worried about.

"Cass?" Miranda waved her hand in front of Cass's face. "Are you?"

"Am I what?"

"Ashamed of her."

It sounded as though Miranda wanted to add a "duh" at the end of that sentence. "No! God, no. She's the most incredible woman I've ever known. I'm proud to be with her."

"Well, something has to be wrong with her if you're not telling *me* about her. Do your parents even know?"

"Not yet. And there is nothing wrong with Rebecca. We've just been wrapped up in each other." *Literally.* Cass hated that Rand was making her feel insecure. Was Rebecca ashamed of *her*? "Listen, I'm sorry we couldn't do lunch today. But, what do you say we get together sometime next week? The four of us."

"If you're not bored by then?" Miranda laughed but stopped when Cass didn't join in. "You really are serious about this one."

"Yeah, I am. So, could you lay off the bored shit, please?"

"Are you in love with her?"

Cass shrugged. She hadn't said the actual words to Rebecca, yet. With a girlfriend who had run away before, a little patience was needed. Even if Cass didn't feel so patient. The positive was, Rebecca didn't seem to mind spending almost every night together. *That* was a good sign.

Miranda pursed her lips. She didn't look terribly happy. Then again, Cass's best friend was the type of person that needed to know everything the minute it happened. If she didn't, she felt left out.

"Fine. Lunch would be good. I'll run it by Connor." She backed away. "I apologize for teasing you, okay? I just never thought I'd see the day Cass Giles settled down. Can't wait to meet her. She must really be something. I'll, uh, text you later for details on lunch."

With that, Miranda was gone as hastily as she said those words.

Cass shook her head. Rand always loved drama while Cass hated it. She preferred to take a more laid-back approach to life. Though that didn't work when you had a deadline. Which she did with the mural. Cass Giles did what she did best. She cleared her mind and painted.

"Hey, babe?" Cass called out.

"In here!" Rebecca called back from her home office. She chuckled as Cass walked in holding Rebecca's ringing phone with two fingers. "You're carrying that thing like it's a viper."

"Yeah, um, not to sound obvious here, but someone named Hunter is calling you. I didn't mean to look at it, I swear. I thought it was mine."

Rebecca stood, took the phone from Cass, and hit the answer button.

"Hang on, Hunter." She put her cell on her desk and wrapped her arms around Cass's neck. "I don't care if you look at my phone, baby. I have nothing to hide from you."

"I didn't want you to think I was snooping." Cass sighed. "And, I certainly don't want to be jealous of whoever's calling you." It wasn't Eve Sumptor-Riley or Rebecca's Aunt Wills. Business calls came through on a business-specific phone registered under the club's name. Hunter was not a name that had been brought up before, and that scared Cass. It was stupid, of course. Surely, Rebecca had tons of friends that would pop up here and there.

"You shouldn't be. Hunter is an old friend, Cassidy. Nothing more."

"Ever?"

"Are you going to ask that of everyone you meet or hear of?" Rebecca asked testily, then sighed. "I'm sorry. I told you before that you are my only exception. No one that has been in my room is in my life anymore."

Cass hung her head. "I know." Rand legitimately got in Cass's head today.

"We're going to talk more about this when I'm done. Okay?"

Cass nodded and made a move to leave, but Rebecca took her hand and pushed her gently into her office chair. After settling herself in Cassidy's lap, Rebecca put the phone on speaker.

"Sorry about that."

"You okay?"

"Yes. Hunter, you're on speaker. I'm here with Cassidy. My girlfriend."

"Cass," Cass muttered automatically.

"Oh! Um, hello. Wow, I had no idea!"

Cass couldn't get a read on this Hunter person's vibe. Of course, she had only said like three sentences, but still. Was she interested in Rebecca? Who wouldn't be? Rebecca is fine as hell. What was Cass up against?

"I know, sorry," Rebecca said softly. "I should have told you sooner, but I've been a bit preoccupied." She winked at Cassidy and kissed her lightly.

"Understandable. It's nice to meet you, Cass."

Cass's eyebrows went up. Hunter definitely sounded sincere. And, she called her Cass. *Good listener. Rebecca needed that in her life.* Cass felt the tension easing.

"Nice to, uh, kinda meet you, too," she said awkwardly causing both Rebecca and Hunter to laugh.

"We have to get together soon and celebrate!" Hunter suggested enthusiastically.

"Do you always celebrate someone getting a girlfriend in your circle?" Cass asked genuinely.

"When it's Rebecca who hasn't given anyone a second look in years, yes!"

"Hey! I'm sitting right here," Rebecca chimed in. She was a little put off by the years remark, but she knew Hunter didn't mean anything by it. "But, I think you're right. We should all get together and have dinner. That includes Mo and Patty. Is that okay with you, baby?"

Well, shit. I didn't have anything at all to worry about. "Sounds awesome to me!" It also reminded her of lunch with Rand and Connor. She hadn't asked Rebecca, yet. But, hell, if they were in the "let's tell everyone we're dating" mode, she didn't think Rebecca would have a problem with lunch.

"Awesome," Rebecca laughed softly. She stared into Cassidy's shining eyes for a moment before remembering Hunter was on the other line. "You'll have to tell us when you're available, Hunter. She's a trauma surgeon," Rebecca explained to Cassidy who responded with a silent "cool."

"Will do. I'm excited to meet the woman that tamed you."

"I don't know about tamed," Cass said.

"I'm still the one with the whip," Rebecca quipped and almost lost it when Cassidy's eyes grew wide with shock. "Hunter knows about Mistress, baby. She's a very good friend who's been there since the night Samantha died."

"Oh." There was a tiny pause and then, "Oh! Wait! Trauma surgeon? Was she? Were you Rebecca's doctor, Hunter?" Cass asked, bringing

Hunter back into the conversation

"Sure was."

"I can't wait to shake your hand and thank you for saving my girl's life." Cass grinned at the slight blush that graced Rebecca's face.

"Just doing my sworn duty, though I'd never turn down a handshake. Especially if it was accompanied by a beer."

"You're on!"

Rebecca's head swam at the fast connection Cassidy and Hunter seemed to have. It was, as Cassidy would say, awesome! *What a relief!* "I don't mean to interrupt the bromance here, but did you need something, Hunter?"

Cass guffawed, and Hunter snorted, each of them spewing out the word "bromance" with mirth.

"Nah, it'll keep."

"No, no." Cass patted Rebecca's ass, getting her to let her up. "I'll let you two talk. Besides, how can you gush about me if I'm sitting here?"

Rebecca and Hunter both laughed heartily. "Get out of here, you nut."

Cass kissed her. "I'll be painting. Come get me when you're done." She jogged out of the room.

"She sounds great," Hunter said quietly.

Rebecca was still staring at the door Cassidy disappeared through. "She is." She cleared her throat and picked up the phone, turning off speaker.

"How long have you been together?"

"Shouldn't we be talking about why you called?" Rebecca asked. It's not that she didn't want to talk about Cassidy. She could do that all day. But she didn't want to be selfish.

"In a minute. You wouldn't want to disappoint your girlfriend by not gushing about her," Hunter answered playfully.

"I think you two are going to get along just fine."

"I'm sure we will. Anyone who makes you as happy as you sound is good with me."

"I am happy, Hunter." *Finally.* "It's been a little more than three weeks. At times, it feels much longer. There's this comfort and familiarity there. To have that along with the excitement she brings me every day is a gift."

"That's fantastic, Becca. How'd you two meet?"

"Oh," Rebecca chuckled nervously. "Well, we met at the club, actually."

"Club as in *your* club?"

"Yes. I had her in my room."

"I—wow. I didn't think you…"

"I don't."

"Hmm. Obviously, there's something about Cass that drew you to her."

"Aside from the absolute sexiness?"

Hunter laughed. "Yeah, aside from that. Get to the part that goes deeper."

It was on the tip of Rebecca's tongue to make some lewd remark about Cassidy going deeper, but she stopped herself.

"She's talented, intelligent, funny… young."

"How young are we talking, Becca?"

"Very. She's, ahem, twenty-five."

"Damn! I never pictured you as a cougar!"

Hunter snickered, and Rebecca held her middle finger up in front of the phone. Hunter couldn't see it, but it made Rebecca feel better.

"Ha, ha."

"I'm kidding, babe. Age doesn't matter. All that matters is how she makes you feel."

"She makes me feel sexy, beautiful, desired. Youthful," Rebecca confessed. "And truthfully, I don't feel the age gap when we're together." The real test will be when they start going out with other people. Which apparently will be soon now that Hunter knew about them. "Now, enough about me. What's going on with you?"

Hunter sighed. "Honestly, Becca, we can talk about that later. You're not going for that, are you?" she asked when Rebecca remained silent.

"Nope."

"Fine. I did it. I broke things off with Susan."

Yes! "That's awesome, babe!"

"Yep, you're definitely dating someone young." She laughed when Rebecca muttered some expletive. "I'm not gonna lie, it's been hard. I haven't seen my folks since because I'm afraid I don't have the strength to keep her out of my life."

"I have someone you can talk to, Hunter. You know that."

"Your aunt who's a shrink? I don't know if I'm ready for that, Becca. I've made it this far on my own."

By avoiding going to see your parents, Rebecca added silently. "Okay. If you're ever ready, just let me know. Until then, I'll be here."

"I know, thank you. Hey, listen, I'll call you about dinner. And, I'll get Mo and Patty on board. Patty's going to be overjoyed that you've found someone! I'm really happy for you, Rebecca."

"And, I'm proud of you," Rebecca responded sincerely. "It's our turn to be happy, Hunter."

"AM I INTERRUPTING?"

Cass looked up from her canvas and smiled at Rebecca. "Never. Are you mad at me?"

"Why would I be mad?"

Cass twirled her paintbrush in her fingers. It was a nervous habit she'd had for years. And, right at this moment, she was nervous as hell. "Because of my insecurity."

Rebecca's eyes softened. "Come here, baby." She held her hand out to Cassidy and guided them to the small couch in the room. "It's become clear to me that we…"

"Please don't break up with me!"

"Oh, baby. It's become clear to me," Rebecca repeated as she held Cassidy's hand, "that as much as we talk, we don't really communicate. Not about true feelings. And, I know that's my fault."

Well, that's not a breakup, Cass thought as she was able to breathe again. "No…"

Rebecca placed a finger over Cassidy's lips, then pushed bangs out of her eyes. "It is. I don't think I ever fully understood the impact it had on you when I ran away. The impact it had on *us*. Since we've been together, I've noticed how you now skirt around the issue of love. You'll say everything but the actual words. I have to wonder if you're still afraid I'll run?"

Cass rubbed Rebecca's knuckles with her thumbs. "No, I don't think so. Not anymore. It's just, you know, you said you wanted to go slow, baby. I'm trying to adhere to that. You have no idea how hard that has been because I am completely and undeniably in love with you, Rebecca."

Rebecca closed her eyes and let that feeling wash over her. "I haven't exactly adhered to taking it slow myself," she said finally with a chuckle. "I'm here almost every night. And, if I'm not here, you're at my place. On the one or two days we haven't been together, we've talked on the phone until we fell asleep."

"I'm sorry. I didn't want to push you. I think I pushed you too hard those nights in the Pink Room, came on too strong despite barely knowing each other. I shouldn't have done that, but I was so desperate to keep you in my life. Now, I couldn't imagine you not being in my life so I was trying not to pressure you."

"That definitely wasn't a complaint, Cassidy. I know I said we shouldn't rush this, but being with you feels right to me. I knew from the moment I saw you in my club that I was in trouble." Rebecca took a breath. "Thing is, I've never felt safer, more desired, or more cherished. I don't think I could possibly explain what that means for someone like me. I thought that if I gave us a timeline, I could make sense of the strength of the feelings I have for you. Maybe I should just come to terms with the fact that not everything has to make sense. It's time to stop isolating ourselves no matter how much I want to keep you to myself," she winked.

"So, you're not ashamed of me?" Cass's heart was soaring, but the conversation with Rand haunted her.

Rebecca looked utterly confused. "Ashamed? Why on earth would I be ashamed of you? Have I ever made you feel that way?"

"No, it's nothing you've done. But, I mean, I guess I can understand why you wouldn't be eager to introduce me to your friends. Your friends are probably all successful, Ivy Leaguers."

Rebecca stood, dragging Cassidy with her. She didn't stop until they were standing in front of the mermaid mural in Cassidy's living room.

"Do you see this?"

Cass looked up at the wall and shrugged. "Yeah. It's a mural."

"No, Cassidy. Do you see? You've taken simple lines and curves and, with a paintbrush, you turned them into something incredible. Do you know what I can do with a paintbrush? Absolutely nothing," she answered before Cassidy could say anything. "You don't need a fancy school to be smart. You don't need a white coat to be successful. You, Cassidy, are talented beyond anything I've ever seen. You have the attention of one of the most influential and respected people in the art industry."

"Because of you," Cass muttered and shuffled her feet.

"No, because of *you*. Eve wouldn't give you this chance because I asked her to. She's giving it to you because you deserve it."

Cass looked at her mural again. "It's always been a hobby or a way to pay bills," she said at length. "No one has ever really taken me seriously, and I guess that made me not take it too seriously." She brought her gaze to Rebecca. "You do. I want to make you proud without embarrassing you in front of your friends."

Rebecca raised a brow. "You do make me proud. Though, I think you have a very skewed idea of my life. Do you know who my closest friends are other than Eve?" Cassidy shook her head. "Hunter, who was my surgeon, and Patty and Mo who were my nurses. That's it. After

Samantha, I couldn't trust anyone else, Cassidy. I didn't want to let anyone in who could possibly hurt me. So, you see? You've broken all of my rules."

Wow. Cass felt sad for Rebecca, but not sorry for her. If she were to examine her own life, she would see that most of her friends were mere acquaintances. Sure, she had those friends who were always up for a party. But, if she were to call them now just to talk, would they have anything to say to each other?

"Rules are made to be broken," Cass said, bringing Rebecca closer to her. "Thank you for letting me in, baby."

Rebecca smiled. "I don't think I had a choice, Cassidy." She tugged Cassidy's head down for a heartfelt kiss and moaned when Cassidy picked her up. Wrapping her legs around Cassidy's waist, she gazed at her lover through lowered lashes.

"I love that you can do this."

"Me, too," Cass grinned, then frowned when Rebecca place her fingers over her lips when she went in for another kiss.

"I have one question before we get too distracted."

"You're a little too late, but shoot."

Rebecca lifted her chin at the mural. The mermaid was still faceless, but still, she wondered. "Was it me?"

It was a little difficult to shuffle your feet when holding someone in your arms. "Um, yeah. I couldn't get you out of my head, so I painted this. But as the days went on, I—I couldn't keep coming home and seeing your face every day. Sorry."

Rebecca kissed Cassidy's pouting lips. "Don't be sorry, baby. You'll make up for it in the bedroom," she winked.

Cass smirked. "Yes, Mistress." She started towards the stairs, then stopped. "Oh, um, I guess it's my turn to say something before I start making it up to you."

"Okay?"

"I bumped into Rand earlier. She surprised me by showing up at my job site. Anyway, I sorta told her that we could have lunch sometime next week. You, me, Rand, and Connor."

"This is really happening, huh? We're coming out to everyone as a couple."

"Seems like it. Is that okay?"

Rebecca kissed her lover again. "Totally. One more thing, Cassidy."

"Make it quick, baby. My arms are getting a little tired and I have a *lot* of things to do to you."

"I love you, too."

Chapter Eleven
REBECCA & CASS

Needs

REBECCA YAWNED. "GODDAMN it, wake up!" She patted her cheeks and contemplated yet another cup of coffee. Knowing that would just accelerate her already stimulated nervous system, she decided against it.

She was cranky. Which didn't bode well for her employees at the club. Unfortunately, due to her crankiness, she had already snapped at the bartender for asking a simple, yet fair question. Hell, it wasn't their fault that she didn't get much sleep the night before. Just as it wasn't Cassidy's fault when Rebecca snapped at her this morning.

It was Rebecca's damn body's fault. Ever since Cassidy actually said the words "I love you" a few nights ago, Rebecca had been feeling off. She didn't understand it. She loved Cassidy. Loved being loved by her. So, why couldn't she sleep? Why did her body…

Rebecca yawned, again. "Ugh!" She opened her laptop and let the melodic sound of Skype making a call soothe her for a moment. The sound disappeared as the call was accepted.

"Well, this is a surprise. Oh!"

"Hey, Aunt Wills."

"Mistress," Willamena said carefully.

Rebecca frowned. Then she remembered she was in her office and had her mask on. "Sorry," she muttered, pulling the long white ribbon to untie the mask. Before removing it, she got up and locked her office door. "I forgot that was on," Rebecca said when she sat back down.

"Is everything okay?" Willamena asked, deciding to not dwell on the mask. For now. "You usually call later in the week. How are things with Cass?"

Rebecca knew that her aunt still felt guilty about not knowing what Samantha was doing. Maybe she would always feel that way, but Rebecca couldn't allow her to think Cassidy could be anything like Samantha.

"Things are wonderful. *Cassidy* is wonderful. It's almost unbelievable how she treats me. Like I'm a queen, Aunt Wills. She loves me. And, I love her."

"Good. I'm sorry, Becca. I know you don't understand…"

"I do, Aunt Wills. But, you have nothing to worry about with Cassidy. I promised you all those years ago that I would come to you if something happened. That still stands today."

Willamena studied her niece in silence. "Very well," she said finally. "I like Cass, Rebecca. I really do. I know I had my doubts at the beginning because of the age difference, but from my talks with her, and seeing how she treats you—even via this high-tech stuff you insist on—I like her *for* you. If I ask questions like that, it's because of my own insecurities."

If Rebecca thought it would help, she would tell her aunt to let go of those feelings of guilt. Of course, she would be a hypocrite since apparently, she couldn't let go of the past herself.

"Becca?"

Aunt Wills's soothing voice cut through Rebecca's foggy thoughts. "Hmm?"

"Where did you go just then?"

Rebecca blinked. "I, um." She sighed. "I think I'm going insane," she blurted out.

Willamena raised a brow. "Well, that's quite the diagnosis. Why don't you tell me your symptoms? See, I *am* a licensed psychiatrist and will be able to tell you if your WebMD diagnosis is correct."

For the first time all day, Rebecca smiled. "I didn't Google it, I just feel… off. It's stupid and frustrating, but I can't seem to stop it."

"I'm going to need details, Becca," Willamena said patiently. Rebecca had been like this since she could remember. If she found a subject that she didn't particularly feel comfortable with, she skirted the issue. It drove the psychiatrist in Willamena nuts. Hell, it drove the *aunt* in Willamena nuts.

"Okay," Rebecca sighed. "Let me preface this by saying Cassidy's and my sex life is magnificent. She makes my body do things it's never done before." She heard a small groan from her aunt. "Aunt Wills? I'm going to need Dr. Woodrow for this one."

Rebecca could practically see the change happen. Where her Aunt Wills was uncomfortable, Dr. Woodrow was completely attentive. A small lean in, a change in her demeanor, and clear eyes completed the transformation. Rebecca often wondered if that's where she acquired her ability to change into Mistress so easily.

"Go on, Rebecca."

Rebecca took a deep breath. "I need you to know that I'm completely satisfied with Cassidy."

"Rebecca, you don't have to convince me that you're happy with your sex life. Unless you're trying to convince yourself?"

"No! I *am*. I've never been happier. That's why this is so confusing to me."

"What is?"

"This—this *urge* my body has."

"What kind of urge?" Woodrow asked patiently. "Do you want to hurt Cassidy?"

"No. God, no. It's the opposite. *I want her to hurt me*," Rebecca whispered.

"Rebecca?" Willamena waited until she had her niece/patient's attention. "I understand why this may concern you. However, it is quite normal."

Rebecca scoffed. "Normal? It's *normal* to want the woman you love to hurt you?"

"When someone has been through what you have, Rebecca, yes," she answered calmly. "What Samantha did to you." Willamena's voice cracked ever-so-slightly and she cleared her throat. "You endured abuse over an extended period of time. It is not uncommon for victims of that type of maltreatment to become addicted to that pain."

"Addicted. To pain." Even though her aunt just told her it was normal, Rebecca sure as hell didn't feel normal. "So, I *am* crazy."

"No," Willamena said forcefully. "I don't want you thinking like that, Rebecca. I want you to acknowledge that your body is responding to trauma that was *not* your fault."

"It was fifteen plus years ago, Aunt Wills! I've changed since then. I've become the dominant one! I've worked very hard not to be that weak anymore."

"It's not weakness, Rebecca."

Rebecca impatiently waved away her aunt's words. "Why? Why is this happening now when I'm happy? Is Samantha always going to be there, ruining my life?"

"I believe you just answered the why. Not Samantha, but your happiness. You said you love Cassidy, yes?"

"Very much."

"And, you trust her?"

"With everything inside me."

"Would you like my professional opinion?" Rebecca nodded. "I believe that you've found the one person that you could feel comfortable enough with, that you could trust enough, to let go of all of your defenses. That is why after fifteen years your body is beginning to have these desires."

Rebecca remembered that night Cassidy told her she loved her. She also remembered how it felt when Cassidy fucked her hard after a raging orgasm. Perhaps it was feeling pain with that kind of pleasure, the pleasure she *should* have felt all those years ago, that brought this on.

"I don't want this, Aunt Wills. How the hell am I supposed to tell Cassidy that I need her to hurt me?" She rubbed her temples, hoping to relieve a headache that was forming. "All this time I've been worried about turning into Samantha. I never even considered I would turn back into the old, weak Rebecca."

"We'll talk about your fears of becoming like that bitch at another time. Like when I'm not being your doctor and I can tell you what I really feel. But, for now, I'm going to tell you that you were never weak, and you're not regressing. In fact, I think this is a breakthrough for you."

"A breakthrough. Are you serious?"

"Quite. I know that decades of experience in psychology isn't that impressive, but sometimes I do know what I'm talking about, Rebecca."

"I'm sorry, Aunt Wills. I don't mean to be so stubborn, I'm just…"

"Born that way?" Willamena joked, causing Rebecca to laugh. "I see this as a breakthrough because you've been very closed off for many years. When you talk to me about the past, you tend to do it without much emotion. Cassidy is good for you, Rebecca. The way she allows you to be you, and I'm assuming to be Mistress when you need to be, has given you the strength you thought you had by being alone. You've always been strong, Becca. But you doubted yourself. Even becoming Mistress, you doubted. I think Cassidy has given you the love that you need—that you deserve—and you're finally learning to be the real you."

"That gives her a lot of power over me," Rebecca stated softly. As much as she loved Cassidy, she never wanted to lose control over herself again.

"On the contrary. You both hold the power. There's no need for a struggle. Just honesty. If you explain to Cassidy what's going on with your body, Rebecca, she will understand. Maybe she'll be confused at first, but that's why communication is so important. It can't be about the physical all the time."

"Hmm." *What a conversation that's going to be.* "You know, you should stick with this psychiatry thing. I think you could be successful at it," Rebecca teased. Her aunt, as a well-respected, often published doctor, was extremely successful in her profession.

"I always say, not bad for someone who got their degree out of a Cracker Jack box."

"I never get anything but stickers," Rebecca muttered playfully. "Thank you, by the way."

"It's my job. And, my pleasure," Willamena said with a smile. "Feeling better?"

"I will after I figure out how to bring this up to my girlfriend."

"Would you like me to be there with you? Via Skype, of course."

"Absolutely not. Having my aunt listening in on an already awkward conversation would not be good. However, if she needs to talk to you, could she?"

"Of course."

"HEY, BABE?" CASS tossed her keys on the table next to the front door. "I'm sorry I'm late!"

She hopped on one foot as she struggled with taking off her paint-stained boot. They had finally secured dinner plans with Hunter, Patty, and Mo, and Cass had been filled with nerves all day. To make things worse, she ran into problems with her mural, hit traffic on her way home, and her phone was dead. With the mood Rebecca had been in the past few days, Cass just knew she was in big trouble.

"Babe?" Cass called out again, this time with a little more trepidation. Normally, being a bit late wouldn't have caused her so much stress. But, obviously, she had already done something to annoy her girlfriend and this was just going to add to it. Unfortunately, she had no idea what she did that has been bothering Rebecca and that worried her. Was Rebecca thinking of leaving again? Had Cass gone too far by confessing her love the other night? *Nah.* No way Cass would believe that. Especially since Rebecca had said it back and the sex afterward was fucking awesome.

So, what else could it have been that was making Rebecca angry? Cass shook her head at her thoughts. No, angry wasn't the right word. Irritable. It hadn't affected their sex life (thankfully). In fact, Rebecca had been a bit more aggressive, much to Cass's delight. Sadly, every other aspect of their lives had been a little stressful, which meant Cass never found the right time to tell Rebecca about Hunter's opinion about Samantha's death. Cass was doing all she could to alleviate the tension. No way she was going to bring up the bitch. She'd wait until she could decipher the problem and fix it.

"In the closet." Rebecca's sweet voice came from behind a half-closed door.

"Since when?" Cass joked, hoping to ease any tension. She walked into the good-sized closet to find a topless Rebecca flipping through her clothes. As usual, the sight floored Cass. For more reasons than just the obvious beauty of the woman before her.

"Ha-ha. I tried calling you."

"I know, babe, I'm sorry. My phone is shit." She brought it out and showed Rebecca the complete deadness of the thing. "Forgot my damn charger."

"You're late," Rebecca said softly. Since she still hadn't gotten the nerve to talk to Cassidy about her *needs,* she had been trying to keep her irritability to a minimum. She hadn't exactly been successful—most notably in bed which worried her—so, when Cassidy decided to be late today of all days it only exacerbated the situation. She was nervous enough about her friends meeting the love of her life. Not that she thought they wouldn't like Cassidy, but there would be no hiding the age difference. That was one hurdle Rebecca had been wary of.

"I'm really sorry, Rebecca," Cass repeated. "Had a mishap at the site and the deadline was today. Not too difficult of a fix, just took me a little longer. Then, of course, the damn traffic."

Rebecca turned around to face her girlfriend. "So, it's not because you're dreading tonight?"

"What? No! I'm not dreading tonight, babe. I may be a little nervous meeting your friends, but definitely not dreading it." Cass pulled Rebecca into her arms. "I'm ready to announce my love for you to the world."

Rebecca smiled. "Me, too. But, first, you need to take a shower and get ready." She stood on her tip-toes, kissed Cassidy tenderly on the lips, then turned back to her clothes to find something that wouldn't make her look old. And something that wouldn't make her look like she was trying too hard to be young. Her entire body stiffened when she felt a faint fingertip on one of the many scars on her back.

Cass felt Rebecca go rigid at her touch and sighed silently. She leaned down and kissed one of the marks gently. In the months they have been together, Rebecca never once spoke about the scars. And, until now, Cass had never done anything to bring attention to them.

"*I always hoped you didn't notice them,*" Rebecca whispered.

"I noticed that first night you stayed with me," Cass replied just as quietly. "But I wanted to wait for you to be ready to talk to me about them."

"I don't think I'll ever be ready for that."

Cass feathered her hands up Rebecca's arms and placed them on Rebecca's shoulders. She squeezed them lightly before backing away. She was disappointed, but she understood. She couldn't even begin to imagine what Rebecca had gone through.

"Badges of honor," Rebecca blurted before Cassidy could leave. "That's what she called them." She slipped on one of Cassidy's t-shirts and turned around. "For *her*. The more scars she could leave on my back, the more powerful she felt. And the more she was in control of me. The worst ones," Rebecca pulled up the shirt enough to show a large stripe that rounded her side and disappeared under the shirt, "happened the night she found out I bought the club. Afterward, she made me stand under the steaming shower."

Cass curled her hands into fists, digging her nails into her palms. *That fucking bitch.* A tear rolled down her cheek and she closed her eyes when Rebecca wiped it away.

"Don't cry for me, Cassidy," she said softly.

Cass shook her head and took Rebecca's beautiful face in her hands. "You have to allow me to be sad for you, baby. And you have to allow me to be mad that I can't kill that bitch for what she did to you."

"Don't say that. You are too good to carry that guilt."

"I could say the same to you." Rebecca tried to turn away, but Cass held steady. "One day, baby, I will get you to believe that you have nothing to be guilty of."

Rebecca gave Cassidy the smile she knew she needed. "Right now, you need to take a really quick shower and get ready." She playfully pushed Cassidy back. "Cassidy? Hunter spoke to me once before about getting the scars removed. Or reduced. If they make you uncomfortable…"

"Hey. Don't do that, baby. I may hate the way you got them, but there is *nothing* about you that I hate or would change."

"Not even my attitude this past week or so?"

"The only thing I would change about that is whatever I did to annoy you."

Rebecca chuckled. "Oh my God, you're impossibly sweet. You didn't do anything. I've just… we need to talk later, okay? Don't look so scared, baby. I'm not going anywhere. Except for dinner without you, if you don't hurry. Now, get that fine ass naked and get in the shower."

Cass smirked. *She said not to be scared, I'm going to trust her.* "Join me?"

"We'll never leave if I do." Rebecca tapped her watch. "Five minutes, babe."

"Only need three!" They both laughed as Cass stripped in record time and ran towards the bathroom. After what they just spoke about, the sound of laughter coming from Rebecca was a gift. She knew talking about the scars had to have reminded Rebecca of the pain of her past. As long as Rebecca would have her, Cass would continue to do whatever it took to remind Rebecca that her present and future would be better.

DESPITE THEIR LITTLE setback, Rebecca and Cassidy managed to make it to the restaurant on time. The drive was quiet, but not uncomfortably so. The two held hands and merely enjoyed being in each other's presence. Rebecca acknowledged that she probably could have had "the talk" with Cassidy then. But, once again, she chickened out, justifying her cowardice with not wanting to ruin the night if Cassidy didn't like what she was hearing.

They were still holding hands when they walked into the restaurant. Cassidy rubbed her thumb over Rebecca's knuckles and Rebecca responded by giving her a little squeeze. It was their way of letting each other know that no matter what happened tonight, they would be okay.

"Rebecca!" Hunter stood and waved them over.

Rebecca gave her long-time friend a huge smile and pulled Cassidy along with her as she quickened her pace.

"Hey, you. Long time, no see." She gave Hunter a quick peck on the cheek before the introductions. "Hunter this is Cassidy." She stepped back to let them get acquainted and hugged Patty. "Good to see you. And you, Mo," she said, giving Mo a quick embrace.

Cass shook Hunter's hand, trying not to stare. The woman was gorgeous. Well, not quite Cass's type, but definitely Rebecca's. How in the hell did Rebecca not hook up with her? She absolutely did *not* want to think of that, so she focused on Hunter saving her girl's life.

"Got the handshake in, now I owe you a beer," Cass grinned.

"You don't owe me anything, but I'll take it," Hunter laughed and gestured for Cass to sit. Her approval of the woman grew in spades as she watched Cass wait for Rebecca to finish her hellos with the others before pulling her chair out for her.

"Patty and Mo, this is my girlfriend Cassidy," Rebecca paused for a second as Cassidy automatically corrected her with "just Cass."

"Never thought I'd ever hear those words coming from you," Mo quipped before taking a swig of beer.

"Me, either. But here we are."

Out of the three women, Rebecca clashed with Mo the most. It wasn't because she didn't like the woman. She did. It just so happened that Mo's personality took a little getting used to. While Rebecca appreciated Mo's frankness, it sometimes went a little overboard.

Patty, on the other hand, was a saint to put up with her wife's frequent immaturity. When Rebecca had met them both during her stay at the hospital, she never would have guessed they were married. They were polar opposites in almost every way except in height.

Patty was a five-foot-two, no-nonsense, chocolate-skinned woman who could put the fear of God into you with one look from her light brown eyes. She was also a few years older than Rebecca and was known as the "mama" of the group. In contrast, Mo—who, unbelievably at times, was around the same age as Rebecca—was a stout butch with short, dirty blonde hair, and a childishness about her that could be as endearing as it was frustrating. Opposites attract, she supposed.

"Well, I can see why you've been hiding this one away," Patty fawned.

"Why? Because she's so young? Seriously, what'd you do, Becca? Rob a cradle?"

"Mo!" Both Hunter and Patty reprimanded Mo with a slap to the back of the head. A common occurrence in Rebecca's experience.

"What! I'm pretty sure she knows she's older!"

Hunter buried her head in her hands and Patty merely stared at her wife until the "tough butch" cowered.

"I apologize for my wife's idiocy," Patty finally said after more seconds of intense staring.

Rebecca shrugged. After fifteen years of Mo, she had been prepared for it. By the look on Cassidy's face, she was not. She placed her hand on Cassidy's thigh under the table and patted it.

"It's fine. Tactless," Rebecca said, looking pointedly at a now contrite Mo, "but fine. She's right. I *do* know that I'm older. But, we seem to be getting along just fine."

"More than fine," Cass muttered. She took a deep breath (or two) before continuing. "Age isn't a factor. *She's* the one who keeps me on my toes. Besides, she's taught me things I could never learn from someone my age. Things I've never even dreamed of."

Hunter choked on her beer with laughter, Patty looked proud, Mo eyed Rebecca with a renewed respect, and Rebecca merely shook her head. She had been in the sex business far too long to be embarrassed by such declarations. That didn't mean Cassidy wouldn't be punished for it when they got home. And Rebecca knew exactly what tool she was going to use.

Cass glanced at her girlfriend and grinned. Oh, she knew she was going to get punished. What other reason would she reveal something so private? She was smart enough to keep it clean and simple but made sure everyone—especially Mo—got the gist. Now, she couldn't wait for dinner to be over to find out what Mistress had in store for her.

"Well," Hunter cleared her throat. "Now that we know of Rebecca's prowess, tell us a bit about yourself, Cass. Uh, the professional side," she said quickly as to not be misunderstood.

"Not much to tell," Cass smiled. "I paint. That's about it."

"She's being very modest," Rebecca chimed in. "She's a brilliant artist." She saw Cassidy lowered her head and blush slightly. *So cute.*

"Brilliant is a little exaggerated, don't you think? I just paint murals around the city."

"Baby, Sumptor Galleries is going to feature you in the new gallery opening soon. That's more than 'just painting murals'."

"Holy shit! That's freakin' big time!" Mo sputtered.

Patty rolled her eyes. "What my wife meant to say is congratulations. That's fantastic!"

"Yeah, that," Mo muttered.

"I'm throwing in my congrats as well," Hunter said with enthusiastic respect. "From what I hear, Sumptor Galleries is one of the most prestigious in the business. Modesty be damned!" She signaled for a waiter who promptly strode over. "A bottle of your finest champagne, please. We're celebrating."

"That's not necessary," Cass protested. The praise was cool and all, but she wasn't used to it.

"Of course, it is. We're celebrating you and Becca being together and your success." The waiter came back with a chilled bottle in an ice bucket. When each glass was filled, Hunter lifted hers in salute. "To Rebecca and Cass. May you continue to make each other happy. And, to Cass's success. One day I'll be able to say, 'I knew her when'."

Everyone raised their glass while calling out "cheers" and making sure to touch everyone's champagne flute.

"Can we order now? I'm starving!"

The group laughed at Mo's half-hearted complaint and Patty's response of throwing a menu at her. Rebecca caught Cassidy's eye and smiled at the glowing face. This was good. This is what they both needed. Not validation, but friends to share their happiness with. Not to mention, Rebecca had missed her friends immensely. She would make it a point to stay in touch better.

"Wait! Did you paint that mural on the strip? You know, the one with the woman and the big t…"

Whatever was about to come out of Mo's mouth was forgotten quickly with another slap to the back of her head.

"I LIKE YOUR friends."

Rebecca looked over at Cassidy and smiled. "They like you."

"Mo's a trip."

"Mo is crazy, but she's ours."

"Do, um, she and Patty know about Mistress?"

"No, just you and Hunter. And, Eve."

Cass whipped her head around. "As in Sumptor?!"

"Mmhmm. Watch the road. I know you only had one glass of champagne, but it always helps to keep your eye on the road."

"Yes, dear." She focused straight ahead. "Why?"

"Why, what?"

"Why does she know?"

"Eve? Because I told her. We've done a lot of business together. I was recommended to her years ago by a client. She wanted to open a club and that's something I excel at. We've become close over the years and have talked about things." She glanced over at a silent Cassidy. "Why does that make you jealous, Cassidy?"

"It doesn't," she muttered, then changed her mind. "Fine, it does. I Googled Eve Sumptor. Do all your friends have to be so damn beautiful and successful?"

"Eve Sumptor-Riley," Rebecca corrected. "She's married. And no one is as beautiful to me as you are, Cassidy."

Cassidy reached over and took Rebecca's hand. "That was pretty stupid, huh? Never thought I'd be *that* girlfriend."

"Aunt Wills would probably tell us that a small dose of jealousy is healthy for us. That it'll keep us on our toes." Rebecca scoffed. "I might tell her to send her degree back to the Cracker Jack box, but who knows? As long as you talk to me about your feelings and don't assume things that only make it worse, I think we'll do fine."

"Deal. Speaking of talking, you said earlier tonight that we needed to talk. Wanna do that now?"

"Oh! Um, it can wait until we get home."

"When we get home, I fully expect to be punished for my indiscretion at dinner."

"I *knew* you did that on purpose!" Rebecca laughed. "Don't worry, you'll get what's coming to you."

"Oh, I hope so." Cass wiggled her eyebrows suggestively.

"And, then, maybe you could, um, take a turn punishing me." There! She said it! Not quite the way she should, but it's a start.

The car swerved as Cass's entire body jerked with surprise and arousal. "You—you want me to? I… you…"

"Baby, calm down before your brain explodes," Rebecca chuckled. "We'll discuss this more when we get home. I've come to realize that I have certain needs that I hadn't anticipated. Hence the mood swings. I've been a little afraid to tell you."

"You're afraid of me?"

"No, no. Definitely not, baby. Quite the opposite." Rebecca breathed in deeply. "Cassidy, when I tell you this, I need for you to listen, okay? Hear me out and then we can discuss if you need to. Promise?"

When Cass looked over at Rebecca the last thing she expected to see was anxiety. It was another moment for her to prove to Rebecca that their relationship was destined for greatness. Cass would make it so. "Promise."

Chapter Twelve
REBECCA & CASS

Hurt Me

"You want me to what?"

"Cassidy, you promised you would listen."

"I am listening, Rebecca." Cass paced restlessly and ran frustrated hands through her already tousled hair. "I'm listening to you tell me that you want me to hurt you."

"No," Rebecca said calmly—more calmly than she actually felt. "You *heard* me say those words and then stopped listening."

Cass flung her arms up in the air. "Because I don't understand how you can ask me to be like her!"

"Is that what you think? That I want you to be someone I hate?" Rebecca stood up to face Cass. "Have you considered the fact that I might be as confused about this as you are? Why do you think I've been so moody the past few days? Hell, I even called my aunt hoping she'd give me meds because I'd gone crazy. And, instead of truly listening, you want to think that it's because I want you to be like *her*?"

Cass stopped in her tracks and sighed. "You're right. I'm sorry." She walked over to the couch where Rebecca sat and perched herself on the coffee table. "I'm listening."

Rebecca gave her a skeptical look but continued. "You know, I've been so distracted that when I called my aunt for advice, I forgot to take off my mask. It was the first time she had seen me as Mistress."

Cass contemplated that. The one thing she knew for certain was how private Rebecca was about her alter ego. For her to be troubled enough to forget must mean this really was bothering her just as much.

"What did she say?" Cass asked. "I mean about what you, um, want?"

"Need," Rebecca corrected softly. "Oddly enough, she said I was normal. Relatively speaking. And, not because she's my relative."

Cass's lips twitched at Rebecca's little joke. Their time together had brought out different sides of their personalities. That included a more lighthearted approach to things. Even when those things were heavy. That was definitely Cass's influence.

"My first sexual experience," Rebecca continued, "was filled with pain. Each subsequent time, the pain got worse. According to Aunt Wills, it's not uncommon for victims of prolonged abuse to… crave something they had become accustomed to."

Cass was no shrink, and that definitely sounded like something Rebecca's aunt would say. Since Aunt Wills had the shrink degree, who was Cass to argue? "That sounds, um, logical, I guess. But you sound a bit doubtful."

Rebecca shrugged. "I still think I'm crazy."

Cass took Rebecca's hand and felt it tremble slightly. "You're not crazy, baby. But, why now? You've been a Dom all these years, why would you want to give up your control now?"

"Because I met you," Rebecca answered honestly.

"I don't understand."

"I spent years building defenses against ever having to go through what Samantha put me through again. Finding you, loving and trusting you, has allowed my body to let go of those defenses." Rebecca took a breath and then dove in with the whole truth. "The other night out on the couch? When you fucked me right after I came? I felt that pain again, but in the way, it was supposed to be all those years ago. Exquisite pleasurable pain. I'm guessing that's what woke up those desires."

Cass was torn between feeling pride and panicked. It was a good thing, no a remarkable thing, to be trusted so much. But the weight of the responsibility of not traumatizing her girlfriend anymore than she already is was hefty.

"I don't know if I can hurt you, baby."

"Cassidy, the reason I can ask this of you is because I know you will never do anything that I can't handle. I know that what you do to me will be out of love and not because you want to control or possess me. I'm not asking you to mark me. I'm asking you to help me in the only way you can."

"Can you understand my hesitation, Rebecca? I've seen your scars. I've been there when you've woken up in a cold sweat after a nightmare."

Rebecca touched Cassidy's worried face. "Then exorcise my demons, baby. Take away the fear."

Cass closed her eyes and silently prayed she was doing the right thing. She would do anything for Rebecca, and if this is what she needed, Cass would do her best not to break both of them.

"What's your favorite word, Rebecca?"

Rebecca grinned at the salute to their beginning. "Cassidy."

The tall woman chuckled. "You're going to have to pick another word. I'm going to make you scream my name all night long."

Laughter filled the air. "Fine, how about platypus? It's such a fun word to say."

"Right!?" Cass stood and held her hand out to Rebecca. They held hands as they made their way to the bedroom. Cass had very little time to figure out how to be what Rebecca needed. She was semi-confident that once they got the awkward beginning out of the way, things would come naturally. And that was one thing Cass was *very* good at. Making Rebecca come naturally.

"Take your clothes off, Rebecca."

The words triggered a bout of anxiety in Rebecca that she wasn't prepared for. "Um, whew. Could you do me a favor?"

"Of course."

"Could you still call me baby?"

"She said that to you, didn't she?" Cass asked gently, and Rebecca nodded. "I should have…"

"No, not your fault," Rebecca interrupted. "I also have a couple of hard limits."

"Hard limits?"

"Boundaries," Rebecca explained. "Things that I absolutely can't do."

"Tell me."

"I can't be tied up. You can hold me down, but no bindings of any kind."

"Okay, I get that. Anything else?"

Rebecca took a cleansing breath and picked up one of the fringed whips they kept handy, giving it to Cassidy. "Not my back."

Cass tossed the whip on the bed and took Rebecca in her arms. "Baby, if I do *anything* at all that makes you uncomfortable or triggers you, tell me and I will stop. If you start getting dragged into the past, I want you to look at me, Rebecca. Look me in the eye and see. Not who I'm *not*, but who I *am*. Always remember who I am."

A tear rolled down Rebecca's cheek. She wrapped her arms around Cassidy's neck and kissed her with all of the emotions she had inside her.

"I love you, Cassidy."

"I love you, too, baby." Cass smacked Rebecca's tight ass hard enough for her to yelp. "Now, let's try out our new roles."

"Yes, ma'am," Rebecca smirked as she took off her clothes and hopped up on the bed. "I'm all yours."

Rebecca swayed her hips and hummed an indistinct tune as she slathered mustard and mayo on a thick piece of wheat bread. She was happy. Aunt Wills had been right. The role reversal and giving up control didn't mean taking away her power. In fact, Rebecca had never felt more powerful. Or more stable. She still didn't know if it made sense to her, but at this point, she didn't care. She was happy.

"Whatcha singin'?"

The knife Rebecca was using clattered as it hit the counter. "Jesus! You scared me!"

Cass chuckled wrapped her arms around Rebecca. "Sorry, I thought you heard me come in. Hey? You okay?" The once singing and dancing woman was now shaking in Cass's arms.

So, Rebecca wasn't *completely* cured of all of her fears. It was going to take more than a week to dispel years of torture.

"Yeah, I'm good. Residual angst." She looked up at Cassidy and laughed. "You have paint on your nose."

Cass lifted a brow and adopted a terrible French accent. "An arteest iz not an arteest if zay do not have paint on zer noze."

"Excusez-moi, mademoiselle arteest!"

Cass harrumphed. "I weel forgive you for eh turkey zandweech."

"Oh, baby," Rebecca laughed heartily. "Your accent is awful! Please do not do that when we go to France. They'll throw us out!"

Cass peered down at Rebecca. "We're going to France?"

"Would you like to?"

Cass had always wanted to travel but never found the time. Or the right person to go with. Until now. "That'd be awesome! Seeing all the sights with you. Doing the touristy thing."

"Then we'll plan it. Maybe we can after your gallery showing. To celebrate your success."

Cass rolled her eyes playfully. "You can't know I'll be successful, babe."

"Sure, I can. I've seen your work." Rebecca turned back to her previous task of making Cass's sandwich. She put the finishing touches on it, plated it, and handed it over. "Want some chips?"

"Please." Cass took a big bite getting mustard and mayonnaise on the sides of her mouth.

Rebecca shook her head. "Doesn't go with the paint," she said, wiping Cass's mouth with a napkin.

"Thanks. So, um," Cass took a swig of water from the glass Rebecca placed in front of her. "Rand called."

"And?"

Cass waited for Rebecca to join her before continuing. "First, thank you for the sandwich. Awesome as usual. Unnecessary, as usual. But, greatly appreciated as usual."

Cassidy was constantly telling her she didn't have to cook or clean or do things for her. But it was another thing ingrained in Rebecca's head. Only now, she loved doing things for Cassidy. Almost as much as she loved it when Cassidy made the effort to do things for her.

"You're welcome. As usual." She watched Cassidy take another huge bite. "Rand?"

"Hmm? Oh, yeah." Cass swallowed and wiped her mouth. "She wanted to know if we were free for lunch this weekend. You, me, her, and Connor. I told her I'd ask you and let her know."

"Well, I have to be at the club at 4 pm both Saturday and Sunday, but we can meet up before that."

"Hmm." Cass took another bite in order to keep her mouth from getting her in trouble.

"What?"

"What what?" Cass asked as innocently as she could with a mouth full of food and a brain full of words she should say.

"What was the 'hmm' for? And the look?"

"I didn't—I'm not..." The look on Rebecca's face told Cass she was having none of it. "Okay. I'm just wondering about the club."

"What about it?"

"Look, baby. I have no problem with you working at or owning a sex club. It's *that* club. That club is your last tie to her, Rebecca. Maybe it would be good for you to cut that tie? Start a new club? One that's just yours."

"We've discussed this, Cassidy."

"Yeah. You *owe* her. But I think that's bullshit. You're keeping that fucking club to torture yourself."

"Enough." Rebecca's voice was dangerously low. "Just because I've let you dominate me in the bedroom does not mean I will allow you to speak to me that way."

Cass tried to hold her own anger in check. How in the hell did this conversation go downhill so fast? Two seconds ago, they were happily eating lunch together.

"No, being your *girlfriend*, someone who *loves* you means that I should be allowed to express my feelings about what you're doing to yourself." She met Rebecca's stony stare. "Or not. Maybe you need a piece of her to stay in your life, so you don't have to give yourself fully to anyone else." Cass pushed away from the table. "Thank you for lunch. I need to get back to painting. Deadlines."

"Cassidy." Rebecca sighed as the woman she truly loved walked out without another word. "Damn it."

She cleaned up the kitchen before locking herself in her office that Cassidy had so graciously set up for her. She was always doing something sweet for Rebecca. And, Cassidy rarely got upset enough to walk out. Perhaps it was time for Rebecca to do something sweet for Cassidy. But, could she give up the club? Shit, was Cassidy right about her?

CASS HATED HOSPITALS. She was always afraid that she'd take a wrong turn and end up seeing something she really shouldn't be seeing. Or worse, get lost and end up in the morgue. She checked her phone again.

"Damn creepy hospitals," she muttered. Somehow her quiet words seemed to echo through the empty halls. "Where the hell is everyone?"

"Can I help you?"

"Shit!" Cass nearly jumped out of her own skin. "Sorry, um, yeah, I'm looking for Dr. Hunter, uh, something." *Why in the hell don't I know her last name?* "Tall, dark-haired woman? Blue eyes."

"Dr. Vale," the lady said almost dreamily. "You're on the wrong floor. Take the elevator down two floors and visit the nurses' station in the ER. They'll page her for you."

"Great, thanks!"

"Is there anything else I can help you with? Maybe we could go somewhere a little more private?"

Cass blinked in confusion. *Did she just proposition me?* "I, uh, have a girlfriend." Of course, that girlfriend was currently mad at her, and they hadn't had sex in three days. But Cass would never do something as stupid as to cheat on Rebecca. She started this mess, now she was going to fix things with her beautiful Mistress.

"She wouldn't have to know." The auburn-haired woman leaned into Cass and was immediately pushed away.

"I would know. Excuse me."

"If you change your mind," the woman called after a retreating Cass. "Just ask for nurse Iris!"

"Not likely," Cass said to herself as the elevator door closed. People like that Iris chick made Cass happier than ever to be with someone like Rebecca. That's why it hurt so much to be at odds with her.

She stepped out into chaos two floors down. The total opposite of where she had just been. Empty halls were replaced by bustling personnel and shouts of medical terms she didn't understand. This was more like the hospitals Cass saw on TV. Spotting a familiar face, she made her way to the nurses' station.

"Patty?"

"Cass! What a surprise." Patty immediately lost the smile she gave her new friend. "Is Rebecca all right?"

"Yeah! Yeah, she's good. Annoyed with me at the moment, but good."

"Ooh, you better get that straightened out, sugar. I've never seen her happier than she is with you. Don't blow this."

"That's why I'm here. Is Hunter available?"

Patty pursed her lips and studied the fine specimen in front of her. She had told the truth about never having seen Rebecca so happy before. If she could have a hand in keeping it that way, Patty was glad to help. She picked up the phone.

"Dr. Vale, please come to the nurses' station." She looked up at Cass. "I don't see her scheduled for a surgery, so unless she was pulled into an emergency, she'll be here."

"I appreciate it."

"My pleasure. Now, you do something for me."

"Name it."

"Get that girl of yours to forgive you and let's get together again for dinner soon."

"Workin' on it," Cass grinned. "And, deal!"

"You rang, Patty?"

Cass turned at the sound of Hunter's smooth voice. "That was for me."

"Hey! Wait, is Rebecca okay?"

Cass chuckled. "Yeah. She's lucky to have people who care so much about her."

"Enough to hurt anyone who ever caused her harm again," Hunter warned.

Cass lifted her arms in surrender. Or defense. Either could work at the moment. "You never have to worry about that with me. But I am here about the person who did hurt her. Do you have a minute?"

Hunter nodded and led Cass to the doctors' lounge. "What's up?"

Cass took a piece of paper out of her back pocket and unfolded it. "I need your advice. And I need your professional opinion, not the opinion of my girlfriend's best friend. Got me?" She handed over the paper and waited for Hunter to read it.

"How did you get this?"

"Does it matter?" Cass sighed. "I have friends, or rather Rebecca has friends in high places that would like to see her stop suffering as much as I would. Look, Rebecca doesn't know I have this, and she won't know if your answer is any different from what I think it is. But, I need to know."

"What do you need to know exactly, Cass? Is it important enough to bring all of this back up for Rebecca?"

"Yeah, Hunter, I think it is. She's been carrying this weight for far too long. So, looking at that," she gestured to the paper, "you tell me. Was there *anything* that Rebecca could have done to save Samantha's life?"

Hunter studied Samantha's autopsy report carefully. She went over it three times before she shook her head. "No. According to these findings, Samantha died the moment she took that last hit of heroin." She turned the document to Cass and pointed out the cause of death.

"Dude, I have no clue what any of that means. That's why I brought it to you."

Hunter gave her a small smile. "Basically, her heart exploded. That's overdramatizing it a bit, but with the buildup in her heart and lungs from prolonged drug abuse, the blood vessels can rupture. Samantha had a heart attack, Cass. A severe one. There was nothing Rebecca could have done to save her. The paramedics would not have made it on time whether Rebecca had called the moment Samantha started experiencing pain or not. Even if they did, Samantha was too far gone to save."

Cass let out a whoosh of air. "You're sure? This is from *Dr.* Hunter?"

"Yes, Cass. That is my professional opinion. I'd stake my reputation on it."

Cass nodded. "Good." She held her hand out to Hunter. "Thank you. I owe you big time."

Hunter held Cass's hand firmly. "You don't owe me anything. I should have thought to do this myself. I knew she was holding on to this, but I…"

"Hey. You saved her life, Hunter. Let me save her heart."

"Sumptor Galleries, how may I help you?"

"Is Eve in?"

"May I ask who's calling?"

"Rebecca Cuinn."

"One moment, Ms. Cuinn." There was only time for a few bars of some song Rebecca couldn't quite place before the line clicked over.

"It's nice being popular." Eve's sensual voice sounded amused. "Hello, Rebecca."

"Popular?"

"It's just been a busy couple of days. What can I do for you?"

"I'm in need of a change."

There was a slight pause on the other end of the line. "Sorry, I was a little taken aback by that. You usually call my cell for personal reasons. What's wrong? I was under the impression life was going quite well for you. How is Cass?"

Rebecca's heart fluttered at the mention of Cass's name. She absolutely hated that they were clashing right now. Especially since it was all Rebecca's fault.

"She's fine. We're fine. And, my life *is* going quite well. I want to keep it that way which is why I need a change. And why I called your office. This is business, not personal. At least, not completely personal."

"How can I help?"

"I need to sell the club. You've mentioned before that you knew people interested in the type of business I'm in. Is that still accurate?"

"I could be interested."

Rebecca's eyebrows shot up. "Please don't take this the wrong way, Eve, but it's not for you. While I'm sure you would make a formidable Dom, you have more important things to focus your energy on."

Eve laughed heartily. "I'm flattered to know that Mistress thinks I could rival her."

"Ah ah, I said you'd be formidable, not competition for me," Rebecca joked.

"My apologies," Eve chuckled. "But, you're probably right. About the more important things, that is. Let me put feelers out. Does it matter if they want to change the direction?"

Rebecca felt that familiar feeling of guilt trying to creep in, and she quickly tamped it down. She was tired of Samantha having a hold on her life. All she ever did was ruin things.

"No, it doesn't matter. It's just time for me to move on. I can't do that living behind the mask."

"So, you're giving up the lifestyle?"

"Not exactly. Just… rerouting it."

"I must say, I'm surprised by this move," Eve said mildly.

"As I said, some things are more important."

"I take that to mean things are more than fine with Cass?"

"They will be. She thinks I'm holding myself back by keeping a part of Samantha via the club."

"I can't say I disagree with her."

Rebecca chuckled. "You've been spending way too much time with my aunt. Have you been taking notes, Eve?"

"That woman is someone I would rather spend less time with," Eve joked. "Unfortunately, it seems I need her increasingly these days. So, my misery means yours, too."

"Gee, thanks. It just so happens I agree, as well. Samantha is my past. Cassidy, I hope, is my future. I need to make things right. This is the first step to doing that."

"I wish I had your balls, Mistress. Doing what you need to do for what you want."

Eve sounded so forlorn, Rebecca felt sorry for her. She was pretty sure that there weren't many people in this world that would think to feel sorry for someone who seemed so incredibly fortunate. If they only knew the real Eve.

"I know you hate it when I talk about certain things, so I'll just say this; You're the bravest woman I've ever known, Eve. The moment you remember that you'll have everything you want."

Eve cleared her throat. "I'll get in touch when I hear something about the club. And, Rebecca? I'm going to suggest that you keep it as is, along with privileges. It is where you and Cass met. That must hold some significance despite the other memories."

Rebecca smiled. She did have a point. "I'll think about it. Right now, I need to go home and seduce my girlfriend." *Home.* Odd how good it felt to say that word. To feel it. The best part about it was it didn't matter where she was. Home was wherever Cassidy was.

Eve laughed. "Go get her!"

Chapter Thirteen
REBECCA & CASS

Oh, My God

CASS'S OLD WORK truck rumbled into the driveway behind Rebecca's Mercedes. As usual, her heart did a little happy dance seeing that her girlfriend was home. Now if they could just get past this bump in the road. Cass was determined to put an end to it tonight. She wanted to be close with Rebecca again. And that didn't just mean sex. Although, sex was always welcome. Always! She hopped out of the cab, ready to take off in a sprint to find her lover when she heard a car pulling into the driveway.

"*Oh, crap.*" Cass plastered a smile on her paint-stained face and jogged up to the car. "Mom, dad! Hey!" Cass opened the door for her mom, hugging her when she got out. "This is unexpected."

"We figured we'd come visit you since you're apparently too busy to come to the house." Beverly Giles stood at least five inches shorter than her daughter, but there was no mistaking her authority. Her slightly graying, brown hair fell just past her shoulders, giving her an almost youthful look. The only trait that mother and daughter shared was blue eyes, and Cass only had one of those. The amber colored one she got from her dad.

Cass rolled her eyes. "You know, Mitch hardly ever comes home, and you don't give him grief over it."

"Your brother doesn't live ten miles away," her mother reminded her.

"Bev, leave our daughter alone. Hey, kid." Russell Giles gave Cass a hug and a quick kiss on the cheek. There was no mistaking that this was Cass's father. She got her height and build from her father, even if he had let himself get a little soft around the edges the older he got.

"Dad. You know, if you'd called I could have tried to make it home earlier and been more prepared."

Russ chuckled. "There wasn't a chance in hell of that. Your mom caught wind of the fact that you might have a serious girlfriend. She didn't want to give you the opportunity to talk us out of visiting."

"This is why people hate lawyers," Bev muttered.

"Because they tell the truth?" Cass asked cheekily.

"Is it true?" her mom asked in lieu of an answer. "Do you have a girlfriend?"

Cass sighed. "I don't know how the hell you guys know everything, but yes, I do."

"I'm guessing that's her fancy ride?" Russ nodded towards Rebecca's car. "And, if her car is here with you just getting home, I'm guessing serious is the right word."

"You should've been a detective," Cass chuckled. "Come on. I'll introduce you. Just *try* not to embarrass me or interrogate her too much."

"You know your dad. Once a lawyer, always a lawyer."

"I was talking to *you*, mom." Cass unlocked the front door, hoping Rebecca wouldn't be too upset with her springing the parents on her like this. Not that Cass had any control over it at the moment. She was relieved (and slightly disappointed) when Rebecca was nowhere to be seen as they walked in. On the one hand, she'd have a chance to give her a heads up. On the other, the emptiness of the room echoed the distance that was between them these days.

"Hmm, cleaner than usual. This girl must be a good influence on you," Bev hip-checked her daughter. The truth was, she was hurt that Cass hadn't come to her with the news. Her daughter was only twenty-five, but her brother was only a few years older and already married with children. The way Cass was playing the field, Bev didn't think she'd ever see her young daughter settling down. She was curious as to what kind of woman could make that possible.

"Ha, ha. It's funny because it's true. She is a good…" If it had been possible to swallow her tongue, Cass would have. As it were, all thoughts melted from her brain, her mouth became dry—other places not so much—and she had a split second to think of *anything* that would keep her parents' attention on her. She grabbed her mom and hugged her fiercely. "Missed you. Both of you! Get in here, dad." She clumsily pulled her dad into the hug and held on tightly. *Oh, my God!*

Rebecca's eyes widened. *Oh, my God!* She foolishly tried to cover her body before realizing that would *not* work. Since there was no graceful way of meeting Cassidy's parents with a crotchless bustier and Mistress's mask, she turned on her heel and ran back to the bedroom.

"So, yeah, um, I'm gonna just, um, go take a quick shower and wash this paint off of me. Then, we can, um, go to dinner. 'Kay?" Cass patted her mom's shoulder and started towards the bedroom, trying not to run.

"Cass?"

Cass closed her eyes and stopped. *Please don't say you saw that. Please, please, please.* "Hmm?"

"Is she here?"

"Oh, um, yeah. I mean her car is here, so she must be in the bedroom." *Almost naked and with her mask on. Holy shit. Is it too late to ask mom and dad for a rain check?* "Be out in a jiffy!"

"That was weird," Bev said to her husband who was smirking.

"Eh, if her young lady is indeed in the bedroom, it makes sense that

Cass would want to have a little alone time."

"Russ! Our daughter wouldn't do *that* while we're here! Would she?!"

Russ chuckled. "I meant, she would probably want to warn the girl that she was about to meet the parents. But, I like the way you think, dear."

"OH, MY GOD!" Rebecca paced around the bedroom repeating the phrase over and over again. Could her luck be any worse? She came *very* close to exposing herself to Cassidy's parents. You only get one first impression, and that would have been disastrous. She was fairly sure they didn't see her, yet she was *still* embarrassed.

"Jesus, baby!" Cass locked the door, hurried to her girlfriend, and began kissing her.

"Cassidy." Rebecca placed two fingers over Cassidy's lips. "Your parents are out there."

Cass groaned. "But you're in here. In this!" Her eyes naturally gravitated to Rebecca's tits that were spilling over the top of the bustier.

Rebecca used those same fingers to lift Cassidy's chin. "Eyes up. Focus."

"I am!" Cass's eyes dipped again until Rebecca cleared her throat. "Come on, baby! It's been *forever* since I've touched you!"

"Three days."

"That's what I said! Forever!"

Rebecca couldn't help but chuckle at Cassidy. "Well, it's going to be a little longer because you have guests."

"*We* have guests," Cass corrected. "Apparently, they know about you." Rebecca's eyebrows rose. "Technically, they only know that I have a girlfriend. I guess Rand told her mom who's friends with my mom."

"So, hiding in here isn't an option?"

Cass frowned. "You don't want to meet my parents?"

"It's not that, baby. I guess I'm just a little embarrassed about almost getting caught like this." Rebecca gestured to her scantily clad body.

"You definitely have *nothing* to be embarrassed about. Your body is rockin'."

"I'm glad you think so, but I'm sure your parents would see things differently."

Not my dad, Cass thought but decided not to voice. "They didn't see you. But, I can't get the gorgeous image out of my head. I could tell them…"

"No," Rebecca laughed softly. "You need to get in the shower and wash this stuff off your cute face, and I need to get dressed."

"Wait!" Cass grabbed Rebecca around the waist. "At least wear this under whatever you change into. Please? Then, maybe we can revisit what you had planned when we're alone again?"

Rebecca nodded with a smile. "How should I dress?"

Cass grinned and shrugged. "Casual? Dad's a meat and potatoes kinda guy, so I thought we could go to a steakhouse not far from here. Is that okay?"

"Of course. Now, go get in the shower."

"Sure you don't want to join me?"

Rebecca rolled her eyes and pushed Cassidy towards the bathroom.

"MOM, DAD?" CASS walked towards her parents with her arm draped around Rebecca's shoulders. "I'd like you to meet the woman I love. This is Rebecca Cuinn."

With a critical eye, Bev Giles studied the woman that had ostensibly stolen her daughter's heart. The elegant blonde certainly wasn't what she had been expecting and she was pleasantly surprised with Cass's choice.

The couple was a striking contrast, yet somehow, they fit perfectly. Her daughter was tall, slim, muscular, and androgynous in her black jeans and light gray Henley. Cass's smaller companion boasted sheer femininity in cream-colored slacks and matching blouse.

Rebecca held her delicate hand out to Cassidy's mother. "It's a pleasure to meet you, Mrs. Giles." After a firm handshake, she turned to Russell. "Mr. Giles."

"Russ, please. And this is Beverly or Bev. Now I can see why Cass has been so preoccupied," Russ replied with a grin that was similar to his daughter's.

"I should apologize for monopolizing Cassidy's time."

"No, you shouldn't," Cass interjected before her parents could respond. "That's my fault, guys. We've sorta been in the 'getting to know you' stage."

"They don't need details, honey," Rebecca said quietly.

"Rebecca is right, Cass." Bev was still stunned that Cass allowed anyone to use her full name. From the time she could speak, Cass was forever telling people not to call her Cassidy. But this woman—not girl—called her Cassidy as though it was the most natural thing. And Cass never even blinked. "Your father and I know what it's like to be in the beginning stages of a relationship."

"Hell, yeah, we do." Russ waggled his eyebrows rakishly and clapped his daughter on the back.

Cass put her hands over her ears and closed her eyes tightly. "Oh, geez."

Rebecca laughed softly. She imagined her own parents would have been just like this with anyone she had brought home. It was a bittersweet moment knowing that would never be. *Don't get caught up in things you can't change, Rebecca.* She cleared her throat and took Cassidy's hands away from her ears. Thankfully, that effectively stopped the "la, la, las" coming from the younger woman. "I wish I had known we would have company. I could have cooked."

"Ah, well that would be our fault," Bev confessed. "We decided to surprise Cass so she wouldn't have a chance to hide you from us."

"Hide Rebecca? Ha! Never!" Cass once again wrapped her arm around Rebecca, standing beside her proudly. "I was selfish, not ashamed. If she would allow me to, I'd buy commercial time during the Super Bowl announcing my love for Rebecca."

Rebecca blushed. It was not an easy task, making someone who spent their time dominating others blush. Cassidy seemed to do it with ease. "Um, why don't we head on out to the restaurant," she squeezed Cassidy's arm and gave her a little tug. "Cassidy is always hungry after a long day of painting."

"Yeah," Cass agreed immediately, sensing Rebecca's uneasiness. "I'm starving. Steakhouse down the street, meet you guys there."

"Right behind ya," Russ announced, rubbing his slightly pooched belly.

CASS SAT CLOSE enough to Rebecca in the booth that their thighs touched. She was just glad that her girlfriend wasn't upset with her for being so brazen about their relationship with her parents. Cass promised she would try to tone it down, but she couldn't help being excited that the three most important people in her life have finally met.

Once they were settled in, drinks were delivered, and food ordered, Bev turned her attention to Rebecca. She wondered if there was a subtle way of asking her age. "So, Rebecca, you seem to be comfortable at Cass's home. Does that mean you're living together?"

"Mom."

"What? It was a simple question, dear."

"Not exactly," Rebecca answered before any arguments could start. "I have my own place."

"Not for long." *Geez, Cass, word vomit much?* She shot Rebecca a repentant look.

Bev looked between the two. This woman seemed to hold some sort of authority over Cass. Another rarity. Cass practically made it her mission to defy authority. "Where did you two meet?"

Another look between the couple had both Bev and Russ intrigued.

"We, um, originally met at a club. During Rand's bachelorette party," Cass explained, obviously leaving out certain details. "But we just happened to run into each other again a few months ago."

"Months?" Bev asked with raised brows. "Isn't it a bit soon to be moving in together or talking about love?"

She shot her husband a "help me out here" look, but Russ opted to stay out of it. He accepted his daughter's lifestyle, but that didn't mean he completely understood it. It was ironic since he had no problems talking about girls with his son. Whether or not it made him a coward, he let Bev take the lead on this one. Besides, he liked Rebecca. He couldn't deny his daughter had great taste in women.

Cass shook her head. "I don't think anything I say is going to change your opinion, but no, it's not too soon. When you know, you know. You used to always tell me that. Now, when I *know*, you're going to question me?"

"I'm not trying to start an argument, Cass. I'm merely wondering how well you know each other. You're so young." Bev's eyes cut to Rebecca. She still couldn't quite put an age to the svelte blonde and that nagged at her. "You do know that Cass is a painter?"

"Oh, here we go," Cass muttered moodily.

Rebecca nudged Cassidy's leg with hers, hoping to keep her calm. "I, indeed, know that Cassidy is an artist. A very talented one."

Bev agreed that her daughter was talented. She just thought Cass was wasting her time doing murals here and there. Bev would never understand why Cass didn't become a lawyer like her father. She certainly had the intelligence. "Of course, she is. But her time would be better spent doing something a little more significant."

Rebecca tilted her head. "I would say it's pretty significant that one of the most prestigious galleries in the country will be showing Cassidy's work in their grand opening."

"Don't bother, Rebecca. I told you, they're not really interested…"

"Now, wait just a minute, young lady," Russ interjected. "What's this about? You're going to be in a gallery? I thought you were just painting murals and houses?"

Cass shrugged. "I was. Rebecca saw something more and called a friend to take a look at my work."

"This is your doing?" Russ asked Rebecca.

"No, it's Cassidy's. Contacts only go so far, Mr. Giles. Sumptor Galleries would not risk its reputation on someone they don't believe in."

"Why didn't you tell us?" Bev asked, clearly upset. "We may not understand your career choice, but we've always been supportive."

"I—I was going to, mom. The opening is still months away and I've been busy working on the canvases."

"Well, I expect an invitation to my only daughter's showing." Bev reached over and took Cass's hand. "I should tell you this more often, but I'm proud of you." She looked over at Rebecca. "And thank you for any role you played in this."

Rebecca smiled. "All I did was make a call."

"Tell me a little more about yourself," Bev suggested, patting Cass's hand before letting it go. "A woman with your contacts must have a story. Are you in the art business yourself?"

Rebecca laughed softly. "Not quite. I'm a business consultant. Eve Sumptor happens to be a friend and client, but I don't specialize in art."

Conversation was momentarily interrupted as their food was delivered. Unmindful of how her actions looked to their company, Rebecca automatically transferred the green vegetables from Cassidy's plate to hers and the mushrooms from her plate to Cassidy's.

"Try the squash, baby," she murmured lightly.

"'Kay."

Russ quietly watched the exchange between the two. As did his wife. This woman had changed their daughter. Fortunately, it seemed to be for the better and Russ's respect for the small woman increased.

"Do you have a specialty, Rebecca?" Russ asked around a mouthful of steak.

"Hmm?" Rebecca had been too preoccupied with her and Cassidy's ritual that she was a bit lost in the conversation.

"Your specialty in business. Do you have one?"

Yeah, she does, Cassidy thought rakishly.

"Oh," Rebecca chuckled. "No specialty. I'm very good at what I do, so it doesn't matter what business I'm working with. I'm sorry if that sounds arrogant, but I've worked very hard to get to where I am."

"I love a confident woman." Bev laughed when Cass wholeheartedly agreed that she did too. "Did you go to school around here?"

"Yes, I went to Berkeley."

"Oh! Cass's brother Mitch went to Berkeley. Class of 2013. Perhaps you've crossed paths?"

Well, shit. Rebecca laughed uncomfortably. *I suppose they'll find out eventually.* "No," she cleared her throat. "I graduated a few years earlier than that."

"What year? Maybe he was coming in as you were graduating?"

"Mom, stop."

"It's okay, Cassidy. First of all, I was in business school, not law, so we would have been in separate buildings. Second, I graduated in '97."

Bev looked up sharply, swallowing hard to avoid choking. "Nine…"

"Bev, let it go." It took Russ a few seconds to catch up with the math, but suffice it to say, Miss Rebecca Cuinn was quite older than Cass.

"You're…"

"I'm forty-one," Rebecca said matter-of-factly.

"Before this goes any further," Cass began. "I want you both to know that I was very aware of *everything* when I asked Rebecca to be with me. We both went into this with our eyes wide open. Please don't judge us."

Bev took a breath. "I'm not judging, Cass. But how much can you two have in common besides *sex*." She whispered the last word, then looked around to make sure she wasn't heard by anyone else.

"We have quite a lot in common," Rebecca offered, trying not to laugh at the situation. Her choices were to either laugh, cry, get angry, or explain the situation. Aunt Wills would be proud that she chose the latter. "We talk, Mrs. Giles. A great deal. Believe me, I had my reservations. I made all of the arguments I'm sure you're making in your mind." She took Cassidy's hand. "Your daughter is very persuasive. And, as long as she doesn't have a problem with the age difference, I won't either."

"I can understand that," Bev said amicably. "I'm sure she's told you that I'm older than her father. But those were different times and we made sure that all of our hopes and dreams coincided with one another's before we took that leap."

"How pragmatic." Rebecca held up a hand. "I apologize for that. Mrs. Giles, Beverly, I deal with business every day of my life. Past relationships have all been about business." She looked at Cassidy lovingly. "With Cassidy, it's not about that. It's about the feelings. She's taught me how to let go of the fear and follow my heart."

Cass grinned at her lover. Not many people had the guts to put Beverly Giles in her place. Rebecca did it with grace and respect. Plus, everything she just said made Cass fall in love even more.

"That's sweet. I want to be happy for you both."

"So, let's be," Russ cut in. "Rebecca is good for Cass. Anyone with eyes can see that. Let's be grateful she found someone that ticks all the right boxes. Intelligence, beauty, success, the ability to keep our kid in line." He ducked when Cass threw a piece of squash at him.

Bev didn't laugh. "What happens if she wants someone younger? Someone more her age at some point?"

"Never gonna happen," Cass answered confidently.

"I won't hold Cassidy back," Rebecca answered Bev unwaveringly. "I've thought of all of the scenarios and have come to terms with them."

"What about children? Don't you think you're a little too old to carry a child to term safely? How will that affect the relationship?"

Rebecca faltered. *That* was one scenario she hadn't thought of. Cassidy had never mentioned children and Rebecca had resigned herself years ago to never having them.

Cass noticed Rebecca's hesitation. Though she was extremely curious to find out what she thought of having kids, they would do that in a more private setting. "Mom, please stop. I'm not a kid. Rebecca and I are grown adults who can make decisions on our own. I'm happy, ma. Really, really happy."

Bev considered her options. Only one would keep everyone at this table from being mad at her. So, she took it. It wasn't a difficult decision since she actually liked the feisty woman sitting across from her. With that in mind, she smiled and raised her glass. "Welcome to the family, Rebecca."

Chapter Fourteen
REBECCA & CASS

Options

CASS WAVED AS her parents backed out of the driveway. "So glad that's over. Love them to death, but," she pushed Rebecca inside as soon as the front door was open. "Do you have it on under this?"

"Yes." Rebecca barely got the word out before Cassidy attacked, kissing her fiercely. As soon as Cassidy kicked the door closed, buttons were flying and bouncing off the hardwood floor. "I liked this shirt."

"I'll buy you a new one," Cassidy murmured against Rebecca's lips. "Right now, I need to get to what's underneath."

She whirled Rebecca around and pushed her up against the door. Cass was desperate enough to lack finesse, but a slightly panting Rebecca didn't seem to mind all that much.

"Take off your pants," Cass ordered as she struggled with her own.

Rebecca moaned at Cassidy's demand, complying without hesitation.

Her young girlfriend was getting very good at dominating. Anticipation built as Cassidy's jeans fell to the floor at her feet. And when Cassidy dropped to her knees in front of her, Rebecca felt her wetness dripping from the crotchless lingerie she wore.

"Put your leg over my shoulder." Cass kissed the smooth thigh as Rebecca draped it over her shoulder. The scent of her lover's sex was intoxicating, and Cass couldn't hold back any longer. Three days without tasting Rebecca was a drought Cass never wanted to experience again. She dove in as though her life depended on Rebecca's ambrosia.

"*Fuck!*" The leg that held Rebecca up, buckled and she struggled to stay upright. Feeling Cassidy's tongue against her aching clit was a blend of bliss and torture. How could she have let such a silly fight come between them? *Never again.* In no time, she felt that familiar peak begin to crescendo. And then Cassidy's mouth was gone. "Wha…?"

Cass didn't give Rebecca a chance to finish that question. As she stood, she grabbed Rebecca behind the thighs and lifted her. Rebecca's back slammed against the front door while Cass reached between them and positioned the dildo at Rebecca's wet and ready opening. She plunged inside so hard that the doorknob rattled, competing with a cry of ecstasy that Rebecca let out.

She didn't relent. Even as Rebecca's fingernails dug into her shoulders and back, Cass never eased up. Her thrusts became harder, faster. She braced one hand on the door as leverage, holding Rebecca up with the other, and she kept thrusting. Everything around her ceased to exist except the woman in her arms. Rebecca. The name became Cass's mantra until the moment she exploded with what was eerily close to a roar. The only thing strong enough to penetrate her euphoria was Rebecca's own shattered yell.

"I LOVE THIS." Rebecca settled back into Cassidy's wet, naked body, letting the scent of the lavender bubbles relax her. Not that she needed to be any more relaxed. Cassidy pretty much turned Rebecca's bones to jelly with a very healthy bout of fucking. After their round at the door, they moved to the bedroom though the change of scenery didn't mean a change of pace. Cassidy was just as relentless. If she hadn't also been attentive to Rebecca's needs, Rebecca would have worried.

"I love *you*," Cass breathed close to Rebecca's ear, then kissed her neck. She had feared that she had gone too far with her aggression. Though Rebecca never complained, Cass drew a bath for her girlfriend to make up for her behavior. She even lit candles! Sure, the candles were something Rebecca brought in, but at least Cass thought to light them for her girl. Now, she was trying to use the ambience to relax. If only her mind would shut the fuck up.

After a brief time of silence, Rebecca sighed quietly. The question in her head wouldn't go away, so she asked it aloud. "Were you punishing me?"

Cass lifted her head in alarm. "What?"

"You've been aggressive before, but never this silent. The only time you're like this is when you are afraid to say something that might start a fight." Rebecca sat up and turned to face her young lover, thankful that she was limber enough to do so in the small, clawfoot bathtub. "Are you mad at me that I never answered the question about children?" Since that's when Cassidy's silence truly began, it was only natural to think that's what was bothering her.

Cass reached for Rebecca's hands. "I'm not mad, baby. It's just… do you not want children?"

Rebecca took a deep breath. What she revealed now could change everything. It could very well be Samantha's final blow. Because if Cassidy left her now, Rebecca wasn't sure she would ever fully recover.

"I—I can't have children, Cassidy."

Cass frowned. "Don't say that, babe. Technology these days is amazing. Forget what my mom said. Women older than you are having healthy babies all the time."

Though she cringed inside, Rebecca let out a laugh. "I think that's the first time you've ever made me feel old." She pressed a hand to Cassidy's mouth that was stuttering apologies and explanations. "Cassidy, I *can't* have children. Samantha made sure of that. One of the surgeries I had that night was a hysterectomy," she revealed softly, praying it wouldn't be the thing that breaks them.

Cass sat back abruptly, sloshing the foamy water. "*Shit.*"

"I'm sorry."

"You have *nothing* to be sorry for!" Cass said immediately. God, she wished they weren't in the tiny ass bathtub. She wasn't as short as Rebecca and couldn't maneuver herself at all. So, she went with the best solution. "Come here," she demanded gently, holding her arms out to Rebecca.

Relief washed over Rebecca as she turned herself back around and allowed herself to be cocooned in Cassidy's embrace. She could feel the swift cadence of Cassidy's heart, affirming that the younger woman wasn't at ease.

"Why didn't you tell me?"

Rebecca was glad that she didn't have to look into Cassidy's eyes as she said this. She didn't know if she could handle the disappointment. "Honestly? I had reconciled with the fact that I couldn't have kids long before I met you. Then, it never came up between us. Maybe deep down I was scared to say it aloud." She tilted her head to look up at Cassidy. "Is it a deal breaker?"

Cassidy shook her head, fighting tears that wanted to break free. But she couldn't cry now. Though those tears would be for Rebecca's tremendous loss, she didn't want to cause any feelings of doubt or guilt. She kissed Rebecca's temple.

"Not a deal breaker at all. Look, if, you know, down the road, we feel like kids are something we need in our lives, there are options."

Rebecca raised a brow in surprise. "Would you carry them?"

Cass's knee-jerk reaction was just that. A knee-jerk. Kids had crossed her mind before. Especially after falling in love with Rebecca. But *her* carrying them? "I, uh, don't know about that. I was talking more about adoption. Millions of kids need homes. If we find ourselves in a position to take one in, maybe we could explore that avenue?"

Rebecca smiled. It was something to keep in mind. "How about we start with a dog."

So, she's a dog person!

"Or, a cat," Rebecca continued, unwittingly screwing up Cassidy's revelation.

"How about both?" Cass grinned, loving the feeling of Rebecca's jiggling tits on her arms as Rebecca laughed. She *barely* resisted taking those gorgeous tits in her hands and squeezing them until Rebecca begged her to stop. *Mmm. Rebecca begging.* Cass cleared her throat. She knew Rebecca needed a little more "recovery" time after their latest romp. With that in mind, Cass veered her thoughts into a different direction. "Um, since we're disclosing information, I have something to confess."

"Oh?" Rebecca hated the sick feeling she got in the pit of her stomach. After a lifetime of disappointment, it was an involuntary response to things she had no control over.

"Please don't be mad at me."

"Cassidy, it's never good to start off with that. Now, I'm going to think you're going to say something terrible."

"It's not terrible!" Cass squirmed a little. She *hoped* Rebecca didn't think it was terrible. "Remember that I did this because I love you."

"Please, just tell me. Making me wait only has me creating my own scenarios and that's never good."

"Okay. Um. I went to Hunter and had her look at the autopsy report and she confirmed everything for me." Cass spoke briskly, not even sure if she was making sense. But she certainly didn't want Rebecca coming up with awful scenarios.

"Wait," Rebecca shook her head and patted Cassidy's arm to let her go. Once again, she nimbly turned herself around to face her girlfriend. "Why don't you start at the beginning and try to be a little more comprehensible. You did what?"

Cass took a breath. "All right. So, I got a copy of Samantha's autopsy report and took it to Hunter for her opinion."

Rebecca stared at Cassidy for a full minute, mouth agape. "You—I." She rubbed her wet hands over her face, forgetting about the bubbles. "How? Let's start there. How did you get the autopsy report?"

Cass shrugged sheepishly. "I used my new artist status with Mrs. Sumptor-Riley to ask her for a favor. That woman is probably more influential than any damn president."

Rebecca was too shell-shocked to appreciate the small joke. "Go on."

"Ahem, right. So, she came through with the report and I took it to Hunter. Baby, I asked her for her *professional* opinion on whether there was anything at all that you could've done to help Samantha."

Blood pounded in Rebecca's ears. How would she react if she knew for sure that her actions killed the woman she spent years with? "And what were her findings?"

Cass took Rebecca's shaking hands in hers. "Rebecca, she staked her reputation on the fact that there was absolutely *nothing* you could have done to save Samantha. She said a lot of medical mumbo jumbo, but the way she explained it, Samantha was dead the moment she took that last hit of heroin."

"But, if I had…"

"No, baby. No ifs. She said that the paramedics would never have made it on time even if you called the moment she started feeling pain. You see? You're holding on to unearned guilt. You can let it go, baby. You can let her go."

Cass held her breath as Rebecca became silent again. Had she gone too far? Rebecca was a very private person and Cass went and involved others in what was surely Rebecca's deepest anguish. *Shit. I fucked up.*

"Say something, please?" Cass begged quietly.

Rebecca's eyebrows furrowed. "I don't know what to say."

"I know I shouldn't have…"

"*Thank you*," Rebecca whispered.

"W-what?" Cass sputtered in surprise.

Rebecca took a breath and for the first time in more than fifteen years, she felt peace. "Thank you for loving me enough to do that for me."

Cass shrugged self-consciously. "I had help. Hunter and Eve both expressed regret that they didn't think to do it years ago."

"They were probably as afraid of the answer as I was. But you *did* it, Cassidy. You did what I couldn't do for years. What *I've* been afraid of doing. Fear that learning the actual truth would destroy me." She turned again, not wanting Cassidy to see the tears. The weight that was lifted off her shoulders was immense. Almost unbearable. But such a relief that she couldn't hold back the tears.

Cass didn't miss the waterworks, but she said nothing. Instead, she embraced her girlfriend with loving arms.

"I'd do anything for you, Rebecca."

Rebecca leaned her head back on Cassidy's shoulder. She didn't think her voice would hold out if she answered to that, so she asked the question that lingered in her head. "What if the results had been different? Would you have told me?"

Cass thought about it for a second. "No."

Rebecca nodded slightly. She appreciated Cassidy's honesty. And the fact that her girlfriend would have shielded her from more pain if needed. Perhaps some would think that was the wrong thing to do, but for Rebecca, it meant the world. It meant Cassidy loved her enough to protect her.

"I am, you know," Rebecca said softly.

Cass frowned in confusion at Rebecca's words. "You are what?"

"Letting her go. I'm selling the club."

It was Cass's turn to be shocked into silence. Yeah, she had argued with Rebecca about it. She said some things she probably shouldn't have said (as she tended to do with her word vomit). But thinking about it now, Cass wasn't sure she wanted Rebecca to sell the place. It was where they met. Where they had some of the most erotic moments of their lives. But it was also the place that held the most pain for Rebecca. If Cass wasn't so selfish, she'd be happier with this news.

"Huh?" Cass rolled her eyes at herself. *The woman tells you she's doing what you asked, and you've lost your communication skills. Dumbass.*

"I don't want you to ever think I'm not giving you all of me."

"Baby..."

Rebecca reached back and pulled Cassidy's head down, so she could kiss her. It was always the most effective way of shutting her up. "I heard you, Cassidy. I know you probably think I didn't, but I heard your fears. They echoed my own. You were right. I held on to that club as a punishment. I don't need to do that anymore. I don't *want* to."

"Wow." Cass's arms tightened around her lover. "Wait, but I just told you about Hunter's findings. Oh, you mean you're *thinking* of selling?"

Rebecca smiled softly. "It feels amazing to know the truth, Cassidy. I don't think I'll ever be able to explain to you the burden you've lifted from my conscience. But that had nothing to do with my decision. Which was made earlier today, by the way. It was you." She looked up into Cassidy's eyes. "I love you. I would do anything for *you*, too, baby."

"*Damn.*" Cass shivered a bit. It wasn't from the chill in the air or being wet from the bath. It was the way Rebecca looked at her. The willingness to let go of the past for her. Cass fidgeted as her libido began to stir. "Um, so, earlier today, huh?"

"Mmhmm." Rebecca chuckled silently, knowing exactly what Cassidy was feeling. The younger woman was terrible at hiding her desire. Rebecca never had any doubts about how Cassidy was feeling. It was one of the things Rebecca loved the most. "That's why I was wearing what I was wearing. I wanted to surprise you."

"You certainly did that," Cass growled close to Rebecca's ear causing her to chuckle.

"Next time, try to warn me if we have guests, okay?"

"Baby, the next time you wear that thing, I'm kicking everyone out and locking the fucking door."

"You're crazy." Rebecca pinched Cassidy's thigh. "And I'll never be wearing 'that thing' again. I'm pretty sure it's still in the living room in tatters."

"Oh, yeah. Heh. Not even sorry." Cass tweaked Rebecca's nipples.

"Don't start something you can't finish, missy."

"I *always* finish with you." Cass wiggled her eyebrows suggestively. "Hey," she kissed a giggling Rebecca's exposed neck. "Are you sure about the club?"

"Yes."

"What will happen to Mistress?"

Rebecca snickered. "I'm going to go out on a limb and say she'll go wherever I go."

"Ha, ha."

"I'm serious. Cassidy, I'm only Mistress to you now. I don't need the club to dominate you. I can do that *anywhere*."

"*Fuck me*, yeah you can. But…"

Rebecca turned, this time getting up on her knees. "Baby, why are you fighting this? I thought this was what you wanted."

"I wanted you free of *her*." Cass shrugged. "I guess I'll miss the Pink Room. It's where I met the love of my life."

"How is it that you can go from raunchy to romantic so easily?" Rebecca teased.

"You bring out the best in me." Cass grinned her devilish grin.

Rebecca shook her head with a smile. "Crazy. Honey, the 'love of your life' will be right here with you. You don't need the club as a reminder. And, if you need a Pink Room, I'm willing to give up my office space."

Cass's eyes sparkled with mischief. "You would allow a playroom in the house?"

"Of course, I would. I am a Mistress after all."

Cass pulled Rebecca closer with one hand, using the other to lift an ample breast to her mouth. "As tempting as that is," she began in between kisses, licks, and sucks, "I wouldn't want you to give up your space. I propose an alternative."

"And what would that be?" Rebecca's breathing hastened with the sensation of Cassidy's hot, wet tongue on her hard nipple.

"We sell our places and buy something bigger. Something that's ours." Cass was taking a big gamble with her suggestion. Rebecca had yet to agree to move in with her permanently. She didn't want to push her too hard, but Cass was ready for that next step. And so much more.

Rebecca took Cassidy's face in her hands, staring into her bi-colored eyes. "That's definitely an alternative. And one that I will keep in mind. Okay?"

"Hot damn. At least that's not a no. Progress. I said that out loud, didn't I?" she asked when Rebecca raised a brow.

"Yes, you did. What do you think we should do about it?"

"I don't know. Anything but the riding crop. Please, Mistress." Cass feigned distress, gripping Rebecca's ass tightly.

"Riding crop, it is," Rebecca smirked. "Get out of the tub, Cassidy. I want you on the bed."

She tried so hard not to laugh when Cassidy moved so fast she slipped, splashing water all over the place. She had to duck her head quickly when Cassidy tried again, swinging her long leg over Rebecca to get out. *I hope she remembers to get a towel. Otherwise, we'll be sleeping on a wet bed. Eh, not the first time.*

Chapter Fifteen
REBECCA & CASS

Nothing but a Number

REBECCA SIPPED HER coffee, flipping through files of potential clients. *Business* clients. She still owned the club but limited her time there for Cassidy's sake. And perhaps her own. Besides, her once side job of consulting was now beginning to keep her busy. Her reputation was such that she was sought out by fortune 500 companies down to mom and pop shops. Rebecca vetted the owners as vigilantly as Mistress did her clients.

She tossed a file into the "no" pile and reached for another one just as the doorbell rang. Slightly irritated with being bothered, she pushed away from her desk and made her way to the front door. She and Cassidy had yet to make things official when it came to moving in together. Still, Rebecca felt at home enough in Cassidy's house to answer the door when her girlfriend wasn't there.

"Beverly!" *Are they* always *going to make surprise visits?* "You just missed Cassidy."

Does she call everyone by their full name? Bev thought, not minding the way it sounded from the dignified blonde. "Hello, Rebecca. Actually, I came here to see you. May I?" She made a move to go into the house when Rebecca stepped in front of her.

"If you're here to try to convince me to break things off with Cassidy, we have nothing to talk about."

Bev sighed. "Please, hear me out. I like you, Rebecca. I truly do."

"Just not for your daughter?"

"I only want to protect her, Rebecca."

"I thought we got past this, Mrs. Giles." *Why now?* Two weeks have gone by since their dinner. Cassidy made it a point to talk to them more often. Never once did she say her mom still had an issue. "Or were you just placating to keep the peace?"

"Perhaps a little of both," Bev confessed. "I've tried to accept this. But my first priority will always be to protect my daughter."

"Understandable." Rebecca leaned against the doorjamb. "The question I have, though, is what do you think I'm doing with Cassidy that's going to hurt her?"

"I don't think you'd do anything deliberately, Rebecca. But Cass is young and impressionable. She still has time to make better decisions in her life."

"And I'm, God forbid, encouraging her to do what she loves," Rebecca finished when Beverly paused. "This is about her choice not to be a lawyer, isn't it? Surely you know that she's not a lawyer because she doesn't *want* to be one. That decision had nothing to do with me. Just as it had nothing to do with you or Mr. Giles."

"It's not just that," Bev insisted. "It's hard for me to reconcile your age difference. Do you know what my daughter was doing when you graduated college? She was *five*, Rebecca. Getting ready for *kindergarten!*"

Rebecca was seriously getting tired of being called out on her age. When she and Cassidy had lunch with Miranda and her husband,

Rebecca's age was the hot topic—at least for Miranda. Cassidy, God love her, did her best to veer the conversation in other directions, but the redhead was relentless. Of course, she tried covering it up by making backhanded compliments. Rebecca saw right through her. Miranda had a problem with her. And now here's Cassidy's mom with the same issues.

"I'm not dating that version of your daughter! I know she will always be your little girl, but she is unequivocally a woman."

"Which brings me to my next concern." Bev glanced behind her, then leaned in. Not enough to encroach Rebecca's personal space, but enough to where she could speak softly. "Women our age are getting to the end of our sexual peak. What happens when that happens to you just as Cass is entering hers?"

It probably wasn't going to help Rebecca's situation by bursting out in laughter. Unfortunately, she couldn't help it. Cassidy's mother was talking to someone like Rebecca—*Mistress*—about sex. "I'm sorry, I don't mean to laugh." She cleared her throat. "I'm going to assume that you don't want details, but Cassidy and I have absolutely no problems in that area. I don't anticipate there will be one anytime soon."

Bev hung her head, laughing softly. Partly because she was embarrassed and partly because she couldn't believe her friend talked her into doing this. "I'm being ridiculous, aren't I?"

The embarrassment on Bev's face softened Rebecca's heart. Not enough to invite the woman in. Mother or not, she came here to break her and Cassidy up. Rebecca had empathy, but forgiveness may take a little longer. As an alternative, she gestured to the steps and sat down.

"I learned long ago that I never had to explain myself," Rebecca began. She looked out over the front yard. It was big for Los Angeles standards, but not so much that she couldn't hear the rumble of passing cars. "I don't ask for permission or forgiveness. What I do with my life is *my* business, no one else's."

"Rebecca…"

Rebecca held up a hand. "That being said, you are Cassidy's mother and I want us to get along. Not just for Cassidy's sake, but for our own."

She turned to Beverly, then, deliberately looking her in the eye. "During college, I was involved in an abusive relationship that lasted way too long."

"I'm so sorry." Bev looked at the composed woman next to her. There was so much more to Rebecca than she first thought. Perhaps her worldliness would be beneficial to Cass. "Was he the reason you turned to women?"

Rebecca gave Beverly a small smile. "Men are not the only ones who can be cruel, Beverly. I was born a lesbian, I wasn't turned into one. Just as I wasn't turned from women because of the inhumanity of one woman." Rebecca exhaled. Ever since Cassidy eased Rebecca's conscience about Samantha, she found it easier to forget about the despicable woman. Talking about her now, bringing her back to mind, wasn't fun. "I'm not telling you this for sympathy points. I want you to understand where I'm coming from when it comes to being with Cassidy."

Bev nodded. Her first instinct was to feel sorry for Rebecca. But that's not what the woman needed.

"It's been many years since my life with Samantha ended, but abuse like that lingers beyond the relationship. I cut myself off from trusting anyone. I built a wall so high I thought it'd be impossible for anyone to scale it. But your daughter," Rebecca shook her head with a laugh.

"Tenacious, isn't she?" Bev responded with a chuckle of her own.

"To say the least. I honestly tried to stay away, Beverly. I knew I was too old for her, but the pull I felt when I looked at her was far too strong. Still, I resisted. Hell, I left L.A. for a couple of months hoping it would cure me of this infatuation I felt for her."

"So *that's* what was wrong with her." Bev explained further when Rebecca looked questioningly at her. "There was a time not too long ago, perhaps the time you're speaking of when Cass was extremely moody. I'd never really seen her depressed before, so it was quite jarring. She would never say what was wrong, but I suppose I now know what caused it."

"If it makes you feel any better, I spent the time in New York being depressed myself. It became so unbearable that I had to come back. I didn't intend on getting in contact with Cassidy, but I felt better just being closer."

"You really do love her, don't you?"

"I do." She glanced at Beverly. "It's a testament to her upbringing how incredible she is. I never expected someone so young to teach me something as profound as my past having no bearing on my future. She saved me, Beverly. I was living with such guilt and shame buried under a bravado I'm not sure is or was real."

Bev took a chance and clasped Rebecca's hand. "I've never been in your situation, Rebecca. But I have to imagine that if you're here, successful, and able to have a loving relationship, you're doing something right."

Rebecca squeezed Beverly's hand. "I'm still in therapy but being with Cassidy has helped me be *me* again. And I'd like to think that I give her that same feeling in return."

"As with her painting," Bev assumed.

"For one. She's pretty amazing, Beverly. The murals don't do justice to the talent she has inside her."

"I'm looking forward to seeing her work in the gallery." As Bev said the words, she realized just how true they were. Seeing Cass through Rebecca's eyes, she was seeing her daughter—the little girl that had stolen her heart twenty-five years ago—in a different light. "You'll make sure she invites us, won't you?"

Rebecca smiled. "She's already put you and Russell on the list."

Bev released Rebecca's hand and patted her knee. "As sorry as I am for the reason I came here in the first place, I can't regret it. I'm glad we got to talk, Rebecca. Maybe next time we can actually go inside and have some coffee," she grinned.

"Now that you're not trying to get my old ass out of this house, you're welcome to come in," Rebecca winked as Beverly snickered. "Would you like to come in?"

"Next time. I've taken up enough of your time today." Bev stood, casually wiping any dust off her bottom. She gave Rebecca a quick hug when the—*slightly*—younger woman stood as well. "Thank you for being there for my daughter. And for letting her be there for you."

"Believe me, it's my pleasure."

"Well now, I don't need to know all of that." Bev held her palms up. "Yes, I know I'm the one who brought up sex in the first place." The two women laughed. "Um, would it futile to ask you not to tell my spirited daughter that I was here today?"

Rebecca pursed her lips in playful thought. "I won't lie to her, but I don't see why I would need to volunteer information."

Bev let out a bark of hearty laughter. "I really do like you, Rebecca. Let's do a less awkward dinner again sometime soon."

"Absolutely. Be careful out there on the roads."

Rebecca waved one last time before going back in the house and closing the front door with a heavy sigh. Her head fell back with a slight thud. While she was glad everything was now worked out with Cassidy's mom, the exchange took a lot out of Rebecca. As it usually did whenever she thought of Samantha and her past.

"Forget about it now, Rebecca," she muttered to herself. "You've done very well the past couple of weeks forgetting about it. You can keep it up."

For a long moment, she stood in that same position, breathing in, breathing out, letting her mind relax again. Rebecca was so close to being fully relaxed when her heart rate jumped dramatically at the frantic knock at the door.

"*Son of a bitch. Don't tell me she changed her mind already.*" Rebecca fixed a smile on her face just in case it *was* Beverly back for more. That smile turned to delighted confusion when she opened the door. "Aunt Wills!"

"Are you okay?" Willamena asked as Rebecca hugged her. "Are you hurt? Is she hurting you?" She pushed past a baffled Rebecca, looking around with a critical eye.

Once the words finally penetrated Rebecca's extremely puzzled mind, she closed the door and turned. "What?"

"Is it happening again, Rebecca?"

"What are you talking about, Aunt Wills? Cassidy would *never* hurt me." Rebecca finally got a good look at her aunt and saw the bags under her worried eyes. "Aunt Wills? What's going on?"

Willamena put her hands on her hips, looking pointedly at her niece. "You tell me. The last time you stopped calling me it was because Samantha was... was." She threw her arms up and whirled around so Rebecca couldn't see the tears.

Rebecca frowned. "Stopped calling?"

"Two weeks, Rebecca! You *promised* to call me every day or at least once a week. So, explain to me why I haven't heard from you in *two weeks*!"

After all of these years, Rebecca never realized just how much what Samantha did affected her aunt. She knew Aunt Wills carried the weight of guilt, but it was as unfounded as Rebecca's was. This? This was more than just guilt. This was anger born out of grief.

"I'm sorry, Aunt Wills." Rebecca walked up to the agitated woman and put her arms around her. "I'm sorry."

REBECCA PLACED A cup of Aunt Wills' favorite tea down in front of her, then sat down beside her.

"Before we delve into this," she began, "I want you to know that Cassidy has done nothing wrong. I thought you knew her better than that."

Willamena lifted a brow. "I have thought things before, Rebecca. I can't afford to be wrong again." She sighed. "I don't truly believe that Cass has it in her to be cruel. But I had to make sure."

"Why didn't you call me?"

"I did. A couple of times. But you never answered." Willamena looked over at Rebecca. "Do you have any idea what it's like to have the image of you broken and bruised every night when I close my eyes? Over the years, it got better. When you met Cass, the visions came back until I realized Cass was good for you. But when I didn't hear from you…"

Rebecca lowered her eyes. She saw those calls come in from her aunt, but there was always something more important than returning them. Or so she told herself. Was she subconsciously avoiding the calls?

"Something did happen recently, Aunt Wills." Rebecca saw her aunt's hands tighten around her cup and quickly explained. "Nothing bad! Cassidy took it upon herself to prove to me that I wasn't responsible for Samantha's death." She explained what Cassidy had done and Hunter's medical opinion.

Willamena sat back and listened carefully to Rebecca's words. She watched her actions and the look in her eyes as she spoke. The psychiatrist in her observed the subtle differences in Rebecca's behavior. As Rebecca's aunt, she noticed the enormous weight that had been lifted from her niece's shoulders.

"You didn't call me back because I make you think of her," Willamena surmised.

"No, you don't!"

"Dr. Woodrow does. And, since the doctor happens to be your aunt, you couldn't distinguish between the two. Do you feel you no longer need therapy, Rebecca?"

"Since I can't 'distinguish' between the two, who am I speaking with now?" Rebecca asked moodily.

"Both. I get that by alleviating your guilt, Cass has allowed you some peace. However, as I recall, you were still having nightmares a mere three weeks ago. Was it all due to your guilt? And, now that is gone, so are they?"

There were times when Rebecca hated having a psychiatrist as an aunt who raised her. *This* was one of those times. Would she ever be able to have a normal conversation with her aunt? Or would Samantha always hold something over their heads?

"They were gone. So was the pain and fear." Rebecca sat back and sighed. How could she be mad that her aunt had the same exact thought Rebecca had earlier. "Maybe you're right. Maybe I was afraid to talk to you because I thought this good feeling would go away. I didn't want to have to think about it anymore. It has been more than fifteen years, Aunt Wills. I'm tired. I want her out of my head. Out of my life. I'm even selling the club."

That news got raised brows from the doc. "That's a huge step, Becca. I'm proud of you."

"I should have called you," Rebecca conceded. "I should have let you know what was going on." She leaned closer. "Have you thought about seeing someone, you know, professionally, for these visions you get?"

For the first time since she arrived, Willamena laughed. "Oh, lord. Do I really sound like that?"

"Kind of, but I was being serious. What happened to me was not your fault, Aunt Wills. I need you to know that. To understand that. To *believe* it."

"I talk to someone," Willamena confessed. "I have been for years, though we psychiatrists prefer to think of it as simple conversation between colleagues. I think there's a clause on our Cracker Jack diploma."

Happy to hear her aunt joking, Rebecca chuckled. "I'll accept that. *If* you try to do what I'm trying and let it go. Fifteen years is a long time to carry a burden, Aunt Wills. Believe me. We deserve better."

"You're right. We do. And, since I happen to love talking with you, how about we cut back on the therapy. As needed. All other times, I'm simply Aunt Wills."

"So, uh, how long is your aunt staying?" Cass made little circles on Rebecca's bare shoulder with the tip of her finger. Her insanely hot girlfriend was naked beside her and Cass couldn't "get it up" so to speak.

"Just a couple of days," Rebecca answered quietly. "Is it okay that she's here? I can have her stay at my place."

"No, no! I mean, yeah, it's great that she's here." *Plus, I hate that you still have a "my place,"* she thought grumpily. "She's welcome anytime. You sure she's okay on the couch?"

"The pull-out is almost more comfortable than this bed, baby. She'll be fine. Besides, she insisted on sleeping there." Rebecca maneuvered herself until she was on top of Cassidy. The younger woman had been a bit rigid ever since they got in bed. Something that *wasn't* normal. "What's wrong, Cassidy?"

"N-nothing." *Don't squirm! Friction right now would be a bad thing.*

"Really? We're usually on our third or fourth orgasm by this time."

"Rebecca," Cass whined. "Come on, babe, don't do that to me."

"I want to do *a lot* of things to you, but you're being a bit standoffish. I want to know why."

"*Your aunt is here!*" Cass whisper yelled as though it was such an obvious answer.

Rebecca looked around their room. "*She's downstairs!*" she whispered back just as dramatically. "I know we can get loud, but I'm sure we can tone it down a bit." She looked into Cassidy's eyes and saw the desire there. But something was still holding her back. "Talk to me."

Cass sighed. Yeah, having Rebecca's aunt here was a little weird, but Rebecca was right in assuming there was something else.

"Does she really think I could hurt you?"

"Oh, baby." Rebecca dipped her head and kissed Cassidy tenderly. She almost regretted telling the sensitive woman why Aunt Wills was there. "No, of course, she doesn't. You have to understand that she holds a tremendous amount of shame for not knowing what was happening to me."

"But you said you kept it from her."

"I did. I took great precautions in keeping it from her. But, as a psychiatrist, she prides herself on seeing beyond what one tells her. Especially when it comes to me. She promised my mother that she would take care of me, and she believes she failed." Rebecca reached up to sweep a lock of hair from Cass's face. "I am the one who failed. I promised her I wouldn't go more than a week without calling her. She's here because I broke that promise."

"Why?"

Rebecca felt a tinge of shame. "Because you had just purged this guilt I carried for Samantha. I wasn't thinking or dreaming about her and that felt amazing. So, I avoided her calls because I thought that by talking to her, by having sessions, I'd bring those feelings back."

"But she's your aunt, babe, not just your therapist."

She lowered her forehead to Cassidy's. "I know, I know. Believe me, we discussed that as well as her continued responsibility." Rebecca lifted her head again. "My point is, she doesn't think you could hurt me. She's just afraid she'll miss something again."

"Man, that's harsh." Cass rubbed her calloused hands over Rebecca's smooth back. She hated that Samantha caused so much damage. Not just to her beautiful girlfriend, but to those who loved her as well. *Fucking bitch.*

"Mmhmm." Rebecca began to roll off of Cassidy when she felt strong arms tighten around her.

"Where are you going?"

Rebecca smiled. "I'm not going to force you to make love to me if it makes you uncomfortable, baby. And being naked on top of you is not helping me."

"But I like you up here." Cass glanced at the door. It was closed, and Aunt Wills was downstairs. If they were quiet… "What, um, what would you do to me if, you know, we were alone?"

Gotcha. Rebecca had always thought actions spoke louder than words. With that in mind, she sat up, straddling Cassidy low on her hips.

Cass's legs automatically spread until she felt the heat of Rebecca's sex on hers. When Rebecca began to rock her hips back and forth, Cass's breath caught in her throat. Rebecca's ample breasts swayed with each movement as Cass's clit was being stroked by Rebecca's beautiful, wet clit.

It was heaven. Absolute, pure heaven. At that moment, no one else existed in Cass's world other than Rebecca Cuinn.

Cassidy reached up and cupped Rebecca's tits, squeezing, kneading... *needing*.

"There's my baby," Rebecca crooned as she upped her pace. As much as she loved Cassidy's 'little friend,' *this* was her favorite. Sex to sex, flesh to flesh, love to love. This was a wave she could ride forever. When she and Cassidy were like this, *nothing* stood between them. Physically or emotionally.

"*Rebecca*," Cass moaned softly. She was so close, and she wanted her lover right there with her.

"*Yes, Cassidy!*"

Cass's hands moved down to Rebecca's hips, grasping them firmly as she lifted her own hips. She pulled Rebecca down with each stroke causing the friction between them to intensify. Neither woman was able to hold back any longer. The coinciding orgasms rocked them both. Cass gritted her teeth to keep herself from shouting out in ecstasy when she felt Rebecca's warmth flow inside her.

Cass wrapped her arms around Rebecca when she collapsed on top of her. "*Jesus!* That was incredible!"

"Imagine what I could do if you were really into it," Rebecca teased.

"I'm *always* into it, baby. Never forget that," Cass grinned. "But if you want to demonstrate again, I'm all for it!"

For the next couple of hours, Rebecca did exactly that.

CASS WIPED SWEAT from her face. Her workout this morning was extra brutal after her romp last night with Rebecca. Not that she was complaining. Hell, if she could, she would have sex with her girlfriend in lieu of *everything* else. Eating, sleeping, even painting. She smiled to herself.

Sex with Rebecca 24/7. Heaven.

"Good morning, Cass." Willamena's eyes tracked down Cass's sweaty body donned only in tight, short shorts and a sports bra. She had never been attracted to a woman, but she was secure enough to appreciate another woman's beauty. Intriguing tattoos adorned Cass's muscular body. A body that showcased six-pack abs that Willamena wasn't used to seeing on a woman. She silently laughed at that thought. *I haven't even seen them on a man lately!*

Cass jumped. "Fuck! Shit! Shit, I'm sorry!" She cringed. Fucking perfect. Yesterday had been her first time meeting Rebecca's aunt face to face and she wanted nothing more than to make a good impression. Now here she stood, half naked, spewing curse words like they were the only words she knew.

Willamena snickered. "I didn't mean to scare you."

"Nah, it's, uh, it's all good. Rebecca isn't usually up this early, so I'm used to having the house to myself. I'm sorry about the, um, cussing and," she gestured to her scantily clad body, "this."

"It's all good," Willamena smirked, throwing Cass's words back at her. "I can see why Rebecca is so enamored with you."

Cass chuckled self-consciously. "I should go put something on."

"Don't be silly. I'm sure I can control my hetero hormones." She gave Cass a humorous wink.

Cass's embarrassed chuckle became full-out laughter. More relaxed, Cass strode over to the fridge and plucked a bottle of chocolate milk out. She twisted the top off and took a long swig. She caught Aunt Wills giving her an odd look.

"Can I get you one?"

"No, thank you. Rebecca showed me where the coffee was yesterday, so I'm quite good." Willamena regarded Cass carefully. "How can you drink that stuff and still look like that?"

Cass looked at the bottle thoughtfully. Rebecca always wondered about her "obsession" with chocolate milk, too. It took a while to convince her it really was good for her. "It's actually a great post-workout drink. Helps me replenish tired muscles, fluids, and energy."

"Hmm. Do you keep a small refrigerator full of chocolate milk upstairs?"

Cass's eyebrows furrowed. "Ah, no."

"Perhaps you should think about it. After what I heard last night, you could have used all of that replenishing."

"Oh, geez! I *told* her…" In the middle of her freak-out, Cass noticed Aunt Wills's shoulders bouncing with laughter. "You're messing with me, aren't you?"

Willamena nodded her head, still laughing.

"So, you *didn't* hear us, I mean, anything last night?" A shake of the head. "That was really mean," Cass pouted playfully.

"And, yet, I'm sure it was pretty accurate," Willamena baited. "Sit with me a minute. I promise not to joke about your sex life with my niece anymore."

Cass winced a bit but obeyed. Despite her worries about being heard while doing the nasty with Rebecca, Cass liked having Aunt Wills here. While smart and insightful, the woman was also witty and fun.

"I need to apologize to you," Willamena said once Cass was seated.

"Huh?" Cass wondered if she had missed something while thinking about how great Rebecca's aunt was.

"I want you to know I don't think you'd ever hurt my niece."

"Oh!" Cass waved a hand in the air. "Don't sweat it. Rebecca explained everything to me last night. You know, before we made hot monkey love."

Willamena both blushed and laughed. "Touché. And she may have explained it, but I needed you to hear it from me. What happened to her will haunt me for the rest of my life. I know it's not fair to her, or to you, to show up here unannounced with accusations."

"Aunt Wills?" Cass interrupted gently. "I get it, yeah? It's fucked up, ahem, excuse me. It's *messed* up how Samantha hurt you both. Yeah, it happened to Rebecca, but it screwed with your head, too. Believe me, I understand. I mean, I was… what I mean to say is I wasn't even in

Rebecca's life back then and I *wish* so much I could have done something to save her from that piece of shit. Excuse my language, again."

"I'm a psychiatrist, Cass. There isn't much I haven't heard. And there isn't much that surprises me. But you do. You're very sweet."

Cass's head dipped in shyness. "That's what Rebecca always says." Normally, she wouldn't enjoy being called sweet. But for some reason, when Rebecca and Aunt Wills said it, it made Cass feel all gooey inside.

"Because it's true. Rebecca hasn't had much of that in her life. Of course, she has friends who care very much about her, but they all have their own baggage to worry about. You just seem… unjaded."

"You mean naïve." Okay, that came out a little harsher than Cass intended.

"No, absolutely not. I don't think you're naïve. Simply unaffected by the world around you." That was the best way Willamena knew how to put it.

"Look, I grew up with a good family, a roof over my head, love, and support. I didn't have to go through the shit Rebecca went through. And, while she told me to never apologize for that, maybe people do think it makes me naïve. Thing is, I *do* know how awful people can be. I've been through the name-calling, the taunts. A little pushing and shoving because I'm too tatted up, too androgynous, not androgynous enough. Too feminine, too masculine, too muscular." She shook her head.

"How do you deal with that?"

Cass thought about her answer for a moment and shrugged. "As an artist, I think I see things differently. I see *people* as art. You know, you have all of these different media. Pencil, paint, charcoal, chalk, clay, photography. You even have different genres of art. And, while I appreciate all types of art, I don't enjoy them all. I don't like abstract, but that doesn't take away from the fact that it's still art. So, I respect it.

"I guess what I'm getting at is, opinions—like mine on abstract—are all subjective. There will always be people who don't like the way I look or act, or who I love. But if I spent my entire life trying to please everyone, all I'd be doing is hurting myself. It'd be like me trying to paint a picture that every single one of the 7 billion plus people on this planet would like, I'd be miserable. Dying, eventually, having been unsuccessful."

A slow smile formed on Dr. Willamena Woodrow's face. "You, Cassidy Giles, are a remarkable woman."

"Cass," Cass muttered bashfully. She twirled the top of her milk bottle on the table. Quite the removal from the insightfulness just before. "And I just say things as I see them."

"Which is part of your charm. Have you ever thought of being a psychiatrist?"

Chocolate milk nearly shot out of Cass's nose when she snorted. "Um, that wouldn't be a good idea. I'm a little too blunt and I don't think the patients would appreciate me calling them crazy."

Willamena laughed. "Yes, we tend to frown on that." She took a sip of her tepid coffee. "In all seriousness, I want to thank you for all you've done for Rebecca. I feel content leaving her in your care."

"Thanks." Cass frowned. "Wait, what?"

The doctor smiled. "In mere months, you have managed to accomplish the one thing I've tried to do for years. Rid Rebecca of her guilt. I believe she's ready to move on from therapy."

"Whoa! But she still needs you!"

"I'll still be her aunt, dear. However, you must've known she was avoiding our conversations. Because I'm her aunt, I don't want her to dread talking to me. If that means I stop being her therapist, so be it."

"What if she needs more than I'm qualified to give her."

Willamena witnessed the mixture of fear and determination on Cass's face. "Oh, my sweet girl. Rebecca needs someone to love her. To treat her with respect and impartiality. You already do that. I'm not going anywhere. I'm merely stepping up my role as an aunt. Which brings me to; what are your intentions with my niece?"

"I, uh, well…" Cass was saved by her girlfriend's extremely good timing.

"What on earth possesses anyone to get up this early?"

Aunt Wills gave her watch an overexaggerated look. "Dear, it's nine o'clock."

"Exactly. Not even double digits." Rebecca sleepily gave her aunt a peck on top of the head. "And you," she began, giving Cass a kiss on the lips. "You've usually finished your shower and have joined me in bed again by now."

"Um, well…" Cass was beyond flustered. First, there was the "intentions" question. Now her girl is talking about being in bed together. In front of her aunt!

"Aunt Wills?" Rebecca never took her eyes off Cassidy. "My girlfriend is broken. What have you done?"

"Absolutely nothing! I simply asked what her intentions with you were."

Rebecca rolled her eyes and pulled Cassidy up from her chair. Her hands wandered down to touch Cassidy's abs. "Go take your shower, baby. I'll keep my aunt occupied."

Stay calm. You're not alone. Stay calm. Cass chanted the words over and over in her head as Rebecca's fingertips trailed over her muscles. She was right. Right about this time, they would be making love. Or, Cass would be receiving a very intense session with Mistress. *Stay calm. You're not alone.* She cleared her throat. "'Kay. Love you."

"Love you, too." Rebecca swatted Cassidy's ass as she passed her. Of course, she knew exactly what she was doing. It would make for a fun time later on when they were alone.

"Minx."

Rebecca laughed softly. "Guilty." She grabbed herself a cup and poured coffee into it, holding up the pot in askance. When Aunt Wills nodded, Rebecca gave her a refill. "What were you two talking about?"

Willamena regarded her niece with pride. Even at forty-one years old, the blonde could pass for her twenties. Willamena took a bit of pleasure in the fact that Rebecca's style was influenced by her. Granted, Rebecca's fashion sense was a tad younger. But the sophistication was all due to Willamena. It was evident even when Rebecca was sitting at the table in pink shorts and nightshirt with her legs pulled up to her chest.

"A little bit of this. A little bit of that."

"Meaning you grilled her?"

"No, Miss Know-it-all. We actually had a very nice conversation about how you're ready to move on from therapy altogether."

Rebecca's legs dropped, and she sat up. "What?"

"My sweet girl. I'd much rather be your aunt than your therapist. I don't want you to be afraid to call me. Or, to think that we must always be in a session."

"I didn't think that. It's just…"

"It's just you want to be rid of Samantha," Willamena continued for Rebecca. "So do I. You were right before. We deserve better. I don't want to be a constant reminder." She shook her head. "I should have insisted you see another psychiatrist."

"I didn't want to see anyone else. I wanted you. Aunt Wills, I trust *you*. I didn't want anyone else to know what happened to me. I didn't want anyone else to fix me. I needed you."

"And now you need me to be your aunt again. Rebecca, Cass has given you a second lease on life. Take it. Embrace it. And let me focus on embarrassing Cass by telling her you both need to keep it down upstairs when you have company."

Rebecca's head snapped up, eyes wide. Then she saw Aunt Wills's smirk. "You are rotten! But I like it. And I love you. You'll still be there if I need you?"

Willamena saw that same ten-year-old frightened little girl she saw after Rebecca's parents passed away.

"Always."

Chapter Sixteen
REBECCA & CASS

Truth and Consequence

CASS WIPED HER paint coated fingers on the front of her shirt and tilted her head. She was on her third painting of the day and it wasn't even lunchtime yet. Cass checked her watch to make sure that was still true. She couldn't trust her stomach to tell her because she was always hungry.

She shook her head, bringing herself back into focus. Today had been a good day so far, production-wise. After a brief two-day stay, Aunt Wills was gone, and Rebecca had left fairly early that morning for meetings. Cass had the house to herself and she was taking full advantage of it. She would have most of the day to spend here in her studio working on canvases for Eve.

Cass carefully removed the still wet painting from the easel, replacing it with a fresh one with a smile on her face. *This.* This is what she loved to do. This made her feel alive. And now that she had someone like Rebecca to share her life with, Cass felt as though she owned the world. She had always been a pretty happy person. Now? She looked back at the painting that stood in the corner, covered by a sheet. Now, she knew what happiness truly was.

The tip of her brush dipped into the paints on her palette, mixing them expertly until she found the color that matched the one in her head. Art had always come naturally for Cass. Ideas would pop into her brain and practically shoot out from her fingertips. The only time she struggled was when Rebecca left her. Since she came back and they're together, not even the prospect of being on display at a Sumptor Gallery could faze her now. Just as she was making her first stroke, the doorbell rang.

"Shit."

Cass hesitated. Stay and paint or answer the damn door? In the end, it was her stomach that made the decision. If she took a break now, she could fix herself a sandwich and be able to put in a few more hours in her studio before her sexy girlfriend got home. That thought put a pep in her step as she made her way to the door.

"Rand?"

Cass's normally well put together best friend looked frazzled. Mascara ran down splotchy cheeks, her eyes were red and puffy from crying, and her hair disheveled. The redhead pushed her way inside.

"Close the door."

Frozen in confusion, it took Cass a moment for things to register in her brain. "What happened?"

"Close the damn door!"

Cass looked out outside, seeing nothing, then shutting and locking it. She guided Rand to the couch and sat next to her, holding her hand.

"What happened, Rand?"

"It's Connor."

"What about him?"

"He's... he's gone insane!" Rand sniffled, and Cass immediately got up for some tissues.

"Here." She handed over the box. "Can you explain what's going on?" Cass didn't like Connor much, but only because he didn't like her. Thing was, the dude was a mild-mannered guy that was kinda boring. The fact that he and Rand were members of Rebecca's club had always been odd to Cass.

"You—you know what our lifestyle is, right?" Rand asked, unknowingly mirroring Cass's thoughts. "Well, ever since we had lunch with you and whats-her-name, things have been off with him."

Considering the state Rand was in, Cass chose to overlook the "whats-her-name" shit. For now.

"Off how?"

"He got more, you know, dominant. It's never been more than I could handle. But it's getting worse, Cass. More like abuse."

"The fuck?"

Cass sprang up and headed for the door. She didn't think, just reacted. Rand ran after her. "Where are you going?"

"I'm going to kill him!" In her mind, Connor became Samantha. She couldn't do anything then, but she sure as hell could do something now.

"Stop, wait!" Rand pulled at Cass's arm. "I don't want him to know I told you!"

"Fuck that, Rand! He hurt you and he's going to pay for it!"

"Can't you just stay here with me? I need you, Cass. Look, I came here because you're my best friend. I love that you want to defend me, but right now, all I need is a place to stay. And maybe a shower."

The grin on Rand's face confused Cass. What the hell was there to grin about? Then again, maybe this was Rand's way of coping. She had always been pretty dramatic, but as far as Cass knew, this was the most traumatic thing to happen to her.

"Fine. You know you're welcome to stay here. But before you do anything else, you need to file a police report."

"No."

"Rand."

"I said no, Cass. This is embarrassing enough! I don't want to drag this out in the open where my family can see. They don't know about our lifestyle and I'd like to keep it that way."

"You have nothing to be embarrassed about. *He's* the problem, Rand. Not you."

Rand responded with a flick of her hand. "Yeah, yeah. I don't really want to talk about it anymore right now. I'm tired. Could I just take a shower and lay down?"

Cass sighed. "Yeah, of course. Did you bring anything with you?" Rand shook her head. "Okay, I'll find you something to wear. The guest bedroom has been turned into an office, but I can fix up the pull-out for you."

"Can't I just sleep with you? I'd feel much safer."

"Uh, I don't think Rebecca would like that."

"You're still with her?" Rand scoffed. "I thought that would have run its course by now. Anyway, if she gets all jealous that you're trying to help a friend, she doesn't have to know I'm here."

One, two, three... Cass clenched and unclenched her hands, reminding herself that Rand has been through a lot. "She'll know since she lives here." *Practically.* "If you want to stay upstairs because you'll feel safer, we can sleep down here."

"*Lives* here? You can't be serious, Cass. She's..."

"Enough, Rand. Look, I get that you're going through something and I want to be there for you. But I can't have you putting my girlfriend down. Please?"

Rand rolled her eyes. "Fine. May I take a bath or is that off-limits, too?"

The only bathtub in the house was in the master bathroom. "Go ahead. You know where the towels are. Just grab some sweats or something from my room. Take your time. When you get out, I'll fix you something to eat and we can talk more about this, yeah?"

"Sure. If I'm up for it." Rand turned to go upstairs, pausing at the first step. "What time will she be here? I was kind of hoping I could just hang here for a while without anyone else around."

The muscles in Cass's jaw contracted. "I don't know when Rebecca will get home." She emphasized the word "home" in hopes it would penetrate through Rand's thick skull that this was exactly where Rebecca belonged. She was thankful that Rand didn't respond before disappearing upstairs.

Cass sank down onto the couch and buried her head in her hands. Rebecca was *not* going to like this. The two certainly didn't hit it off the way Cass and Hunter had. In fact, as Cass could tell from her very short, very odd conversation she just had with Rand, there was an underlying animosity. She didn't know why, but it sucked. Now Cass invited Rand to stay with them without talking to Rebecca first. Surely, she would be the one person who could understand. Right?

"Things were going so well," she muttered.

"Baby?"

Cass's head jerked up and she popped off the couch like it was spring loaded.

"Hey, babe! Um, you're home early." Cass checked her watch. *Very early.*

"What's wrong?" God, Rebecca hated that damn feeling she got in the pit of her stomach. The one that told her something was wrong.

"Huh? Nothing."

"Cassidy."

Oh, for fuck's sake. Tell her! She already knows something is up. "Yeah, okay. So, Rand showed up."

Rebecca raised a brow. Why was Cassidy so nervous just because her best friend came by? "All right." She watched as Cassidy shuffled her feet and stalled. "Cassidy, we've talked about this. You stalling only makes me think of my own scenarios."

"Right." Cass sighed, wondering how to explain something she didn't quite understand herself. "Rand came crashing through here extremely upset." She glanced towards the stairs, totally noticing that Rebecca looked that way as well. "She didn't say much, but what she did say…"

This was where Cass began to feel a little strange. Was she betraying her best friend's confidence by telling Rebecca what she learned? Or was she doing Rand a favor by getting advice from someone who has been through this? Another glance at the stairs and Cass made her decision.

"Okay, you obviously know about Rand and Connor's lifestyle. Well, Rand said that Connor has been a little off lately. And that when he, you know, dominates her he takes it too far. She says it's more about abuse now."

"She said that? Exactly that way?" Cassidy nodded and that bad feeling in her tummy grew. "Did you call the police?"

"No, she said she didn't want to involve them. That it was too embarrassing."

"I see." Rebecca didn't know how she could argue with Miranda's decision. Didn't she make the same years ago? "What about confronting Connor?"

Cass shook her head. "Won't let me. I wanted to go over there and show him…"

"Cass?" Rand bounced down the stairs completely naked. "Oh! I didn't know we had company!" Rand giggled but made no attempt to cover herself up.

Cass immediately turned away, covering her eyes for even more protection from the sight. "What the hell, Rand?! Why don't you have clothes on?"

Rebecca, on the other hand, narrowed her eyes at the sight. That bad feeling just turned into turmoil. So many questions were going through her head. The most glaring ones being, what the hell was Miranda Loring-Daly doing in *her* house? Why the *fuck* was she naked? And who the *fuck* says things like "I didn't know *we* had *company*!" in someone else's home?

"Oh, come on. It's not like you haven't seen this before."

One more question, Rebecca thought as her eyes left Miranda and landed on a blushing Cassidy. A raised brow asked the question that she knew wouldn't be answered. At least not at this moment.

"Will you go put something on!"

"Sure, sure. I came down to ask if I could borrow a pair of sweats or something. I sort of forgot to bring an overnight bag."

"Yeah, whatever. Just get dressed."

Rebecca turned just in time to see Miranda smile at her, spin, and bound back up the stairs as if she had not a care in the world. Turmoil became a perfect storm.

"I'm sorry I didn't say…"

"You've slept with her?" Rebecca interrupted.

"Not, um, technically," Cass stammered. She couldn't believe Rand said that in front of Rebecca! Not that Cass had anything to hide, but she sure as hell would've told her in a much more tactful way. *This* is what was confusing her. Rand wasn't acting like herself at all.

"Not technically?" Rebecca shook her head. "You know what? I don't care. What I care about is another woman walking around our house naked."

"I—I didn't think she'd do that. She was upset and asked if she could stay here because she was afraid to go home."

"So, she decided that taking a bath in *our* tub would make her feel better?" Something was *way* off with all of this, but Rebecca couldn't be upset with Cassidy. She actually looked as confused as Rebecca felt. Of course, Rebecca was aware of Cassidy's wish that she could have saved Rebecca years ago. This was her chance to help Miranda. If only the situation didn't feel so… wrong to Rebecca.

"I just wanted her to feel safe and comfortable, baby. After all my talk about wanting to help you," Cass said, eerily mirroring Rebecca's inner thoughts, "I feel so out of my depth here, Becca. It doesn't help that she's being all weird and shit. I mean, is this normal?"

Rebecca's heart ached for her lover and she reached over to rub Cassidy's arm. "There is no normal when it comes to something like this, Cassidy."

"Thank God you're here to help me."

Rebecca shook her head slightly. "I think it would be better if I went to the club." She hesitated for a heartbeat. "And then to my place."

"What! Why?" Cass became a tad bit panicked. Okay, more than a tad bit. "Baby, please don't leave me!"

"Honey, I'm not leaving you. Miranda already doesn't like me much and I just think it would be easier for her to talk to you if I'm not here."

"I don't know if I can do this by myself, Rebecca." Cass nearly dropped to her knees to beg Rebecca to stay. Obviously, fear that she wouldn't know what to do to help Rand bothered her. But the biggest fear was that Rebecca wouldn't come back. Cass knew she should be over that doubt by now, however, as long as Rebecca had her own fucking place the fear would remain.

Going against every instinct in her body, Rebecca stuck with her decision. She could very well be making the biggest mistake of her life, but if Miranda truly was a victim of abuse, Rebecca needed to take a step back and not be selfish.

"You can. All you need to do is listen to her." She touched Cass's worried face. "I love you."

Rebecca nearly changed her mind when Cassidy didn't respond in kind. She knew her lover wouldn't be happy with her. Hell, Rebecca knew that Cassidy hated that she still had her place. And while she hated using it like this, Rebecca had to believe that she was doing the right thing. She kept telling herself that as she walked to her car, got in, and drove away.

A tear rolled down Cass's cheek. "*I love you, too, baby.*" She would probably kick herself for the rest of her life for not saying the words *to* Rebecca before she left. And if something happened to her… Cass promptly pulled out her phone and dialed.

"Hello?"

"I love you, baby. So much. I should have said that before you left but I was being an ass. I'm sorry."

Rebecca smiled. "Thank you. Good luck with Miranda. And if you need me, I'm always there. Do you hear me, Cassidy? I'm not going anywhere."

Relief washed over Cass. As shitty as this situation with Rand was, it gave Cass strength to know that she wasn't alone. That Rebecca understood her fears and made it a point to put her at ease. No, she didn't like that Rebecca wasn't going to be with her tonight, but she could rest assured that it was temporary. If Cass had anything to say about it, this little arrangement would be over permanently after tonight.

THREE HOURS, TWENTY-FOUR minutes, and thirty-five seconds. Thirty-six. That's how long it had been since Rebecca left Cassidy. But who's counting? Cassidy hadn't called since the brief—yet, very sweet—call right after Rebecca pulled away. She wasn't sure how she felt about that. Undoubtedly, she had faith that Cassidy could handle the situation. And no matter what she thought of Miranda, she trusted Cassidy with her heart. So, why did she still have this sinking feeling?

"Mistress?" Carlie knocked timidly *after* opening the door to Mistress's office.

"Yes, Carlie?" Mistress said patiently.

She reminded herself that she could possibly be done with all of this soon. It had been a couple of months since she made the decision to sell the club, and she had to admit, it was a harder process than she realized. Despite the club's beginnings, the place was important to her. She became who she was today in this club. And, of course, she had the same thoughts as Cassidy. They met here. Their time in the Pink Room was the stuff of wet dreams. She couldn't sell it to just anyone. Perhaps she was being difficult, but since Cassidy felt the same way, Rebecca felt better about it.

"You, um, have a visitor. I didn't make any appointments!" Carlie added quickly.

Mistress frowned behind her mask. Cassidy would occasionally visit her at the club, but it was always in the Pink Room. She would never compromise Rebecca's privacy by coming to her office. Besides, Cassidy was still busy with Miranda as far as Rebecca knew.

"Who is it?"

Carlie looked behind her, tilting her head up. "Ah..."

The guest poked their head around the door. "Um, hi. I was given an invitation to this place, and I wanted to talk about membership?"

Mistress blinked. "Right. Please, come in. Carlie, no interruptions, please."

"Yes, ma'am." Carlie gave one last look, then closed the door behind her.

Mistress stood, opening her arms to her guest. "What the hell are you doing here?" She pushed away. "You're not really looking for a membership, are you?"

Hunter laughed. "No! I assumed it was better to act as if we didn't know each other. Besides, I don't think having a membership here would win Ellie over."

Rebecca waved her hand. "You were never here." Hunter was finally rid of that wretched Susan and had her eyes set on a sweet—and hot—diner owner. Rebecca didn't know much about Ellie except for the facts that she taught Rebecca's yoga class and she could bake like an angel. In Rebecca's eyes, as long as she was gay, available, and honest, Ellie was perfect for Hunter. "Now, answer my question. *Why* are you here?"

"Can you, uh." Hunter waggled her finger up and down at Rebecca. "You look great in that mask, but I'm not used to seeing you like this. May I talk to Rebecca?"

"Oh!" Rebecca removed her mask. "Better? It's such a habit to wear it while I'm here that I don't even realize it's on."

"Better. I shouldn't be here. I don't want to jeopardize your privacy."

"It won't matter anymore soon. I'm selling the place."

Hunter's eyes widened. "Whoa. I know I've been preoccupied lately, but this is big news. Why haven't you said anything?"

"Precisely for that reason, Hunter. You're dealing with getting over Susan, dealing with some tough times at work, and trying to figure out if the woman you have the hots for is a lesbian." Rebecca gestured around her. "Me selling this place isn't that important in the grand scheme of things."

"How does Cass feel about it?"

"She's fine with it. Hunter? You're stalling. I don't like it."

"Geez, maybe you should put the mask back on, *Mistress*." Hunter sighed heavily. "Okay. I'm getting nervous."

"About?"

"Ellie." Hunter sprang up. "I'm not good enough for someone like her, Becca."

Rebecca got up, walked around her desk, and caught Hunter's arm as she paced by her. "I should have warned you that talking to my aunt has side-effects."

"She's so good."

"My aunt? Yeah, I think so."

"No. I mean, yeah, but no. Ellie. Did I tell you she got Dani to talk? Not to me. At least not yet, but she's talking. Ellie did that. She did what *trained* doctors couldn't do."

"That's truly impressive, Hunter. But that doesn't mean you're not good enough for her." Rebecca took Hunter's hand and guided her friend back to the guest chair. She kept the large, soft hand in hers as she sat next to Hunter. "I've never pressured you into telling me more about Susan. And I'm not doing that now. From what I know, she's married, she seduced you when you were younger, and she has some sort of hold on you that you finally broke free from. None of that makes you a bad person."

"You said it yourself, she's married."

"You made a bad choice. Jesus, Hunter, you've more than made up for naïve foolishness. You're a trauma surgeon. You've saved countless lives. You're charitable. You're one of the sweetest people I've ever known."

"You're biased," Hunter muttered.

"I'm sure you think that. Truth is, I made my own decision about you after considering everything I know about you, Hunter. I think Ellie deserves the same opportunity, don't you?"

"I guess you're right." Hunter studied Rebecca for a second. "Is everything okay with you? Not that you're not being completely supportive, but you seem a little, um, distracted. You and Cass?"

"We're great." Rebecca attempted a smile but didn't quite pull it off. "That's true, we are great. *She's* great. There's just a small hitch right now."

"Do I need to kick her ass?" Hunter threatened half-heartedly. She couldn't imagine Cass being stupid enough to mess things up with someone like Rebecca. Or vice-versa.

Rebecca chuckled. "No. She's done nothing wrong. In fact, she's doing everything right. She's with her best friend right now helping her through a situation."

"And, you're upset about that?"

"No. Yes. I don't know."

Hunter shook her head in wonder. "I don't think I've ever seen you this flustered. Want to tell me about it?"

Rebecca didn't hesitate to tell Hunter about the little scene with Miranda.

"Wait, she came down the stairs naked?" Rebecca nodded. "And said something asinine like "I didn't know *we* had company"? What did Cass say about that?"

"Honestly, I don't think she even noticed. She was completely flustered by the whole naked thing."

"So, a woman struts in naked, acting as though it's her home, and you just left her alone with Cass?"

This time Rebecca stood to pace. "Well, when you put it that way, what I thought was a good idea now seems like a terrible one."

"Why would that be a good idea if you doubted her, Becca?"

"Because!"

"That explains everything," Hunter scoffed.

"Love is a bitch sometimes, Hunter. Do you know that when Samantha cheated on me—which was practically every fucking week—I didn't care. Hell, I was *grateful* that it wasn't me! But the thought of Cassidy being with someone else literally gives me heartburn. I can't stand the thought! Which is exactly why I left them alone."

"Okay, babe, you're going to have to explain that one to me." Hunter had no clue what was going to happen with Ellie. But, man, Rebecca wasn't making love sound like rainbows and unicorns.

"I don't know what's real in here," Rebecca said, pointing to her head. "*If* Miranda has been abused and I hindered her from getting help from Cass, anything that happens to her is my fault. She would never talk if I was there, so I left."

"You don't believe her? About being abused?"

"That's the thing, I don't know what I believe. Even Cassidy says Miranda is acting weird. How do I know that she hasn't been abused and this whole naked thing is how she's acting out?"

Hunter stood and walked over to Rebecca. "So, you made the only decision you could."

Rebecca nodded. "Cassidy is doing the right thing. I know she didn't hesitate in believing Miranda. That's who she is. I couldn't force my doubts on her."

"She's good, too, Becca."

"I know. Maybe too good for me."

"Bullshit." Hunter rolled her eyes when Rebecca lifted a brow. Yeah, she got it. She needed to stop doubting her worthiness for Ellie. It wouldn't be easy, but she would try. "I hope you know that Cass is head over heels in love with you. I don't think *anything* could make her hurt you."

Rebecca smiled. "I know. I trust Cassidy with my heart. I don't, however, trust Miranda. I'm afraid Cassidy is going to get hurt somehow."

"If that happens, at least she has you to make it all better."

NINE HOURS, FIFTEEN minutes, and forty-three seconds. Cass's fingers tapped her thigh as the seconds ticked by, reminding her that the woman she loved wasn't with her. That Rebecca hadn't called her. And that she wasn't sure if Rebecca would pick up if Cass called her. Why the *fuck* did she just let Rebecca go? And what good did it do? Rand still hasn't talked to her. Well, she's talked, but not about the abuse. She talked about her and Cass and their past. There was a lot of "Do you remember when we…" and really playing up the closeness they had growing up together.

Through all of it, Cass tried to remain attentive and supportive. Every time she tried to steer the conversation back to why Rand was there, Rand got upset. *That's normal, right?* Cass sighed in the dark. *God, I wish Rebecca were here.* It probably wouldn't have helped Rand, but it sure as hell would have helped Cass. As it was, she was alone, on the couch, missing the love of her life.

She almost laughed out loud at the absurdity of her gushing. The love of her life. As hokey as that sounded, especially from one who was only twenty-five, it was true. Cass was the luckiest son of a bitch ever to have found someone like Rebecca. She tried so hard not to be pissed that Rand was now sleeping in Cass and Rebecca's bed while Rebecca was gone. Rand would have understood that this was Rebecca's home. Right? Even this very different, very confusing Rand would understand.

"Cass?"

Cass looked through the darkness towards Rand's voice. She could only make out her silhouette. "Yeah?"

"Are you sure you don't want to sleep upstairs with me? I'd feel much safer."

"I'm sure. Look, you're safe, Rand. No one will get past me to get to you."

"You always did look out for me."

Rand had moved closer, but Cass remained where she was. Something was wrong. Rand sounded… wrong.

"Yeah, well, we're best friends," Cass said slowly.

"It's always been more than that for you, hasn't it?"

"What? No."

"Come on, Cassidy. It's just us here. You can tell me the truth. Remember that night when we…"

"It's *Cass*. And, nothing happened that night, Rand." Cass was moving from confused to pissed. It was becoming clear to her now that *this* was what Rand had been doing all night. Reminiscing. And now Cass was getting a clue as to why.

Rand giggled, and the sound grated on Cass's nerves. It reminded Cass as to why she started pulling away from this friendship even before she and Rebecca got together. Rand had been very demanding of Cass's time since they were teens. Whenever she needed something done that her other "girly" friends couldn't do, she called Cass. And when Rand decided she wanted to "experiment," well that fell to Cass, too, obviously.

If Cass were honest with herself, the friendship began deteriorating that night. Rand *begged* Cass to give her the "lesbian experience." Though she felt used, Cass reluctantly agreed. Only Cass couldn't go through with it. They got as far as being naked together before Cass decided that sex with Rand was not what she wanted. The feeling she had now was all too reminiscent of that night.

"*Everything* happened that night. You showed me what I truly wanted that night."

"Yeah?" Cass sneered. "Me deciding I didn't want to be with you is what made you want to laugh at your friends' jokes about me? It made you marry an abuser like Connor? Are you saying because I *didn't* have sex with you, this is all my fault?"

Rand laughed. "Please. I don't know why you're denying what happened. What does it matter if people find out? We can be together now."

Cass jumped when she felt Rand's naked body straddling her. "Are you fucking insane?" She used her considerable upper body strength to lift Rand off of her. "I'm with Rebecca! I *love* Rebecca! I'm sorry that Connor hurt you, but that doesn't give you the right to do this!"

"There's no way you could love someone as old as that woman. *I'm* your age. *We* would be perfect together."

"Don't talk about Rebecca like that."

"She's as weak as Connor is. Don't pretend you didn't see the way they looked at each other. Let them have each other."

Cass frowned at the woman she thought she knew. "You're delusional. Rebecca is a lesbian and in love with me." She heard Rand scoff and was thankful for the darkness. Not only because she didn't want to see Rand naked, but because she knew that scoff all too well. It was often paired with a look of entitled disgust. "Was any of it true, Rand? Did he really hurt you?"

"Mild-mannered Connor?" Another scoff. "Does it matter if he did or didn't? It got us to this point."

Cass felt sick to her stomach. Her so-called best friend had lied to her. About something incredibly serious. What this must have done to Rebecca. She was just getting over her own nightmares only to be thrust into someone else's and it wasn't even true.

"Call one of your friends, Miranda," Cass said coldly. "Stay with them or go back to Connor. I don't care what you do but get out of my house. Don't contact me again."

"Cass, wait! He did hurt me!"

She heard the panic in Rand's voice. She also heard the insincerity. For years, Cass was able to tell when Rand lied to her. This one night, she let her guard down. She *chose* to believe something she thought Rand could never lie about. And now she understood to look in Rebecca's eyes. She knew. *I'm a fucking idiot.*

"Stop. I don't know what the fuck happened to you, how you changed so much, but I'm done. You don't fucking lie about being abused! And you don't try to seduce someone who you know is in love with someone else. I don't know, maybe that's just who *you* are now, but," Cass wiped her hands together, "I'm out."

"You can't be out! We're best friends!"

She picked up the blanket she was using and threw it in Rand's direction. "Not anymore. You have two minutes to get your ass upstairs, get dressed, and get out. Otherwise, I'm throwing you out with only that fucking blanket. If you think I'm joking with you, try me." She switched on a lamp and glared at her former friend. "One minute and forty-eight seconds."

Rand huffed, threw the blanket back at Cass, and ran upstairs. Cass sank to the couch, much like she did when Rand first got here. What the fuck was she going to do if this caused her to lose Rebecca?

"Please forgive me, baby."

Chapter Seventeen
REBECCA & CASS

Forgive and Forget

TEN HOURS, THREE minutes, and twenty-two seconds. A tear splashed onto the screen of Rebecca's cell phone. She should call. But what if she interrupted something? Another tear. God, what if she interrupted something? She shook her head vigorously. No. Cassidy would never do that to her. Rebecca's heart knew that for certain. Now, if her head would just get a hint.

Problem was, she had been sitting at her place, alone, for what felt like years instead of hours. Stupid, fucking scenarios kept going through her head and she hated each and every one of them. Her stomach was churning too much to eat. As much as she could use a drink, she needed to keep a clear head. Hell, the only thing she has done since she left the club was change into pajamas and plop her sad ass down on the couch. She didn't even turn on the damn TV out of some stupid fear she would somehow miss Cassidy's call. The call that never came. Jealousy was a fucking asshole.

"This is bullshit!"

Unable to stand it any longer, Rebecca decided that Miranda Daly was not going to keep her away from Cassidy no matter what kind of trauma she may or may not have been through. Cassidy was home to Rebecca. And she needed to be home. She strode to the door with purpose, tears still in her eyes. Picking her keys up from the side table, she opened the door and nearly fainted with relief and happiness.

"Cassidy."

Cass had a split second to take in Rebecca's tear-stained cheeks before crushing herself to the smaller woman. "I'm sorry!" She repeated the apology over and over, kissing Rebecca's entire face as she did.

"Come in," Rebecca managed after a particularly deep kiss.

"Where were you going?" Cass allowed herself to be pulled inside and guided to the couch. Honestly, she wasn't altogether sure her feet worked anymore. She had been on autopilot all the way here. Now that she was with Rebecca, autopilot switched off.

"Home to you."

Those three little words caused a dam inside Cass to break. She had always thought that the only three words that could ever mean so much to her were "I love you." She was wrong.

Rebecca held on tightly as Cassidy sobbed in her arms. She cooed unintelligible words, stroked her hair, and wondered what she could have said that caused such a reaction. Or what could Cassidy have done?

"*Talk to me*," Rebecca whispered.

"You were right," Cass mumbled against Rebecca's bosom.

"Right?"

Cass sniffled and looked up. "You didn't believe her."

"I never said…"

"You didn't have to, I saw it in your eyes. I couldn't understand it at the time. But now… How did you know?"

Rebecca shook her head. "I didn't know. That's why I didn't say anything." She sighed when Cassidy looked at her expectantly. "There were a couple of things that made me doubt."

"What were they?"

"You told me that Miranda had accused Connor of using his dominance over her to abuse her. But, honey, Connor isn't the dominant one. Miranda is."

Cass sat up further. "Why didn't you tell me? And don't say it was a privacy thing, Rebecca. This was important."

"It wasn't just that. I could have been wrong. I don't know what they do in their personal lives, Cassidy. For all I know, they could have left the club and changed roles. We have."

Cass took a moment to let that sink in. "Okay, what else?"

"There were no marks on her. When she came downstairs, nude, you turned away. But I saw her. There were no marks indicating abuse."

Cass stared into Rebecca's eyes. "But you thought that didn't mean she wasn't being abused so you kept quiet?"

"I thought I was reading into things. If I had been wrong, I would be the jealous girlfriend that prevented you from helping a friend." She pushed Cassidy's long bangs out of tired eyes. "What happened? Did she tell you she was lying?"

Cass twitched. "I tried getting her to open up, but she refused to talk about that. At some point, I just became too exhausted to keep trying. I wasn't in the greatest state of mind since I wanted to be with you and you hadn't even called me."

"I was giving you space. The phone does work both ways, by the way."

"Yeah, I know, but I was afraid you wouldn't pick up. Stupid, I know." She exhaled heavily. "Anyway, long story short, she insisted on sleeping upstairs…"

"Wait. You may want to make this the long story and explain that little tidbit."

"I slept on the couch, baby. She made up this bullshit thing about being too scared to sleep near the front door. I'd been having this weird feeling all night that something wasn't right with her. I kept attributing it to the trauma. When she would talk about the past, I thought she just wanted to think about simpler times." Cass shook her head. "It wasn't until she came back downstairs that my gut started screaming at me."

Rebecca bit the inside of her cheek. All sorts of things were running through her imagination, and she didn't like any of them.

"Go on."

Cass *so* didn't want to say this part. But she refused to keep anything from Rebecca. "She started saying shit like we belonged together. And that Connor wanted you, so he could have you. I think I knew she had really lost it when she brought up something from our past. But she had a totally different version of it than what really happened."

"Does this have to do with her saying you'd already seen her naked?" Rebecca realized then that trying to talk with clenched teeth wasn't that easy.

"Yeah." Cass told Rebecca everything. Every detail of that night and every detail of what happened right before coming here. She also made it *extremely* clear that she immediately got out of the position Rand tried to trap her in.

"She certainly has no issues with nakedness, does she." Rebecca struggled to keep that little green-eyed monster at bay. "So, you've never had sex with her?"

"Never. I've never been attracted to her like that. Despite what she wants to believe. Even if I had been, being used by her like that would have been a total turn-off."

"I can't believe she tried to seduce you." Rebecca stood and started pacing. Seemed like she was doing that a lot tonight. It didn't help her mentally, but at least it gave her something to do besides finding Miranda and kicking her ass.

Cass shook her head, getting up to interrupt Rebecca's pacing. "I've never seen her like this before. I mean, she's always been a little outspoken, but this delusion she has? That's new. And to lie about something like this?"

Rebecca knew better than anyone else how dangerous delusional people could be. She also knew how many times Miranda and Connor have been in the Black Room. It wasn't that she was afraid of Miranda. She just didn't like the unpredictability surrounding people like that. "She's not still at the house, is she?"

"No way. I told her to go stay with one of her friends. I'm done."

Rebecca studied Cassidy for a moment. There didn't seem to be any remorse behind those words. She wondered if it would come later. When the shock of everything wore off. Whatever happens, Rebecca would be there.

She snaked her arms around Cassidy's neck, standing on her tiptoes for better access to Cassidy's lips. "Do you know what I would like?" Rebecca asked softly.

Cass's arms automatically wrapped around Rebecca's waist. "Tell me," she murmured.

"I would like," kiss, "to go to the bedroom," kiss, "and forget today ever happened." Kiss. "Maybe we could make up for the last ten hours."

Cass grinned. "That sounds like the best idea *ever*." She bent slightly and picked Rebecca up. Beautiful, toned legs wrapped around her, squeezing her. She carried her precious cargo down the hall to Rebecca's bedroom. Once there, she carefully set Rebecca down on the bed. "I don't, um, have…"

Rebecca kissed Cassidy again, deeply. "You. I only want you," she whispered against her lips.

Oh, baby, you have me. "Anything you want."

They undressed each other, taking their time exploring as though it was their first time.

"I love your body." Cass emphasized her statement with kisses and nibbles that followed the trail her hands made.

"I'm so happy you do."

Rebecca giggled when Cass hit a certain spot. It was so different than the one she heard earlier that evening. Rebecca's giggle sounded like heaven to Cass. She nudged Rebecca back onto the bed and positioned herself on top of her. A quick maneuver found Cass's arm between the two of them, and she slowly slipped two fingers inside her lover.

Rebecca arched into Cassidy, humming with delight. God, just the sensation of Cassidy's hard body on top of her made Rebecca incredibly wet. Such a difference from the first time they made love. She couldn't believe she was ever frightened of being with Cassidy like this.

"Don't leave me again. Please."

Even Cassidy's heavy breathing didn't mask the fear in her voice.

"I didn't leave you, baby." Rebecca cupped Cassidy's face and looked her in the eye. "I don't want to be without you."

Cass moaned. How is it that Rebecca knew exactly the right thing to say at exactly the right time? She shifted her body until the core of her need collided perfectly with Rebecca's smooth thigh. Rebecca rewarded her by lifting her leg slightly, putting divine pressure on her swollen clit. Then, she felt Rebecca's fingernails dig into her ass and knew she was getting close.

She added another finger inside Rebecca, matching her thrusts with each grind on Rebecca's thigh. *"Jesus!"*

"Don't stop! God, Cassidy, I'm so close," Rebecca panted.

The sound of glass breaking startled them both, chasing that wonderful peak into oblivion.

"What the fuck?" Mindful of Rebecca's comfort, Cass slowly withdrew her fingers. *Damn it.* "Stay here." She rolled off the bed and picked up her boxers.

"Cassidy put a shirt on," Rebecca said calmly as she reached for her robe.

"Oh, right." Cass looked around until she found her shirt. "You're not going to stay put, are you?" Rebecca merely raised a brow as she tied her robe. "Didn't think so. Will you at least stay behind me?"

"Come on." In the interest of keeping the peace, Rebecca pushed Cassidy ahead of her. In the interest of keeping them both safe, she grabbed a bat that she kept near the bedroom door.

Cass walked slowly down the hall with Rebecca hanging onto the tail of her shirt with one hand and a bat in the other. Even as tense as the situation was, the thought of Rebecca getting some swings in on some punk trying to ruin their awesome night made her smile inwardly. She flipped on the light, eyes scanning keenly. There was no sign of anyone in the house, but the large picture window facing the backyard was shattered.

"Cassidy, be careful. You're barefoot."

Cass nodded, motioning for Rebecca to stay where she was. She carefully tiptoed her way through the debris and picked up a brick. *What the hell?* Rage welled up inside her as she peered out the destroyed window.

"What is it?" Rebecca gingerly made her way to Cassidy. Her lover's rigid posture put all of Rebecca's senses on alert.

"I thought…" Cass sighed. No use in thinking Rebecca would do anything she didn't want to do. Grudgingly, she handed over the brick.

I know who you are, Mistress.

Rebecca frowned, jumping when Cass yelled out the window.

"Rand! Show your goddamn face, you coward! You think you can do this to my girlfriend and get away with it?!"

"Cassidy." Rebecca laid a calming hand on Cassidy's arm. She felt it quiver with fury. She didn't like it. "Please."

Cass turned towards Rebecca and her anger immediately faded. "I swear I didn't tell her anything."

"I know." She ran a soothing hand down Cassidy's stomach. "Unpredictable," Rebecca muttered.

"Huh?"

"You said Miranda was acting delusional. When Samantha's delusions started, she became unpredictable."

Cass let that sink in. Did she really believe that the girl she grew up with could become someone like Samantha? Looking around her at the mess she *knew* Rand created, she could believe. She picked Rebecca up and made her way out of the glass.

"Where's your phone?" Rebecca pointed to the end table next to the couch. Setting Rebecca down on a safe part of the floor that was not littered with debris, she picked up the phone and dialed. "Yeah, I'd like to report vandalism. Someone threw a brick through our home's window." She rattled off the address, answered a few questions, and hung up.

Rebecca reached for Cassidy's hand and pulled her down next to her. "Are you okay?"

Cass shook her head. "I'm sorry about this."

"You have told me from the very beginning that everything that Samantha did to me was not my fault. Was that bullshit?"

"No!"

"Then blame the person doing this, Cassidy. Not yourself. You taught me that."

Cass leaned back and pulled Rebecca into her arms. "What will you do if she exposes you?"

Rebecca shrugged. "It doesn't matter, Cassidy. I hid who I was back then because I thought I had something to be ashamed of. Anonymity helped me hide from myself." She looked up into Cassidy's eyes. "I have nothing to hide from anymore."

CASS ZIPPED HER jeans up just in time to answer the door. *That was quick*, she thought when she saw the strobe of the lights from the cop cars through the front window. Not even ten minutes had gone by since she called 911 and here they were. Thankfully, Rebecca had been level-headed enough to suggest that they put clothes on while they waited.

"You guys are quick." Cass scanned the badge the officer held up. "Come on in."

"Thank you." He took a step inside, eyes alert. "My guys are checking the perimeter while I take your statement. I'm…"

"Detective Chi?"

Cass felt a stab of jealousy when the cop's face lit up with a huge smile.

"It's, uh, lieutenant now," the cop responded with a boyish grin.

Cass scrutinized the older Asian man with a critical eye. How did he know Rebecca? Was he a client? Did cops do that kind of thing? She almost snorted with laughter. Of course, they did. They're human. There probably wasn't a human alive that wouldn't pay for a chance to be with Rebecca Cuinn. And, since she didn't like that line of thought, she tuned back into the conversation.

"Wow. Impressive." Rebecca gave the man a hug much to Cass's displeasure. "I'm happy for you. This is my girlfriend Cassidy."

"Cass," Cass responded automatically, shaking the guy's proffered hand.

"Cassidy, this is *Lieutenant* Lou Chi. He helped me that night."

It dawned on Cass then that she was being ridiculously jealous of the man who quite possibly saved Rebecca's life.

"Hi, um, it's nice to meet you." *You're such an idiot*, Cass scolded herself silently.

"Likewise," Lou responded sincerely. "Want to tell me what's going on here?" He nodded at the brick and listened carefully when the couple explained what happened.

"Did you see this," he checked his notes, "Miranda Daly throw the brick?"

"No, but I know it was her," Cass stated with confidence. She went on to explain what had transpired that day as "evidence."

"I see." He picked up the brick with gloved hands. "You both touched this, correct? Just want to make sure we eliminate your prints."

"Yes," Rebecca answered. She tilted her head in that special Rebecca way. "Why are you here, Lou?"

Lou frowned. "We're investigating a 911 call."

"But why are *you* here. This is a petty crime. You're a lieutenant."

Cass watched the back and forth between them like it was a tennis match. Head swiveled from person to person.

Lou sighed. "I heard the call come through on the scanner. I recognized your address and came by to make sure you were okay." It was the tilt of the head to the other side that had him spilling his guts as though he'd just been waterboarded. "I've been keeping an eye on you, okay? I f—screwed up that night when I didn't lock that bitch up the first time I knew she was hitting you. You don't know how guilty I feel about the terror you went through because I was too damn selfish to arrest her."

"I asked you not to," Rebecca reminded him. Out of the corner of her eye, she saw Cass's nostrils flare, and she laid a hand on Cass's thigh.

"That doesn't matter, Rebecca. I'm a cop and I should have done my job. If I had, you wouldn't have nearly died." He glanced in Cass's direction. "No way I'm letting that happen again."

"Me either," Cass practically growled. She didn't appreciate being lumped anywhere near the pile of shit that was Samantha. "That's why I called this in."

Lou gave Cass a respectful nod. "Good." He tapped the note on the brick. "About this. I'm assuming you know who Mistress is?" he asked Cass directly.

"Yeah, I do."

"And will this be a problem for either of you if it were to get out?"

"No," Rebecca answered. "What's written on there doesn't matter. It's who did it. She needs help."

"Do you think she's really been abused by her husband?"

Cassidy shook her head, but it was Rebecca who answered. "It would appear that she just used that as an excuse to get close to Cassidy."

"Does she somehow know about your past?" Lou asked as delicately as he could. "If this is who you say it is, maybe she feels Cass would feel more obligated to protect her "best friend" rather than be with you?"

"I never told her. I never told *anyone*." Cassidy directed the answer to Rebecca instead of Lou. She needed her lover to know that she would never betray her confidence. "There's no way she could know."

Rebecca cleared her throat. "There is one way she could know." She recounted Cassidy's mother's visit, leaving out a few details that were for Cassidy only.

"I have so many questions," Cass said with a touch of

disappointment. Rebecca had kept something from her. Why? They would have to talk about this more in depth later. "You told my mom and you think she told Rand?"

"Yes, I told your mom. I needed her to understand who and what you are to me." She turned to Lou for a moment. "Miranda's mom and Cassidy's mom are best friends. There's a chance that the two had a conversation that could have been overheard."

Cass sulked as the two talked. It was childish, yeah, but she still couldn't figure out why Rebecca lied to her. Okay, maybe technically she didn't lie, but she didn't tell her. *Same difference*, she thought grumpily.

"Sir?" A fresh-faced uniformed officer knocked lightly on the ajar door.

Lou stood. "Yeah?"

"We found a suspect lurking around the perimeter."

Cass moved to get up when she felt Rebecca's fingers tighten around her thigh. She looked over and Rebecca shook her head slightly.

"Description?"

"White female, mid-twenties, red hair. Extremely upset."

Lou looked over at Rebecca and Cass. "Sound like someone you know?"

Cass lowered her head. *Fuck.* She knew she was right, but confirmation still sucked. "Yeah, that's Miranda."

Lou nodded to his officer. "Let her cool off a bit in the back of your cruiser." He turned his attention back to Rebecca who was gently rubbing Cass's back. Lou knew what guilt looked like. He saw it in the mirror every day since finding Rebecca close to death. Cass was feeling it right now. "Rebecca? Do you want to press charges?"

Rebecca faltered. She was torn because this was Cassidy's best friend, regardless of what the younger woman said before. Miranda needed help with whatever it was she was going through now. Rebecca just didn't know if jail time was the right kind of help.

"Yes." Whatever Rebecca's hesitation was, Cass was having none of it. "We're pressing charges."

"Cassidy."

"No, baby. I will *not* allow this to happen to you again. *No one* will hurt you."

"She needs help," Rebecca tried again. She didn't know why she was opposing what she knew was the right thing to do. Perhaps it all came back to the fact that she wanted to protect Cassidy from the hurt Rebecca knew would come once the anger wore off.

"Not your responsibility, babe. Nor is it mine. *My* responsibility is keeping you happy and safe. If help is what Rand needs, she can get it in jail. Or wherever they put her." Cass looked up at Lou. "We're pressing charges."

Lou nodded and felt the weight of a fifteen-year-old burden lift from his shoulders. He no longer had to keep an eye on Rebecca. She was safe now.

"What will happen now?" Rebecca asked.

"She'll spend the night in jail before we take her to arraignment in the morning." He flipped his notebook shut. "I'll keep you updated on all of the proceedings."

Cass and Rebecca stood, both taking their turn shaking Lou's hand.

"Would it be okay if we visited Connor and told him about what's happening?" Cass asked. "I just have a feeling that he's going to be totally blindsided by this."

"That was actually my next stop. I wanted to be sure the allegations against him aren't valid." He caught Rebecca's pleading look and relented. He hoped to hell he wasn't making another huge mistake. "However, it is pretty late. I'll have one of my officers visit him in the morning to take his statement. You need any help getting that window fixed?" he asked lifting his chin towards the large opening.

"Nah, we can take care of it. Thanks."

Lou smiled. He definitely liked Cass for Rebecca. "Great. Whatever you do tonight, please be careful. Don't take any unnecessary chances, yeah?"

"We won't," Rebecca assured. "It was nice seeing you again, Lou."

"You, too, Rebecca. Cass, the circumstances suck, but it's been a pleasure meeting you."

Rebecca waited until Cassidy ushered everyone out, receiving assurances that they would do drive-bys until the window was fixed. Once the door was closed, she took Cassidy's hands in hers.

"I'm sorry. I know it upset you to find out about your mom's visit like that."

"Why didn't you tell me?"

"Because she asked me not to, baby." Rebecca sighed. Beverly knew Rebecca wouldn't lie to Cassidy. Since it's out there now, she needed to tell Cassidy everything. "She came here to try to convince me to leave you."

"She what?!"

Rebecca held on tightly when Cassidy tried pulling away. "Hear me out before you get all growly."

"I'm not growly," Cass growled.

"Mmhmm. Come here." She pushed Cassidy down on the couch and sat on her lap. Not only did she like it there, Rebecca knew it was an effective way to keep Cassidy's attention. "She was worried about you, baby. It's a mother's job to make sure their child is making the best decisions for themselves. Even if it was a little misdirected, she had good intentions."

"Making you break up with me isn't good intentions, babe."

"Are you going to listen?"

Ooo, that was Mistress! Cass momentarily entertained the idea of being bad. Then she remembered that there was a fucking broken window, glass all over the damn place, and they still needed to break the news to Connor. *Damn it.*

"I'm listening, baby. Sorry."

As a reward, Rebecca gave Cassidy a sweet kiss before continuing. "She did come here to try and convince me that we weren't good for each other. She was so hung up on age and the problems that could incur, she couldn't see what was underneath it all. She even worried about our sex life," Rebecca laughed.

Cass cringed hoping against hope that it was not true. That her mom didn't talk sex with someone like Rebecca. "Oh, fuck. She did *not* talk to you about that did she?"

"Yes, she did. However, that's when she realized how silly she was being and was embarrassed."

"That's why you told her about Samantha?"

"What I said to Lou was sincere. I told your mom what happened to me so she could understand the love I feel for you. So she could see that you mean more to me than our difference in age or sex. She still sees you as her little girl. I needed her to see you as the woman who has done more for me—emotionally and physically—than anyone else." Rebecca wiped a tear from Cassidy's cheek. "I agreed not to tell you unless asked because I didn't want to be the reason for a rift between the two of you when there's no need for one."

"She betrayed you, though," Cass said softly.

"Oh, honey. What happened to me isn't some shameful secret. I don't mind that your mom talked to her best friend about it. If Miranda heard…" Rebecca's brows furrowed. "Has she ever lied like this before? Faked something that she saw happening to someone else?"

It took a bit of time for Cass's mind to catch up to the change in subject. She was just feeling all warm and fuzzy inside, listening to what Rebecca felt about her. Now she had to switch gears and think about the person she'd rather not think about.

"Um…" Cass had the stories that Rand was spewing all night in her head. She sat up suddenly, nearly jostling Rebecca off her lap. "Sorry. But yeah, she has. In high school she would always be calling me, crying over something that happened. It was all pretty mundane, you know? High school problems. But I always listened, whether I wanted to or not. I would even leave dates early because she was hysterical. Oh, and if it involved someone who was in some sort of fight with her, I was the one she would come to for "protection." I found out a couple of times that she either lied about a situation or didn't tell the whole truth. Fuck. It never occurred to me what she was doing. How fucking blind and naïve can I be?"

"Hey, stop. You were young, and she was your friend."

Cass snorted with derision. "What's my excuse now? You just told me how you convinced my mom that age didn't matter and I'm here proving you wrong."

Rebecca moved until she was straddling Cassidy. "What you did tonight by believing Miranda without hesitation was the absolute right thing to do. My first reaction, even with my past, was doubt. One of the many reasons women who are abused don't come forward is out of fear they won't be believed. You gave Miranda a safe haven. It is much easier to live with being wrong about believing a liar than doubting what could've been a deadly truth. The only one who did wrong tonight is Miranda. And perhaps me for leaving you alone with her."

Cass hadn't thought of it that way. Yeah, shit happened tonight because she trusted Rand. Like the damn window. But this shit could easily be dealt with. Rebecca was right. If she had turned Rand away and it ended like what Rebecca had gone through, Cass would never have been able to live with herself. She now understood Lieutenant Chi's desire to watch over Rebecca over the years.

"Thank you for saying that." Cass looked over at Rebecca's shattered window. "I'll clean that up and have it repaired."

"I'll hire someone to clean it and insurance will take care of the repairs." Rebecca checked the time. "Let's stop by Connor's on our way home."

"Home? You know, if you really love this place, we could move in here."

Rebecca smiled. "It was never about loving this place. It was about the fear of giving up everything again. Tonight, I realized that I didn't have to give up anything with you. Because without you, I have nothing."

"Jesus, baby." Cass crushed Rebecca to her. "I don't think I can explain how you've made me feel tonight. And I don't want to say something stupid like ditto." She looked up. "Give me a little time? I promise I will show you exactly what's in here." She placed Rebecca's hand over her heart, melting a little when Rebecca smiled brightly.

"I'm not going anywhere."

Chapter Eighteen
REBECCA & CASS

The Aftermath

CASS TOOK A deep breath. Connor already didn't like her. That certainly wasn't going to get any better when she tells him what's been going on.

"Are you okay?"

Rebecca's sweet voice brought a smile to Cass's face. "Yeah, I'm good. Just trying to figure out why I thought I wanted to do this."

Rebecca scooted closer to Cassidy. The *only* thing she liked about this clunker of a truck was that the bench seat allowed her to be as close to Cassidy as she wanted to be. Well, that and the fact that the seat was much easier to have sex on than the bucket seats in her Mercedes. "Because you're a good person and you thought hearing it from someone he knew would be easier."

"He hates me, babe. What do you think he's going to feel when he finds out Rand did all this to, um, be with me?"

"Betrayed by his wife. Look, you're not going to become bosom buddies, but this is the right thing to do. And, I'm right here with you."

Cass looked down at Rebecca's breasts. "I only want to be bosom buddies with you."

Rebecca laughed. "Stop looking at my tits, you fiend, and let's go."

Cass opened the door and hopped out. She then turned and helped her significantly shorter girlfriend out by lifting her from the waist. God, she loved this truck.

"Would you like me to talk to him?" Rebecca asked.

"Nah, it should be me, I think." Yeah, she was all confident and shit until it came time to knock on the door. She decided to approach this with the same mentality she used when working out. Get in, get it done.

"Why are you hopping around?"

"Getting ready." Cass bent her neck from side to side, satisfied by the cracking that resulted.

"Are you going to fight him?" Rebecca hid her smile behind her hand. There were times when Cassidy showed her age. Luckily, Rebecca found those moments very charming and cute.

"Only if I have to," Cass mumbled but stopped bouncing on her toes. *Okay, here we go.* She raised her hand, hesitated, then knocked. "Maybe it's too late," she suggested after waiting a mere three seconds.

"Give him time, baby."

Just then, the door opened, and Connor was there frowning at them.

"What are you doing here?" he asked irritably.

"Just a courtesy call, man. I—*we*—thought you should know that Rand is, um, in jail."

"In jail? Are you crazy? She said she was going out with friends. What the hell did you do?"

"I didn't do anything!"

While the two exchanged words, Rebecca studied Connor. One thing stood out to her the most.

"Connor?" The arguing stopped at once and they both turned towards Rebecca. "Could we come in?"

"N-no. It's late."

Rebecca gave him the head tilt. "What happened to your eye?"

Connor's hand involuntarily went to his face. "Basketball. Some dude elbowed me. Still made the shot."

"Since when do you play basketball?" Cass asked crassly.

Rebecca discreetly touched Cassidy's arm. "That must have hurt."

Connor glared at Cass but shrugged. "I can take it."

"I'm sure. Well, we just stopped by to let you know that the police will be here in the morning." She saw his knuckles whiten as he gripped the doorknob.

"Why?"

Cass didn't understand what the hell was going on, but she stayed quiet, letting Rebecca take the lead. Had she noticed something Cass didn't?

"Because Miranda made accusations against you that they need to discuss with you."

Connor's face scrunched with confusion. "What kind of accusations?"

Cass felt Rebecca's slight nudge. *Great. Now she wants me to talk.* "Connor, Rand came to me, hysterical, saying you were abusing her."

"That's fucking bullshit! I never touched her!" Connor practically snarled at Cass. "This is all your fault! It's *always* about you!" He moved to close the door but was stopped by a delicate hand.

"Connor, we know she's lying. And we're pretty sure we know why. Blaming Cassidy for this doesn't help any of us." She took a chance and laid a hand on his arm. "Did she give you the black eye?"

"No!" He jerked his arm away and was ready to slam the door on them.

"When my ex's beatings left marks that were visible to others," Rebecca called out right before the door clicked shut, "she would tie me to the bed to ensure I didn't go out in public."

Cass's heart constricted at the image of a battered Rebecca tied to the bed. It was one more piece of Rebecca's past, and Cass hated it. But it also had Connor opening the door back up. She couldn't wrap her brain around the fact that Rand was the one abusing Connor. She would never have suspected that. Hell, even when she saw the black eye, it didn't occur to her. Rebecca really had seen something that Cass completely missed. *Thank God she's here.*

"You were?"

"Abused, yes. For many years. So, I get your hesitation, but you need to tell the police."

"You don't get shit! Look, I'm sorry about what happened to you, but I'm a *man*. Do you have any idea what my life would be like if my friends found out that…" Connor looked around. "Come in."

Cass followed Rebecca in, trying not to look Connor in the eye. For some reason, she thought if he saw any kind of sympathy coming from her, he would take it as pity. The truth was, it wasn't pity she felt, but anger that she hadn't seen this before. She *knew* Rand and Connor. Went to their wedding. She never saw a damn thing. Was it because Connor was a man? Was she so "unjaded" as Aunt Wills suggested that she couldn't imagine a man being abused by a woman?

"Real men don't get abused by women. That's what people are going to say." Connor gestured to the couch, opting to sit in his recliner.

Rebecca sat down in the middle of the couch so she could be close to Cassidy. "When we told you of Miranda's accusations, you were very clear that you never touched her."

"Never."

"She hit you, you're bigger than her, and yet you never once hit her back. I'd say *that's* a real man," Cass suggested with sincerity.

"Do you think my male friends will say that?" Connor scoffed. "They'll call me a fucking pussy. It's not the same. There's no sympathy for men who allow women to beat them."

Annoyed with the term, Rebecca nearly pointed out just how tough a pussy could be. Try getting a baby out of a damn penis. But she refrained.

"Do you think it's easy for women to admit they're being abused?" Rebecca asked softly. "I was a strong, independent woman when I met my ex. I made the horrible mistake of getting involved with her despite my reservations. Then I was stuck. I couldn't tell anyone. How in the hell could I face people and tell them what I had gotten myself into? There are so many reasons we don't tell, Connor. There's the fear of being hurt even more or not being believed. Then there's the victim-shaming, the embarrassment, and in some cases, women have no other alternative than to stay. But when I look back, my biggest regret is that I didn't open my mouth before it was too late."

Connor sat up in his chair, elbows on his knees. "How'd you get out?"

"She died," Rebecca answered simply.

"Did you...?"

"Kill her? No. She had a heart attack while beating me. We both almost lost our lives that night." Funny how that was getting easier and easier to say. "Listen, I can see that you care for Miranda as well as your reputation. But at what cost?"

Connor looked at the floor, contemplating. "I know who you are, Mistress," he said at length, still not looking at them. "After we had lunch together, Rand became convinced that you were manipulating Cass into being with you. It was all she ever talked about. She was obsessed." He looked up finally, eyes locking with Cass's. "Obsessed with you."

"I gave her no reason to be, man. You gotta believe that. I love Rebecca. She's it for me."

"What about your past with Rand?"

"If she told you we slept together, she lied." Cass went on to tell Connor the truth about what happened between her and Rand that night when they were teenagers, surprised when he laughed.

"To hear her tell it, you two had a torrid affair. It's why I never really liked you." He shook his head. "Anyway, she made it her mission to find out more about you, Rebecca. She would follow you. One day, she came home so excited that she found dirt on you. She followed you to the club, took pictures. Said she was going to go to Cass once she had evidence that people were going into your room." He laughed mirthlessly. "Can you imagine her surprise when she saw Cass going in there?"

Rebecca glanced over at Cassidy. Well, that was one mystery solved.

Connor caught the exchange that told him there was more he didn't know. It occurred to him then that he still had no idea why his wife was currently in jail instead of him. "Hang on, if Rand is running around accusing me of abuse, why is she the one in jail? Can't possibly be for lying."

"Vandalism," Cass offered.

"Vandalism? My wife? I think you better start from the beginning."

"I tried telling you before. Are you going to listen this time?"

"Cassidy," Rebecca admonished softly.

"Sorry." Cass inhaled and blew it out slowly. "Okay. Like I said before, Rand showed up at my house acting very strange. Yeah, she was hysterical, but also kinda off. She told me you were using your, um, lifestyle to abuse her. I gotta say, man, I couldn't see you doing that, but what choice did I have than to believe her? It's happened before." Cass risked a quick look at Rebecca.

Connor nodded. He understood Cass wanting to believe her best friend. It wasn't any secret that there was no love lost between the two of them, so who did he expect her to side with?

"How did you figure out she was lying?"

Another look passed between Cass and Rebecca. "She wouldn't give me details when I tried to get her to open up about it. Then, she, uh…"

"She came on to Cassidy," Rebecca finished for Cassidy.

Connor barked out a mirthless laugh. "Of course, she did."

"Yeah, well, that's when I asked her if she was lying to me. She admitted she was. I threw her out, told her I was done with her."

Connor's brows rose. "Don't tell me she tore your house up after that."

"No, she threw a brick through the window at *my* place," Rebecca said. "Along with a note saying she knew I was Mistress."

"Damn."

"She needs help, Connor."

He looked over at Cass. "And it's my responsibility to get her help?"

He pointed at his eye. "This is what happened when I told her she needed help."

"It's not your responsibility to help her, Connor. But help yourself. If you press charges, she could be mandated to get therapy." Doubt clouded the man's face. If only she could get his ego out of the way. "It wasn't until very recently that I came to understand that Samantha's, my ex, death wasn't my fault. But a part of me will always wonder what could have happened if I had come forward. Would she have gotten help?" Rebecca shook her head. "You don't have to live with that burden, Connor. You don't have to live like *this*. Take the chance that I didn't. Please."

Connor watched Cass pick up Rebecca's hand and kiss it gently. He stood and walked over to a desk in the far side of the room. Digging a key out of his pocket, he opened a drawer and took out a manila envelope. When he sat back down, he waved it in front of him.

"Divorce papers. I filed a couple of weeks ago when I came close to hitting back." Connor caught Rebecca's gaze. "I don't know if I can do this. You know, the only reason I went to your club was because she needed something "more" out of sex. I loved her enough to try anything. Of course, when she told me our roles wouldn't be exactly what I thought, I was hesitant."

"But you did it anyway."

He shrugged. "At first, I thought it could be exciting. Giving up some of that control. Thing is, she was extremely aggressive from the beginning. The first time it got physical beyond the sex and BDSM she wanted to do things I wasn't comfortable with. When that information gets out?" He shook his head.

"I have a friend at the police department. He helped me years ago. I can give him a call, have him come here to talk to you himself. If we ask, I'm sure we can convince him to keep it quiet," Rebecca suggested.

"That'll last for as long as it takes to get a trial going, right?" Connor opened the envelope. "Maybe I'll travel. I've always wanted to see the world." He took the contents out of the envelope and handed them over to Rebecca.

Flashes of the horrors she went through with Samantha ran through Rebecca's mind when she saw the photos. Unable to look at any more, she handed them over to Cassidy.

"*Jesus.*" Cass swallowed down the bile that threatened to come up. How could Rand do this? "You documented the abuse."

"Insurance. Rand tells me all the time that if I tried to leave her, she would make sure I lost everything. She would do exactly what she did with you. Accuse me. She said no one would believe me if I told them the truth. She was right. I never planned on using those unless I absolutely had to." Connor addressed Rebecca again. "Your friend? I'll talk to only him. Think he can get her sent to a hospital or something?"

"I think he'll do his best." Rebecca gave him a small smile.

Cass, on the other hand, was sure of one thing. Miranda would fight tooth and nail before going to a mental hospital.

"You're not going to press charges?" she asked handing him back the photos.

"I'll tell my story. But no trial. I don't want to drag her parents through that shit. If she doesn't fight spending time in a hospital to get help and signs the divorce papers, I won't pursue jail time. After that, I wash my hands of this. Of her." Connor rose from his chair, ready for this night to be over.

Rebecca took his cue and stood as well, bringing Cassidy up with her. "You're doing a very brave thing, Connor."

He grunted. "I'm not doing this to be brave. I don't want to be the stepping stone for other men to feel safe to admit they are being abused. I just want it over."

"The bruises and scars will fade, but it'll never stray far from your mind." Rebecca looked up at Cassidy and smiled. "Until you find someone who takes it away."

Connor chuckled. It was a weird feeling to smile and laugh. It felt as though he hadn't done that in a long time. "As great as I think you two are together, I think I'm going to focus on myself for a while."

"I have the number for a terrific therapist if you're interested," Rebecca smiled. "She can even do sessions over Skype no matter where you are in the world."

"She?"

"I'm sure she could refer you to a very qualified male colleague if you prefer."

"Nah, it's good. I'll, uh, think about it." He held his hand out to Rebecca, surprised by how strong the elegant hands were. "Thank you. Both of you. You had no reason or responsibility to come here and give me a heads up. Especially after the way I've treated you," he told Cass.

"Forget it. Rand gave you a good reason not to like me." Cass lowered her head. "I'm sorry I didn't see what was going on. I should have known *something*."

Connor shook his head. "There was no way I was going to let you see what she was doing to me. Hell, I denied it to myself until I couldn't anymore." He chucked Cass on the shoulder amicably. "Don't worry too much about this shit. I know what I said earlier, but this isn't on you."

"Yeah." Cass didn't believe that, but now wasn't the time or place to argue. "Keep me posted if you can?"

Connor agreed, thanking them again before escorting them out.

Cass stood outside of Rand and Connor's home and breathed in the chilled air. Everything still seemed so normal—except how she felt.

"What now?"

Rebecca looked up at Cassidy, whose eyes were closed. The fatigue was obvious. So was the confusion. Rebecca knew when this all sank in, it would be difficult for Cassidy to accept the truth about Miranda. She anticipated some anger and sadness and silently vowed to be there for Cassidy every step of the way.

"Now we go home."

Chapter Nineteen
REBECCA & CASS

Questions & Answers

SNAP! "FUCK!" CASS growled. That was the fourth damn brush today that she had broken. Not only was she ruining her fucking supplies—including her favorite brush—but she wasn't liking any of the stuff she was putting on the canvas. Which was fucking perfect since her showing at Sumptor Gallery was in a couple of weeks.

The shrill of her phone only served to annoy her even more. Obviously, she had forgotten to silence it when she came in to paint and that wasn't Rebecca's ringtone, so fuck it. Though, Cass couldn't blame Rebecca for keeping her distance lately. The stress of the opening had Cass a bit cranky. Perhaps Cass could make up for it by cooking dinner tonight. She snorted. *Yeah, that'd probably make things worse.*

A light knock on the door made Cass's pulse quicken. Only one person in the world was allowed in this room. "Come in," she called out.

Rebecca stuck her blonde head in and held up her phone. "Sorry, I know you're busy, but there's a call for you."

Cass frowned. "Who is it?"

"Connor."

"I'm, uh, trying to get this shit done. Can't you take it? He called you."

"No, he called you, but you didn't answer. And I'm not your secretary, Cassidy." Rebecca took a deep breath. After almost three weeks of this attitude, Rebecca was nearing the end of her patience. "You asked him to keep you updated. Deal with it."

Cass caught the phone that Rebecca tossed to her. *She is not happy with me. Damn it.* "Yeah, hello?" Cass tapped her fingers on her easel as she listened. "No, no, it's okay. I've just been swamped. What's up… And you think that's the best course to take… Well, that's good, then, right?" She looked over a Rebecca who looked back with expectancy—and a hint of exasperation. "So, what does all of this mean for you… For how long… Yeah, I wish you all the luck, man. Thanks for the update."

"So?" Rebecca asked after Cassidy stayed silent.

"If you wanted to know, why didn't you just talk to him?" Cass watched as Rebecca's nostrils flared. *Oh, you are a fucking idiot, Cass.*

"I promised myself that I would be patient as you went through this," Rebecca said coolly. "I knew that you'd have to let these emotions run their course. I've even allowed you angry sex in hopes that it would help you move forward. But you are stuck on the anger. I love you, Cassidy. But I won't go through this again."

Cass's stomach dropped. Her heart stopped. "Connor said that Rand finally agreed to counseling and a divorce as long as he didn't release the photos publicly," she said quickly. "At Connor's request, the judge ordered her to stay in a rehabilitation hospital, instead of jail, for a minimum of three years and she'll be fined $10,000. Connor has decided that traveling is his best option. He's pretty sure her parents are going to blame him for everything that's happening." She stopped there. It all seemed so unimportant now. It didn't matter what Connor did, or where

Rand ended up. Not in Cass's mind. In her mind, nothing mattered except convincing Rebecca to stay with her. "*Please. Don't leave me,*" she whispered.

Rebecca stared at the woman in front of her, witnessing the fear in those incredible eyes. She was sorry for being the one to put it there, but something had to give. "I'm doing the best I can, Cassidy. I truly am. But how can I help you when you refuse to talk about it?" She looked around the room. "You pretend that it's the stress of the opening. Yet, you've been like this since the night you found out about Miranda. Do you think I can't see how it has affected you? Affected *us*? It's ironic that the woman who taught me it wasn't my fault, blames herself for something she had absolutely no control over."

Panic rose like bile inside Cass when Rebecca turned to leave. "Wait! Where are you going? I can do better!"

The trepidation in Cassidy's voice caused Rebecca's step to falter. She turned her head to look at her lover. "I'm not asking you to get over it, Cassidy. I just need you to move past the anger. Now, I have to meet a client."

"A client!"

Rebecca rolled her eyes. Oh, yeah. Her patience was quickly turning to nil. "A *business* client. I'll be back later." And with that, she was out the door.

Be back. Not home, but back. The only solace Cass could find in that was at least Rebecca was coming back. *Unless she changes her mind,* Cass thought grumpily. She blew out a frustrated breath. Rebecca was right. Cass was stuck on this anger and she needed to do something about it fast before she lost the most precious thing to her in the world. Rebecca's love.

"CASS! THIS IS quite the surprise."

Cass rubbed the back of her neck, feeling a bit self-conscious.

"Hey, Aunt Wills. Do you have a minute?"

"For you, I have," she checked her appointment book, then the clock, "ten." The normally good-natured Cass looked so downtrodden that Willamena considered rescheduling her next appointment. "What can I help you with?"

"Do you ever get tired of people coming to you with their stupid problems?"

Willamena tsked. "First of all, no problem is stupid. Well, *almost* no problem. Second, what kind of psychiatrist would I be if I didn't want to help people through their toughest times?"

"Not a very good one?" Cass guessed, receiving a smile and a nod from Aunt Wills in return. "I'm really fucking things up with Rebecca. I think she's going to leave me and with this damn anger I have, I can't blame her."

Willamena frowned. "Cassidy?"

Oh, that sounded like Cass's mom when Cass got in trouble. And Cass realized how what she just said sounded. "No, no. Nothing like that. I haven't hurt her. I mean, not physically. But I'm being a real dick and she's over it."

"Our Rebecca certainly isn't one to take dickery for that long," Willamena said with a straight face. She was sure it was a rarity that Cass Giles was angry or depressed for long. She had to admit to being a little distressed by it. Though Rebecca had told her side of what happened recently, Willamena could clearly see there was more to Cass's side.

"Dickery," Cass snickered but sobered immediately. "Help me, Aunt Wills."

"I'm assuming this has to do with Miranda."

Cass hung her head in shame. "I see Rebecca has talked to you about it. Probably telling you how much of a bitch I'm being."

"Actually, she's told me very little. I imagine she's done that for your benefit as well as Miranda's husband's. She told me that she mentioned my name to Connor and didn't want to influence me in any way."

Willamena hesitated, wondering how much she should reveal. Certain that Rebecca would be okay with her telling Cass a few things, she continued. "She called me as a preventive measure. She was afraid that the nightmares she had just gotten over would come back because of the subject matter you both are dealing with now."

"Shit. I didn't even think about that." Cass flopped back and rubbed her face with frustration. "I've been fucking selfish lately."

"Cass, would you like to tell me your side before continuing on with your self-deprecation?"

Cass reluctantly told Aunt Wills all about how she had been duped by her so-called best friend. She even told her about their early days together and how it all made sense now to Cass what Rand was doing. She couldn't believe she had been so damned blind. Every little lie and manipulation was so fucking clear in hindsight.

"Your anger stems not only from recent events but from your past?" Willamena asked carefully.

"Yeah, I guess. She played me like a fucking violin. I can see now how she played the damsel in distress every chance she got. If there wasn't drama, she would create it. Of course, I didn't see that then. And this shit she's been doing to Connor. How the fuck did I miss that? So fucking clueless," she muttered with a shake of the head.

"May I ask you a question?"

Almost as though she forgot she was on a Skype call with Rebecca's aunt/therapist, Cass's head popped up. "Um, yeah."

"Do you think I'm clueless?" Willamena asked pointedly.

"Of course not!"

"But I'm a professional, Cass. I am highly trained to see patterns in people that help me determine who they are. I *literally* do this for a living. Yet, I had no idea what was happening to my own niece. The person I love the most in this world."

Cass sputtered. "But—but that's different!"

"Why?"

"Because you weren't here with her! You didn't see her every day or spend time with the both of them, Aunt Wills. Not like I did with Rand and Connor. She was my best friend!"

"And Rebecca is my niece!" Willamena shouted back in a rare show of frustration. "I *know* her. I should have seen it. I should have heard it in her voice. I should have known when she stopped calling me." The doctor sat back in her own chair and smoothed her already impeccable hair. "We both have to come to terms with the fact that we can't see what someone doesn't want us to see. Even me. My very limited knowledge of Miranda tells me she's manipulative and narcissistic. Someone like that is very good at hiding the truth from people. Particularly those closest to her. Do you think her parents had any clue she was abusive?"

Cass pictured Mr. and Mrs. Loring. Nice people. Perhaps a bit too doting on their only daughter, but Cass didn't think they'd cover up something like this. And she certainly didn't think they could lie well enough. Hell, Cass remembered back when she had first come out. She went over to Rand's like she did every day, but for the first time ever, she was turned away. Rand's parents answered the door which should have been Cass's first clue that something was up. They were uncomfortable, stumbling over their words as they told Cass that Rand was sick. She learned later that they had concerns about Rand being around a lesbian. Rand gave them hell for that. It was the one genuine thing Cass could give Rand credit for. It took them a while to come around, but it happened eventually. Whatever their hang-ups were about Cass's sexuality, she didn't see them ever condoning an abusive daughter.

"No. Okay, I get it. I have no fault in this." That was actually harder to say than she thought it would be. Knowing and feeling something are totally different. "How do I get all of this," she swirled her hands around her head and heart, "on the same page."

"Based on what Rebecca has told me, you're not going to like my answer."

"Lay it on me, doc."

"You need to talk to Miranda."

"You're right. I don't like your answer."

Willamena chuckled. "I told you. But it is honestly the best thing you can do, Cass. You can't know the answers until you ask the questions. There are moments when I wish I had the opportunity to speak with Samantha. Then I remember that would require her to be breathing. I know I'm a doctor and shouldn't say this, but I can live with not having closure for the rest of my life as long as she stays dead."

"Nothing wrong with that, Aunt Wills," Cass stated proudly.

Willamena gave her niece's lover a small smile. "You, on the other hand, have the opportunity to say what you need to say to Miranda and close this chapter in your life."

Cass frowned. The thought of talking to Rand didn't sit well with her. However, the prospect of losing Rebecca because Cass couldn't get her head out of her ass was far worse. "Fine. I'll talk to her. Can you do me a favor, though?"

"Perhaps."

"Can you convince your niece not to leave me?"

"Oh, Cass. She was never going to leave you. Why would she be selling her house if she planned on leaving you?"

Cass's eyes grew wide. "She's selling her place?!"

"Oh, dear. Something tells me she didn't mean for you to know that now. Crap."

The muttered "crap" somehow filtered through Cass's muddled brain, tickling something that felt close to hysterical. She burst out laughing. She laughed until she cried. Cried until she sobbed. Sobbed until she started hiccupping.

"I would hand you a tissue, but…"

Cass gave Aunt Wills a watery smile. "Sorry."

"Don't be. I suspect you needed that more than you realized. A word of advice?" Cass nodded. "Know that Rebecca can handle you like this. She doesn't always need you to be strong. I know she's your, ahem, Mistress at times. But let her be there when you need her emotionally as well. She's much stronger than we sometimes give her credit for. And she's been through quite a bit in her life. Learn from her. Lean on her."

"Yes, ma'am."

Willamena rolled her eyes at the term. She always hated how old it made her feel no matter how silly it was. "Do you need to talk some more? I could push back my next appointment."

"Nah, I'm good. I think. Thank you."

"Anytime, dear."

"Hey, Aunt Wills?" Cass was most likely going to regret this, but she had to know. Aunt Wills was an amazing woman with the patience of a saint. She proved that by listening to Cass spout obscenities and insecurities during her downtime. "Why aren't you seeing anyone?"

"Who says I'm not?" Willamena winked at a dumbfounded Cass. "Goodbye, Cass. My love to Rebecca."

With that, the connection was broken. Oh, Cass was so going to grill Rebecca on this one. But first things first. She took out her phone. After a quick search, she found the place Connor mentioned Rand being at. Her thumb hovered over the green call button for a long time before finally getting the nerve to press it. She made the appointment she had been avoiding, feeling a slight pressure leaving her chest.

The next call was a little more difficult. Despite what Aunt Wills had disclosed, Cass was nervous about Rebecca's response to her call. As the line rang Cass's doubt grew. Perhaps she should have given Rebecca more time to forgive Cass's damn idiocy.

"Hi, baby."

Taken aback by Rebecca's sweet greeting, Cass faltered. "Um, hi. Am I interrupting anything?"

"No, I just finished the meeting. It was a waste of time, so I'm having an iced coffee to make it up to myself."

Cass smiled picturing Rebecca at her favorite coffee shop. She'd be sitting by a window with the sunlight filtering in, making her blonde hair shine.

"Cassidy?"

"Oh, sorry, babe. Was just picturing you." Cass suddenly wanted a paintbrush in her hand to capture the scene in her head. Even more, she wanted Rebecca home and in her arms. "Rebecca?"

"Still here."

"Are you, um, coming home tonight?" She heard Rebecca sigh softly and Cass's pulse spiked. *Please say yes. Please say yes.*

"Yes, baby. You've been frustrating lately, but that doesn't mean I want to leave you."

"'Kay. I'm really sorry about my attitude."

"I know. And I know that you've been stressed out. This thing with Miranda came out at the worst possible time when you're already under pressure with the gallery opening."

"That's not an excuse." The background noise on Rebecca's end changed from soft music and muted talking to traffic. *I wonder where she's going now.*

"I'm not making excuses for you, Cassidy. I'm reminding myself what kind of toll this is taking on you."

The beep of Rebecca's Mercedes signaled she was now at her car. *You can't know the answers until you ask the questions.* "Where are you headed now?" Cass asked as nonchalantly as she could.

Rebecca laughed quietly. "I'm coming home, Cassidy. I'm done for the day if you want to spend some time together."

"Yes!" Okay, that was quite enthusiastic, but Cass didn't care. "I was thinking about making you dinner."

"Oh! That's—I thought I would pick up some take-out and we can just relax. Maybe watch some movies?"

Cass laughed heartily. "I'm that bad, huh?"

"Only at cooking, babe."

Oh, that flirtatious tone always got Cass's juices flowing. Literally. "Take-out and movies sound perfect."

"Thought so. Chinese okay?"

Cass heard the smile in Rebecca's voice and it made her happy. "Anything you want, babe."

THE COFFEE TABLE was littered with containers filled with all of Cassidy's favorites. The couple propped themselves on the couch, Rebecca with her legs tucked under her, Cassidy had her socked feet propped up on the table.

"Must you have your feet next to the food?"

"I'm not touching it." Cass playfully wiggled her toes closer to the lo mein.

"You're such a child," Rebecca laughed.

"You weren't saying that an hour ago." Cass waggled her eyebrows suggestively and stuffed half an egg roll in her mouth. She didn't care one iota that it wasn't hot and fresh anymore. When Rebecca had arrived home, need overtook them both. Food was forgotten. Miranda was forgotten. Once again, all that existed was the two of them. It was fast and furious, but it was also loving. Cass allowed herself to submit and give all to Mistress and it felt amazing to let go. That burden she had been holding for the past couple of weeks lightened even more.

"Hmm, as I recall, you were saying a lot of "yes, ma'am's" an hour ago." Rebecca winked at her lover. She loved seeing this relaxed side of Cassidy again. She wasn't foolish enough to think the issues were resolved or that there wouldn't be more disagreements between them. Life wasn't perfect. As long as they could work through them together, things would be okay.

"You got me there, Mistress." Cass bumped Rebecca on the shoulder and fed her a mouthful of noodles. "Think we could talk a little instead of watching a movie?"

"Of course." Rebecca had been waiting for this moment. She had sensed a change in Cassidy from the moment Cassidy called her.

"So, I, uh, called the hospital where Rand will be at. I'm going to talk to her. You know, closure and all."

Rebecca raised her brows. "You talked to Aunt Wills, didn't you?"

Cass shrugged. "Yeah. I should have talked to you…"

"Cassidy, it doesn't matter who you talk to as long as you're talking." Rebecca put her hand over Cassidy's. "And as long as you know I'm here and can handle it."

"I think I understand that a little more now. Aunt Wills basically told me to let your experiences guide me." She turned her hand over and linked her fingers with Rebecca's. "I'm scared, Becca."

"Of what, baby?"

"My anger towards her. Hating her for the rest of my life." She looked over at Rebecca. "Do you still hate Samantha?"

Rebecca took a moment to think about her answer, then shook her head. "No. I learned long ago that holding onto that hate was hurting me as much as holding on to that guilt was. For some reason, the hate was easier to let go. Maybe that's because she died, I don't know."

"I don't want her to be dead. Rand, I mean. But a few days of this shit and I turned into a dick. I can't do that to you or myself for the rest of our lives, babe. No more dickery. That's what your aunt called it," Cass smirked.

Rebecca laughed. "She did not!" Cassidy nodded emphatically. "She's crazy. Don't you dare tell her I said that!" Rebecca laid her head on Cassidy's shoulder. "I think going to talk to Miranda will be good for you. Hard, but good."

"What would you say to Samantha if you had the chance?"

"Nothing." There was no hesitation this time. "I think the most honest she ever was with me was the night she almost killed me. I defied her, and she wanted to control me. Completely. If I wanted to understand her mindset, I could ask my aunt. But there's nothing more I need from her."

Cass contemplated that as she popped a dumpling in her mouth. "Think Rand will tell me why?"

"I think she'll try to manipulate you," Rebecca answered honestly. "She'll blame everyone but herself. Don't go in there thinking she'll give you all the answers you'll need, Cassidy."

"Why should I go then?"

Rebecca turned just in time to see Cassidy eat another dumpling. Her seventh one, but who's counting? Certainly not Cassidy when it came to calories. Lucky. "You go, not to hear what she has to say, baby, but to say what *you* need to say."

"Will you go with me?"

Rebecca smiled, feathering Cassidy's bangs off her face. "If that's what you want. Would you like me to kick her ass, too?"

"Oh man! I would ask Eve for a loan to see that!" Cass laughed so hard she nearly choked on her dumpling.

"Make sure you save enough for my bail, *darling*."

Cass crossed her heart in a silent promise as she ate more food. She caught Rebecca looking at her funny. "Wha?" she asked with a full mouth.

"You are such a bottomless pit!" Rebecca lifted Cassidy's tank top revealing her six pack. "Seriously, where do you put it?"

Cass tapped her thighs. "Goes down my legs. I can eat so much because I'm tall." She topped off her ridiculous statement with a cheeky grin.

"Oh my God! You're insane!" Rebecca fell back on the couch, laughing hysterically.

Cass's hand froze reaching for more food. "Insane? Did you just call me insane?" Cass grabbed Rebecca's ankles and pulled her towards her, causing a shriek from her girlfriend. "Oh, no, no, no. What would Aunt Wills say? You're going to have to apologize for that," she said as she crawled on top of a still laughing Rebecca.

"Not a chance, weirdo."

Cass tsked. "Weirdo? You know what that deserves, right?"

Rebecca's eyes widened. "No! I'm sorry, Cassidy! Truly!"

"Nope. You had your opportunity, sweetheart. You must now face the consequences."

"Please don't, Cassidy. I'm begging you!"

"Mmm, I like it when you beg. But it's not going to help you this time."

"Cassidy!"

Cass began tickling Rebecca relentlessly. God, she loved the sound of that laughter. Whatever was wrong in the world could be fixed by the musicality of Rebecca's laughter.

"Bet you're sorry you called me names now." Cass brought her mouth into the action by gleefully nibbling on Rebecca's neck. Oh yeah, she knew all of Rebecca's spots. The ones that turned her on and the ones that tickled her.

"Please!" Rebecca panted between giggles. "I have to pee!"

Cass immediately let up which turned out to be a huge mistake. Before she knew what happened, Rebecca had turned the tables on her. *She* was on her back and Rebecca was straddling her waist.

"You lied!" *And I'm not minding it one single bit.* Cass lifted her hips slightly.

"Slow down there, cowgirl. I didn't lie. What do you say to cleaning this stuff up and going to bed?"

"Can we resume this position when we do?"

Rebecca smiled down at Cassidy. "No. I want you to make love to me. In order to do that, you need to be on top." She leaned down, her lips close to Cassidy's ear. "And when I say make love, I mean slowly, thoroughly, and more than once."

Cass's entire body shuddered with pleasure. It was on the tip of her tongue to say "yes, Mistress" but she instinctively knew that Mistress was not here now. "My pleasure, baby."

"It'll definitely be mine." Rebecca gave Cassidy a satisfied smile. When she made a move to stand up, Cassidy caught her around the waist.

"Are you really selling your home?"

Rebecca chuckled. "You'd think a psychiatrist would be better at keeping secrets." She kissed Cassidy gently. "*This* is my home, Cassidy."

"I can sell, too. We can buy something…"

Rebecca kissed her girlfriend again to shut her up. "I like it here. Your studio is here. Your gym. The mermaid," she smirked as she referred to the mural on the living room wall. The mermaid which now exhibited Rebecca's face. "You've even given me my own space. It's perfect."

"You're perfect," Cass said dreamily. "Why didn't you tell me? Was I being that much of a dick?"

"I wanted to surprise you. Remind me to thank my aunt, by the way."

Cass smiled. "Don't be too hard on her. She was pretty upset when she found out I didn't know already. She even said," Cass motioned for Rebecca to come closer. When she did, Cass whispered dramatically, "*Crap*!"

Rebecca snorted. "Dickery and crap. You're influencing my very proper aunt, dear." She pushed herself off Cassidy and began closing the containers that still held food.

"Me! Ha!" Cass helped by collecting empty containers. "Oh, and another thing, why didn't you tell me she was seeing someone?"

Cass collided with Rebecca's back when the smaller woman stopped. "She's what?"

Cass flicked a piece of rice off Rebecca's chest. "Uh, seeing someone? I assumed you would know who."

"No, I don't. But I'm calling her tomorrow to find out."

"Aww, man! Now she's going to know I blabbed!"

"Serves her right for blabbing about my surprise for you."

Chapter Twenty
REBECCA & CASS

Closure

"Do you want me to go in there with you?" Rebecca unnecessarily smoothed Cassidy's collar. Yes, she was being overprotective, but she was concerned about how talking to Miranda was going to affect Cassidy. Rebecca had dealt with women like Miranda many times over the years, starting with Samantha. But this entire situation was testing Cassidy's faith in humanity.

"I do. But I think I should do this myself." Cass shrugged. "Gotta learn sometime, right?"

"I'd rather you stay the sweet, happy-go-lucky woman I fell in love with."

Cass smiled down at her girlfriend. "I'm always happy when I'm with you." She dipped her head and gave Rebecca a quick kiss. "Let me get this over with. I still owe Eve a couple of canvases."

"I'll be right here if you need me."

"Good thing since I always need you." Cass winked saucily. Of course, her good-natured bravado was all an act. She was aware that Rebecca knew that as well. Cass silently thanked her for not calling her on it. She squared her shoulders and nodded at the guard standing at the door of the room she would be talking to Rand in. *Here goes nothing.*

Rebecca watched the door close behind Cassidy and sighed. She had spent many, many years learning how to keep her emotions in check. With Cassidy, all that learning flew out the damn window. *If Miranda hurts Cassidy any more than she already has, there would be hell to pay.* She eyed the guard. *Manipulation isn't hard. Especially if you found a gullible enough victim.*

CASS SAT IN the uncomfortable metal chair and waited. Her knee bounced in rhythm to some random song she had in her head. It kept her from overthinking what she was going to say. Rebecca had told her to speak from the heart. She just didn't know if her heart was involved any longer when it came to Rand.

"I knew you'd come to see me!"

Cass looked up as Rand came through the door, a guard at her side. She couldn't comprehend this sight of Rand. White scrubs, white slip-on shoes were a sharp contrast to her fiery red hair. The paleness of her skin was highlighted by the lack of makeup. Which was weird in itself. Cass couldn't remember the last time she saw Rand without makeup. Cass shook herself. She wasn't ready to have compassion for the woman in front of her.

"I'm not here to *see* you, Rand. I'm here for closure."

"I told them you would be here," Rand continued as though Cass never spoke. "You know me being here is a mistake, right? He forced me here." She let out a short laugh. "He abuses me and I'm the one…"

"Stop! I know exactly what happened, Rand. I know what you've done to him. I saw the pictures."

Rand's eyes widened slightly before they turned cold. "He made me do that to him. Now I know why. He…"

"You can't stop lying, can you?" Cass held up her hand, cutting off Rand's response. "I didn't come here to listen to you. For once, you're going to listen to me. I've been wracking my brain trying to figure out what happened with you. Recently, I was reminded of the time you stood up to your parents for me. At the time, I thought it was genuine. Even yesterday I thought it was the *last* genuine thing you did for me. But now?" Cass shook her head. "Now I think it was all selfish. It wasn't me you were standing up for. It was you. I did something you couldn't do yourself."

Rand scoffed. "You think I'm gay?"

"Yeah, I do. And, while I'm no professional, I'm pretty sure you have some sort of personality disorder. Maybe they'll figure that out while you're here. I'm almost hoping that's the case, Rand, because I don't want to hate you." Cass leaned her elbows on the wobbly table that separated them. "The other night when you insisted on reminiscing, I realized that you and I have very different memories about the past. I see who you are and what you were doing very clearly now. You used me. You came to me every time you had a problem. And if there wasn't one, you would make one up. Maybe it helped you pretend I was your girlfriend, I don't know. Even after you hooked up with Connor, it was still me you came to for help. Hell, maybe you did what you did to him because he wasn't who you wanted to be with. If so, that's even shittier, Rand. How dare you punish someone else for your inability to be true to yourself."

Cass faltered slightly when she saw Rand's bottom lip quiver. And despite the hateful look on her face, there were tears threatening to fall. Cass didn't even know if she was on the right track. Rand never confirmed she was a lesbian. On the other hand, she didn't deny it either. Either way, nothing excused her behavior with Connor.

Cass sighed wearily.

"Like I said, I don't want to hate you, Rand. So, I'm saying goodbye."

Rand sat back in her chair with a scowl. "Fine. Throw away years of friendship, and what I *know* you feel for me."

"See? That's where you mess up. I don't have those feelings for you. I never did. Why do you think I couldn't sleep with you? There wasn't anything there like that. And I certainly didn't like being used as some token lesbian experience."

"You couldn't sleep with me because you felt too much," Rand countered defiantly. "I've seen you with other women, Cass. Don't forget that. I see how you kick them to the curb when they try to get too close. You were afraid of your feelings for me."

Cass shook her head. *Delusional.* She found herself feeling sorry for Rand, convinced now that there was a deeper reason for her delusions. "You're wrong on so many levels. And if that is what you think I did, you obviously weren't paying attention. Most of those women were looking for one thing only. The ones that stayed longer thought they could change. Not me, themselves. But mostly, the chemistry was never right. I never "kicked them to the curb," Rand. It wasn't until recently that I found someone I clicked with on all cylinders." A lightbulb went off in Cass's head. "Which is why this all started with you, isn't it? You saw me with Rebecca and you couldn't handle it."

"She doesn't deserve you." Rand folded her arms in front of her. "You're such a fucking hypocrite. You judged me when you found out about my membership at that stupid club. Turns out, you're *fucking* the owner! I know she's Mistress. You should have told me you were into that stuff. I could show you things if you would just submit to me."

Cass laughed mirthlessly. Pity or not, Cass had her limits. "Like you did Connor? No thanks. Besides, there's not a damned thing you could teach me that *my* Mistress hasn't taught me. Extensively. You are right about one thing, though. I judged you. I apologize for that."

When Rand reached out to touch her hands, Cass sat back. The last thing Rand needed was false hope. Of course, now she was getting a scathing look.

"I thought you were saying goodbye," Rand spat out.

"I am," Cass said softly. "I truly hope you get the help you need in here. I hope you come to terms with who you are." She stood.

"Wait! You're all I have left! My parents won't understand this, and they'll leave me just like everyone else. You can't leave me, too!"

"Your parents love you, Rand. Yeah, they freaked a bit when I came out, but they got over it. Maybe this will be a little harder to understand, but you're their child. They'll stand by you." Cass looked Rand in the eye, noticing how glassy they were. They must have started her on meds. "I can't be here for you because of what you did. You tried to manipulate me using a very *real* issue for the woman I love. You vandalized her house, and you did the unthinkable to Connor. He didn't deserve that."

Say what you need to say. Cass received that advice from two extremely smart women. She admitted she was skeptical that she would feel any different. They were right. Despite the guilt trip Rand just tried to lay on her, Cass didn't owe her a damn thing. She could walk out of here with a clear conscience. That's exactly what she did.

REBECCA STOPPED PACING the moment she heard the door open. With a critical, but loving, eye she studied her lover. No tears, no frown. In fact, Cassidy was smiling at her.

"I take it things went well?" she asked, making her way to Cassidy.

Cass opened her arms, readily accepting Rebecca's hug. "As well as it could. I'm good, baby. You ready to get out of here?"

Rebecca looked up at Cassidy. One thing she loved about Cassidy was her inability to lie. It was because of that she knew Cassidy was telling the truth now. She was good.

"Give me a minute?"

"Whoa, whoa, whoa." Cass tightened her arms around Rebecca when she moved towards the door. "Are you going in there to kick her ass? Because as much as I'd like to see that, I really do think she has issues this place may be able to help her with."

Rebecca reached up to cup Cassidy's face. "You truly are the sweetest person I know. I'm not going to touch her, baby. But there are things I need to say myself."

"Oh." Cass frowned at her stupidity. Rebecca was so good at keeping her cool that Cass could sometimes forget how much this situation affected her. "Right. I should have thought of that."

"Don't be silly. I'll be right back."

"Babe, I don't think they'll…"

"Ms. Cuinn?" The first guard Cass encountered looked over his shoulder. "No more than five minutes. I could get fired for this."

"I only need one."

Cass shook her head as Rebecca disappeared through the door giving the guard a smile that could charm the pants off anyone. It sure as hell worked on her. Every. Single. Day.

"Why do I have to stay in here? I want to go back to my room."

"Sit down."

"But…"

"This would go faster if you just listen to him, Miranda."

Miranda turned and scowled at her visitor. "I don't want to talk to you."

"That's fine because I don't particularly care about what you have to say." Rebecca sat in the metal chair in her Mistress pose. Straight back, crossed ankles tucked beneath the chair, and hands clasped in her lap. "This is about your little threat. You should know that I couldn't care less who knows who I am. Not even Beverly and Russell. Neither does Cassidy. So, if you were planning on using that to manipulate Cassidy in some way, you can forget it."

"You don't deserve her," Miranda snarled.

"Perhaps. But for some reason, she loves me as much as I love her. Which is why I will not allow you to hurt her again. She seems to think you can get help in here. Make sure you do." Rebecca leaned forward slightly and dropped her voice to a menacing whisper. "Because if you try to make things difficult for Cassidy when you get out of here, you will have to deal with me. And I'm not nearly as sweet as Cassidy is."

She stood, smoothing the front of her black slacks. There was a part of her that felt sorry for Miranda. But the part of her that was protective of Cassidy? That part didn't care one-bit what Miranda was suffering from. Perhaps that was callous of her. Yet, after everything she had endured from Samantha, even a mental illness didn't make hurting someone else acceptable.

"Be well, Miranda."

Rebecca walked out of the room, leaving behind Miranda's angry words. She didn't listen. There was a time when all she *could* hear were the angry words. Those times were over. Rebecca smiled at Cassidy when she came into view.

Cass peered over Rebecca's shoulder and watched as the guard escorted a sullen Rand out of the room.

"Okay?" she asked.

"Mmhmm. Ready to go home?"

"Totally."

Chapter Twenty-One
REBECCA & CASS

The Opening

"BABE! YOU'RE GOING to wear a hole in the floor!"

Cass glanced at the closed bathroom door. *How the hell does she know I'm pacing?* "I'm nervous!" Cass called back.

Rebecca opened the door and stopped short. Nervous or not, her girlfriend looked fucking hot! Cassidy continued to pace, her pale pink shirt unbuttoned and flowing open with each turn. God, Rebecca loved that Cassidy never wore a bra. The tight black jeans had Rebecca wondering if Cassidy would be packing tonight. She hoped so. If Rebecca had to spend the entire night lusting after her, she didn't want any delays when they got home. She caught Cassidy's arm.

"I know you're nervous, baby. But everything is going to be fine."

"Huh?" As it happened so often, all of Cass's blood flowed to southern regions of her anatomy when she got a vision of Rebecca.

Thoughts disappeared rapidly seeing Rebecca in her dress that she couldn't even remember what she was nervous about. Fuck. That dress. It took all of Cass's strength to *stop* herself from tearing it off Rebecca right here and now. The pale pink matched her shirt, but that was where any similarities ended. Where Cass was androgynously dressed, Rebecca was pure femininity. Though she was clueless about fashion, she knew that the tight, knee-length dress fit Rebecca like a glove. She got a drool-inducing peek at Rebecca's cleavage due to a very nice cut out that went from neck to belly button. And if Rebecca's bare shoulders were anything to go by, Cass was pretty sure the dress was backless. *Jesus. She's trying to kill me.*

Rebecca smirked. She knew Cassidy and knew exactly what was going on in her head. She loved that she could have that effect on her. "I said everything is going to be fine."

Somehow, Cass's brain caught up with the conversation. "But people are going to see these paintings. Judge them."

"Babe, people see your murals every day. What's the difference?"

"The difference is, these are artsy people who know what they're looking at!"

"And they're going to love it."

"How can you be so sure?"

"Because I've seen your work, baby. You're talented. And Eve saw that, too. You wouldn't be her featured artist if she didn't."

Cass threw back her head and groaned. "You had to remind me."

"Hey, look at me."

"I can't."

"Why?"

"Because I want to fuck you when I look at you and I don't think we have time for that."

Cassidy's candid answer caused a jolt of electric arousal in Rebecca's body. And it was such a Cassidy answer at a time when they were having a serious conversation that it made Rebecca laugh.

"Well, how do you think I feel with you walking around with your shirt open and your tits on display?"

Cass looked down at her small breasts. "These aren't tits." She then ran a finger down Rebecca's cleavage. "*These* are tits."

Rebecca grabbed Cassidy's hand. "Don't do that," she breathed, then cleared her throat. *Get back on track, Rebecca.* "Cassidy, whatever the response is tonight, know that I'm proud of you. I'm proud to stand by your side, to be your girlfriend, to love you."

Cass's eyes left Rebecca's cleavage and softened. It was exactly what she needed to hear. She had never worried before if someone liked her work. She didn't do it for anyone else but herself. This was just like that. And if Rebecca was proud no matter what, that's all Cass needed.

"Thank you," she said softly. "Wanna stay home and make love all night?"

"Tempting." Rebecca opened Cassidy's shirt and cupped her small breasts with a sigh. "But since you're the artist of the night, we should go. Besides your parents and our friends will be there."

"Then you're gonna have to stop pinching my nipples, babe. If you don't, I can't be responsible for how late we'll be." She was a bit disappointed when Rebecca began buttoning Cass's shirt. "Hunter is bringing Ellie, right?" she asked trying to get her mind on literally anything else.

"Yes. Tonight just might be the night for them," Rebecca winked.

"Ugh. Come on, babe! I was trying to get my mind *off* of sex! Now I'm thinking about Hunter and Ellie doing it!"

Rebecca raised a brow. "Excuse me?"

"Don't you raise your brow at me! It's your fault I now have that image in my head!" She turned away to finish getting ready and yelped when Rebecca smacked her ass hard. She hid her smile. *Oh, yeah. Tonight is going to be fun.*

"This is incredible." Bev looked around in awe at all her daughter's art surrounding her. She squeezed her husband's arm. "Why didn't I pay attention to how good she was?"

"Neither of us did, dear. We wanted more for her." Russ shook his head. "No, we wanted what *we* wanted for her. I wanted her to follow in my footsteps." He took in every nuance of one of Cass's paintings. He knew absolutely nothing about art, but even a newbie like him could see the brilliance. And not because his daughter did it.

"Hey, guys." After some prodding from Rebecca, Cass was finally making her way over to her parents. Of course, she appreciated them being there, but she also knew how they felt about her "hobby."

"Cass!" Bev enveloped her daughter in a fierce hug. "You are amazing! I can't believe I've wasted the opportunity to have Cass Giles originals hanging in my home."

Cass let out a relieved chuckle. "There's still time."

"Damn right there is," Russ huffed. "But we're paying for it like everyone else here."

"Nah, I'll…"

"Nope," Russ interrupted. "We weren't supportive before, so we're going to support you now by paying full price."

"That's not necessary, dad, but I appreciate the sentiment. Listen, all I need from you guys is acknowledgment that this is more than a hobby and it's all good."

"You deserve more than that, dear, but you have our acknowledgment and support. We're so proud of you."

"Thanks, mom."

"Now, where's that lady of yours?"

"She's mingling. Getting the lay of the land." Cass decided not to confront her mom about her little visit. It served no purpose except causing her mom stress. After everything that had happened recently, drama was the last thing Cass needed. Especially tonight.

"Well, make sure we get to see her tonight, okay? In the meantime, we're going to mingle as well. We want to see everything."

Cass smiled. "G'wan." She watched for a bit while her parents stood at each painting for a good amount of time. She could admit that it felt good. She never needed her parents' validation, but it certainly didn't hurt having it.

She made her way to her girlfriend who was studying one of Cass's paintings. Cass had forgotten that this was truly the first time Rebecca had been able to look at Cass's work. Of course, if Rebecca had wanted to watch her paint, Cass would have allowed it. But she had said she wanted the experience of seeing them in the gallery the way everyone else was going to.

"Can you believe this place? When Eve Sumptor opens a gallery, she *opens* a gallery." Cass wrapped her arms around Rebecca's waist and glanced around. The elegant woman she spoke of was across the room with her business partner Lainey who Cass finally had the opportunity to meet. The two were standing close together, laughing softly, completely focused on each other. Their husbands were nearby, talking amiably, with Eve's husband eyeing them surreptitiously. Interesting. She wondered if he knew his wife and Lainey were in love with each other. Did Rebecca know? She shrugged it off and turned her attention back to the woman she loved.

"Hmm?" Rebecca snapped out of her art induced trance and looked up at her girlfriend. "Sorry, baby. I was just admiring your work."

"No need to apologize for that," Cass grinned.

Rebecca returned the smile before returning her gaze to the painting. The colors were brilliant reds, oranges, and blues. At first glance, you would think it was an abstract. But once you got closer, you could see the couple holding hands. Perspective made them look far away, yet they became the complete focus of the painting. Just looking at it gave Rebecca a sense of hope and love.

"I'm so glad I waited to see these in the way they were meant to be seen," Rebecca murmured softly.

"All because of you, baby."

Rebecca bit her lip. They have had this argument time and time again.

No matter how many times she told Cass she had nothing to do with getting her in the gallery, Cass would continually give Rebecca credit.

"How do you do it?" she asked instead of getting into that discussion again. "You've been so stressed with everything that has been going on with Miranda and getting ready for tonight. None of that shows in your work. It's all very inspiring."

Cass shrugged modestly. "I just paint what I see. What I feel when I'm with you."

Rebecca looked up at Cassidy to thank her for the beautiful words, but Cassidy's eyes were glancing at the people surrounding them. These were words said to impress Rebecca, but words from the heart.

"I look around me," Cass continued, oblivious to Rebecca's stare. "And I see all of these things keeping people apart. Fear," she said as she remembered how Hunter had left already because of the fear she wasn't good enough for Ellie. "Consequences." Her eyes landed on Eve and Lainey. "So many things fighting against true happiness. I could have let Rand tear us apart. Hell, I almost did with my damn mood. But when I'm with you, when you tell me you love me, or look me in the eyes, or when we make love, this is the way I see the world."

Rebecca turned in Cassidy's arms, wrapping her own around Cassidy's neck. "I love you."

Cass dipped her head, kissing Rebecca lightly on the lips. "I love you, too, baby." She loved this feeling right here. Rebecca in her arms, smiling up at her, happy. There were two months before Rebecca came back to her when she didn't think a night like this would be possible. Normally, Cass laughs at herself when she thought this way. She had known Rebecca for less than two days when she walked away. It should have been absurd to have been so affected. But the impact Rebecca had made on Cass had been far too great to ignore.

"Ahem." Eve smiled at them both. "I apologize for interrupting this beautiful moment. However, there are people waiting to meet the artist."

"Do I have to?" Cass asked with a bit of whine. Talking to Rebecca about her work was fine. Talking to strangers, not so much. She'd much rather stay in the background, quietly eavesdropping on what people are saying about her work.

"One of the perks," Eve winked. "Rebecca is welcome to come with you. Though it looks like she has no choice with the way you're gripping her hand."

Cass automatically relaxed her grip, apologizing softly. "See what you got me into?" she asked playfully.

Eve stopped in her tracks and turned back to Cass. "Is that what you think? That my friendship with Rebecca is what got you this gig?" Cass shuffled her feet a bit and shrugged. "Cass, I adore Rebecca. I respect her opinion. But there is no way I would select someone as the featured artist for the grand opening of Sumptor Galleries in LA as a favor. And I never take recommendations without doing my own due diligence. I've seen your work all around the city. It speaks for itself. And what you've given me for tonight exceeded expectations. Rebecca may have introduced me to your work, but you got yourself into this mess." She winked again in that true Eve fashion and walked away fully expecting to be followed.

Rebecca did the only thing that came to mind after hearing Eve's little speech. "Told ya." She stuck her tongue out and sashayed away.

Cass laughed at her "dignified" girlfriend and took off after her. She could do this. Hell, with Rebecca by her side, she was pretty sure she could do anything.

TONIGHT HAD BEEN amazing. Cassidy's work was a hit. And Cassidy herself charmed everyone clamoring to meet her. The only hiccup was a bit of drama between Hunter and Ellie that Rebecca hoped was being resolved. But her current worry was how uncharacteristically quiet Cassidy was being on their drive home. Rebecca had thought she would be excited, talking a mile a minute about her experience tonight. There was nothing but silence. Rebecca allowed the silence, opting to try to get Cassidy to open up when they got home.

As she turned into their driveway, she stole a glance at Cassidy. It wasn't necessarily sadness or stress in her features, but more of a daze. Rebecca began to wonder if everything that happened tonight was just now hitting Cassidy. She had been so calm and collected during the showing that Rebecca had been incredibly proud. Was Cassidy finally letting it all sink in?

"Baby? We're home," Rebecca said softly as to not startle Cassidy.

"'Kay."

It was like watching Cassidy rely on muscle memory to get her inside. Once the door was closed behind them, Rebecca stripped a dazed Cassidy of her jacket and led her to the couch. With a small push, Cassidy fell back on the sofa which seemed to jar her brain loose. Or at least her tongue.

"They liked my paintings," Cass said, her voice filled with awe. "Did you see them, baby? They bought my stuff. Not just prints, but the originals."

"Mmhmm. Lift."

Cass absently lifted her hips, her mind completely consumed with the events of the night. "They wanted to meet me. Some of them even knew me from my murals!"

"I know, baby. It was fantastic." Rebecca smiled at Cassidy. The younger woman was so cute when she was awestruck. And entirely oblivious to the fact that she and Rebecca were both naked. Well, except for Cassidy's "little friend."

"I mean, it was like I had fans! I never imagined I would... whoa!" Cass's hands came up, making contact with Rebecca's smooth, velvety soft, very naked skin. It took only a nanosecond to realize that she was also naked and inside Rebecca who was rocking her hips slowly. "How did you get my pants off?"

Rebecca smirked. "I asked you to lift."

"I've been out of it, haven't I? Sorry." Cass's hips began to move in time with Rebecca's. As usual, it didn't take her long to catch up and be ready to perform. Hell, just seeing Rebecca's naked tits swaying in her face was almost enough to set her off.

"Don't be. You were very cute."

"Ugh, don't call me cute when you're riding me, babe. I wanna be sexy."

Rebecca kissed Cassidy passionately. "You are sexy. And I'm very proud of you. Now fuck me."

The truth was, seeing Cassidy being a commanding force tonight had aroused Rebecca to the point of being painful. She had spent the entire night watching people wanting Cassidy's attention—including women who were more interested in the artist than the art. Cassidy handled everything with dignity and a touch of authority that melted Rebecca. Literally, since she was incredibly wet by the time they left. Unfortunately, Cassidy spent the entire car ride in a trance and Rebecca couldn't even get a preview of things to come. Now they were alone, and Cassidy was all hers.

Cass was surprised by Rebecca's obvious need. What had she missed since they left the gallery? Then she remembered the way Rebecca had looked at her while other people surrounded them. She remembered how Rebecca would touch her every chance she got. Oh, fuck yeah, she remembered that. A brush against her breast. A quick slap on the ass. Oh, and that delicious, hidden grab of the dildo trapped in her pants. Cass had wanted to drag Rebecca to some secluded corner of the gallery and fuck her brains out right then and there. That's when the buying frenzy began, and it felt like Cass was pulled in a million different directions, none of them towards the woman she loved.

"Now *this* is the kind of opening I could get behind every night," Cass panted and squeezed Rebecca's ass. "Mmm, behind. Can we do that next? Please?"

Rebecca laughed, then moaned when Cassidy's finger played with the area she wanted. "All yours, baby. Any time."

"God, I love you." Cass's hips bucked up as Rebecca pushed herself down on the dildo. The sound of being inside Rebecca's wet pussy had to be one of her favorite sounds ever. Then Rebecca let out a breathy sigh, and that became Cass's favorite. *Heaven.*

"*I love you.*" Rebecca's hands clenched in Cassidy's hair, her hips pumping faster. "Do you have any idea how much I wanted to fuck you at the gallery? If only I were an exhibitionist."

Cass's eyes widened and her pussy clenched. "In front of everyone?"

"Especially the bitches who thought they could get your attention. Imagine their faces if they could see you thrusting inside of me."

"Jesus. I don't even know who you're talking about, but I'm about to fucking explode, baby!" Cass used her considerable leg strength to push them both up from the couch. Rebecca's legs immediately wrapped around her waist, squeezing to keep Cass inside her. Not that it was necessary. Cass wasn't going anywhere until Rebecca shattered for her. She carried Rebecca to the wall that started it all with the mermaid. Cass's siren.

Rebecca gasped when her back hit the cold wall. She loved it when Cass got like this. Aggression used to scare her. With Cass, it made her feel as powerful as she did vulnerable. Such a heady sensation.

"Hang on to me, Becca." Rebecca obeyed, her hands locking behind Cass's neck as tight as her legs were around her waist. Cass's hands went to the wall for support, and she thrust upwards with all her might. If Rebecca wanted to be fucked, Cass was going to give her exactly that.

"Harder!" Rebecca begged.

Cass braced her feet, her calves and quads screaming with each plunge. The pain didn't stop her. Instead, it spurred her on as much as Rebecca's sharp sounds of pleasure did. When Rebecca's nails dug into her neck, Cass knew Rebecca was there. Thank fuck because there was no holding back her orgasm at this point.

"Come for me, Rebecca! Give it to me! Come on, baby, let me feel it!"

"Oh, fuck!" Rebecca's head whipped back, narrowly missing the wall behind her. "Cassidy! I'm coming!"

One last, hard thrust and Cass was right there with her. Both women cried out with pent-up ecstasy. For a moment, Cass's calves locked up in that position, but that was totally fine with her. It kept her buried deep inside Rebecca as she erupted around Cass. The feeling of Rebecca's essence running down Cass's leg was sexy as fuck.

"Holy shit!" Cass kept Rebecca locked around her but lowered them both to the floor. "Fucking amazing."

"Agreed," Rebecca managed. "Want to do it again?"

"Fuck yeah, I do. But you may need to massage a few cramps out of my legs first."

Rebecca snickered. "I can do that. We could also go to the bed where it's much easier to maneuver."

"We could," Cass considered, stroking an invisible beard.

Rebecca narrowed her eyes at her girlfriend. "What are you plotting?"

"Who me? Just thinking about how I want to get at your ass. Doggy style? Reverse cowgirl?"

Rebecca burst out laughing. "Well, I trust you to figure it out. Want some water?"

"Do we have any energy drinks? I'm going to need all I can get." She waggled her eyebrows at Rebecca who continued to laugh.

"I'll see what I can rustle up." She gingerly lifted herself off the dildo. *I'm going to feel that in the morning,* she thought with a naughty smile. "Be right back."

Cass flipped over to watch that sexy ass walk away, wincing when the dildo caught on the carpet. *Good thing I have more of these!* She smiled wickedly. *Maybe I can get a turn in with each of them.* Another thought filtered through her sex haze and her smile turned anticipatory. She hopped to her feet, grabbed her shirt, and made her way to the room she used as her studio.

"We only had chocolate milk, so that will have to…" Rebecca stared at the empty spot she had left Cassidy in. "Cassidy?"

"Hey, babe!" Cass called from her studio. "Could you come in here for a minute, please?"

"Now?" Rebecca said to herself. It *was* the only room they hadn't fucked in, yet. Cass was pretty particular about that space. Of course, it made Rebecca want to christen it even more, but she respected Cass's space. Maybe Cass was finally going to give her what she wanted. She pushed the partially opened door with her naked ass. "Here." She handed Cass her bottle of milk. "You're dressed."

Okay, dressed wasn't completely accurate. The shirt was open all the way and it didn't come close to covering Cass's ass. Nor did it cover the dildo that bounced slightly every time she moved.

"Thank you. I, uh, wanted to show you something."

"Does it involve me bending over one of these easels?"

Cass hesitated. As she looked between an empty easel and Rebecca, her mouth began to water. Interesting. For some reason, this room had been on the no-sex list. There was one thing in life that Cass was uptight about and that was her studio. Having Rebecca in here now, all naked and glowing from their earlier fuck, that was seriously going to change. *Hmm. I wonder what she would say to me painting her body.*

"Maybe after." Her voice quivered with expectation. "But right now, I wanted to show you a painting I did. One that wasn't for Eve. Or anyone else. Except you."

Rebecca lifted a brow in surprise. "Me?" Cassidy nodded gesturing towards a draped canvas. "What is it?" Rebecca asked excitedly. Whatever it was, she was going to love it.

Cass chuckled. "You have to take off the sheet, babe." She prodded Rebecca forward, taking the water out of Rebecca's hand and setting both their drinks on a nearby table.

Rebecca stood in front of the covered painting, a peculiar nervousness in her belly. She took the ends of the cover and slowly began to lift it. As the painting came into view, it took a minute for Rebecca's brain to register what she was seeing. It was a painting of Rebecca, standing in this room, looking at this painting. The only difference was "painted Rebecca" was fully clothed and Cassidy was behind her, on one knee, a small box in her hand. Rebecca turned to ask Cassidy about it. Her hand flew to her mouth in absolute shock when she found Cassidy kneeling, holding up a small box.

"Cassidy!"

"I can never find the words to accurately describe what I feel when I'm with you, Rebecca. That's why I rely on my brushes to do it for me." Cass cleared her throat and tried to keep her emotions in check. "I wish I knew how to tell you how much you mean to me. What you've brought to my life. God, Becca, if you could just feel what it does to me when you tell me you love me, you'd know how I've longed to do this since the day we met."

Cass faltered. So much for keeping her emotions in check. But she could see the tears in Rebecca's beautiful eyes and hoped they were the good kind. Damn, she wished she was better at this.

"I—there's so much to say. I wish I knew how to articulate."

Rebecca walked over to Cassidy—forgetting that she was naked—and placed a trembling finger over Cassidy's mouth.

"You've said it all with your actions, Cassidy. From day one you *showed* me what it's like to truly be loved." She dropped to her knees, bringing herself to Cassidy's level. "I don't need any other words."

They were both openly crying now. "How about five more? Will you marry me, Rebecca?"

Rebecca crushed her mouth to Cassidy's. "Yes!" she answered when she finally came up for air.

"Yes?"

"Yes!"

Cass let out an excited "whoop" and enveloped Rebecca in a mighty hug. Their bare breasts came in contact with each other and both women felt the jolt of arousal once again. But, before that…

She took Rebecca's left hand in hers and slipped the ring on her ring finger. It was a simple round pavé ring, but it suited Rebecca. Both were sophisticated, elegant, and beautiful. Cass looked deep into Rebecca's eyes.

"You're totally sure?"

Rebecca smiled. "Totally."

Cass grinned. "Good. Now, about that bending over an easel thing. Care to show me how that would work?"

Epilogue
REBECCA & CASS

The Beginning

A BLAST OF cool air hit Rebecca as she stepped into the gallery. She smiled at the collection of new "Cass Giles" that adorned the walls. Not even the passing of the months had diminished the interest in Cassidy's work. It kept her fiancée busy, but Rebecca couldn't complain. They were both happy. After the past couple of months, happiness was exactly what they needed.

"Hello, Rebecca."

Rebecca smiled at Eve. "I was surprised to get your call. I thought you had gone back to New York with Lainey already."

The mentioning of Lainey's name provoked a sad smile from Eve. "She had family matters to attend to and I had a few things here I needed to take care of. How is Ellie doing?"

The sudden change of topic told Rebecca that Eve was not willing to speak of the subject any longer. Instead, Rebecca turned her thoughts to Hunter's now wife. Not long after the gallery opening, Hunter was hit with a devastating blow when Ellie wound up in the hospital after being forced off the road. It was a scary time for the entire group who had become very close friends. Rebecca had spent countless girls' nights with Ellie, Patty, Ellie's daughter Jessie, and Ellie's best friend and her daughter Blaise and Piper. Nearly losing Ellie had been devastating to everyone, but none more so than Hunter.

"She's getting better every day. She's using her legs more, which is fantastic. The trial has been brutal, but with Hunter and Jessie by her side, I think she'll be okay."

"Along with the rest of you. Such a tight-knit group." Eve was interrupted briefly by her new curator.

"Excuse me, I'm sorry. Hello again, Ms. Cuinn." Lauren smiled brightly at the woman who recommended her for the job. "Mr. Riley is on the phone." Lauren's subtle German accent was charming.

"Tell him I'll call him back, please."

Lauren dutifully nodded and left as quietly as she arrived. As she watched the young woman disappear, Rebecca pondered the hint of resentment she detected in Eve's voice. They were as close as Eve could be with anyone (not named Lainey), but Rebecca was astute enough not to ask about it. She wished so badly that Eve could have everything she desired. The woman did so much for others and, yet, her own life—as perfect as it seemed—was a mess.

"You're part of that group, you know," Rebecca said softly.

There were many times when Eve was in town that she and Lainey were invited to hang out. Unfortunately, Eve wasn't the type to be in the company of that many people in an intimate setting. Perhaps people thought she was snobbish, but with the past Eve had, Rebecca didn't blame her for being an introvert. Hell, wasn't Rebecca the same way? She didn't have many friends. But those she had now have become some of the most important people in her life. Eve needed that support system in her life. If she would just allow it.

Eve eyed Rebecca with a smirk. "Out of curiosity, which group would I be in? As I understand it, couples are not allowed to be in the same group. Would I be with the women for girls' night, or would I be playing poker with the boys?"

Rebecca tilted her head. "Are you admitting you and Lainey are a couple?" She took a *very* big chance and caught Eve's arm before she could walk away. "I apologize, but you walked into that one. However, you do raise an interesting question. Ellie made the rule so we could talk about our significant others. But you don't seem to fit in the poker scenario."

"I assure you, I'm a very good poker player."

"Oh, I don't doubt that. You have the best poker face I have ever seen. I just don't think the guys would be able to function around you."

Eve surprised her by laughing. "What you're saying is I wouldn't fit anywhere. Sounds about right."

"That's not what I meant, Eve. Don't anger the Mistress."

Eve raised a brow. "You think you could get me to submit?"

Rebecca smiled at the challenge. She knew it was playful flirtation. She also knew there was only one person who could actually make Eve submit.

"I could. But…"

"Please don't finish that," Eve pleaded quietly.

"Eve, you deserve happiness."

"I didn't ask you here to discuss my problems. That's what I have your aunt for."

"Sometimes all you need is a friend to listen," Rebecca countered.

Eve sighed. "My issues are far beyond anyone's help, Rebecca. Perhaps even your aunt."

"I'm going to say one thing, and then I'll drop the subject." Though Eve rolled her eyes, she nodded. "I understand the consequences, but I also know how fleeting life can be. I spent many years with someone I shouldn't have been with and it nearly killed me."

"That's different. Adam doesn't hurt me," Eve clarified.

"Not physically. And I'm not saying this is Adam's fault," Rebecca said quickly before Eve could argue with her. "But not being with the person you're truly in love with kills your soul with each passing day. I was away from Cassidy for two months and it was incredibly painful. I can't imagine how you feel seeing Lainey every day, feeling as though you can't be with her."

"Rebecca, I appreciate what you're trying to do. And I'm happy that you're happy. But as we've discussed before, my situation is very different. Do I want to be with Lainey? Of course, I do. I missed my shot."

"I don't believe that. But," Rebecca continued, surrendering her argument. For now. "When you're ready to fight, I'll be here to support you."

"You are…"

"Stubborn?"

"Annoying." Eve winked. "Now, can I tell you why I asked you here?"

Since Rebecca knew she was getting no further with this topic, she nodded in agreement. Besides, she was curious as to why she was summoned to the gallery.

"You came to me months ago asking me to help you sell the club. I have sent you countless potential buyers and you've denied all of them. Do you really want to sell?"

Rebecca blinked. "I—um, yes?" The question caught her off-guard. So much had happened between the time she decided to sell and now. Miranda, the gallery opening, getting engaged, Ellie's accident, Hunter and Ellie's wedding, the trial. Selling the club was never a top priority. She still wanted to sell. Right? She lifted her hand to scratch her head and was startled when Eve caught it.

"Something you want to tell me?" Eve asked staring at the engagement ring.

"Oh!" Rebecca had forgotten that she and Cassidy had kept their engagement a secret. The night that Cassidy proposed to her was the best night of her life. Then they found out that Hunter and Ellie were having problems with Susan. After that, one thing after another kept happening and it never seemed like the right time to be ecstatically happy. Recently, things had settled down and Rebecca decided it was time to wear her ring. The thing she kept forgetting to do now was actually *tell* people. "Cassidy asked me to marry her." Rebecca smiled broadly, turning her hand this way and that to give Eve a better view.

"Congratulations!" She gave Rebecca a quick hug. "When did this happen?"

"Months ago," Rebecca laughed. "But…"

"But you're a good friend and you kept your happiness to yourself during challenging times," Eve guessed.

Rebecca lifted a shoulder. "There's that. And we were being selfish, wanting to keep it to ourselves for a while. A while just turned out to be much longer than we expected."

Eve chuckled. "Well, it's a beautiful ring. I'm happy for you and Cass. Is that why you're hesitant on selling?"

"Not hesitant, really. But with everything else, it sort of slipped my mind. Which is why I thought it would be best to let you handle it."

"Alright. Well, it hasn't slipped mine. I received an offer a few days ago. It was a fantastic offer."

"I see. Do you have the offer? I can take it to Cassidy and we'll discuss it."

"No need. I made an executive decision and accepted the offer."

Rebecca's jaw dropped. "You did what? How? Why? That was not your decision to make! I don't care who you are, Eve Sumptor, this is *my* club. I…" She stopped cold when Eve practically shoved a paper in her face.

"Read, Mistress."

Rebecca snatched the papers from Eve's hands and flipped through them angrily. Her eyes snapped up after she read the name on the papers.

"Is this a joke, Eve?"

Eve shook her head. "No joke. There are conditions which are listed, but I don't think you'll have any objections."

"You should have talked to me."

"Perhaps. I'm an extremely good business woman, Rebecca. My track record speaks for itself. It's why you came to me in the first place. In situations like this, it's better to ask for forgiveness than to ask for permission."

Rebecca gave her a cunning smile. "Be glad I'm not your Mistress."

"I'm counting my blessings," Eve grinned with a wink.

SHE TOOK IN her surroundings as she walked into the club. Posh leathers in red, black, and white shared the space with lace in the same color scheme. Men and women who work here are donned in leather as well. Masks hid their identities, but not their intentions. They chose their subs for the night—or an hour at a time—by handing them a color-coded card.

She dodged all of them and headed straight to the VIP area. Settling in on the plush leather couch, she continued to watch those around her. The men in masks carried themselves with an air of arrogance. She imagined it was needed to be a good Dom. But it was the women, as usual, that caught her attention. It wasn't arrogance for most. It was a confidence that couldn't be denied. She wondered if the masks helped and if they were vulnerable when the masks came off.

A shot glass of amber liquid was placed in front of her, cutting off her view of the main floor.

"I didn't order this," she said to the young waitress.

"It's from Mistress." Her voice held a bit of confusion and awe. "She also asked me to give you this." She placed a pink card on the table and walked away.

Picking up the card and the drink, she tossed the latter back in one gulp. The burn made her smile. Fireball. Perfect. She stood and made her way to the back of the club where the "playrooms" were. Once she made it to the pink door, she knocked lightly.

"Come."

The woman sat rigidly in her chair, ankles crossed, and hands clasped in her lap. Though her face was hidden behind a black mask, her eyes were able to roam over her companion. A full-blown smile bloomed.

"You look incredible."

"And you look like you're in my seat." Rebecca sauntered up to Cass and straddled her hips. She was almost sorry that Cassidy was in jeans and a t-shirt and not the bustier that went with the mask. It would be weird seeing her like that, but Rebecca was curious enough to hope for it one day. "And this," she reached back and untied the mask, "isn't you. I can't believe you did this."

"Are you mad?" Cass asked hesitantly. Whenever Rebecca straddled her, she lost brain function. But not enough now to know that she could have seriously messed shit up.

"That you bought the club behind my back? I should be, but I'm not. How?"

Cass's hands held onto Rebecca's hips. She truly looked incredible, dressed similarly to the way Cass was the first night they met. Tight, black jeans and a white button-down shirt. Only when the buttons were undone on her shirt, the cleavage was considerably... more. So, to keep her hands from wandering up that way, she kept them firmly on her slim hips.

"I, uh, asked Eve for a loan."

"Cassidy!"

"Hang on, now. She turned me down. I'm probably indebted to be her artist for the rest of my life, but she said the money wasn't needed."

Rebecca shook her head with a smile. "You didn't actually buy the club, baby. You're my partner."

"Huh?"

Rebecca took the contract out of her back pocket. "You didn't read these before you signed them, did you?"

"Uh, no. I mean, it's Eve. You trusted her to handle this for you, right? At least that's what I thought when she handed me papers. I guess I trusted her, too."

"I gave her the power to do that when Ellie was hurt. We were spending a lot of time with Hunter and Jessie at the hospital, and I didn't want the burden of the club at the time. I was *supposed* to get final approval on the buyer, but she never told me you made an offer."

"I asked her not to. I wanted to surprise you." Cass lowered her hands a bit, rubbing Rebecca's ass. "Communication kinda broke down during that time, didn't it?"

"We're getting it back, baby. So, let's talk about this. You want to keep the club? Run it with me?"

Cass shook her head. "I don't want to run it with you. I put that mask on for like five minutes and felt claustrophobic. Plus," she grinned. "I'm no Mistress."

"Oh, I don't know," Rebecca murmured as she kissed Cassidy. "You dominate me pretty good."

"Pretty good?" Cass smacked Rebecca's ass sharply causing her to yelp. "Just pretty good?"

"Well, like you said," Rebecca bit Cassidy's lip nearly hard enough to make it bleed, "you're no Mistress."

Cass laughed as she licked the tender spot. "Before you punish me, may I tell you my dream for this place?"

Rebecca sat up a little but was still close enough to feel Cassidy's breath on her. "Please."

"It's cleansed of the demons, yeah?" Rebecca nodded. "What's left is the beautiful moment we met. I want to keep it for that reason. This room."

"But?" Rebecca ran her fingers through Cassidy's hair and felt her shiver beneath her.

"But you don't have to hide anymore. We can hire someone else to run the place, and the only time you have to wear the mask is when you're in this room with me."

Rebecca lifted a brow. "When we met, you wanted me to take the mask off."

Cass shrugged. "I was young and stupid then."

Rebecca laughed. "It was less than a year ago, you goof!"

"Okay, okay." Cass grinned. "I wanted to see if your face was as hot as your ass." She frowned. "Wait. That… that didn't come out right."

"God, I love you." Rebecca kissed Cassidy the best she could while cracking up. "Okay, ahem. So, we hire someone to manage the place, keep the Pink Room closed to anyone but us, and use it often. I'm free to keep pursuing other options."

"In business only!" Cass smiled. "But yeah. That was kinda my plan when I went to Eve."

"All for this room, huh?" Rebecca purred.

"All for you, baby. You worked hard for this place. Almost died for it. You deserve to be here without the guilt or hurt. Let it make you happy now."

Rebecca's heart melted. Maybe Miranda was right. Maybe she didn't deserve Cassidy. But she was going to cherish her for as long as she had her. And if Rebecca—and Mistress—had anything to say about it, that would be forever.

She crawled off Cassidy's lap, provoking a whiney protest. "Go to the foot of the bed, Cassidy, and get undressed."

Cass scrambled to obey. When she got to the bed, she turned and smiled. "Yes, Mistress."

Just the beginning…

Acknowledgments

WHEN WRITING A book, you become aware that what is in your head may not be how readers will comprehend what they've read. That sensation happened to me during one particular section of this book. My hope is that people will read it exactly the way it was meant to be. I wanted the reader to feel the confusion and figure it all out at the same time the character did. It's a gamble, but then again, so is putting out anything that you write. Authors spend countless hours pouring their hearts out knowing full well that there will always be someone who doesn't like it. But we do it anyway because we have to. That's what writing is for me. A necessity.

I cannot thank ANYONE before I thank the woman who made me who I am today. Literally. My mom. Recently, my mom was diagnosed with Alzheimer's. It is progressing more rapidly than we imagined and I am doing my best to care for her as well as she cared for me. My mom is never far from my mind. I dread the day when I disappear from hers.

It took a little longer writing this book because real life became my central focus. From fundraisers to training for triathlons to raise money, to starting a business in order to help my mom more, my heart and mind were on my mom, not writing. But those moments I needed them the most, Rebecca and Cass offered me a gateway out of reality. I'll forever be grateful for that. I hope they give you that same gift.

Lisa—As always, your input helped me bring out the best in these characters. I love that I can text you or talk to you about an idea I have, and you'll elaborate on why it will or won't work. You're not afraid to tell me when something doesn't make sense and that's exactly what an author needs in a beta reader. That makes you the best beta read ever! Thank you!

Karen—As I said before, it's always fun having you as a beta reader. You let me know whether I've pissed you off or made you have emotions (a rarity, I know ☺) as though we're talking about real people in our lives. Of course, to me, they are real. Thank you for indulging my weirdness.

Daisy – You continue to support me and cheer me on with each book. And now with what's going on with my mom, you've been there for me and my parents 100% without complaint. I don't know what I'd do without you.

Angela McLaurin (Fictional Formats) – I'm so glad to be working with you again! It's like you know what is in my head and make it a reality on the page. Thank you!

Jim McLaurin – It is ALWAYS great working with you! I love that you not only show me what I've done wrong, but you let me know what you think I've done right. Thank you!

Writing sex scenes is STILL the most difficult part of writing for me. Of course, there's a lot of sex in this book. It's Rebecca and Cass. They certainly keep me on my toes! And though I know this won't appeal to everyone—even some of my own friends—I made a decision not too long ago not to be scared about writing what I want to write about any longer. Luckily, that doesn't stop any of my friends from supporting me, something I love them for. Even though this is a lesbian book, I hope readers can see that it's not always about who you love, but how you're loved.

As always, my message to my readers – This book deals with some difficult issues. I know that it could possibly be a trigger to someone who has been through some of the problems these characters have been through. I apologize for that. Truly. I read and write because it's cathartic. I hope reading is the same for you. I would like you to always want to say, "just one more chapter." ☺ Peace, love, and light!

About the Author

I've been in Houston, Texas since 2009. I continue to write novels as a way to release the voices in my head. ☺ Recently, due to family issues, I've gotten back into designing promotional items as a way to help my parents with medical expenses. Though I miss my family, moving here was one of the best decisions I've ever made. I've been able to live wonderfully and write my heart out, something I truly need. I've always enjoyed the arts in one form or another. Music sets the mood, reading stimulates my brain, and writing allows me to utilize my imagination in any way I want. I've been writing stories since I was a teen and figured out writing was my passion when I finished my first novel, *Something About Eve*.

As a merchandiser for singer/actress Deborah Gibson, I've had the opportunity to be involved in wonderful experiences, travel around the country and meet exciting people. It's experiences like this, I believe, that help me create unique, and (hopefully) lovable characters.

This is usually where I discuss what's coming next. But until I sit down and write that first line, it could be any one of three books that I have in mind. It'll be as much of a surprise to me as it will to you! ☺ Thank you for reading!

Where you can find cameo characters

Eve and Lainey
Something About Eve
Flawed Perfection
Coming Home
Coming Out

Dr. Willamena Woodrow
Eve's Blogs
Fifty Shades of Pink
Coming Out

Ellie and Hunter
Coming Home (Ellie only)
Coming Out (Their story)

Patty and Mo
Coming Out

Connect with Jourdyn Kelly online

My Website (http://www.jourdynkelly.com/)

Twitter: (https://twitter.com/JourdynK)

Goodreads (goodreads.com/author/show/2980644.Jourdyn_Kelly)

Secret Society on Facebook (https://www.facebook.com/groups/JoKels/)

Facebook (https://www.facebook.com/AuthorJourdynKelly)

Instagram (https://www.instagram.com/jourdynk/)

Amazon Author's Page (http://www.amazon.com/-/e/B005O24HK8)

Printed in Great Britain
by Amazon